DESIRES

SOUTHERN SECRETS SAGA, BOOK 3

JEANNE HARDT

James —
Desires will
often lead to
trouble ...

Jeanne
Hardt

CHAPTER 1

I'm home.

Claire stared at the eggs frying in the pan. Andrew's kitchen suited her. Simple and clean. Of course, she'd eventually add a woman's touch to the entire house. Finish what she'd started almost two years ago.

Sighing, she looked upward. *I hope you can forgive me for movin' on so fast, Gerald.*

"I changed him."

Startled by Andrew's voice, she jerked to face him. "Thank you. I reckon Michael appreciates it, too." He beamed, holding their son.

The baby patted his daddy's face and giggled. He'd taken instantly to Andrew—as if he'd always been there for him.

Michael had his features. Black hair and eyes as dark as coal. Evidence of the Cherokee blood flowing through their veins.

My handsome men.

She focused again on the eggs, then stirred the oats and checked the biscuits in the oven. She couldn't help but glance over her shoulder to see what they were doing.

Andrew had taken Michael to the living area and set him down on the woven rug. The two were stacking wooden blocks.

"He has other toys," she said. "They're still at Henry's. We left so suddenly we didn't take everythin' with us."

"We'll go and get them." Andrew smiled, no doubt trying to ease her. "I know it'll be difficult for you, but you should get your belongings."

Difficult? No, it terrified her. "Henry won't understand us bein' together. This won't be easy for *anyone.* Especially Beth."

Andrew stroked Michael's head, then crossed to her and wrapped his arms around her. "It may not be easy, but we both know it's right. We belong together." He glanced at Michael. "We're a family."

She nestled into his embrace. "*We* believe it, but Gerald hasn't been gone long. They won't accept it."

"They will in time." He lifted her chin and looked into her eyes. "As long as this is where *you* want to be, we can work through it."

"I don't wanna be anywhere else. I love you, Andrew."

"I love you, too. More than ever." He kissed her on the forehead. "Don't worry about anything. We'll be fine."

He gave her a squeeze, then took a step back. His brow furrowed as he grasped her arm and examined it like a doctor, not the lover he'd been last night. He gently ran his fingers along the bruises that remained from the numerous needles that had penetrated her skin. "Does it hurt?"

"No. It looks worse than it feels."

"I'm sorry you had to go through it. Even though you didn't feel it at first, once you became conscious, I know the treatments were painful."

"The pain saved my life. The bruises will fade." She gave him a reassuring kiss, then returned to the stove to finish making their breakfast.

"Dada!" Michael protested his absence, holding up a block.

"Someone needs you," Claire said, grinning, and Andrew went back to their son.

She loved the openness of the house. She could see everything with a simple turn of her head. Aside from their bedroom, the floorplan was open with the kitchen to one side and the living room to the other. A narrow stairway at the end of the main room led to a loft overhead. She'd not been up there yet, but assumed Andrew used it for storage.

Her kitchen had a sink with an indoor water pump similar to the one she'd used at Henry's. Preferable to going outside to a well. She had two rows of cupboards beside her small wood stove and oven, and a table with four chairs.

The living room had a small sofa in front of a large stone fireplace. The only other furniture in the room was Andrew's roll top desk. Her stomach knotted at the memory of what she'd found there—and what had started her long nightmare.

They'd been able to put all that behind them, though Gerald had paid the ultimate price for their deceptions. No matter how much she'd loved him in the end, she'd caught him up in a series of events that led to the end of his life.

Please forgive me.

Hearing Michael giggle, she smiled. Was it right for her to be this happy?

"That's a *C*, Michael," Andrew said. "*C* is for cat."

Watching them play with the blocks she and Gerald had made for Michael's first birthday wrenched her heart even more. Yet, the joy on Andrew's face made up for it. After all, he was Michael's *real* daddy. He deserved to be in his life.

Michael clapped his hands. "Dada!"

"Yes, I'm your daddy," Andrew said, scooping him up.

Claire stirred the oats one more time, then went back to her family on the floor. "He adores you. Reckon he understands you're his daddy?"

Andrew smiled. "Maybe so."

"How will I manage bein' 'round such handsome men all the time?"

"Sorry. You're stuck with us now." He gave her a kiss.

"I'm not complainin'." She smoothed Michael's dark hair. "Are you hungry?"

"More." Michael stretched out his arms.

"He says *more* when he wants to eat." She took him from Andrew. "I'll get him some oats."

Andrew poured himself a cup of coffee, then helped dish up the food. She sat at the table with Michael on her lap, spooning him cereal. Now and then she snuck a bite for herself.

"Andrew . . . there's a lot we need to talk 'bout. My head's spinnin' from all that's happened. I'm nervous 'bout what we're gonna tell folks. It's not that I'm ashamed bein' here, but . . ."

"*Are* you ashamed, Claire?"

She let out a long breath. "Maybe. I reckon we shoulda waited a while, but I didn't wanna spend another day without you. Is that terrible?"

"I don't think so. I didn't want to wait, either. Once I knew we *could* be together, it was all I wanted." He reached across the table and laid his hand on hers. "I wanted Michael in my life, too. You have no idea how I felt when I realized he was my son. I'll never forget seeing you with Gerald and wishing you were carrying *my* child. I had no idea you actually were."

"I was scared. Since I thought you were my brother, I was afraid he wouldn't be right when he was born. I prayed God would make him smart, and He did. Our baby's perfect."

"Yes, he is." Andrew's smile spoke volumes, displaying pride for their son.

"Andrew?" Multiple questions spun through her mind, but this one weighed heavy. "Why aren't you marryin' Victoria? You told me you *had* to marry her, but then last night you said you didn't. What happened?"

Sitting back in his chair, he sighed, shaking his head. "There's so much to tell."

"Then tell." She cast an encouraging smile.

He remained quiet, then cleared his throat. "Do you remember when we first met and I told you about the Negro woman I tended who died in childbirth?"

"Course I do. You blamed yourself, but it wasn't your fault. It broke my heart seein' you so upset."

"Yes, I blamed myself, but eventually realized there was nothing I could've done to save her. Unfortunately, Tobias, the woman's husband, blamed me. He was set on revenge. After he found out I was involved with Victoria, he went after her instead of me. He wanted to hurt someone I cared for."

Claire's heart beat a little faster. She recalled Jake Parker gossiping about Victoria being ravaged by a Negro. "What happened?"

"He followed her one day when she left the mercantile. He grabbed her and forced her into a storage building, intending to have his way with her. Thankfully, he didn't. She managed to get away. If she hadn't, I'm certain he'd have killed her." His voice had softened to a whisper.

Claire laid a reassuring hand on his arm and he closed his eyes.

"He hurt her, Claire. Bit her so hard on the neck that it left a scar. But even worse than the physical pain, the experience changed her. Her father blamed *me*."

"Why?"

Slowly, Andrew lifted his head and looked directly at her. "Because I told him we were being followed and wouldn't say who it was, even though I knew. Mr. O'Malley is involved with the Klan, and I had no doubt what he'd do to Tobias. I don't condone men taking the law into their own hands. But my silence could've cost Victoria's life. After it happened, O'Malley believed that no man would ever want her. So he made me promise to marry her. He said I owed it to her."

Claire stared in disbelief.

"Claire, how could I argue with the man? In many ways he was right."

"I'd heard rumors 'bout her. Folks said some awful things. Some said he'd made a baby with her." She sighed. "I feel sorry for her, but I still don't understand what changed. Why don't you hafta marry her?"

"John Martin released me from my obligation."

"My daddy?"

"Yes, your daddy, my *father*. Or so I thought my entire life. When he arrived for the wedding, he and Victoria shared an instant attraction. I tried to ignore it, but it wasn't easy. He charmed her. Even more so when she realized his wealth."

"So . . ." *I hate to think where this is goin'.*

"So, your father's marrying her." He crossed his arms and shook his head. "I wasn't sure how to tell you."

"Victoria will be my . . . *stepmother*?" A laugh escaped her. The mood of the conversation had certainly changed. "She's younger than me. What is she, twenty?"

"Nineteen." Andrew grinned, but it quickly turned to a frown. "I'm worried about what she's getting into. You and I both know John isn't a good person. He may have charmed his way into her life, but it won't take her long to realize he's not what he seems."

Claire had fed Michael almost the entire bowl of oats and had hardly eaten any herself. Luckily, the baby was much too little to understand their conversation. "I take it the weddin's still on, but with a different groom?" She cuddled Michael closer. "Why'd her daddy agree to it?"

"John can be persuasive. He saw a pretty woman and had to have her. And from what he told me, he already has." His brows rose as he took a sip of coffee.

"He told you?"

"He boasted about it. That's why I'm worried about her. But, she's made her choice. She's angry because she claims I lied to her. I didn't tell her about you or Michael, so she feels I deceived her. I tried to warn her about John, but she wouldn't listen." He took another drink. "Strange as it may seem, John did us a favor. If he hadn't wanted to marry her, I'd still be obligated. You and I could never be together. It's probably the kindest thing he's ever done for us."

"He never showed us any love. That's for certain." She scooted her chair back and returned Michael to his blocks on the floor. Then, needing to feel him near her, she walked behind Andrew, bent over, and held him.

"I should thank John for one other thing," Andrew whispered.

"What?"

"Creating you." He pulled her onto his lap and kissed her, causing her heart to increase its speed.

She stroked his cheek. "Our livin' arrangement won't be easy."

"Why?"

"Well . . ." She grinned. "When you touch me, I want more. I won't be able to get much else done. I'd like to just sit here on your lap all day."

Michael toddled over to them. "Up!" He raised his arms.

"Seems someone's jealous," Andrew said, chuckling. He lifted Michael from the floor and placed him atop Claire. "I'll have to hold both of you."

Michael tapped his daddy's face, then yanked on his nose.

Andrew laughed even harder. "Our living arrangement is perfect."

Perfect? Unfortunately, not quite. Her emotions had her so up and down, she didn't know whether to smile or frown. Incredibly in love and filled with desire for the man holding her, but plagued with guilt.

She stood, holding Michael, then lovingly ran her fingers through Andrew's hair. If only they could shut out the rest of the world, they'd be blissfully happy. Sadly, that wasn't possible. "We *do* need to get those things from Henry. Michael will sleep much better in his own bed. 'Sides, we don't want him to get used to sleepin' with us."

Andrew studied her face. Could he see her unease? Look into her soul and know how worried she was?

"Tell you what, Claire." He rose from his chair. "Though I was told to take some time off for my wedding, I need to go by the hospital to check in. Sooner or later they'll know I didn't get married. The last thing I want to do is upset Mr. Schultz."

"Mr. Schultz?"

"The administrator. We don't always see eye to eye."

"Oh. So I should wait here until you get home?"

He grinned. "No. I may not be marrying Victoria, but I intend to get married. I want you with me so we can go to the justice of the peace after we leave the hospital. I want our relationship to be completely proper, and I know you do, too."

Still holding Michael, she circled her other arm around Andrew and squeezed. "I want to marry you more than anythin'."

"I hoped you'd say that." He kissed her forehead. "After we're married, we can pick up those things from Henry."

She looked down. "I'm scared 'bout seein' him."

"I'll be with you. And if you're concerned about it, we don't have to tell him we're together."

"No. I want him to know. He can't think there's a chance I might move back in with him, or *ever* marry him. What I'm worried 'bout is him tellin' Beth." Claire set

Michael on the floor and started clearing away the breakfast dishes.

"She's been your friend a long time. It may take her a while to accept, but eventually she'll understand." He moved behind her and began rubbing her shoulders. His touch soothed her tension.

"I hope you're right. But this may be sumthin' she'll *never* forgive."

She loved that Andrew always tried to see everything in a positive light, but she knew Beth well. Once she learned the truth about Michael, she'd be crushed.

"I'll get the wagon ready," Andrew said, then kissed her cheek and walked away.

She was about to marry the man she'd always wanted, but her heavy heart overshadowed her joy.

Nothin' 'bout any of this is gonna be easy.

CHAPTER 2

Andrew hooked Sam up to Claire's wagon.

The worry he'd seen on Claire's face tore at his heart. He'd always believed that if they could be together, everything would be fine. Now, he wasn't so sure. Even so, he didn't doubt their love for each other.

That's all that really matters. He had to believe things would fall into place.

When he stopped the wagon at the front door, Claire came out, holding Michael. She'd put on a pale blue dress with a matching hat. He'd never seen her in one of the new-style hats with her hair twisted fashionably on her head. Before, she'd always worn a sunbonnet.

"You look beautiful," he said, and helped her up.

"Thank you. I decided to dress up since we're gettin' married. It's not exactly a weddin' dress, but I hope you like it." She repositioned Michael on her lap, then adjusted the fabric beneath him.

"It's perfect. Truthfully, I would've married you in your bedclothes. I just want to marry you."

She tipped her head to one side and grinned. "The justice of the peace might have disapproved."

He chuckled and took his place beside her, then reached out and gave her hand a squeeze. "Are you ready for this?"

"Ready as I'll ever be." She let out a long sigh.

"Sure you don't want to change your mind?"

With a soft smile, she shook her head and looked him in the eye. "No. *Never.*"

He leaned over and gave her a kiss, then faced forward and popped the reins.

Tension hung in the air between them through the course of their ride to the hospital livery. She'd often hug Michael a little closer. Worry lines between her brows grew deeper as they neared the city. Other than *I love you,* he didn't know what to say to ease her.

It has to be enough.

After leaving the livery, they walked the short distance to the hospital.

"Sure you want me to go in with you?" Claire asked, brows weaving.

"Yes."

"But . . . won't it make you uncomfortable?"

All the while he'd been worried about her, and she in turn had been concerned for him. "Not at all. I'd like to shout from the mountaintops that you're my wife. I can start at City Hospital."

"I'm not your wife yet. Maybe you should wait before you start shoutin'."

"All right. I'll wait for now, but not forever." He grinned at her, receiving a look of trepidation in return. He might need to keep their secret a little longer.

She placed her hand in the crook of his arm as they walked up the steps to the front door. "This hospital is incredible." She paused and gazed upward, pointing to the tall white colonnades. "I like it better now that I'm on the outside lookin' in."

He nodded. "Let's keep it that way. I don't ever want to see *either* of you on the inside, unless it's to visit me." He cupped his hand over Michael's head. Claire hadn't loosened her hold on him. Perhaps their son gave her the comfort he'd been unable to.

As they walked through the front door, Claire released his arm and stepped away. Hopefully out of respect for his position at the hospital and not from shame.

Sally, the front desk clerk, hurried toward them. "Dr. Fletcher? I didn't expect to see you, but I'm happy you're here." She smiled broadly. "Everyone's talking about what you did for Mrs. Alexander."

Before he could remark, Sally shifted her questioning eyes to Claire.

"You never met Mrs. Alexander, did you Sally?" he asked.

"No, sir."

"Well, *this* is *Claire* Alexander."

"Oh, my!" Sally held her hand to her heart. "You're lovely. And . . . *well.*"

"Thank you. And yes, because of Dr. Fletcher I *am* well."

"Your baby's beautiful." Sally grinned at Michael, then let him grip onto her finger.

"Thank you." The moment Claire said it, she looked downward.

She's ashamed. Why?

"Dr. Fletcher?" Sally took a step back. "I thought you took time off to get married."

Claire's head popped up.

"I did, and I'm going to." *Time to prove to Claire that I'm not ashamed of her or our son.* "I'd like you to be the first to know that Claire has agreed to be my wife."

Claire's eyes widened. He hadn't shouted it, but he'd certainly said it.

"What?" Sally couldn't have looked more confused. "What about Miss O'Malley?"

"Victoria decided she doesn't want to marry me. She's marrying someone else."

"Oh. *My.*" Sally gulped. Andrew knew Sally didn't care for Victoria. Still, the poor girl seemed to be in shock. "I have the wedding invitation you gave me. It's supposed to be the event of the year. Everyone's talking about it."

Andrew nodded with a smile. "You should still go. Same *event of the year*, just a different groom. It could be entertaining and you'd have even more to talk about."

"But, Doctor . . ." Sally crossed her arms. "I've never been a gossip." She faced Claire again. "Honestly, I don't know *what* to say."

"Why don't you congratulate us?" Andrew placed his arm around Claire's shoulder. Tension blanketed her, and she cast a timid smile.

"Congratulations!" Sally chirped. He believed she'd waste no time spreading the word. After all, he'd essentially given her permission.

"Thank you, Sally," Claire said, but then shifted her gaze downward again when Sally's eyes roamed between him and Michael.

"Yes, thank you," Andrew added. "Do you know if Dr. Mitchell is with a patient?"

"I don't believe so," Sally said. "He may be in his office. Oh . . . and I'm glad you came by because I have something for you." She scurried off to her desk and returned with an envelope. "A man dropped this by for you."

Andrew took it, immediately recognizing John's handwriting. "Thank you."

With Sally still gaping at him and the baby, he guided Claire down the hall to Dr. Mitchell's office.

When they approached the door, the man was coming out. "Dr. Fletcher? I didn't expect to see you." His brows wove in a similar fashion to Sally's, then he cocked his head, looking at Claire. "Mrs. Alexander? I thought you'd returned home to the bay."

"I-I did. But . . ." She froze in place.

"Do you have a minute, Harvey?" Andrew asked, using the man's given name to show he had business of a personal nature, and motioned into his office.

After taking their seats, Andrew dove right in and explained to his friend what had transpired. Harvey sat, saying nothing, seemingly in awe of the situation. Claire also sat quietly and let Andrew do all the talking. Getting this out in the open would allow them to get on with their lives without people constantly questioning why they were together.

"So," Andrew concluded, "we're going to the justice of the peace to take care of legalities. I don't want our situation to tarnish the image of the hospital. Our actions were done in innocence. Well . . . that is . . ."

Harvey raised a single hand. "I understand." He gave Claire a warm smile, then gestured toward Andrew with a toss of his head. "His behavior these past two years finally makes sense. He'd been pining for you. When you became his patient, I could tell he loved you. But I didn't understand the extent. Now I do."

"Will Andrew lose his position?" Claire leaned toward Harvey. "I know folks here have high standards."

"The hospital needs him." The man looked at her over the top of his glasses. "He saved your life and the lives of many others. If Mr. Schultz questions his character, I'll defend him. And, I sincerely wish both of you well. You've been through an ordeal and deserve some happiness in your lives."

Tears trickled down Claire's cheeks. "Thank you, Dr. Mitchell." She sniffled, drawing Michael's attention.

"Mama." He patted her face, looking as if he might cry, too.

"Mama's fine, Michael." She took his tiny hand and gave it a kiss. Then he arched backward and extended his arms to Andrew.

"Dada."

Andrew took him, and he laid his head on Andrew's chest.

Harvey smiled. "Seems you're already headed in the right direction."

They all stood and Harvey excused himself to see to his patients. Still holding Michael, Andrew led Claire outside. They exited to Sally's cheerful goodbyes.

Harvey had taken the news better than Andrew had expected, and Claire seemed slightly more at ease. Still, she wasn't the woman he'd met on the beach. Her carefree spirit had been doused by life. Somehow he had to find a way to bring her back again.

He motioned to a bench. "Before we go, I'm curious about what's in this letter." He waved the envelope. "It's from your father."

Claire tucked her skirt beneath her and sat. "You sure you wanna know now? Can't imagine anythin' good that man might have to say." She squinted up at him in the sunlight. Thankfully, her tears had vanished.

"Yes, I do. I want a clear mind when we say our vows."

He tore the envelope open. *A legal document.* He scanned it quickly, then chuckled. "He actually did it."

"What?"

"He drew up the papers legally changing my name to *Fletcher.*" Shaking his head in disbelief, he sat beside her. Michael wiggled over onto her lap.

"Good timin'," she said with a genuine smile. "I can legally be *Mrs.* Andrew Fletcher."

The envelope held another piece of paper. A letter from John. He cleared his throat to read it aloud.

> *Andrew, May 8, 1873*
>
> *As you requested, I have filed the necessary papers to legally change your name from Martin to Fletcher. You will find a copy enclosed with this letter.*
>
> *I can envision the surprise on your face as I write this. You had doubted I would take care of this matter. I know you have little regard for me, but I raised you, and though you may not believe me, I genuinely care about your wellbeing.*
>
> *I imagine you're with Claire. You will be taking care of my girl, and I will be taking care of yours. Odd how things happen in life. We will both be satisfied with a woman. Truthfully, I believe I acquired the better of the two, and I*

thank you for leading Victoria into my arms. There is no need to thank me for Claire.

It's unlikely I will see you anytime soon. Victoria and I will be leaving for Bridgeport immediately following our wedding.

Take care of my grandson as well as my daughter. I am certain you will do a better job than I ever did. I am not ignorant. I know I failed you both as a father. I was never meant to have children and have no intentions of having any more.

Enjoy Alabama. It suits you.
John Martin

Andrew stuffed the letter into the envelope. "He has some nerve." He couldn't hide his bitterness, but when he looked at Claire, her tears had returned. He wished he'd kept the letter to himself.

"He thinks so little of me," she muttered, sniffling.

"The man's a beast who thinks only of himself." He drew her to him. "Don't let his words hurt you. We'll never have to see him again."

"He thinks Victoria is better than me." Tears streamed down her face. "Are you sure you don't want her? She's beautiful, and refined, and—"

"She's not you." Not caring who might see them, he covered her lips with his. She eagerly returned his kiss. "I love *you,* Claire. You're far more beautiful than Victoria, because your beauty goes through and through. I thank God I'm marrying you and not her."

Michael watched them, wide-eyed.

"Today I believe I'm the happiest man in the world. You're giving me the family I've always dreamed of." He kissed her again, then kissed his son. "So dry your tears and marry me."

"I love you so much." She pulled a handkerchief from her satchel and wiped her face. "I'm ready now."

After retrieving their wagon, they headed to the court-house and said their vows. The short simple ceremony ended in no time, but made them man and wife. The one thing they'd both wanted since the first time they'd met.

CHAPTER 3

Claire twisted the ring around her finger. "Can't believe I'm really your wife."

Andrew took her hand, then raised it to his lips and kissed it. "Are you happy?"

"Course I am." She looked away. Would her nerves ever settle?

"Why don't we get a bite to eat before going to Henry's? It might help."

She nodded without speaking. Andrew read her like a book.

He took her to Sylvia's Pantry, a small diner beside the hospital, and led her to a table in the far corner. "I eat here frequently. The food's quite good."

They ordered the daily special, beef stew. Claire ate heartily. She had a long way to go before her body was as strong as it had been before the accident. "You're right. It's good. Much better than havin' me pack your dinner every day."

"Eating here helped me a great deal. For a time after you left, I didn't eat much at all."

"I'm sorry." She couldn't stop her eyes from filling with tears. *Why can't I be done cryin'?* She broke off some of her fried cornbread and gave it to Michael, after feeding him several bites of stew. "We both suffered, Andrew. But I wanna try an' put all that behind us. Make today our new start. I know *I'm* happy."

"Even through your tears?"

"I'm a mess, but I'm happy."

"I am, too. In time we can talk about everything, but I hope you don't mind me asking you one thing that's troubled me."

She looked directly at him. "You can ask me anythin'."

"Why'd you give Michael the middle name, *Andrew*?"

The memory made her smile. "I wondered when you'd ask."

"Well?" He leaned back in his chair, grinning.

"It was Gerald's idea. Kind of a long story, so I'll shorten it." She took a deep breath. "One mornin' he asked me who Andrew was. You can imagine how it made my heart race not knowin' why he brought your name up. He told me I'd been sayin' *Andrew* in my sleep, over and over again. So I lied and told him I'd been thinkin' of baby names."

"Did he believe you?"

"Not only did he believe me, he liked the name. Turned out he had a great granddaddy named Andrew Alexander. Luckily, when Michael was born, I convinced him to use it as a middle name. I woulda had an awful time havin' to call him Andrew every day of his life. His looks alone reminded me of you." She shook her head to wash away the memory. "Poor Gerald."

"Forgive me. It seems I keep making you sad. But at least now I understand why he laughed when I met him and told him my name."

"He laughed?"

"Yes. He said it had something to do with a conversation he'd had with his wife that morning."

"I remember that day like it was yesterday. Knowin' you were so close tore me up inside. I missed you terribly."

He brushed her cheek with his hand. "You'll never have to miss me again."

They quietly finished their meal, then headed down the road to Henry's.

Claire's stomach knotted the second his house came into view. Oddly, the shop doors were closed. *Unusual for a Friday.* "Maybe he's gone somewhere," she muttered.

"I have a feeling he's home," Andrew said. "The place looked this way when I came to see him after Gerald died."

"It's not like him. He always took pride in his business. Why's he lettin' it go like this?"

"After you and Gerald left, he took to drinking." Andrew pulled the wagon to a stop. "He's a broken man."

More to feel guilty about. How many lives had her lies destroyed? Not wanting Andrew to see her tears fall, she turned away.

"Claire?" He grasped her hand. "Why don't you wait here with Michael? I'll go in and make certain he's all right."

She silently nodded, and gazed at their son lying peacefully in her arms. *You're too young to understand the awful things your mama did.*

She never wanted him to know.

* * *

Joy shouldn't be so painful.

Andrew jumped down from the wagon and headed for Henry's front door. Because of the man's hearing impairment, he pounded with his fist.

When no one came to the door after numerous attempts, he decided to go around back and knock on the kitchen door. Within moments it swung wide and he found himself face to face with Henry Alexander.

"You back here again," the man grunted. A waft of alcohol filled Andrew's nose. Henry's eyes were half-shut and his cheeks were red, not to mention the slurred speech.

"May I COME IN?" Andrew raised his voice, while looking directly at the man.

Henry stepped back, then staggered against his cane as he made his way to the table. The moment he sat, he reached for a flask and guzzled a long drink.

Andrew took the seat across from him. "Do you want to drink yourself to DEATH? You need some HELP!"

"Don't want it." He downed another swig. "Don't care no more."

"You SHOULD. You have a lot of LIFE ahead of you, but you NEED HELP."

Andrew had met Henry at a time when he was happy and working hard. Now, he barely recognized the man and sincerely wanted to help him. Understanding what it felt like to have a broken heart helped.

"I want CLAIRE!" Henry yelled. His head bobbled from side to side. "She turned me down." He blinked with glazed-over eyes.

This will be harder than I thought.

"About Claire . . ."

"What?" Henry could barely hold his head upright.

"She's here. With Michael." As soon as the words left his mouth, Henry managed to get on his feet. Holding onto his cane, he pushed through the swinging kitchen door and headed to the front window. Andrew followed him.

Claire could easily be seen in the wagon holding Michael on her lap. Henry whipped around and almost fell. "She can't see me like this!" Sobbing, he staggered back to the kitchen. Andrew tried to help him, but he jerked away.

The man frantically worked the water pump and splashed cold water on his face. "My head hurts."

"Of course it does. You should SIT DOWN." This time, when Andrew took hold of his arm, Henry allowed his help.

* * *

Tempted to bite her nails, Claire focused on Michael instead.

"Let's go. I can't stand waitin'."

Since Andrew had gone around to the back, she went the same way. Looking around the property, her heart broke. For nearly two years this had been her home. Maintained and cared for. But now, after such a short time, the grounds were in shambles.

She walked to the barn and to her dismay found Rosie in need of milking. Her swollen udders looked painful.

"Mama's gonna help Rosie," she said, setting Michael on the ground. He clung to her leg. "It's all right, baby."

She patted his head, then took a seat on the milking stool. Michael squatted down beside her and tipped his head, intrigued. Then he giggled when the milk squirted into the pail.

"Poor girl," Claire muttered, patting Rosie's side. The cow let out a contented *maw*.

After relieving Rosie of her milk, Claire hoisted Michael onto her hip and lifted the nearly full pail. Her stomach fluttered.

Time to face Henry.

As often as she'd walked into Henry's house, she'd never been scared before. Not like this. Having to avoid his affections had been one thing, but how much had Andrew already told him?

Taking a deep breath, she pushed on, then stopped, facing the back door. It seemed appropriate to knock.

Setting the milk down, she rapped softly.

You're a nervous fool, Claire. Scolding herself helped, and she squared her jaw.

Andrew opened the door. After passing Michael into his arms, she set the milk pail in the sink. Then she boldly gave Andrew a hug, thankful to find him well.

"What's goin' on here?" Henry mumbled. His words were slurred.

He's been drinkin'.

Lifting her chin, she looked directly at him. "I've come for our things."

"What?" He tried to stand, but fell back down into his chair.

"You're DRUNK!" She moved closer, towering over him. "What's WRONG with you? Rosie was so swollen with milk she could hardly move! How can you let things go like this?" No longer feeling ashamed, she'd become furious. She shook her finger in his face. "SHAME on you!"

"Shame on *me*?" He wiggled his finger toward Andrew. "What was you doin' holdin' onto that man?" He glared at her.

"That *MAN* happens to be my husband!" She no longer cared what Henry thought. He'd hurt her and Gerald, and a wicked part of her wanted him to hurt, too. "I can hold him however I want!"

"HUSBAND?" Henry snarled. "What the HELL?"

She placed her hands on her hips. "We were married today. And I'd appreciate it if you'd stop yellin'. You're scarin' Michael." He'd buried his head into Andrew's shoulder.

Henry breathed heavily. His droopy eyes somehow managed to fill with fire and he directed the flames at Andrew. "What you doin' marryin' my woman?"

"She's never been yours, Henry." Andrew spoke with calm. "I love her. I'm going to take care of her and Michael."

"No!" Henry pounded his fist on the table, startling the baby, who let out a whimper.

Andrew held him tighter and patted his back. "Let's get your things and go, Claire," he said, nodding toward the hallway.

"Ain't right!" Henry yelled. "She was s'posed to be mine!" He took a long drink from a flask, then laid his head down on the table.

"NEVER," Claire hissed. Her entire body shook.

Andrew wrapped his arm over her shoulder. "C'mon. There's no talking to him reasonably when he's like this."

"Get your things and leave!" Henry growled. "Take all of it! Don't want nothin' here remindin' me a her' Take the damn cow, too!"

Claire left the room as fast as she could. Andrew remained by her side, holding Michael.

She stomped up the stairs. "Can't believe he's done this to himself." She stopped on the stairway and faced Andrew. "He blames *me*."

"It's not your fault. Don't ever forget that."

She'd certainly not forced the man to drink or to try having his way with her. He'd done all that himself. She carried the guilt for many sins, but not those.

Walking into her old room, her breath caught. Seeing the pine bed Gerald had made for them wrenched her heart. She ran her hand over the engraving:

GERALD AND CLAIRE ALEXANDER,
SEPTEMBER 2, 1871.

You were so proud of our bed, Gerald.

Even the humorous memory of how it squeaked on their wedding night brought pain now. He'd learned how to tenderly love her, and she'd learned to truly love him back. Tears trickled down her cheeks.

I miss you.

"Are you all right, Claire?" Andrew touched her shoulder, returning her to her new reality.

"Yes. Let's just hurry. This is too hard." She fingered the quilt at the base of the bed. "This was a weddin' gift from Mrs. White. Oldest member at the Baptist church. When she gave it to us, it was covered in dust . . ."

Andrew stepped back and stood in the doorway. She moved to the vanity where she'd sat many nights brushing out her hair. Sometimes, Gerald would do it for her. She picked up the wooden box that held her comb and brush and set it on the bed with the quilt.

Then she went to the little stand that housed her chamber pot. She removed it and showed it to Andrew. "This may come in handy." She managed to smile. The thing had been given to her when she was pregnant with Michael, so she wouldn't have to go to the outhouse in the middle of the night.

Andrew returned her smile, but his discomfort was obvious. It couldn't be easy for him, watching her relive memories with another man.

Her trunk sat on the floor beside the wardrobe. It still held a good deal of her clothing and quite a bit of material. She opened it and placed the items she'd selected inside, then topped it off with more clothing.

Once they'd finished there, they went to the nursery and Andrew set Michael down. Claire gathered up all the things she'd made for him. He let out an excited squeal when she handed him his stuffed bunny.

He clutched it close. "Mine!"

"Yes, Michael, that's your bunny," she said, smoothing his hair.

He toddled over to Andrew and extended his favorite toy, grasped in his little fist. "Dada!"

Andrew scooped him up, then made the bunny dance, prompting more giggles. "Why don't we put him in his crib while we carry your trunk out?"

"Good idea."

Andrew laid him down with his bunny. "We'll be right back, Michael." She couldn't get over the ease he had with him.

He's gonna be such a good daddy.

They hauled out the trunk as well as Michael's rocking horse, then returned upstairs for the crib. Michael had almost fallen asleep.

She lifted him into her arms. "Sure you can get the crib by yourself?"

He chuckled. "I can manage." He flexed his muscle to prove himself, not knowing how it stirred another painful memory. Not wanting to hurt him further, she quickly turned away and hastened with Michael down the stairs and out the door to the wagon.

Andrew placed the crib in the back. "Why don't you go back up by yourself and make sure you've not forgotten anything." With a tender smile, he took Michael from her.

"All right."

How could he know her so well after so little time together?

We have an indescribable bond.

The very reason she'd not been able to forget him. If only she could let go of Gerald.

She went through the rooms a final time. The necklace Henry had given her lay on the vanity. She grabbed it and headed back down the stairs to the kitchen.

Henry hadn't moved—passed out in a drunken stupor. She shoved the necklace under his hand.

When you wake up, you'll know I'm gone for good.

Walking out the door, she didn't look back.

She climbed into the wagon and took Michael. "Let's get Rosie."

Andrew nodded, then steered them toward the barn. "Even though Henry was drunk when he told us to take her, I think it's best we do. When he sobers up, we can always offer to return her. She needs care. More so than the horses."

"Horses need tendin', too," Claire whispered. "Least they have a field to graze in. Might be a good idea to come an' check on them in a few days. Make sure they have water."

"I can do that." He pulled the wagon to a stop. Before Claire could blink, he was leading Rosie from the barn by a rope that he'd tied around her neck. He secured her to the back of the wagon, then climbed back in. "We'll need to go slow."

Fine by her. As long as they were headed *away* from Henry's. She'd prefer never to see the man again.

"He really does need help, Claire." Andrew had once again managed to read her mind. "I can see about sending someone to offer it."

"You're a good man, Andrew Fletcher." Better than she deserved. With affection, she rubbed his leg.

"He'll kill himself if he doesn't stop drinking."

"Maybe that's what he wants." She let out a long breath. "Angry as I am at him, I hate that he's hurtin'."

"I'll see what I can do."

She scooted closer to her husband and laid her head on his shoulder. Michael had fallen asleep in her arms. "Wish we could go a *bit* faster," she whispered.

"Why? Aren't you enjoying the ride?" He glanced over his shoulder. "Rosie seems happy."

Claire giggled. "I wanna get home so I can curl up in your arms again. I can't stop thinkin' 'bout it." Truthfully, she needed the loving reassurance of his touch. Something to help her let go of Gerald.

"I'm glad." He stared straight ahead. "Seeing you in your old room, I was worried."

"Never doubt how much I love you." She took his chin in her hand, forcing him to turn his head. Then she kissed him.

As she nestled against him, she sensed some of the tension leaving his body.

They made it home just in time to avoid the rain. They quickly unloaded the wagon and Andrew returned it to the barn while she laid Michael in his crib. They'd placed it in the corner of the living room.

"Rosie went right into her new stall," Andrew said as he came in through the front door.

"Shh . . ." Claire held a finger to her lips. "Michael's asleep."

Andrew tiptoed across the floor. "For how long?"

"Least a couple hours." Her heart thumped.

"Then let's not waste a minute."

They walked quietly to the bedroom. Rain pattered against the rooftop.

Wasting no time at all, Andrew pushed her hair away from her neck and glided his lips along her skin, making her shiver.

"I know of one person who'll be happy for us," she rasped.

Andrew raised his head. "Who?" He resumed his kisses.

"Aunt Martha." His mouth covered hers with hunger. Not wanting to talk anymore, she urged him toward the bed.

"I believe you're right," he said, breathlessly. "But she thinks I'm your brother."

"We know better now." She closed her eyes.

His hands roamed her body, stripping away her clothing. "Yes, we do. We should go see her. Tell her the good news." He pushed her undergarments to the floor.

"Not now," she panted.

Naked, she melted into his arms.

He lifted her off the floor and laid her down on the bed, then quickly shed his own clothes.

"No. Definitely not now." He lay down atop her and pressed his lips to hers.

Their bodies entwined, saying everything else that needed to be said.

CHAPTER 4

Beth pounded on Mrs. Sandborn's door. Her heart beat as hard as her fist.

"Mrs. Sandborn! Open up!"

She'd not slept a wink. If she'd been in her right mind, she'd have come here the second Claire left.

"What in tarnation?" Mrs. Sandborn yanked the door open. "Beth?" The woman's eyes filled with panic. "What happened? Is it the baby?"

"Yes! I mean . . . no!" Beth shook her head. "I need to talk to you."

"Well, ya didn't hafta beat my door down. Come inside. You look pitiful."

Beth shuffled past her and headed to the kitchen. The boarding house had been her home for so many years that she still felt she belonged here. She plopped down in a chair.

Mrs. Sandborn handed her a glass of water. "Drink this, then tell me what's wrong."

The water soothed Beth's dry throat. She gratefully finished off every last drop, then wiped her mouth with the back of her hand. "Claire's gone. She took Michael and went back to Henry's!"

"Why?"

"Said it was where they belonged. But it ain't! Henry's the reason my brother's dead! Why would Claire do that?" Beth sniffled, choking back tears.

Mrs. Sandborn reached across the table and grabbed her hand. "Claire's doin' what she thinks is best. It ain't easy losin' a husband. But I hafta agree with ya. She left a might quick."

"Don't reckon her mind's quite right just yet. I'm worried sumthin' awful. Thought maybe you'd let me borrow a horse so I can go an' check on her. Don't wanna see Henry, but I hafta know Claire an' Michael are all right."

"Course you can borrow a horse. When ya gonna go?"

"Don't know. Storm's a brewin'." Beth fidgeted with the empty water glass. "Things just ain't right no more. I miss Gerald. And with Claire an' Michael gone . . ." She couldn't stop tears from falling. "It hurts."

"Oh, baby." Mrs. Sandborn scooted her chair beside Beth's. "I love ya like my own. Gerald, too. It's hard for me to believe he's gone. I've lost loved ones before, and it ain't never easy. I'm here for ya." She pulled Beth into an embrace. "I understand you're worried 'bout Claire, but ya need to take care a yourself, too. You look plum worn out. You need some rest."

"Can't sleep. 'Specially now." She dried her tears and traced invisible patterns on the tablecloth.

"I know what'll help." Mrs. Sandborn clapped her hands together and scooted away from the table. "How 'bout a nice big slice of apple pie? It just came outta the oven."

"No, thank you." Beth frowned. "I'm watchin' what I eat. I've put on a lot a weight an' I'm tryin' to improve my appearance."

"Ah . . ." Mrs. Sandborn dismissed her comment with the wave of her hand. "You look just fine. A piece a pie won't hurt a thing."

"Better not. I have a fella might be callin' on me. I wanna look good for him." She smiled for the first time since Claire left.

"A fella? Don't stop there. Tell me more."

Beth stood and meandered through the kitchen. In all her life, she'd never had a man to speak of. "Remember Martha Montgomery's farmhand, George? It's him. He's real nice."

"Yep, I remember him. He don't talk much."

"That's cuz he has a stutter. Reckon he's self-conscious of it, but I think it's sweet. 'Sides, I can talk enough for both of us." She let out a laugh.

Mrs. Sandborn slapped her thighs. "Now that's my girl!" She got out of her chair and wrapped an arm around Beth's shoulders. "Terrible things happen in life, but there's always good out there if you're willin' to find it. You're a fine woman, an' you deserve a good man."

"I'm twenty-seven years old. I'd given up on ever havin' a man in my life. Got used to the idea of dyin' alone. I ain't exactly purty. Nothin' like Claire. Most men don't even notice me. But George is different. Claire told me he never married—lives with his folks. He helps take care a them."

"Sounds like a *real* good man."

"Yep." Beth returned to her chair. "He's forty-sumthin', but I don't care."

Mrs. Sandborn sat beside her. "Age don't matter none once you're over twenty. Long as a man's breathin', he's fine by me." A faraway look shadowed her face. "I do miss my Leonard. Never was such a good man."

"Why'd you never remarry?" Her husband had died early on in the war, so she'd been widowed over eleven years.

"Ain't met no one who could measure up to him. I'm happy with my memories."

"I ain't got memories with any man. I want some." Beth wrinkled her nose. "I ain't never even been kissed." Resting her chin in her hand, she leaned on the table. "Is it as nice as it looks? I seen Claire an' Gerald kiss lotsa times and they seemed to enjoy it."

"It's nice." Mrs. Sandborn cleared her throat. "Some things is even nicer." She winked.

Heat rose into Beth's cheeks, certain what *things* the woman had implied. "Can't even imagine *them* things. Scares me to death."

Again, Mrs. Sandborn dismissed her with the wave of a hand. "Nothin' to be scared of. It's natural. How God made us. 'Sides, you're gettin' ahead a yourself. The man hasn't even called on you yet. All that other stuff comes *after* the weddin'. Start with the first kiss, then go from there."

Beth twisted her mouth, pondering her words. "It's strange talkin' to you 'bout all this. Mama died 'fore she could tell me 'bout men. Claire an' I used to talk 'bout them, but when she married Gerald she told me them things was private. She didn't like talkin' 'bout it."

"What a man an' woman do when they're alone *is* private. But you don't hafta be afraid of it. Long as your man is good and carin', you got nothin' to fret over." She patted Beth's cheek.

"I just hope he calls on me." Beth let out a loud sigh. With the kind of luck she'd been having lately, she'd probably never hear from him again.

"If he asked to, then I reckon he will." Mrs. Sandborn stood and peered out the kitchen window. "You best get yourself home before the rain comes. An' get some sleep. You need it."

"All right." She gave the woman a hug. "I'll come by for the horse when the weather clears." She gave her another, much harder squeeze. "Thanks for everythin'."

Beth hurried home, hoping not to get caught in the rain. When she got there, she crawled into bed, even though it was only midafternoon. She drifted off to sleep thinking about George, that first kiss, and whatever else might come about.

CHAPTER 5

The warmth of the morning sun covered Claire's cheek and woke her. She loved the feel of Andrew's bed—now *their* bed—but even more so, the feel of Andrew himself.

"Mmm . . ." she purred. Content as a lazy barn cat. Rain had pattered against the rooftop most of the night and had lulled her into blissful sleep after hours of love-making.

Thankfully, Michael had also been lulled and slept through the night.

"Good morning, Mrs. Fletcher," Andrew whispered in her ear. His fingertips cascaded down her arm, making her shiver.

"Mornin', Dr. Fletcher." She quivered against him. They'd been lying on their sides and she faced away from him, but she turned onto her back to look him in the eye. His hand followed her movement and covered her breast. "Can we stay here all day?" She closed her eyes, relishing his touch.

"There's nothing I'd like more." His lips touched hers with a simple kiss, then he climbed atop her, obviously ready for something more.

A loud cry erupted from the living room. "Michael . . ." She sighed. "I reckon that changes things a might." She gave Andrew a quick peck on the cheek. With a soft moan, he rolled off and flopped back onto the pillows.

She giggled and put on a nightgown. "We have plenty of time for that later. Our son needs us." Andrew had been watching every move she made. "What?" She cocked her head and posed with her hands on her hips.

"You're beautiful. I can't stop looking at you."

"Well, you best get out a bed. If you wanna keep watchin' me you'll hafta move to the livin' room." With a grin, she flitted out of the room.

Michael stood in his crib grasping the rail. "Mama!" His chin vibrated and tiny tears covered his chubby cheeks.

"I'm here, baby." She lifted him, then laid him on the sofa to change his diaper.

Andrew came out of the room, stretching. "I'll make coffee." Dressed only in pajama bottoms, she couldn't help but admire his firm muscular chest. He got her heart racing again simply by standing there.

I'll never get tired a lookin' at you, Andrew Fletcher.

They had two more days to enjoy before he had to return to work. She intended to make the most of their time together.

Though she planned to put her womanly touch to the interior of his house, she'd do that after he went back to work. For now, she'd reserve her attention for him alone.

Once she'd changed Michael, he was content sitting on the floor playing with his toys. The stuffed bunny stayed right by his side.

"I need to go out an' milk Rosie. Mind watchin' Michael while I do?"

"Why don't I bring him outside and show him the chickens and horses while you're milking?"

"All right." She liked the idea. "I'll fix breakfast once I'm done. It'll be good to have some fresh milk."

They'd have to find a routine. Likely, she'd be up before the baby most mornings to milk the cow, but it would take some getting used to. Living with Andrew would be nothing like living with Gerald and Henry.

I hope it'll be even better.

Andrew scooped up Michael, who gripped his bunny tight. "He sure loves this," Andrew said.

"Yep. It's his favorite toy. I have to sneak it away every now an' then to wash it."

The day couldn't be more beautiful. The sun shone bright overhead and the air smelled fresh. The rain had washed the land clean. Content, Claire breathed deeply. Their night together had taken away some of her trepidation.

Rosie seemed pleased to see her. If cows could smile, she believed this one would. She patted her side and took a seat on the milking stool.

Andrew stood close by with their son. "There's someone I'd like you to meet."

"Who?" She got into rhythm, yanking and pulling the udders.

"Alicia Tarver."

"A woman?" Warily, she looked up at him.

He grinned. "Yes. She's been a very good friend. And she has exceptional children."

"Tarver?" Claire returned her attention to the cow. "I know that name." It came to her suddenly, heating her cheeks. "That boy—the one who walked in on us—wasn't he a Tarver?" She stopped, closed her eyes, and placed her forehead against Rosie's belly.

"Yes." He chuckled. "You have a good memory."

She shook her head and resumed milking. "Hard to forget the most embarrassin' moment in my life. When that boy came in . . ." She giggled. "Oh, well. Least now we're married. If he happens to walk in on us again, I won't be *quite* so uncomfortable."

"Clay's fifteen. I think that experience taught him to knock. He was embarrassed, too."

"Did he ever tell his daddy 'bout us. You said you thought he might." She glanced up at him over her shoulder.

Every trace of a smile disappeared from his face. "Yes, he told him."

"Andrew? What's wrong?"

He set Michael down, then grabbed a bale of hay, moved it close to her, and sat. Michael immediately raised his arms and Andrew picked him up, holding him tight.

"I forgot you didn't know," he finally said. "It's strange. I sometimes feel like you and I have never been apart, but then things like this come up and I realize just how much of our lives we didn't share."

She shifted on the stool to face him. "What happened?"

"Clay's father, Elijah, is dead."

Pain filled Andrew's eyes, and she wished she could wash it away. "How'd it happen?"

"The Klan hung him. Victoria's father sent them after him. She thought it was Elijah who'd tried to molest her. Everything was mixed up and complicated. I blamed myself for most of it." He spoke without looking at her.

I should've been there for you.

"Elijah was the best friend I'd ever had. He died on my birthday. They came after me, too, because they knew we were friends and that I'd tried to help him. But O'Malley told them not to kill me. Only to scare me." He blew out a long breath. "They did."

He finally looked at her. "Please, don't cry." He dabbed at her cheeks. "We've had enough tears. A lot has happened since you left, but I didn't want to overwhelm you with everything."

"You've faced such horrid things. How'd you make it through?"

"Alicia helped. And the memory of you." He brushed his hand over her cheek, then with a grin, Michael patted her face. The sweet gesture warmed both of them, making them laugh. Something they both needed.

"Our precious boy," she said, smoothing his hair.

"Yes. Alicia would like to meet *both* of you. I've told her a lot about you. I believe she could become your good friend, too."

"I've never had a colored friend. I wouldn't know what to expect."

"She's no different than anyone else. Her color shouldn't scare you. She's a beautiful person with five incredible children. Her youngest was born the day you left. I delivered her. They named her Betsy, after my mother."

"That would make her 'bout nine months older than Michael."

"Yes. Maybe they'd enjoy playing together."

She decided she'd gotten enough milk from Rosie and stood from the stool. "Odd thinkin' how times have changed. My granddaddy owned slaves, now my boy will be playmates with a colored child."

"Things have changed for the better." Andrew rose, holding onto Michael. "There's still a long way to go, but at least our county's headed in the right direction."

Claire rubbed Michael's little back. "Granddaddy Montgomery might roll over in his grave, but I know you're right. I'd love to meet them."

They returned to the house and she busied herself preparing breakfast.

Her life had certainly changed directions. Hopefully Alicia Tarver would accept her *and* Michael. Andrew seemed to have the ability of fitting in anywhere, but why would any Negro in Shanty Town want to be *her* friend?

Once again she perched Michael on her lap to feed him breakfast.

"He needs a highchair," Andrew said. "It would make it easier on you. I'll have to add that to the list."

"I'm glad you've got a good job. Havin' a family can be expensive."

"Don't' worry about money. We'll be fine." He cocked his head sideways, then popped himself in the head with the palm of his hand. "I'm still paying for Victoria's ring. It's being deducted from my pay at the hospital." He shook his head. "It's not right. I need to speak to Mr. Schultz about it. Maybe I could send John the bill."

"It seems like the proper thing to do. Or . . ." She let out a long sigh. "Consider what you've already paid as a weddin' gift. 'Sides, they gave us sumthin' more valuable."

"You're right." He gave her one of his most amazing smiles. "I have you. You're worth more than any ring."

Andrew dove into his food, eating heartily. She loved that he appreciated her cooking. He wiped up every last bit of gravy from his plate with one of her buttermilk biscuits.

"You're spoiling me, Claire." He licked his fingers.

Michael held up his hands, covered in gravy. "More!"

"He likes it, too," Andrew said, laughing.

This felt good. Exactly what she'd always wanted. A happy home with the man she loved. She set her mind right, determined to let the past go. From here on out, her life would be happy. Come hell or high water.

* * *

After almost two years of talking to Alicia nonstop about Claire, Andrew couldn't wait to introduce her as his wife. No doubt Alicia would be thrilled for him.

He hummed while he hitched Sam to the buggy, then helped his nervous wife up onto the seat.

They could've walked the short distance, but with the baby riding was easier.

"You sure she'll like me?" Claire asked, and fidgeted with Michael's clothing.

"She'll love you." He gave her a reassuring pat on the leg.

As they approached the little house, Andrew spotted Clay in the field. He pointed. "That's Clay. You never got a look at him before." Andrew grinned, remembering how she'd hidden under the blankets.

"He's tall!" she exclaimed. "Only fifteen?"

"His father was a large man. His sons are taking after him."

She bounced Michael on her trembling knee. He felt certain that once she met Alicia, her nerves would calm.

Once he'd stopped the buggy and helped Claire down, by the time he rapped on Alicia's door, Claire was clinging to Michael like a security blanket.

The door creaked open.

"Hello, Samuel," Andrew said. "We came to see your mama."

Samuel's nose crinkled. He stared at Claire and Michael with his big brown eyes. "Mama! Doc Fletcher's here with a woman an' a baby!"

Alicia jerked the door fully open. "Doc?" Her eyes widened, taking in Claire, then her surprise faded and her face brightened. "This must be your Claire."

"Yes. And our son, Michael."

She covered her mouth with one hand, shaking her head. "Well don't just stand there." She waved them in. "I got a pot a coffee just waitin' for someone to drink it."

Andrew had shared many hours sitting at her table, drinking coffee and receiving advice. Sometimes she'd just listen, but most of the time she'd tell him exactly what she thought. He'd always appreciated her frankness *and* her honesty.

Alicia hadn't stopped staring at Claire. "My, oh my, Doc. No wonder you was pinin' over this woman. You're beautiful, Miss Claire."

Claire's cheeks glowed red, and her eyes shifted to the floor. "Thank you, Mrs. Tarver."

"Call me Alicia. I just know we's gonna be friends." She motioned for them to sit at the table.

Timidly, Claire set Michael down.

"Your boy looks just like you, Doc." Alicia held her hand to her breast. "Can I hold 'im?" She bent down to his level and he held out his hands.

"I think he wants you to," Andrew said.

Alicia picked him up and cuddled him. "Look at you. Doc junior. You're a sight!" She kissed his cheek and he giggled. "Such a big boy! Course, all babies look big compared to Betsy. Jenny took her outside to play. Joshua, too." She nodded to Samuel. "Go get your sister and the two little uns."

With a loud huff, Samuel walked out the door.

Alicia swayed with Michael. "Miss Claire, I gots my hands full, but they keeps me goin'. Go on an' have a seat, I'll get the coffee." She passed Michael to Andrew, then gathered the coffee cups.

Claire sat down and Andrew sat beside her. She looked nervously around the shanty. At Henry's she'd been uncomfortable, but this was something more.

Alicia handed her a cup. "Careful, it's hot." She smiled at Claire. Had *she* sensed her nervousness as well?

"Thank you." Claire took a sip. "You're a good mama. Can't imagine havin' more than one child."

"It can happen." She looked sideways at Andrew and grinned. "I'm shore you know how."

"I *am* a doctor," he replied with a grin of his own.

"I likes seein' you smile, Doc." She handed him a cup of coffee, then took a seat. "Miss Claire, I thank God you came back to 'im. He ain't been right for some time. I can tell you're just what he needed. Hope you don't plan to leave again anytime soon."

"Oh. No," Claire said, wide-eyed. "I'm here to stay. We got married yesterday."

"Married?" Alicia set her cup down and waved her hands in the air. "Praise the Lawd!"

Andrew laughed. "Amen."

The door swung open and the children paraded in. They stood beside their mother giving Claire the once-over.

"This is Doc's wife," Alicia said. "You can call her Miss Claire."

Claire transformed before Andrew's eyes. Love for the children beamed from her face and tension melted from her shoulders. "I'm happy to meet you. This is my . . ." She paused. "*Our* son, Michael." She locked eyes with Andrew. His heart beat strong, feeling the love and pride in her voice. She'd been liberated. This was probably the first time she'd openly told the truth about him.

"Doc gots a baby?" Samuel asked, wrinkling his nose.

"Yes, he does," Alicia sat flatly. "Miss Claire, that there's Samuel. He gives me fits. The other children are Jenny, she's my second oldest. She's twelve. Joshua there is seven and little Betsy is almost two."

Betsy crossed to Andrew and tugged at his pant leg. Then she pointed to Michael.

Alicia laughed. "Reckon she wants to play."

Andrew set Michael down and Betsy led him by the hand to the middle of the floor where she picked up a rag doll. They sat down and babbled at each other. Instant playmates.

"Ain't that the sweetest thing?" Alicia exclaimed.

"Yes." Claire laughed with genuine joy. "Michael's never been 'round other children. He seems to like her."

The others joined in. Soon they were all playing and laughing.

"They's good children," Alicia said. "Nice thing 'bout havin' more than one. They looks after each other."

Claire scooted her chair closer to Andrew, then nestled her head against him. Was she thinking the same thing he was? Hopefully they'd have another child soon.

Alicia grinned. "Easy to tell you's newlyweds. Must be kinda hard not havin' much time alone. What with the baby an' all."

"It's all right," Claire said, smiling. "We're just happy to be together. That's all that matters."

"Maybe so. But I knows you'd enjoy some alone time. When you's comfortable with the idea, bring Michael over for a night. One more child won't bother me none."

"Thank you," Andrew said. "We may do that. There's no one I'd trust more with my son."

"Mmm . . ." Alicia tilted her head back and closed her eyes. "I likes hearin' you say that. Wish Lijah coulda been here to see your boy." She opened her eyes and gazed at the ceiling. "Lijah? You see this? Doc finally gots his Claire an' his baby, too." She turned her attention to Claire. "My Lijah's up there watchin' over us. Reckon he's smilin' down on us."

"I'm sure he is." Claire reached across the table and took Alicia's hand. The look on Alicia's face indicated that the action both surprised and pleased her. "Andrew told me 'bout him. It must be hard on you."

Alicia nodded. "It hurts to lose someone you love. *You* know. But God has a way a makin' things all right, long as you listen to Him. Never fill your heart with hate an' anger."

"It still can't be easy." Claire was completely relaxed. This was the woman he loved. At ease and full of compassion.

"It *ain't* easy," Alicia whispered. "But that's why we gots friends. To hep us through." She patted Claire's hand. "I'm glad I gots a new friend, an' the children do, too."

They stayed for several hours, talking, drinking coffee, and becoming well acquainted. When they left, Claire gave Alicia a hug with a promise to come back soon.

"Don't forget my offer," Alicia said as they were leaving. "You'll be wantin' some *alone* time."

"We won't forget," Andrew and Claire replied in unison.

Laughing, they climbed into the wagon and headed home.

CHAPTER 6

Beth woke to a sunny Saturday morning. She yawned and stretched, finally having slept through the night. Tomorrow would mark two weeks since Gerald drowned; changing the lives of everyone she loved. Especially Claire.

Looking around her little home, she smiled at the generous gift Claire had given her. She was the best friend anyone could ask for.

"I gotta go see her," she mumbled and threw on a robe. She then walked out onto the front porch and sat in one of the rocking chairs. The more she thought about Claire, the faster she rocked.

The weather couldn't be more perfect for a ride. With a clear sky and no rainclouds in sight, she made up her mind and hopped onto her feet.

Dressing quickly, she hastened down the road to the boarding house. Time to borrow Mrs. Sandborn's horse. She'd learned how to ride when she was a girl. But after her daddy died in the war, they had to sell their horses just to get by.

Henry better be treatin' Claire right.

The long journey gave her time to think about everything that had happened. None of it was fair. Gerald never should've drowned, but she'd had to make a choice. She could only save one of them, and she'd chosen Claire.

Michael needed his mama.

Still, her heart ached for her brother—the daddy Michael would never know.

She needed to dismiss the painful thoughts. If she cried, her vision would blur and she might fall from her horse. Then she wouldn't be good to anyone.

Shifting her thoughts to George, her spirit lifted. Until a terrible thought struck all at once.

What if he rides to my house an' I ain't there?

She'd been told he worked for Martha, Monday through Friday, so he could possibly decide to call on her on a Saturday. Worry replaced her depression. If the man drove all the way from Martha's to find an empty house, would he ever come back again?

Maybe they'd pass on the road. For a moment, she calmed.

She'd forgotten how much a horse jostled her insides, but she pushed on.

As she neared Henry's, her thoughts shifted again. Surely Claire would have his house neat and tidy, but would she go near his bed?

No. Claire would never do that. Only man she ever wanted was Gerald.

Of that she was certain.

She smiled remembering the way they used to kiss. *So much in love.*

She'd always think of her brother as the man who loved her best friend and gave her a son. Excited to see her nephew, she pushed the horse a little faster.

Reaching Henry's, everything seemed too quiet. When she found the *closed* sign on the door of the blacksmith shop, she became even more perplexed. The man never closed on a Saturday.

She'd been told her uncle had started drinking again after Gerald and Claire left him, but surely Claire would set him straight and get him working again.

She took her horse to the barn. Oddly, Claire's wagon was nowhere to be seen, nor was her mare, Cocoa.

Beth's stomach fluttered. *Sumthin's wrong.*

She hurried to the front door and knocked, but after getting no answer, went on in.

Stale air surrounded her. All of the curtains had been pulled, making the house eerily dark.

"Henry!" She yelled, but got no answer. "Claire? Where are you?"

Silence.

The discomfort in her belly grew with each passing second.

A loud moan coming from Henry's room turned her head. She cautiously approached his door. "Henry?" Her voice trembled.

Another moan. Even louder.

Her hand shook as she gave his door a slight push. She peeked inside and found the man face down on his bed, fully clothed. He reeked of alcohol. Relief turned to anger and she pushed the door open wide. "Henry!" She stomped to his bedside and shook his shoulders. "Where's CLAIRE?"

He flopped onto his back, brows weaving. He opened one eye, and then the other. "Huh? Beth? That you?" His words sounded like mush.

Breathing hard, Beth headed to the kitchen. She pumped a glass of water, then returned to Henry and threw it in his face. "Yep! It's me!"

"Damn it, girl!" Henry shook his head and tried to sit upright. "What'd you do that for?"

"You're drunk!" She should've gotten a full bucket of water to throw at him. "Now tell me. Where's CLAIRE?"

"Why'd ya come lookin' for her *here*?" He grabbed the corner of a blanket and dabbed at his face.

"She told me she was comin' here!"

"She did?" The man started to laugh, making her even angrier. "Yep! She was here all right."

Beth had almost lost her patience. *Senseless drunk.* "Well, WHERE is she?"

"You won't believe me, even if I tell ya."

She tightened her hands into fists. "Try me!"

"Ya won't like it." His head bobbed from side to side.

"Uncle Henry!" She stomped her foot. "Just TELL me!"

He waved a finger in the air. "She came here yesterday with that Dr. Fletcher." Again, he tried to sit. He peered at her, squinting. "They got married." His demeanor completely changed and he burst out crying, blubbering like a baby. "Hear me? My Claire got married!"

"*Your* Claire? She gaped at him. "Alcohol's made you CRAZY! You don't know what you're TALKIN' 'bout!"

"Do too! I ain't that drunk. They was here. She was huggin' all over 'im. They took her things an' left!" He shook his finger at her.

"What makes you think they're MARRIED?" He couldn't be right. The old man had to be confused.

"She told me!" His body jerked, sobbing. "She was wearin' his ring. He said he loves her. How could he? He ain't known her long!"

Weak-kneed, Beth sat down hard on the edge of the bed. She knew differently. They'd known each other since before Claire and Gerald were married. Dr. Fletcher had come looking for her.

No, it can't be.

Somehow Henry managed to sit upright. "What's wrong? You quit yellin'. Cat got your tongue?"

She shook her head. "No. I just . . . I don't understand."

He tapped her on the back. "What? Look at me when you talk. I can't hear ya!"

She faced him. "I DON'T UNDERSTAND!" She covered her face with her hands. There had to be an explanation. "Claire loved *GERALD*!"

Henry dropped back against the pillows. "Gerald's dead," he mumbled. "Reckon Claire was lonely."

"No!" Tears pooled in her eyes. "Gerald ain't been gone long enough for her to be lonely!"

"Anytime alone is too long." Henry closed his eyes.

"HENRY!" She shook him hard. "Where'd she GO? Where's HE LIVE?"

He opened one eye. "Don't know. Sorry." He grabbed a flask from the bed stand, then guzzled a long drink.

She stood and moved away from him. Talking to him anymore like this was useless.

Claire wouldn't get married again. Not so soon.

Besides, Dr. Fletcher was engaged to that rich, snobby woman.

Henry's wrong.

She left him snoring, clutching his precious flask. She probably should've thrown it out the window, but she'd deal with him later. For now, she needed to go to the hospital and see if they'd tell her where Dr. Fletcher lived. Seemed it'd be the only way to find Claire.

* * *

With a light spirit and spring in her step, Claire moved the broom around the kitchen floor. Meeting Alicia had gone better than she'd expected. She'd indeed made a new friend.

One who didn't judge me.

It felt incredibly good to call Michael Andrew's son. Of course, anyone who saw the two of them together could easily tell.

No denyin' that bloodline.

Andrew had taken Michael out to see the animals since he'd not done it earlier in the day. She stayed behind to tidy things up a bit.

"Can't wait to make new curtains," she mumbled, fingering the threadbare things that hung over the kitchen window.

"Oh, dear Lord . . ." Her heart constricted and she had to grip the edge of the sink to keep from crumbling onto the floor. "Beth . . ."

Somehow she'd found them.

Beth dismounted from Mrs. Sandborn's horse. The same horse Claire had ridden when she'd left the bay to seek out Gerald.

She ducked down, away from the window. But it did no good.

The rap on the door made her heart stop completely.
Just breathe.

Frozen to the floor, she couldn't make a simple step forward. The second knock was much louder.

Her friend had come a long way. Claire had no choice but to answer the door. Besides, sooner or later, Beth would find out about her and Andrew.

I wish it'd been later.

She opened the door one slow inch at a time. They stared silently at each other. After several long moments, Claire couldn't take it any longer. "Would you like to come in?"

"What?" Beth gaped at her. "Is that all you can say? You invite me in as if there ain't nothin' strange 'bout it?" She frowned and shook her head. "I don't wanna come in."

"Please?" Claire reached out, but Beth took a step back. Claire had to persist. "We need to talk."

Beth defiantly crossed her arms. "I went to see Henry, thinkin' you'd gone there. He said you an' Dr. Fletcher got married. If that's true, we got nothin' needs sayin'."

Seems Henry had been sober enough to remember a few things.

Claire looked at the floor, then slowly raised her eyes to meet Beth's. "Yes, it's true."

Beth backed further away. Air hissed from her nostrils. "What 'bout Gerald?"

"He's gone, Beth. And I—"

"He's *dead*! Not *gone*!" Her face contorted, looking completely unlike the girl who'd been Claire's best friend for as long as she could remember. "How could you marry someone else so soon? My brother's body is barely cold! It ain't right!"

Michael's giggle turned Beth's head. The timing couldn't have been worse.

Andrew lifted Michael into the air, then brought him down, tickling him. Caught up playing, he obviously hadn't noticed Beth.

Michael let out another loud laugh. "Dada!"

Oh, my . . .

Beth's face became ashen. "What's goin' on here?"

"Oh, Beth . . ." Claire made another attempt to reach out to her friend, but received ice in return.

"Y'all act like Gerald never was."

"Come inside an' I can explain." Tears she believed had finally dried reformed in her eyes. Beth didn't budge. "Beth, I love you. You're my best friend. My *sister*."

"I *ain't* your sister no more." She shook her head, her face hard as stone.

Her proclamation forced the droplets in Claire's eyes to spill down her cheeks.

Andrew's laughter drew her attention. If she could have, she'd have willed him back to the barn, but he approached, holding Michael. How had he not seen Beth?

"Daddy loves you, Michael," he said as he walked. He might as well have plunged a knife into Beth's chest. The anger on her face instantly turned to pain.

Finally, he took his eyes off the baby and looked up. He stopped immediately upon seeing Beth.

"Dada," Michael said, patting Andrew's face.

Beth's eyes grew wide. Her head moved back and forth looking between Andrew and Michael. Then she whipped around and faced Claire. "What'd you do, Claire?" Her eyes narrowed. "You lied to Gerald, didn't you?"

"I—Oh, Beth. You gotta let me explain." Her tears streamed.

"No! I was blind. Now everythin' makes sense. Lucy Beecham knew an' I slapped her in the face for sayin' it!" Beth's face contorted even more. Angry and wicked-looking. "I don't know who you are anymore, Claire." She burst into tears of her own.

"Beth," Andrew stepped forward. "Please give us the chance to explain." He set his hand on her shoulder.

She jerked away. "How could you? I trusted you! It was never 'bout shirts, was it?" She rapidly wiped the tears from her eyes. "I don't never wanna see either of you again!" She pushed past Andrew and prepared to mount her horse.

"Please don't say that!" Claire cried out after her. "You're my best friend!"

"No, I ain't!" Beth climbed atop the mare. "My best friend never woulda done what you did! I thought you loved Gerald! Everythin' was a lie!"

"I *did* love him! Please believe me!" Unbearable pain pierced her heart.

"I ain't got no business bein' here." She tugged on the reins, turning the horse to leave.

"Please come inside, Beth." Andrew made an attempt of his own.

"No!" she snapped, then guided the horse close to Claire. "I made the wrong choice. I shoulda saved Gerald." Turning the horse around, she dug in her heels, and sped away.

Claire erupted into a sob. She raced into the house and lay down on the bed. Drawing her legs up tightly to her chest, she let the tears flow. She could never make this right. How could she have believed her life would be better now?

* * *

Andrew kissed Michael on the cheek, then followed Claire inside. If only he'd noticed Beth, he could've stayed away. But his son had him caught up in joyful play and his attention had been solely on him.

Would there be any way to make Claire feel better? It had been hard to hear Beth's words, but for Claire it had to have been excruciating.

He set Michael on the floor with his bunny and blocks and went to the bedroom to console his wife. He found her curled up in a ball, lying on her side.

Perching on the edge of the bed, he rubbed her back. "Claire," he whispered. "She'll need time. I know she didn't mean what she said. She's hurting right now." Her body shook beneath his touch, trembling from heavy sobs. "When you're able to explain, she'll understand. She's been your friend a long time. I know she cares about you."

Claire sniffled. "She has every right to hate me. I know lyin' to Gerald was wrong. But she said it was *all* a lie. That's not true."

"I know." He slowly let out his breath, making every effort to remain calm for her. Since rubbing her back hadn't helped, he moved his fingers to her hair and repeatedly drew them through it. "I know you loved him, and you love *her*, too. It's tearing me up inside seeing you this way."

"Was I wrong? How long would've been long enough to wait for you? Who makes the rules?" She rolled over to face him. "She doesn't know I loved you first, and that I was without you for a very long time. I didn't want Gerald to die, but he did. An' then—like some kinda miracle—God brought *us* back together again. So why's it wrong?"

He lay down beside her and drew her in close. "It isn't wrong. But we both know other people won't see it that way. They don't know everything that happened. All they'll see is a widow who didn't grieve long enough for her husband." He sighed. "I don't know. Maybe we should've waited."

"No." She peered into his eyes. Her tears had stopped. "Please don't say that."

"I'm sorry, but like you, I don't know who makes the rules about such things. Honestly, I doubt there *are* any rules." He pushed her hair away from her face. "I know I didn't want to wait. Maybe *I* was wrong. All I'm certain of is that I love you and Michael. Give Beth time, but please don't let this tear your heart in two." He traced his fingers around her lips. "I want to see you smile. You're allowed to be happy, Claire. Love shouldn't cause this much pain."

She placed her hand against his cheek. "Lovin' you is all I ever wanted. Our lives took a detour an' I'm tryin' to get us back on track. You *do* make me happy, an' I hate you've had to see me cry so much. But I hurt Beth so badly . . ."

He kissed her, then cradled her in his arms. "We'll be all right as long as we have each other. I'll always be here for you."

"Mama." Michael patted his hands against the side of the bed.

Andrew smiled at his wife, then lifted their son off the floor and laid him between them. Michael's little eyes studied his mother as if he knew she was in pain.

The three of them lay together, comforted as a family. For a time they were able to forget the troubles that waited outside the walls of their home.

CHAPTER 7

Beth rode in a daze. The horse's hooves clopped heavily on the hard ground, but the only thoughts that filled her mind were images of her *nephew* with his real daddy.

Michael ain't even my blood.

She gripped the saddle horn tight. Luckily she rode a sure-footed horse. Her blurred vision kept her from steering the animal in any form or fashion. The mare just kept running on—encouraged by Beth's constant kicks to her side.

Inescapable loneliness weighed her down. Her parents were long gone, and her brother had died because she'd been deceived and made a poor choice in saving the life of her *best* friend. She'd loved her like a sister.

Why'd she hafta lie?

Even the doctor Beth had respected and admired had ultimately betrayed her.

No wonder he looked ill when I told him 'bout Claire an' Gerald.

"An' to think I wanted to marry that man," she mumbled.

Wonder what happened to his fiancée?

The thought of Claire replacing snobby Victoria brought a brief smile to her face, but it quickly disappeared.

Claire's just as bad as that hateful woman. Least Victoria never pretended to care 'bout me.

Claire had always acted like she didn't remember who Dr. Fletcher was, when all along she knew him well. *Biblically.*

The more she thought about it, the harder she gripped the horn. She'd clenched her jaw so tight her cheeks hurt.

I hate her for what she done.

But then, she thought about her brother. Gerald had never been happier. Could that make Claire's lies forgivable?

She shook her head. *Never.*

"I just wanna get home."

She sat upright in the saddle and froze. Somehow she managed to pull the horse to a stop.

It ain't my home.

Claire had given her the little house on the bay as a *wedding* gift. When she married Gerald and moved with him to their Uncle Henry's house, she'd said she didn't need it anymore. Beth loved it, but . . .

I don't want no part a her!

The perfect solution struck, and she dug her heels into the mare's side to get her moving again. She'd pack her things and move to Henry's. Being the only family she had left, it seemed the right thing to do. Besides, he needed her.

I'll get 'im off the bottle.

Mentally making a plan stopped her tears. The old man had turned into a drunk, but she blamed Claire for that, too. From now on, she'd always choose her family over a supposed friend.

Time flew by as fast as her horse galloped. She'd not thought about George the entire way until he appeared sitting in a rocking chair on her front porch.

Slowing her horse, she attempted to wipe her face.

I must look a sight. Not how she wanted to look when George came calling. Her puffy eyes were nearly swollen shut, and surely her nose glowed bright red.

George craned his neck, then stood.

Yep. He seen me.

She dismounted and traipsed reluctantly toward him. Her breath caught. *He brung flowers.*

He held a slightly wilted bouquet of daisies.

Musta been waitin' quite a spell.

He wore his usual coveralls and straw hat, but didn't have a piece of straw dangling from the side of his mouth. She'd never seen him without it. Maybe he'd chosen not to, hoping to make a good first impression.

She'd failed miserably.

He extended the flowers. "I g-got these for ya." Immediately, he looked at the ground.

Had he looked away out of shyness, or because she looked such a mess?

Though the flowers had wilted, they were the most beautiful daisies she'd ever seen. She took them from him and her fingers brushed across his hand. Just touching his skin caused her heart to patter. "Thank you, George."

As she moved the flowers toward her nose for a sniff, she burst out crying.

George's eyes opened wide, staring at her.

"Oh, George!" She grabbed onto him and bawled.

His arms had been dangling at his sides, but ever-so-slowly they moved around her. He patted her back in the same manner her mama used to comfort her.

"She lied to me," she whimpered, gasping for air.

"Who lied?"

She lifted her head from his shoulder and looked him in the eye. "Claire. She's gone an' married Dr. Fletcher!"

He blinked and studied her. Their faces were inches apart. She'd never been so close to a man.

"Why, why d-don't we sit down?" He motioned to the rockers.

No longer caring about her appearance, Beth wiped her nose on the sleeve of her dress and sat. George scooted the other rocker beside hers.

"Everythin' Claire told me 'bout Gerald was a lie!" She blurted out. "She said she loved him. Made everyone think she had his baby. But she didn't! Dr. Fletcher's the baby's real daddy! Claire had *him* 'fore she had Gerald. How could she do that?" Everything spilled out of her. Talking to George was easy. Of course, he rarely spoke. That probably helped a might.

He swallowed hard, but didn't utter a sound.

"My brother's body has been in the ground two weeks." She pointed a stiff finger toward the grave. "The soil over yonder's still loose. She claims to be a Christian, but no *real* Christian would do such a thing!" Beth gripped the armrests of her chair and rocked fast, accompanying her anger.

"Miss Beth," George stammered. "I-I can see you're angry. But, but you shouldn't j-judge Miss Claire. You d-don't know what's in her h-heart."

Has he lost his mind? "I saw with my own two eyes what they was doin'. They acted as if Gerald had never walked the earth. They was all cozied down in their little house. An' *married*! I ain't never gonna forgive her."

He shook his head and frowned. "Not good, n-not forgivin'. I th-think you're a fine woman, Miss B-Beth. I-I don't like seein' ya so upset."

He'd spoken more words than she'd ever heard from him, but nothing he could say would make her think any better of Claire.

She stopped rocking. "George, you just might be my salvation." She stood erect and squared her jaw. "I need a ride back to Mobile. I don't wanna stay here no longer. I aim to move in with my uncle. He's the only family I got left, and it just so happens he needs me. Will you take me?"

He sat up straight. "You'll be livin' in Mobile?" He didn't stutter once.

"Yep." Having made up her mind *and* her proclamation, she sat back down. "I know you came a long way to call on me, an' I appreciate you bein' here. Sorry you found me in such a state. An' I hate you had to wait so long. My manners seem to have gone somewhere down the road. Shucks . . . I ain't even offered you a cool drink. How long you been sittin' here?"

"Three hours."

"Dang!" She quickly covered her mouth. Swearing hadn't been wise. Especially in front of a prospective beau. "I really am sorry." She patted his knee and received a terrified look in return. With a sheepish grin, she pulled her hand back. "You really are an answer to prayer, George. I mean, you came in your wagon. It's like you knew I was gonna need you. If you'll give me a bit to pack my things, we can leave right away. An' don't fret. I ain't gonna take no furniture. Uncle Henry has plenty." She jumped to her feet. "Want some sweet tea punch while you wait?"

He smiled and nodded. "Thank ya."

She went inside and put the daisies in a glass of water. *So sweet.* Then after taking George some punch, she returned inside to pack. It didn't take long to gather her personal items. Almost everything she had belonged to Claire, and she intended to leave every bit of it behind.

In the barn she found a padlock for the front door. She'd lock up the house and send Claire the key. The only thing she truly hated leaving behind was Gerald. He'd have to lie there in the ground next to Claire's mama for all eternity. None of it seemed right.

With the glass of daisies in her hand, she walked to his grave. She dug a small hole next to the marker and pushed the container into the earth. "Gerald, a real nice man gave these to me, but I want to leave 'em with you. I reckon he'll understand. I know you're in Heaven, and you know how much I miss you.

"I'm glad you didn't live to see what Claire done. I thought we knew her, but we was wrong. Hope you can forgive me for not pullin' *you* outta the water. I could always count on you. You never woulda lied to me 'bout nothin'.

"I hafta leave now, but I'll come visit you again one day. I know you was mad at Henry, but he's the only family I got now. He's a mess." She patted the soil where she assumed Gerald's head might be. *Why'd you hafta die?* "Henry needs me," she whispered and got to her feet. Sniffling, she stared at the mound of dirt. "I love you, Gerald." She wiped away fresh tears and returned to George.

"We gotta take the chickens. There's a mesh coop in the barn. I hate leavin' my garden, but the rabbits will like it."

Without saying a word, he helped her load her belongings, including the chickens. They tied Mrs. Sandborn's horse to the back of the wagon, then headed down the road.

Beth felt confident that Mrs. Sandborn would take the chickens. She didn't want to haul them all the way to Mobile. Besides, Henry had more than enough.

The woman seemed happily relieved to see her and helped George unload the brood. But her mood changed when Beth told her what she'd discovered in Mobile.

"Oh, my," Mrs. Sandborn said, pulling Beth into an embrace. "I'm so sorry. But that don't sound like Claire. Reckon you shoulda heard her out?"

"Why? What's to hear? She had relations with a man who wasn't her husband an' they made a baby. Then, she told Gerald it was his. I hate her for it!"

Mrs. Sandborn stepped away. Her face hardened and her eyes narrowed. "Hate's a strong word. Claire's been your friend nearly all your life. I know you're angry she misled Gerald, but even *he* wouldn't want ya carryin' around those kinda feelin's."

Beth wouldn't hear it. "It woulda killed him if he'd known what she done! He trusted her. We *both* did. All the while I worried 'bout Henry tryin' to take advantage of her. But *Claire* was the one who took advantage. Truth be told, she *did* kill Gerald!"

"Don't blame Claire for Gerald dyin'." Mrs. Sandborn frowned and shook her head. "That ain't right. Gerald's death was an accident. No one wanted him to die."

"You sure 'bout that? Maybe Claire hoped for it all along so she could go back to *him*." Just thinking about Dr. Fletcher made her heart pound. And *not* in a good way. "I'll *always* blame her. I shoulda saved Gerald." She whipped around and headed for the front door.

"Beth!" Mrs. Sandborn's sharp tone made Beth stop in her tracks. "Don't go out there like this!"

"Like what?" Beth fisted her hands on her hips.

"Bitter." She matched Beth's defiant stance. "You've got a good man sittin' out there waitin' on ya. No doubt he cares 'bout you or he wouldn't be here. Don't let him see ya like this. Take a deep breath an' let your anger go. It ain't healthy."

"I can't!" Beth huffed. "Not now, anyways. If you'd a seen 'em, you'd understand. Michael looks just like him. Why didn't I see it before?"

"Because you loved them." Mrs. Sandborn crossed to her, and with a loving smile rested her hand on Beth's shoulder. "I believe with all my heart that Claire loved your brother. Give her a chance to explain."

Even Mrs. Sandborn's tender touch couldn't melt the ice that had hold of Beth's heart. "No. I ain't never gonna speak to her again."

A single tear fell onto Mrs. Sandborn's cheek, but Beth couldn't appease her and walked out the door.

For a brief moment, she paused on the porch steps. Mrs. Sandborn stood in the doorway, watching her.

Beth sighed. She hated hurting the woman, but it couldn't be helped. "Thank you for everythin' you ever done for me. Don't know when I'll be back. I'd appreciate if you tell Reverend Brown that I've gone to live with my uncle."

"I will." Mrs. Sandborn dabbed at her face with the corner of her apron. "I'll miss ya, Beth. You know I love you."

"You, too." Unable to even *smile* at the woman, Beth climbed into the wagon beside George.

He clicked to the horses and they rode silently until they were a good distance from the small town.

She shifted her eyes to give him a once-over, then stared at the road. Luckily the rain had settled the dust. If not for the anger brewing inside her, she'd have enjoyed this. Surrounded by beauty. A clear, cloudless sky and fresh clean air. Best of all, a man who for some unknown reason decided he liked her.

Cuz a Claire, I can't even be happy sittin' beside a man.

She should be bubbling over.

She completely turned her head to look at him and found him smiling at her. Without even thinking, she returned it.

He'd shaved.

Not bad lookin'.

He had kind, loving brown eyes.

Her heart pattered.

"It's g-good to see ya smile," he said.

"Reckon so," she sighed. His brows wove. "George, I hope you know how much I appreciate this. I know it wasn't what you had planned."

"I—"

"Come to think of it, what *did* you have planned?"

"N-Nothin'. Really. J-Just wanted to be with ya."

"Well, you are." She let out a laugh.

George chuckled. "I'm g-glad you're movin' to Mobile."

"You are?"

"Yep. You'll be closer. If ya ain't at home when I c-call, I can come back. I w-won't hafta wait." He grinned.

Feeling heat rising in her cheeks, she looked away, then casually smoothed her skirt.

"Why me, George?" *Might as well ask.* She was twice his size and not the kind of woman any man had ever paid mind to.

"Huh?"

"Why call on me? I ain't nothin' special."

His face looked almost . . . *sad.* "Don't say that. Y-You got a big heart. I seen how ya cared for Claire."

Why'd he hafta bring her up?

Her lip curled into a snarl. "Some good it did me."

He shook his head like a disapproving parent. "M-Maybe you need to tell me everythin'."

She tipped her head, studying him, then readjusted in the seat. With hours of riding ahead of them, they had time. With such a long story to tell, she'd need it.

George didn't utter a sound. She went on and on about Claire and Gerald, giving every sordid detail.

"So, you see, she might a been my best friend, but I'll never forgive her for what she done." Beth smacked her palms against her thighs. "*Never.*"

George jerked on the reins and stopped the wagon.

Beth's body lurched forward and she had to grab hold of the seat to keep from tumbling out. "Why'd you do that?"

"You're t-too good a woman to n-not forgive."

She looked away. "I can't."

No doubt she'd disappointed him just as she had Mrs. Sandborn. Why couldn't they understand? This was something unforgivable. She had every right to hold a grudge against Claire.

She crossed her arms over her chest and faced him. "Now it's your turn. Tell me 'bout *your* family."

He didn't smile. She'd doused his enthusiasm with her negativity. He'd probably never call on her again and would be glad to be rid of her at Henry's.

After clicking to the horses to get them started again, George began talking. She gave him the same courtesy he'd shown and remained quiet while he spoke. His impediment would frustrate most folks, but she didn't mind. And the more he talked, the less he stuttered. Even if he'd been disappointed in her, maybe in an odd way, she helped him.

She learned that he'd devoted his adult life to caring for his folks. His daddy had debilitating arthritis and his vision had started to fail. He had difficulty doing simple chores, let alone taking care of their farm. They'd sold most of it, so that's why George had to work for Martha. They needed the money. His mama did all she could to help his daddy, but the big man was impossible for her to lift if he happened to fall.

"She r-reads to him." George smiled. "Mostly in German, b-but I've given 'em books in English, too. They n-need it."

"So . . ." She needed clarification. "Do they *speak* English?"

"Not as g-good as me." He grinned.

Without immediately realizing it, through the course of their conversation, her anger had subsided. Good thing, too. Soon she'd have to face Henry and she needed a clear head.

"Your last name's Barnhardt, huh?" He'd told her more

than once and in her mind she'd already tried it out. Beth Barnhardt didn't sound half bad. But she'd gotten ahead of herself.

He nodded.

"It's nice."

"Glad ya like it." This time, he smiled in a different way. Soft. Tender. Maybe he'd been trying out her name, too.

George stopped the wagon right in front of Henry's house. "It's b-big," he said, pointing to the pillared front.

"Yep. An' Henry ain't takin' care of it proper. Himself neither. I aim to change that."

"You're a g-good woman, Beth."

Maybe he'd forgotten his earlier disappointment in her. "Thank you." Heat returned to her cheeks. "Do you mind waitin' while I go in an' make sure he's all right?"

"Want me to go in with ya?"

"No. But thank you for offerin'." She placed her hand on his knee. He gaped at it, so she pulled it to herself. "Wait here. I'll come back to let you know how he's doin'."

He gulped. "All right."

She'd never known such a timid man. At least she'd learned more about him. Truthfully, if he didn't call on her again, she'd be devastated.

After grabbing her bag from the back of the wagon, she went to the front door. She decided to beat on it this time before entering. But, it did no good. She got no answer.

When she went inside, she found him the same way she'd left him. Face down on his bed, snoring like a freight train. His flask lay on the floor, apparently having fallen from his grasp.

With a sigh, she went back to George. "He's fine. Out cold, but still breathin'. I got my work cut out for me."

"Like I s-said. You're a good woman." He removed his hat and held it against his chest. "May I c-call on you again?"

She beamed. "Anytime you like." Tempted to kiss his cheek, she held back. *Don't wanna scare him off.* "I *want* you to call on me."

He grinned from ear to ear. "I will." He helped her unload the rest of her items from the back of the wagon, then hopped up onto the seat. "I'll be callin' soon."

"Fine," she choked out the word. He'd affected her more than she'd realized.

She waited to go inside until he'd driven out of sight. Caring for George had come about easily. *Everything in time*, as Mrs. Sandborn had said. But they weren't getting any younger, so hopefully time would speed up a might. She wanted to spend more of it with him.

Now the hard part.

She raised her chin in the air and paraded through the front door, then grabbed her pack and headed up the stairs to the old nursery. She'd slept there last Christmas, in the single bed that had been placed beside Michael's crib. The crib was gone, so she assumed Claire had taken it.

Under no circumstances would she sleep in Claire and Gerald's bed.

I'll tear it apart and burn it tomorrow.

Once that pleasant task had been completed, she'd move the old wrought iron bed back into that room and stay there. She felt she deserved the biggest and best room in the house. After all, she intended to take care of the place as well as its master. *Some master. Drunk on his tail.*

She'd let him sleep off his drunkenness, but wouldn't let him lie around forever. If he slept too long, she'd wake him with another glass of water.

CHAPTER 8

The moment Andrew stepped inside the house, an incredible aroma welcomed him and started his taste buds anticipating another one of Claire's fabulous meals.

She'd finally stopped crying. Maybe cooking had gotten her mind off the encounter with Beth.

He crept up behind her and encircled her waist. "How are you able to turn a simple chicken into something so delicious?" He kissed her cheek.

She shifted in his arms and faced him. "It's a gift," she said with a soft laugh. "And it's necessary. You have lotsa chickens. I need to get creative so you won't tire of my cookin'."

"I'll never tire of anything you do." He pulled her in closer for a real kiss this time. A tug on his pant leg stopped him. "Are you jealous, Michael?" He lifted him and held him between them.

Claire wrinkled her nose. "He needs a bath. Where's your bathin' tub?"

"In the barn. I'll bring it in after we eat." He got a whiff of what she'd referred to. "For now, I'll change him while you cook."

She giggled. "Thank you."

"And after we put him to bed, I have another tub big enough for grownups." He jiggled his brows.

"Sounds nice." She displayed a smile, but something else lay behind her eyes. Would he ever have his old Claire back again?

Regardless, he loved her. She remained the person he'd fallen in love with, but they'd both become scarred since their first meeting.

I'll help her heal, no matter how long it takes.

If only Beth had listened to her . . .

He cleaned Michael up just in time to sit down to eat. While Claire set the food on the table, he bounced his son on his knee. "We should pay Martha a visit before I have to go back to work. I'll enjoy seeing the look on her face when she sees the three of us together."

He bent down to give Michael a kiss and was rewarded with a tug on the nose. "What is it about my nose that he likes so much?"

"Sumthin' to grab onto I reckon." She patted the baby's head. "He loves you. I can tell."

"So, the nose grabbing is a sign of affection?"

"He's a baby. Nose grabbin' works. He stole *your* heart, didn't he?"

"From the moment I saw him."

She held onto a skillet with one hand, then jabbed a fork into a large chicken breast and placed it on Andrew's plate. "As for Martha . . ." She put a thigh on her own plate. "Good thing you're a doctor. Her heart may fail."

She let out a laugh. "But in all seriousness, I reckon she'll be happy for us. She knows we cared about each other."

After returning the pan to the stove, she handed Michael a biscuit, then sat.

Andrew reached across the table and took her hand. "I wouldn't have been able to save you without her. She rarely left your side."

"It's hard for me to imagine what y'all went through while I was unconscious in that hospital bed."

"It's something horrible I don't ever want to go through again." Michael wiggled out of his lap and went to his mother. "Claire, I know you don't remember it, but you woke up in my arms."

"I did?" Her voice seemed tentative, maybe even . . . *ashamed*? She scooped Michael up and began feeding him tiny bites of meat.

"The last night you were in the hospital, I was beside myself. I wanted to hold you, believing you'd die." Saying it brought back a familiar wrench in his heart. "Martha sat at the door to keep anyone from coming in, so I could lie with you one last time. I got in the bed and cradled you to my chest. Then hours later, you woke up. But . . ." He stared at his plate.

"What?"

"You called out for Gerald." *I shouldn't have said it.* Why make her feel worse?

She pushed her chair back, set Michael down, and knelt beside Andrew. "Don't think 'bout that. We went through a lot. I'm glad you held me. Never believe for a minute I'd rather be with him."

He cupped her cheek. "I'm sorry. I shouldn't have brought it up. But I was thinking about Martha and what she did for me that night. She knew I loved you. And even though she believed I was your brother, she didn't say a word about it. She didn't want me to hurt any more than I already did."

"She's a good woman." She took his hand and inter-locked their fingers. "Let's go see her tomorrow. Since you don't go back to work till Monday, we have time. She needs to know 'bout us."

"That's a wonderful idea." Her smile helped ease the painful memory. "Let's get supper finished so we can get about our *other* business."

"And what might that be?"

"Something that makes *both* of us smile."

Michael giggled.

Andrew lifted him up. "I know you don't understand what we're talking about, do you?"

Michael yanked on his nose. "Dada."

"Yep," Claire said, grinning. "A sign of affection." She patted Michael's head, looking sideways at Andrew. "I'll show you mine later."

"Do *you* pull on noses?"

The devilish grin he got in response made his heart race.

* * *

Claire cleaned the dishes as fast as she could, while Andrew bathed Michael.

She'd promised Andrew she'd only think of him now, but she'd been unable to wash away the memories of Gerald. Even the thought of bathing together reminded her of her late husband.

It's not fair to Andrew.

She'd have to try harder.

While she boiled water for their bath, Andrew settled Michael down for the night. Watching the two of them warmed her, until guilt crept in.

Let it go.

By the time Michael had fallen asleep and they prepared to bathe, Claire was nearly spent. Emotion had taken its toll.

Andrew helped her undress. "The warm water will help." He brushed his lips along her neck.

He knows I'm an uptight mess.

She shivered and quickly removed her undergarments, then stepped into the tub. After securing her hair in a twist, she slid into the water and rested her head against the back of the metal vessel. Though she wanted to close her eyes and bask in the warmth, she kept them open to watch her husband.

His sleek, fit body was a work of art. He'd been perfectly formed. *God's masterpiece.*

"What are you looking at?" he asked, grinning.

"Everythin'." She splashed a bit of water in his direction. "Get in before it gets cold."

He took his place facing her. "Shall I wash your back?"

"Please do." She handed him a bar of lye soap and a sponge, then turned around.

He glided the soap along her skin, and she contentedly closed her eyes. "Mmm . . ." His hand kept moving and eventually found its way to her breasts. "That's not my back, Andrew."

"I know," he whispered in her ear.

She rotated to face him. "I hope so. Doctors *should* know the difference."

"I know a great deal about the human body." He drew her close and kissed her. Long and deep.

"Andrew . . ." she rasped. "I thought we were bathin'."

"We are." He gave her a quick peck. "Want to do *my* back?"

"All right." She took the sponge and moved it over his body. He hadn't faced away from her, so she reached around him to wash his back. Their bodies entwined in a mixture of tepid water and soap suds. Sensuality took hold, and she dotted his chest with tiny kisses.

"I thought we were bathing," he teased.

"We are."

He removed the pins from her hair and it fell across her shoulders. Gently, he drew his fingers through it, then bent forward and kissed her with hunger.

The water had nearly cooled, but her body lit up like a flame. "Let's get outta here and into bed."

Silently, he nodded.

Water dripped from their bare skin as they stood. They wasted little time drying off and hastened to the bedroom.

Their bodies tangled together, ready to release the passion that had been building all day. They made love like two hungering souls devouring the righteous bliss of their affections. Their pain melted away into reassuring pleasure.

* * *

Beth filled the glass full and marched into Henry's room. Without hesitation, she flung the cold water in his face.

"Damn it!" His arms flailed. Glaring, he sputtered and spit, then pushed himself upright. "I thought ya left!"

"I did, but I'm BACK!" She leaned in, just inches from his face. "An' I'm STAYIN'!"

His wide-eyed horror amused her, but she made a point not to laugh. She had to prove her seriousness. So she pulled her shoulders back and stood beside him, waiting for his disapproval.

"I didn't ask ya to stay!" A bigger growl couldn't have come out of a bear.

"Don't care!" She faced him directly so he could read her lips. "I ain't forgiven you for what you done to Gerald, but you're my uncle an' I aim to set you straight."

"Damn women! Nothin' but trouble!" His eyes squinted shut and he winced. "My head hurts."

"Imagine that!"

"Shh!" He waved his hands.

"Ain't gonna shush. How much whiskey you had today?" He turned his head, so she grabbed his chin and made him look at her. "Reckon you don't know, do you?" She picked up the flask from the floor and found it empty. "You ain't gettin' no more."

"Says who?" He scowled. The man she'd always thought handsome, looked like an ogre. "You ain't gonna tell me what I can and can't do. If I want more whiskey, I'll get more whiskey!"

Beth firmed her stance and placed her hands on her hips. "You got two choices. I can haul your tail to the hospital and let *them* dry you out, or you can stay here an' let *me* take care a you. But . . ." She pointed her finger in his face. "If you stay, you do what *I* say. So, what'll it be?"

"If *I* stay here?" He mumbled something unrecognizable. "It's my damn house."

She pursed her lips and tapped her foot. "Well?"

"You gonna cook?"

"Yep. An' I happen to be a might *good* cook."

His upper lip twitched. "Fine! Stay. But it's *my* house! Don't you forget it."

"I won't." She gave him a hint of a smile.

"Can I have just a bit a whiskey?" He held up his fingers, displaying a small portion.

"No!" Her smile vanished and her outburst made him cringe. "If you wanna get rid a them headaches, you gotta lay off the whiskey. Won't be easy, but I'll help you. First and foremost, you need a bath." Having focused on him, she'd ignored the smell, but now it surrounded her. "Smells like sumthin' crawled in the walls an' died!"

"Ach!" He dismissed her with the wave of a hand.

"How long's it been since you bathed?"

"Don't remember."

"Tub still in the shed?"

"Yep."

She turned and left. A genuine smile formed on her face, but she made a point not to let him see it. He had to be handled with an iron fist, and any sign she might give in to him could ruin everything.

After setting the tub in the kitchen, she prepared the water, then drug Henry from his room. Because he'd been wounded in the war, he walked with a cane. In his stupor, he needed even more assistance, though he wouldn't let her help him undress. That turned out to be a good thing. The last thing she wanted was to see the man naked.

She gave him his privacy, but stayed close and checked on him from time to time. Meanwhile, she wandered through the rooms admiring the furnishings.

Much nicer than Claire's.

Henry's wealth was displayed throughout the house. She paused to admire the portrait of her Aunt Sarah that hung above the fireplace mantel. But then she frowned when she noticed the necklace Sarah wore. The same one Henry had given to Claire. Everywhere she looked, reminders of her *friend* remained.

"Beth!"

Huh?

"Beth! Come 'ere!"

She raced to the kitchen, heart pounding. "You DROWNIN'?"

"Nope!" He chuckled. "Just makin' sure you was still here."

Tempted to smack him, she shook her head. He was facing away from her and she wasn't about to go around and look him in the eye. "I ain't goin' NOWHERE!"

"Good!" He glanced over his shoulder and smiled, then sighed and settled back against the tub.

Maybe he's as lonely as I am.

She returned to the living room. They were quite a pair. Both had crushed hearts.

She wanted to stay angry at the man for what he'd done. But since she had to live with him, she decided to focus all her wrath on Claire.

She'd forgive him, but *never* her.

CHAPTER 9

"Are you all right, Claire?" Andrew reached over and gave her a quick pat on the hand.

She instantly stopped fidgeting. How many times had she twirled the loose string on the toe of Michael's stuffed bunny around her finger?

"Truth be told, I'm a might nervous." She clutched Michael closer. Her security. Having him in her lap kept her from biting her nails.

"No need to be. I think Martha will be happy for us." He sat tall. *Confident.*

She wished she shared his enthusiasm.

Though *she'd* been the one to suggest they visit her aunt, she'd decided it might be a bad idea. The sixty-seven year old woman could be more outspoken than a senseless drunk. She never shied away from speaking her mind.

Will she *think I've discounted Gerald?*

"I hope you're right," she finally said, after stewing a few moments.

Sam, Andrew's mare, clopped along and pulled the buggy down the last bit of road to Martha's. Claire's stomach continued to churn.

Andrew gave her a sideways grin, then pulled on the reins and stopped. "We'll be fine." He hopped down. "Want me to take Michael?"

"Just hold him while I get down, then I'd like to carry him inside."

Was it right to use the baby for her own security? *It can't hurt.*

They walked side by side up the pathway to the porch. Claire glanced at the swing, remembering all the times she and Martha had sat together. Tempted to sit there with Michael, she hesitated. *No, I hafta get this over with.*

Andrew pointed to the front door. Again, he displayed a playful grin.

She couldn't return it. "You're enjoyin' this a bit too much."

"I can't help myself. I'm looking forward to telling her our news." He rapped hard on the door.

Heavy footfalls came from the other side. "Who in the . . ." Martha swung the door open wide. "Land sakes!" Even with her missing front tooth, her enormous smile couldn't have been more beautiful. "Claire Belle! Doc! What're you doin' here?" She waved them in.

"You said I could come an' see you soon," Claire said, nervously bubbling over. "So, here I am. That is . . . here *we* are."

Martha scratched her head. "Why y'all together?" Her brows drew in and she whipped her head around to face Andrew. "She relapse?"

"No." He let out a laugh. "It's nothing like that." With raised eyes and a nod of his head, he gestured for Claire to tell their news.

She'd told him she wanted to be the one to tell. But now, the words stuck in her throat like a lump of dry bread. "Martha." She clutched Michael so tight he began to squirm. "That is . . . Um . . ." She set the baby down on the living room floor.

Martha fisted her hands on her plump hips. "Spit it out, girl."

"We have some news. Reckon we should sit?" Claire hastened to the sofa and sat down hard.

Martha's eyes narrowed. "Do I *need* to sit down for this?"

"Maybe." Claire twisted her fingers into knots.

Andrew crossed the room and sat beside her, then took her hand.

"Reckon I *do* need to sit down," Martha muttered. "What's goin' on?" She plopped down onto an overstuffed chair.

Claire smiled, then looked to Andrew for encouragement and took a large breath. "Andrew an' I . . . well . . ." She held up her hand and displayed her wedding ring. "We got married."

"What?" Martha shrieked. Her booming voice startled Michael and he toddled quickly across the floor onto Andrew's lap. "You can't marry your brother! It ain't right!"

"Don't worry, Martha," Andrew said, while bouncing Michael on his knee. "John Martin isn't my father. He raised me, but I was adopted. I didn't know until after you and Claire left the hospital. I went to tell her as soon as I found out, but you were already gone."

Looking like she might combust, Martha fanned her face. "I don't believe it. You sure?"

"Yes." Andrew stroked Michael's hair. "John told me after I told *him* about Michael. I expressed my concern over our son having parents akin to each other." He looked up from the baby and directly at Martha. "After I punched him in the jaw, that is."

She slapped her thigh, eyes popping wide. "You let that damn man have it, did ya?" Her grin lit up the room. "Well, I'll be a . . ." She chuckled and wiped her eyes. "'Bout time. I'd a hit him myself, but it ain't ladylike." She coughed, then turned her head and spit on the floor.

As quickly as she'd been humored, she sobered. "So, why'd he wait so long to tell ya?"

"He'd promised my mother he wouldn't. She'd led everyone to believe she'd given birth to me."

Claire lovingly rubbed his leg. "Least he had the decency to tell. He coulda gone on with the lie an' we woulda never been able to be together."

"Yes," Andrew added. "Aside from fathering Claire, it was probably the only decent thing he's done in his life." He lifted her hand to his lips and kissed it.

Martha grunted. "That's all fine an' good, but you should be ashamed a yourselves!"

What? Claire's heart sank. Not what she'd wanted to hear. Andrew obviously felt the same because he put his arm around her and scooted closer.

"Martha," he said, calmly. "We thought you'd understand. You know how much we love each other."

Claire's heart beat hard. *Why'd we ever come here?* Her throat became even drier, but for a much different reason. Any second now, the tears would come.

"Damn," Martha muttered. "Reckon you didn't come here to hear this. I know you love each other. But couldn't you have waited? Least a little longer?" She shook her finger at Claire. "Gerald's body ain't been in the ground long! How do you reckon Beth's gonna feel when she finds out?"

"She already knows," Claire whispered, staring at her lap.

"Ah, heck . . ." Martha stood and crossed to her. "I'm sorry, Claire Belle."

Claire rose to her feet and wrapped her arms around the woman. "I hurt her, Martha." Though she'd tried to hold them in, her tears fell. "But I did what you told me."

Martha stroked her hair. "What's that?"

Lifting her head from her aunt's shoulder, Claire glanced at Andrew. "I followed my heart. It led me to him. I love him. I always have."

"I know. Better than most anyone. I saw how broken you was after you left him. You went through an awful time an' deserve some happiness. But . . ."

"But?" Claire released her and took a step back, moving closer to Andrew.

"Ya caught me off guard. Don't know *what* to think." Her mouth twitched from side to side, then she nodded at Andrew. "Never will forget how you looked at Claire in the hospital. Ain't never seen such love."

With Michael still in his arms, Andrew stood beside her. "So you should understand why we didn't want to wait. We'd been apart a long time. I wanted us to be a family— like we always should've been."

Martha cupped her hand over Michael's head. "I understand, but I feel bad for Beth. Does she know 'bout *all* a this?"

"She wouldn't give us the chance to explain," Claire said. "But she guessed that Andrew is Michael's daddy. She thinks I lied 'bout everythin'. Doesn't believe I ever loved Gerald."

"Can you blame her? Put yourself in her shoes. She trusted *both* of you."

Her aunt's words depressed Claire even more. Martha hadn't said anything she didn't already know, but hearing it aloud made it painful. Like a knife to her heart.

"Claire Belle?" Martha rubbed her back. "I hope in time you can tell her everythin'. She might not wanna hear it, but maybe she'll understand." She let out a huff. "Sorry. I know you expected me to be happy for ya."

"Well," Andrew said. "We haven't exactly been showered with wedding congratulations."

Martha's face contorted into a different type of confusion. Her brows drew in close. "Weddin' congratulations," she mumbled. "Ain't you s'posed to be marryin' that rich girl? The one who wears them dresses too small?"

Andrew chuckled. The mood in the room had taken a turn. "Victoria?" He set Michael down on the floor.

"Yep. *Victoria.*" Martha said her name with disgust. "Thought the weddin' was next Saturday. What happened?" She returned to her chair, followed by Michael.

"Up." He reached out to her.

She lifted him off the floor and perched him on her lap. "Didn't mean to ignore you, Michael."

He yanked on her nose.

"That means he likes you," Andrew said with a laugh. "And it's good you're sitting down again. The wedding's still on."

Andrew guided Claire back to the sofa.

Martha's face crinkled like a prune. "You ain't makin' no sense!"

"Martha," Claire said. "Victoria's marryin' my daddy."

"John Martin?" Martha had always had large, bugging eyes, but they doubled in size, wide as saucers.

"Yes!" Claire exclaimed, relieved that the conversation had turned.

Martha spat on the floor. "Damndest thing I ever heard." She covered her mouth and looked at Michael. "Sorry. I'll try an control my words round the baby. But how the *hell* did that happen?"

"They were drawn to each other," Andrew said. "His wallet happened to be larger than mine, and he admired her . . . *assets*."

"I seen her assets," Martha chortled. "Hard to miss 'em!"

"Oh, Martha!" Though she felt guilty doing so, Claire giggled. A sad situation, but laughter certainly helped.

Martha blew out a long breath. "Reckon they're well suited. He did you a favor, Doc. That woman was never right for ya. But I never thought you could be with Claire. God has an odd sense a humor."

Her words sunk in deep. "I thought all along He was punishin' me," Claire whispered. "Teachin' me a lesson."

Andrew took her hand and gave it a squeeze. His reassuring smile sent warmth all the way to her toes.

Martha cleared her throat. "Well, did ya learn sumthin'?"

"Course I did." Claire clutched Andrew's hand and leaned against him. "No matter what, I should listen to my heart an' try to do what's right."

Martha's plump legs jostled Michael up and down. "You two *are* right for each other. I think you shoulda waited

longer, but . . . ah heck! What the hell! Congratulations!"
Michael grabbed her nose and this time didn't let go.
"Sorry for cursin'."

Claire let out a laugh. "He's too little to understand, but
when he gets older, you'll need to be careful. We can't have
him repeatin' those kinda words."

"I'll try." Martha shook her head. "How is it John Martin keeps comin' back to haunt us? Hope he stays away an'
leaves ya alone. I don't trust him."

"I doubt you'll have to worry about him," Andrew said.
"He's returning to Bridgeport with Victoria after the wedding. It's unlikely he'll ever come back to Alabama."

"Hmm . . ." Martha scratched her chin. "Much as I dis-
like that girl, I feel sorry for her. She don't know what she's
gettin' into."

"Do you think he'll hurt her?" Claire asked.

"He hurts every woman he touches," Martha huffed. "It
ain't right to despise someone, but it's hard not to hate that
man. Worst kind there is. Talks sweet, but has a devil's tail.
She'll be livin' in Hell 'fore she knows it." She spat on the
floor.

Claire burrowed into Andrew's body. "I feel sorry for
her, too."

"So do I," Andrew said, running his hand along her
arm. "I tried to warn her, but she wouldn't listen."

"Least ya tried," Martha said. With a loud groan, she
stood and set Michael down. Then she crossed the room
and laid a hand on Andrew's shoulder. "She'll find out for
herself one day." She stepped back and clapped her hands.
"I'm tired a bein' gloomy! Let's stop talkin' 'bout this crap
an' have some sweet tea punch!"

She strode out of the room.

"Your aunt has a unique way of putting things," Andrew said. He kissed Claire on the tip of her nose. "I think she's incredible."

"Me, too." Claire smiled, then gave him a real kiss. "I think she's happy for us. Maybe still a might disappointed, but I reckon it's gonna be all right."

"It will." He drew her in and cradled her against his body. "I love you, Claire."

In his arms she believed everything would eventually be fine. Maybe one day her heart would believe it, too.

CHAPTER 10

Monday morning came too soon for Andrew. He sat up in bed and stretched, ready to get out, when Claire pulled him back down.

"This brings back some awful memories," she whispered. Her hand glided across his bare chest.

He knew exactly what she meant. The last time he'd left her to go to work, she'd discovered the letter from their father that changed everything. "You have nothing to worry about." He brushed his fingers along her beautiful face, then kissed her forehead. "I have to go. I have a family to support now."

"I know." She stared into his eyes. "I'm still gonna miss you."

"Just be here when I get home. That's all that matters. The time we're apart makes us appreciate being together." He ran his hands down her back and drew her in closer. With a sigh, she gave him a sweet kiss, but then followed it with something more enticing. He grinned. "Claire, I *have* to go. Mr. Schultz doesn't tolerate tardiness."

"Well then, I wouldn't wanna damage your reputation." She rolled onto her back, looking up at him. "Can't help it if I can't keep my hands off you."

He laced his fingers through her hair. "I'll be home before you know it."

"Think 'bout me." She blinked slowly. Her long lashes highlighted her big brown eyes.

"Of course."

She sat up and shooed him away with a swish of her hand. "Now go on. I'll have a surprise waitin' for you when you get home."

"A surprise?" He got up and started dressing. "What might that be?"

"If I told you, it wouldn't be a surprise." She bit her lower lip, then giggled.

Andrew shook his head and finished getting ready, while Claire made coffee and eggs. Michael hadn't stirred in his crib, so they crept quietly around the house.

After eating a quick bite, Andrew gave Claire a kiss goodbye, then walked away. Not an easy thing to do.

When he arrived at work, Sally greeted him with a cheerful *hello*.

"Hello, Sally." He formally dipped his head. "Did you have a pleasant weekend?"

"Yes, I did." She shuffled through a stack of envelopes, then handed him one. "This is for you. I'm not sure who it's from."

"Thank you." The thing hadn't been mailed. *Dr. Fletcher* had been written on the front in block letters. It bulged from something more than a letter.

He'd planned to report in with Mr. Schultz, but since he'd arrived early, he returned outside. He sat on a bench and opened the envelope, then drew out a letter.

> *Dr. Fletcher*
> *Tell Claire I don't want her house. I don't want nothing of hers.*
> *I padlocked the door. This key will open it.*

The bluntness of the words made his heart ache. Worse yet, he worried how Claire would take them. He tumbled a small metal key through his fingers and continued reading.

> *I moved in with Henry. He's my family. The ONLY family I got left.*
> *No need for either of you to come here ever again. Claire got all that was hers. Tell her to keep the cow, too. Henry don't want it. Like me, he don't want nothing that will remind him of her.*
> *Just stay away.*
> *Beth*

Andrew closed his eyes, wishing he'd never seen the letter. Then he folded and placed it back into the envelope with the key. Knowing it would hurt her, he wouldn't give it to Claire. At least not anytime soon.

With a heavy heart, he walked down the hallway to the administrator's office and rapped on the door.

"Come in," Mr. Schultz bellowed.

Andrew pushed the door open, shocked to be greeted by a smile. "Dr. Fletcher! It's good to see you!"

Odd. Unlike Sally, the man had never been the cheerful sort. But he'd changed somewhat since Andrew had miraculously saved Claire's life. The hospital had received commendations from all over the country for his use of an untried procedure.

"Thank you, sir."

"I've heard rumors," Mr. Schultz said, rubbing his chin. "Rumors about you and Mrs. Alexander. Are they true?"

Sally had obviously spread the word. "If you heard that she and I are married, then yes, they are."

Mr. Schultz took a seat at his desk, then folded his hands atop it. His demeanor had darkened. "Does Patrick O'Malley know?"

"No, sir." He took a seat across from him. "Mr. O'Malley and I have no further business with each other. Victoria decided to marry someone else. My father, as a matter of fact."

The man's face turned ashen. "Your father? He must be twice her age."

"Yes, he is. But Victoria chose him and he didn't refuse her." Andrew spoke with little feeling. If he thought about the situation too deeply, it would upset him.

"Hmm." Mr. Schultz grunted. "Well. Unusual to say the least, but . . ." He loosened his collar. "I can understand *why* he would want her."

Andrew studied him. He seemed a little *jealous*. "Yes, sir."

The man cleared a great deal of phlegm from his throat. "I was concerned—about the rumors. Patrick O'Malley contributes a great sum of money to our hospital. I feared you'd potentially damaged that relationship."

"No, sir. I believe Mr. O'Malley will continue to support the hospital. And since Victoria will be moving away and financially supported by someone else, O'Malley may have even more money to spend."

Mr. Schultz dabbed at his brow with a handkerchief. "That is very good news. As for your new *wife*, are you certain this isn't simply a doctor-patient infatuation? Aside from the fact that she's recently widowed, I'm sure you're aware those things can happen. Perhaps you've rushed this."

"I'm well aware that patients can become enamored with their doctors. We briefly studied about it in medical school. But I assure you, Claire was in my heart long before she became my patient. Neither of us saw the need to wait."

"Hmm." Once again, he shuffled the papers on his desk. "Now I understand why you took on the burden of her debt." With a huff, he stood. "I doubt your hasty decision will serve you well." He motioned to the door. "Your patients are waiting." The stern man had returned.

Andrew left his office, undaunted by the man's shifting demeanor.

Soon his relationship with Claire would be known by all. He didn't have to hide any longer. That alone eased his burden.

With a spring in his step, he headed down the hall to examine his first patient.

* * *

The instant Andrew left, memories of the horrible day that eventually led to Gerald's death, covered Claire.

Stop lookin' at it that way!

She stomped her foot, angry for allowing guilt to continue its harmful taunt.

With Michael still sleeping, she decided to get her mind off things by cleaning and straightening the house.

"Mama!"

Household chores would have to wait.

She scooped Michael up, then quickly changed him. She'd take him with her to milk Rosie, then she'd feed him breakfast.

In a few short days, they'd fallen into a routine. With Andrew back at work, the routine had changed, but still felt comfortable. And, it felt *right*. As long as she kept guilt at bay.

Michael pointed to Rosie. "Ow," he said, grinning.

"That's right!" Claire beamed. Andrew must have taught him the new word. "Rosie's a cow." She emphasized the *c*, but Michael repeated the word without it. It didn't matter. She was sure her son would be a genius like his daddy.

After milking, she gathered eggs. More than she'd ever be able to use before they'd spoil.

"Michael? Let's go see your new friend, Betsy. We can take her mama some eggs. Would you like that?"

He grinned and clapped his hands. Maybe he understood.

After feeding him his oats, they headed down the road to Alicia's.

Michael walked beside her at first, holding his bunny by one ear dragging it behind him, but the road had deep ruts that his wobbly little legs couldn't manage. So, she decided to carry him. Michael on one hip and the basket of eggs looped through her opposite arm.

She lifted her face to the brilliant sunshine. Walking felt good. Fresh air and a feeling of contentment. But as she neared Shanty Town, uneasiness crept in.

I don't belong here.

Andrew was accepted because he doctored the folks. They all knew him, but not her.

She clutched Michael tighter. Luckily, Alicia's house sat at the edge of the small community.

Silly? Maybe. But tension had not eased between whites and colored folks.

They won't hurt a woman with a baby.

She hastened to Alicia's front door and pounded hard.

Samuel opened it. "Mama! It's Doc's wife an' baby!"

Alicia's face lit up upon seeing her, but instantly turned to a frown. "Miss Claire? What's wrong?" She pulled her inside. "You sick?"

"N-No." Claire handed her the eggs. "I thought you might need these."

Michael wiggled out of her arms and onto the floor, then toddled across the room to Betsy. The two erupted with giggles. If only she could be as colorblind as her son.

"Thank ya," Alicia said. She set the basket on the kitchen table, then motioned for Claire to have a seat. "Want some coffee? You looks like ya needs it."

"Yes. Thank you." Claire loosened her sunbonnet and pushed it off her head, leaving it dangling down her back. She glanced over her shoulder at the children. "Looks like Michael doesn't need me anymore." She forced a smile.

Alicia set a cup of coffee in front of her. "That's children for ya. They takes to each other easily. Grownups should learn from them." She looked directly at Claire. "Sumthin's troublin' you."

"I . . ." Claire took a quick sip of coffee. "Forgive me. I truly like you. You've been more than kind. But I've never been 'round colored folks. I wanted to see you—and bring the eggs, but the closer I came, I got nervous. Afraid some-one might see me an' *do* sumthin'."

"Do sumthin'? Like . . .?"

"I don't know. Hurt me somehow."

"Miss Claire . . ." Alicia laid her dark hand over the top of Claire's snowy white one. "Bein' colored don't make folks bad. It's what's in their hearts that do. They's lotsa good folks here just tryin' to get by. We loves our children an' want what's best for 'em. Just like you does." She pulled her hand back. "We's free, but in many ways, we's helpless. That's why we thank God for Doc Fletcher. He's saved more lives here than I can count. If'n more folks was like him, we'd have more hope for our children."

"Hasn't the government helped you?" Claire swallowed hard.

Alicia chuckled. "Shore. They gave out money to get us started, but most folks din't know what to do with it. Lijah tried to teach 'em. They loved him. Respected him. But even the new laws couldn't protect him. Some folks still make their own rules. They hates us just cuz we's colored."

"But that's wrong." Claire's fear had turned to heartache, knowing Elijah had been hung for something he didn't do. "How do *you* not hate?"

"God say we should love. *Forgive*. That's how."

Claire had been a Christian all her life, but had never seen such faith. Her eyes pooled with tears. "I'm glad you're my friend."

"Me, too." She patted Claire's hand and stood. Crossing to the stove, she got her own cup of coffee and returned to the table.

They sat quietly for a few moments.

What would I do if sumthin' happened to Andrew?

Losing Gerald had been horrible, but she doubted she'd want to go on living if Andrew died.

"Miss Claire?"

She met Alicia's gaze. "Yes?"

"Don't think 'bout the bad things. Set your mind on good. Then your heart will heal."

How had this woman been able to see into her heart? Andrew had said Alicia was perceptive and smart. She was beginning to understand what he meant.

Claire nodded, then let out a sigh. "Where are your other children?"

"Clay an' Jenny is out in the fields. My hard-workin' boy took over tendin' the farm after his daddy died. Jenny helps best she can." Alicia shook her head from side to side. "Boy wanted to be a doctor. Doc was learnin' him for a time. But now . . ."

"It's a shame." What more could she say? Clay had no choice but to tend the fields. She stared at her coffee cup.

"Don't you fret, Miss Claire. We takes what God puts in front of us. Clay's usin' what his daddy taught him. The boy's happy doin' it. Lijah would be proud."

"I know you are, too." This time, Claire reached across the table and took Alicia's hand. "I'm glad you're here. I truly do need a friend."

And like water pouring from a pitcher into a glass, she spilled everything out. She told Alicia what had happened between her and Beth, and also about their visit with Martha. Somehow she spoke without shedding a single tear.

Alicia sipped her coffee and listened, not saying a word.

"It hurts," Claire said and closed her eyes.

"Course it does." Alicia refilled their cups. "I was happy for you an' Doc, cuz I knew everythin' what happened. When folks doesn't know everythin' they makes up their own minds what's right. They judge wrongly 'thout all the facts. One day, your friend will forgive ya. In time, God'll find a way to bring you back together. He'll soften her heart."

"How can you be sure?"

Alicia let out a soft laugh. "Cuz she loves you." She shook her finger when Claire was about to protest. "Love can get angry, but real love never goes away. She be angry, but she loved you too long for it not to be real."

A heavy weight lifted from Claire's shoulders and she sat a little taller. "How do you do it?"

"What?"

"Make sense of everythin'? I've never met anyone with a faith like yours, an' I've been goin' to church all my life. But I've never felt the peace you seem to wear so comfortably. I've always believed in God, but I don't think I've trusted Him the way you do."

Alicia's head tipped to one side. "Miss Claire, if I didn't have my faith I'd be a bitter woman. What good would that do my children? God puts peace in my heart." She chuckled. "Don't get me wrong. I ain't no saint! One day I'll hafta reconcile some things with the good Lawd, but I know He loves me, an' he knows I ain't perfect. Just a poor colored woman tryin' to get by." She grinned.

They talked for hours. Time slipped away, until Claire realized that if she didn't return home soon, Andrew might come home and find her gone again. She didn't dare put him through that.

Michael hadn't had a nap and as soon as she picked him up off the floor to leave, he rested his head against her and closed his eyes.

Alicia tucked his bunny under his arm.

"Thank you," Claire whispered. "He'd be lost without it."

"I understan'." Alicia's warm smile would stay in Claire's heart forever.

"Oh . . . Alicia, I know this is soon, but would you mind watchin' him for us tonight? I'd like to do sumthin' extra nice for Andrew, and—"

"Nuff said. Bring him anytime. You can leave him *now* if you'd like."

"No. I'm sure Andrew will wanna see him when he gets home. We'll bring him by after supper." With Michael pressed between them, she gave Alicia a hug. "Thank you for everythin'."

"No need to thank me. I'm your friend. You're a good woman, Miss Claire, an' *I'm* thankful Doc finally married ya."

Refreshed, Claire walked away.

God put an angel in my life.

Alicia had reminded her that no one was perfect. Everyone sinned and forgiveness was attainable. If only she could forgive herself.

* * *

Andrew's heart beat hard. His home had come into view. Had it sped up anticipating seeing Claire again, or fearing what he'd found the last time he'd come home to her.

She'll be there.

His confidence had grown, but it didn't wash away the painful memories.

He drove to the barn and unhitched Sam, then gathered one of Claire's surprises from the seat of the buggy and walked briskly to the house. She'd promised a surprise for him, and he delighted in retaliating.

As he approached the door, a welcoming scent filled the air.

She's cooked something good.

Her meals had never disappointed him.

Leaving her surprise on the stoop, he inhaled the wonderful aroma, then with a smile on his face, went inside.

His beautiful wife stood in his simple kitchen wearing an apron over her cotton dress. Her face glowed with a smile the second he entered. She ran across the floor and embraced him, then gave him a kiss.

"That's some welcome," he said and kissed her again. He glanced around his spotless home and immediately noticed blue gingham donning his kitchen window. "I love them." He pointed to the curtains. "How'd you get them done so fast?"

"I'm simply astonishin'." She grinned and batted her eyes, sparkling like the Claire he remembered from long ago. *Please stay.*

"I've always known that." He pushed his fingers through her hair. "Still, you amaze me. The house looks wonderful, and something smells delicious."

"I promised to get creative with your chickens, so I made a pot pie."

"Well . . ." He pulled her in close. "I love my surprises. You outdid yourself." He moved his lips close to her ear and lightly nibbled her earlobe. "Did you miss me?"

Her body quivered. "Andrew Fletcher!" She backed away and playfully smacked his chest. "Course I did. But don't start that now. We hafta eat supper first." She pointed to a chair at the table.

"More!" Michael beat his hands against the chair.

"Michael!" Andrew swooped him up. "Have you been good for Mama today?"

"Yes, he has," Claire said. She removed a pan from the oven. "We went to Alicia's an' he played with Betsy."

"Oh? Good coffee?" Andrew bounced him on his knee.

"Yes. An' even better conversation. She's remarkable. I'm glad you introduced us." She walked around behind him and bent close to his ear. "She's gonna keep Michael for us tonight." With a quick peck on his cheek, she returned to the stove. The implication of what he had to look forward to set his heart thumping again. "More surprises for me?"

With a coy tip of her head, she bit her lower lip. "Nothin' you haven't had before. Hope that's not too disappointin'."

"Never."

"More!" Michael protested.

"Now, Michael," Claire said. "Mama an' Daddy are havin' some fun. I'm gettin' your food."

Good time for one of *his* surprises. "I have something for you, Michael," he said and set him down. He opened the door and brought it in from the stoop.

"A highchair!" Claire exclaimed. She ran her hands over the back of it as he pushed it into place at the end of the table. "It's perfect, Andrew. Where'd you get it?" She picked Michael up and sat him in the chair. He grinned and patted his hands on the table.

"Do you remember Mrs. Stevens, the hospital matron?" Claire nodded. "Her husband's a carpenter who makes wood furniture as well. He happened to have this highchair in his shop. But that's just part of *my* surprise."

"An' to think surprises were *my* idea." She grinned. "There's more?"

With lips sealed tight, Andrew took his seat at the table. Claire's eyes widened and she waved her hands in a circle, prompting him to continue.

"I've hired the man to add on to our house. He said he could start next week."

"Oh, my!" Her reaction made him laugh. Eyes filled with joy, she looked like a child who'd just been given candy. Exactly what he'd wanted to see. But then her face fell. "Can we afford it?"

They'd never discussed finances. He hadn't seen the need. No doubt she'd been used to pinching pennies. She'd lived alone for a long time and even when she'd been married to Gerald, he was certain money matters had come into play.

"Don't worry about that. We'll be fine. Our land and home are paid for. John gave me some of my mother's money when I moved here, allowing me to buy everything outright. Our food takes care of itself through bartering and our garden, so I've managed to tuck away some extra money."

She reached for a plate and dished up a large portion of pot pie, then set it down in front of him. "I shoulda known you wouldn't be reckless."

He took her hand and kissed it. "I have a family to care for. I won't be irresponsible."

After scooping a portion for herself, then spreading out some for Michael and blowing on it, she sat down. "So, what all is Mr. Stevens gonna do?"

"Since Michael will probably want his own room one day, I've asked him to add on two bedrooms, a bathing room, and a full front porch. I've also asked him to fix up the loft so it could be used as a bedroom as well."

"Four bedrooms? Reckon we'll need that many?"

"If we continue our nightly play, *yes*." He winked, and her cheeks turned crimson. "Why, Miss Claire." He used his best attempt at a southern drawl. "Are you embarrassed?"

She scooted her chair back, moved behind him, then squatted down and encircled him with her arms. "No. You just got me thinkin'. Now hurry up an' eat so we can work on fillin' those rooms."

She returned to her seat and devoured her food. Andrew did the same. Unfortunately, Michael took his time. Once he'd finished, Andrew whisked him off to Alicia's. He didn't stay for coffee.

CHAPTER 11

Saying goodbye to Andrew had been harder than ever after a night of lovemaking.

Claire giggled, thinking about his droopy eyes as he headed out the door. They'd gotten little sleep, but it'd been worth it. The only thing they didn't like was waking up and not having Michael there. The house seemed too empty. So she hurried off to Alicia's to bring him back home just as soon as Andrew left.

"He was fine," Alicia said and placed him into Claire's outstretched arms. "But I reckon you'll need some rest today. Take a nap when the baby does." She laughed and patted Claire on the shoulder.

"I may do that. But it's so beautiful outside I plan to do some gardenin'. I'll let Michael help." She took his little hand and helped him wave goodbye. "Thank you!" she called out as they walked away.

Once home, she went to the barn and got a shovel. She intended to move some bushes from the woods to the side of the house. Eventually she'd get some flower bulbs so they could have a little color next spring.

"Dada!" Michael called out and pointed.

Claire looked up from the hole she'd started to dig. Her breath hitched, then her stomach knotted. She dropped the shovel and lifted Michael into her arms. "That's not dada," she whispered.

The large man strode along the road coming from Shanty Town. His dark skin glistened in the sunlight, reflecting sweat that beaded on his brow. Since the weather wasn't that warm, he had to have been walking hard.

Well aware folks knew Andrew was a doctor, she shouldn't be so nervous. But her belly twisted in warning. She prayed he'd keep on walking, but he headed straight for them. She tightened her hold on the baby.

As he neared, his size overwhelmed her. Taller and larger than Andrew. He had to be over three hundred pounds.

He stopped with only a few feet between them. "The doc live here?" His gruff voice gave her chills.

"Well . . . y-yes." She couldn't hide her nervousness. And the way he smirked, she could tell it pleased him. She had to look away from his dark, pitted skin. "I'm afraid he's not here right now." Why had she told him? She could've led him to believe he'd be out any moment.

"When will he be home?" He took a step closer.

Be strong. Don't let him know you're afraid.

She pulled her shoulders back and met his gaze, then winced at his rotting teeth. "Are you ill?"

"No." His lip curled into a snarl. "Just need to see 'im. When will he be home?"

"Soon," she lied.

His eyes moved over every inch of her. "Who are you?"

She protectively shielded Michael from the man's penetrating gaze. Could she outrun him? "His wife." She took a few steps back. "You should come back later." She bolted for the front door.

In a few long strides, he overtook her. He wrestled Michael from her arms and threw him to the ground. Then the man's constricting grip imprisoned her.

"Don't hurt my baby!" She struggled. Kicked. Hit against him as hard as she could. But it only made him laugh.

Michael's head had struck the ground. Blood trickled from an open wound. Worse yet, he didn't cry. He lay there, not moving.

Tears streamed down her face as she continued to struggle. "Let me go!" She stomped on his foot.

"You ain't got red hair, but you's feisty!" He forced her into the house and locked the door, then pushed her to the floor.

The impact hurt, but she didn't care. She had to get to Michael.

Jumping to her feet, she raced for the door. But the man grabbed her and stopped her with a hard slap to the face. "Forget the baby. You best worry 'bout yourself. It's you I came for. Tobias told me you had red hair. Musta been wrong. Was in a lotta pain 'fore he died."

His powerful grip dug into her arm, but she jerked at it, ignoring the pain. Her cheek stung, and her mind raced.

Tobias, the man who hurt Victoria.

Her thoughts turned to Michael, making her chin quiver. *He needs me.* "What do you want with me?" She couldn't keep her voice from shaking. Her eyes darted around the room looking for a weapon.

"Poor little thing," he hissed. "You scared?" He grasped both of her arms and brought her within inches of his face. "You *should* be."

She turned her head. His foul breath made her gag. "Who are you?"

"Jeremiah. Tobias's brother." His evil laughter filled their tiny home. "The last man you'll ever see."

He's gonna kill me. My baby might already *be dyin'.*

With tear-filled eyes, she looked upward, but not at the wretched man. *Please, God. Help us.*

She prayed for courage. "Don't do this. I've never done anythin' to hurt you *or* your brother."

He grunted. "You *killed* my brother. That thing you jabbed in his back infected him. No man should die that way. 'Specially my kin." He released one of her arms, and she tried to pull away. "Ain't gonna work." He held up some rope he'd removed from his pocket. "Tobias wadn't too smart. Forgot to tie your hands. I came prepared."

He wrestled her down to the floor, then turned her onto her stomach and sat on her. She struggled to breathe against his weight. He bound her hands behind her back and yanked the rope tight. It dug into her flesh.

"Bible say eye for an eye." He bent so low that his rough face scratched against her cheek. "God gave me the right to do what I aim to. You believe in God?" He pulled on the rope, chuckling.

If he tightened it any more, it would cut to the bone. She winced at the pain. "I believe, but He'd never want you to hurt me or my baby." Tears streamed down her face.

He forcefully turned her over so she was lying on her bound hands. Helpless.

He glared at her. "*I'm* God." His eyes moved to her breasts.

No. She wanted to scream it, knowing full well what Tobias had tried to do to Victoria. But fear froze her in place.

"Tobias was right 'bout one thing." He licked his lips, then squeezed her breast. "Big an' fine." But then he drew his hand back and snarled. "I ain't like Tobias. Ain't gonna poke no white woman. Once I'm through with ya, I's goin' back to Shanty Town. Hear there's a colored widow woman fine to look at. Aim to have a go at *her*. Not no white whore."

She pinched her lips shut. She didn't dare say Alicia's name aloud. *No.* But how could she help Alicia when she couldn't even help herself. *Or Michael.*

Tears dripped down the sides of her face.

He pushed her hair away from her neck. "Where's the scar? Tobias say he bit ya." He chuckled, low and sinister. "I'll leave more than a scar."

"I didn't kill your brother," she said, sucking in air. "I swear it wasn't me."

"You're lyin'. You said you's Doc's wife. It was you." He studied her, then ran a single finger along her neck. "But how should I do it?"

She looked away from him.

God, please make it quick. An' don't let Michael suffer.

He stood and wrenched her from the floor, then dragged her to the bedroom. With a single shove, he tossed her onto the bed.

"No!" she screamed as she flopped backward. Immediately she rose up and tried to stand. *I hafta get to Michael.*

Her protest set him laughing again. "You ain't goin' nowhere. Don't ya see? We's gonna have some fun."

A knife shimmered in his hand.

Claire swallowed hard. "Please don't."

"Ain't gonna listen to you no more." He looked around the room and deviously laughed when he found one of Michael's small blankets. A sound she'd never forget. He twisted it, then forced it into her mouth, gagging her. He tied it behind her head. "Don't wanna hear ya scream."

He touched the tip of the blade to her cheek and pressed, piercing her skin. Yes, he'd toy with her. Hurt her until he'd had enough, then plunge the knife into her and take her life. She knew enough of evil to understand his intentions.

She closed her eyes. *Why?*

She and Andrew had just begun their lives. They had love. *Joy.* A child they planned to watch grow. She'd cheated death before . . .

Oh, Andrew . . .

A loud thud and Jeremiah's body fell onto her.

What?

Her eyes popped open.

Clay?

He stood over them, horrified, clutching the shovel. Blood oozed from Jeremiah and onto Claire. He'd been struck with the sharp metal edge. It split his head wide open.

Claire groaned and wriggled beneath the dying man.

Clay stared, then pointed. "What'd I do?"

Claire pushed with all her might and still couldn't get the huge man off her.

Finally, Clay moved. He tossed the shovel to the side and grabbed the back of Jeremiah's shirt. The man flopped onto the floor with a thump.

Claire grunted and jerked her head, gesturing for help. With shaking hands, Clay untied the gag.

"Untie my hands!" she yelled. "I gotta help Michael!"

Unsure *why* Clay had come, she accepted it as an answer to prayer. She had no time for an explanation. He unbound her and she raced out the door.

Michael hadn't moved. "Bring me a towel!" she screamed at Clay and sped to the barn. She saddled Cocoa, fussing at herself for having to waste time to use it. But she'd have to carry Michael and needed the security, and the wagon wouldn't be fast enough.

When she knelt beside Michael's body, Clay handed her a towel. His face held no expression. "That man I hit. I think he's dead."

"You did right. He woulda killed me." She rapidly bound Michael's head, then stood and placed him into Clay's arms. After giving Clay a quick kiss on the cheek, she mounted Cocoa. "Hand me Michael. I gotta get him to his daddy."

Still dazed, Clay lifted the baby toward her. She held him close. While she grasped him with one arm, she clutched the saddle horn with her free hand. Her heels dug into the mare's side and they raced away.

The towel covering Michael's head had already become stained with blood. Her heart pounded hard along with Cocoa's thundering hooves. Her baby lay limp in her arms, but she held him tight, not about to give up hope.

She nearly raced the horse up the hospital steps, but stopped at the bottom and jumped down. With Michael clutched to her breast, she flew through the front door.

"Sally!" Claire yelled. "Where's Andrew?"

Wide-eyed, Sally didn't utter a sound. She fled down the hall and in no time returned with Andrew running beside her.

"Oh, God. Claire . . . Michael?" He took him from her. His brows dipped with worry. "Come with me." She could tell he was trying to hide it from her, but fear lay beneath his solemn expression. How could it not when she and the baby were covered in blood? "What happened?"

He didn't stop moving and she stayed on his heels. "A man—Oh, Andrew! He said he was Tobias's brother. He did this!"

"Tobias?" Andrew's face paled. He pushed open a door and she followed him in.

"Yes. He . . . he . . ." She sniffled, fighting back tears. The man on her bedroom floor didn't matter anymore. "Will Michael be all right?" He'd laid the baby on an examination table and removed the cloth.

Without answering, he pressed a stethoscope to Michael's chest. The worry on his face made her physically ill. She covered her mouth to keep from retching.

"His heartbeat's strong," Andrew whispered. His lips formed a half smile. "But he needs to wake up." He examined the deep gash above his right eye. "He'll need stitches."

"Our poor baby . . ." Unable to hold back, she erupted into tears. "I couldn't help him!"

Andrew pulled her into an embrace. "Shh . . . This isn't your fault." He placed his hands to the sides of her face and peered into her eyes. "You didn't cause this."

"But . . ." She pointed to the baby. "What if he doesn't wake up?"

"He will."

Andrew released her and began cleaning the wound. "Come hold his hand while I stitch him."

She rapidly nodded and took Michael's tiny hand in her own.

The second Andrew inserted the needle, Michael squalled. Claire had never heard a more beautiful sound. Both she and Andrew let out a tearful laugh.

"Hush, Michael," she soothed against his cheek. He'd started to squirm, so she had to hold him tighter. "Mama's here. Daddy's makin' you all better."

It took eight stitches to close the wound, and throughout the procedure he hadn't stopped crying. Once done, Andrew picked him up and held him close. "Oh, Claire . . ." Andrew blinked slowly several times, taking her in as though he'd never seen her before. He reached out and touched her cheek. "My God, you're hurt, too." His fingertips barely touched her skin.

"I'm fine."

"No, you aren't." He stepped closer, gaping at her dress. "*His* blood?"

"Yes."

A second of relief filled his eyes, until he moved them to her face. "He hit you. A bruise is forming." He guided her to a chair. "Sit down so I can get a better look."

She didn't argue. Her knees had felt like they might give way any moment.

With Michael clutched to his body, Andrew knelt in front of her. "Where else are you hurt?"

She showed him her wrists. Though they'd stopped bleeding, they throbbed. The rope had dug deep and stripped away some of her skin.

"Can you hold him?" Andrew nodded toward Michael.

"Course I can." He'd calmed and no longer cried. He nestled into her body. Nothing had ever felt so wonderful.

Andrew stood, then rummaged around in a drawer and produced a bottle of salve. After studying the small cut on her face, he rubbed it with the medicine and also put some on her wrists. "I'm glad *you* don't need stitches." He let out a long breath.

"Me, too. I've had my fair share of needles." She tried to encourage him with a smile, but it didn't work.

"Make certain he stays awake." He smoothed Michael's hair. "It's important." Moisture clouded Andrew's dark eyes.

"I will."

Tears spilled over onto her husband's cheeks.

"Andrew." She ran her fingers through his hair. "I'm fine. Michael's fine. Nothin' else matters."

He wrapped his arms around both of them, kissed Michael's cheek, then kissed her long and deep. Without words, he said what she'd been feeling. They could've lost each other.

With a heavy sigh, Andrew pressed his forehead to hers. "Tell me what happened."

Now that she knew their son would live, she recanted the whole story. Not leaving out a single detail, the more she told him, a different kind of pain grew in his eyes. He stood and paced as she finished speaking.

Finally, he stopped, but turned his back to her. "Maybe I should've listened to O'Malley and moved into the city."

"No. I love our home. We can't let one bad man change the way we wanna live."

"But he could've—"

"He's dead, Andrew. He can't hurt anyone."

Andrew looked downward, shaking his head. "Still . . . If he'd—"

"Stop." Her abrupt tone made him look at her. "Don't say it, an' don't think it."

He stood erect and lifted his chin. "You should take Michael home. I'll tell Mr. Schultz I need to leave, then I'll get the city marshal and bring him to the house. I don't like the man, but I have no choice."

"You don't like the marshal?"

Andrew looked from side to side, then leaned close to her. "He's affiliated with the Klan," he whispered. "One of the men in O'Malley's back pocket."

"Our own city marshal? Things are worse here than I ever thought."

With a frown, Andrew nodded. "I'm certain he'll have questions for Clay."

"Don't know why he came by, but I thank God he did. Poor boy was in shock when I left him. But if what you say 'bout the marshal is true, will he be safe?"

"Safer than his father was." The faraway look in Andrew's eyes broke her heart.

She reached out to him and he drew both her and Michael into his arms. He held her so tight he nearly took her breath. He pressed his cheek to hers. "I love you."

"I love you, too." They locked eyes. Then a pat on the face from Michael made her drop her gaze. "I'll take him home."

"I'll be there soon. I promise."

As she walked away, she glanced over her shoulder.

Andrew wiped tears from his eyes.

* * *

I could've lost everything.

The thought repeated through Andrew's mind. Though Claire had told him not to think it, he couldn't wash it away.

Fortunately, Mr. Schultz had understood his need to leave, though he'd mumbled a comment Andrew heard loud and clear. *Trouble seems to follow you.*

The man was right. People he loved kept getting hurt. *Why?*

"You're bein' a might quiet."

With a quick look to the side, Andrew acknowledged the marshal. He'd agreed to accompany Andrew home, though he'd grumbled about having to go so close to Shanty Town.

"I have a lot on my mind," Andrew said. He faced forward again, his eyes glued to Charger's backside.

He'd told the marshal what had happened and got scarcely more than a grunt in reply. Andrew wished there was another lawman who could handle the situation, but the marshal was the only one available.

Unspoken animosity hung in the air. The man's affiliation to the Klan sickened him. He could very well be sitting beside one of the men responsible for Elijah's death.

"So," the marshal said, then spit over the side of the buggy. "A filthy nigga tried to murder your wife an child. That 'bout sums it up. Ain't that right?"

"An evil *man*," Andrew said. "One who wanted to hurt *me*."

"Hmph. Cuz a his brother, you say? Man named Tobias?"

"Yes. Tobias Lewis. The man who attacked Victoria O'Malley. The man who should've hung the night you strung up Elijah Tarver." Andrew turned his head just enough to leer at the man. His heart pounded. He'd taken a risk speaking his mind.

The man's upper lip twitched. "Watch what you say, *Doc*."

The longer the marshal spoke, it confirmed what Andrew believed. Though the men that night had covered Andrew's face, he recognized the man's voice as one of those who'd tied him up and threatened him.

Andrew didn't reply. Enough had been said.

But then, the man broke out laughing. "Thought you was marryin' O'Malley's daughter. That nigga change your mind?"

If only the marshal had remained silent. "Victoria changed *her* mind. She's marrying my father."

The marshal laughed even harder. "Your daddy? Wish I coulda seen O'Malley's face when that happened!" He slapped his knee, but then his laughter subsided into something more sinister. "Looks like you have no one protectin' you no more."

O'Malley had told them not to hurt him because of Victoria, so the man was right. He'd lost his protection. "I have a family now. If you take your position seriously, you'll do what's right by all of us."

Again the man grunted, then spit.

When Andrew stopped the wagon in front of his house, they were immediately greeted by Claire. She still held Michael tight in her grasp. He blinked wide-eyed at Andrew, then reached for him. "Dada."

Andrew gladly took him.

The marshal stared at Claire. "This your wife?"

"Yes," Andrew said. "This is Claire."

"Marshal," Claire said, acknowledging him. She dipped her head and motioned for him to enter. The man strode inside without another word.

Claire questioned Andrew with her eyes.

"I told him everything I knew," Andrew whispered. "I think he wants to talk to Clay."

Claire sighed and they walked together to the kitchen table. The marshal hovered over Clay, arms folded across his chest.

He's trying to intimidate the boy.

Clay trembled and twisted his fingers together. "You gonna arrest me?"

Without answering, the man headed to the bedroom. After passing Michael over to Claire, Andrew followed him.

The marshal snarled in disgust, then shoved his foot against Jeremiah's rear end. "Filthy nigga."

Andrew pushed by him and knelt beside the body. He pressed his fingers to the man's neck, feeling for a pulse. He hadn't expected to find one, especially after seeing the amount of blood pooled on the floor. But his instincts as a doctor always prompted him to follow through.

"The man's dead," the marshal said flatly, then spat on his body.

Andrew jerked a blanket from the bed and covered him. He no longer wanted to look at the man. Pure evil dese-crated the floor of his bedroom. Would Claire be able to sleep here ever again?

"You got a might pretty woman out there," the marshal said. "Know what that piece a filth coulda done to her?"

Andrew looked away and didn't reply.

"You wanna protect your wife, move into town an' get away from the coloreds."

"We like it here," Claire said, defiantly stepping into the room. "This is our home."

"Well, ma'am . . ." The marshal spoke in a kinder tone to Claire, but no matter how the man acted, Andrew didn't trust him. "I'm thinkin' of you an' your child. These niggas don't respect no one white. Even children. Understand?"

"I understand perfectly well." She bounced Michael in her arms. "There are bad people in this world. Colored *and* white." Eyes filled with anger, she stared him down.

With a low growl, the marshal stomped his way out of the bedroom and headed toward the front door.

"Marshal?" Andrew stopped him. "What should we do now?"

The man looked around the house, as if taking mental notes. "Clean up the mess."

"That's all you have to say?"

"Way I see it . . ." The marshal rubbed his chin. "That nigga got what he deserved." He gestured with his head toward Clay. "That boy did Mobile a favor. Not many niggas will kill their own kind."

Andrew pushed aside disgust for the man. "Don't we need to file a report? Or sign something?"

"No need. Just get rid a the body. Don't care what you do with it."

"You don't care?" Claire asked, wide-eyed.

The marshal's eyes narrowed. "Fine, then. Bury 'im in that nigga cemetery in Shanty Town." He shook a finger at Andrew. "Be glad he didn't have your wife. You woulda never touched her again. Mark my word."

Claire covered her mouth and turned away.

"Take me home," the marshal said and moved toward the door. "I seen all I care to."

"Go to the buggy," Andrew said, finding civility almost impossible. "I'll be there in a minute."

The man grunted and walked out.

"Claire." Andrew put his arm over her shoulder. "I'll be back soon. We'll take care of this ourselves."

With a sad smile, she nodded, then sat next to Clay.

Andrew left them there. He'd return the marshal to the city, but hoped he never had to deal with him again.

* * *

Claire glanced over her shoulder toward the bedroom. Though she couldn't see him, she knew he was there, blood draining from his body onto their floor. She shuddered and shook her head.

Reckon I shoulda closed the door.

Michael whimpered and pulled her from her thoughts. His eyes were droopy. The poor baby needed sleep, but for now she had to keep him awake. She bounced her knees a little harder. Hopefully by the time Andrew returned, he'd tell her she could lay Michael down for a nap.

Clay's heavy sigh drew her attention.

"It's gonna be fine, Clay. You did the right thing."

"But I killed him," he muttered. With his elbows resting on the table, he covered his face with his hands.

He'd told her why he'd come by. Michael's bunny had been left behind at Alicia's, so she'd asked him to return it. That little stuffed animal had been the answer to Claire's prayer.

She took hold of one of Clay's hands. "You saved me an' Michael."

"That man—he had a knife. He was gonna cut you bad." Clay turned to face her. "I couldn't let him." He looked as though he might start crying, but he sucked in his breath and his face hardened. "I almost din't come in. When I seen Michael on the ground, I aimed to hep him. But then I heard you cryin'. When I looked through the winda, I seen that man cut you. So I grabbed the shovel and opened the winda to get inside."

She squeezed his hand. "You were brave. You made a decision like a grown man. Your daddy would be proud."

He gave her a weak smile. "But it don't feel right killin' a man."

"Killin's not supposed to feel right. Still, you made a good choice."

"Reckon so." He stared downward, miserable as ever.

"You should talk to Andrew 'bout it."

"Who's Andrew?"

She laughed. "Dr. Fletcher."

Clay wrinkled his nose. "Doc's name's *Andrew*? Glad I calls him Doc."

"Doc!" Michael exclaimed.

"No, Michael," Claire said, sweetly. "To you he's Daddy." She stood and perched him on her hip. "Clay, would you like some sweet tea punch?" She hoped to take his mind off his troubles.

"Ain't never had it."

"Well then, reckon it's time. Mind holdin' Michael while I fix it?"

Finally, the boy's face lit up with an enormous smile. "Not at all."

She passed Michael over. The baby pointed to his stuffed bunny lying in the middle of the living room floor.

Clay took him to it and the two began a simple game of peep-eye with the toy.

"I'm glad I finally met you, Miss Claire," Clay said, while moving the bunny in and out from behind the sofa, making Michael giggle.

"Me, too, Clay." She smiled at him, then looked away before he could see the tears that had started to form.

If Clay hadn't come . . .

She scrunched her eyes tight. It was time to put aside the *ifs* and concentrate on what she had. Life was too short to wallow in regret and guilt. She needed to make the best of it and appreciate every breath she took.

The front door swung open.

"Andrew!" She raced to him and latched on, then smothered him with kisses.

He held her tight.

"I'm so glad you're home," she said and kissed him again.

Andrew nodded toward the bedroom. "I've been worried." He raked his fingers through her hair and looked at her with so much love she could've melted into the floor.

"Today's been one a the worst in my life. But it taught me that we need to appreciate every minute we have together. We never know when it might be taken away."

He clutched her closer, then kissed the top of her head.

She tended Michael while Clay helped Andrew wrap Jeremiah's body in a blanket. They loaded it into the wagon and headed for the cemetery.

While they were gone, Claire tried to scrub the floorboards clean, but the blood had permeated the wood. She finally gave up and placed a woven rug over it.

She couldn't shake the memory of the man sitting on her, touching her where no one but her husband ever should. Even his scent lingered. A bath might help, but she'd never wash away the memory.

* * *

Claire lay beside Andrew, much too quiet for his liking. She'd been that way ever since he'd returned home from burying Jeremiah Lewis. He'd assured her that from what he'd learned from talking to people in the shanties, Tobias had no other family. But now, even his gentle touch didn't seem to soothe her.

He rose onto his elbow and looked down at her. Moonlight poured in through their bedroom window and highlighted her beautiful features. "Are you going to be all right?"

She inched her body closer. "Eventually. I keep thinkin' 'bout Michael. I just wanted to get to him. Even when Jeremiah pulled out that knife, I kept seein' our baby lyin' in the dirt not movin'. It was horrible."

Her words punched him in the stomach. "I wish I'd been here for you."

"You can't be with me all the time. 'Sides, you help folks every day with what you do. They need you at the hospital. An' I know how much you help folks in the shanties. Alicia told me 'bout some a the things you've done."

"Still, I don't like to see you hurt." He drew her in and she nestled against his chest. "Clay asked me about Jeremiah and what the marshal said."

"I'm glad he talked to you."

"I told him Jeremiah wanted to hurt me, and the best way he could do that would be to hurt *you*."

"He needs his daddy." She let out a long breath. "Life's so unfair."

"If I'd lost you—"

"Don't say it, Andrew."

He kissed her forehead, then pushed the covers back and got up. As quietly as he could, he crept to Michael's crib and picked him up. Then he went back to their bedroom and laid him down in the center of the bed. "For tonight I think we all need to be close." He got back under the covers beside his son.

"Thank you," Claire whispered.

They fell asleep holding onto one another, sharing warmth and love.

CHAPTER 12

Beth huffed.

The seventeenth of May. Doc Fletcher's weddin' day.

"I hate him," she grumbled and yanked a brush through her hair. *Bet he broke Victoria O'Malley's heart by standing her up at the altar.* Stomped on it like he did hers.

Since the man had had his way with Claire without being married to her, he'd probably had a romp or two with the snobby redhead. She'd never approve of such immorality.

If that hospital knew what was good for them, they'd dismiss him.

After disassembling and setting fire to Gerald and Claire's old bed, Beth had made herself comfortable in their room. She liked the vanity, even though she often pictured her former friend sitting here preparing for bed—brushing out her long locks, then slithering between the sheets beside Gerald.

Anger and hate burned away at Beth's insides. She threw the brush on the floor.

With an exasperated grunt, she picked it up and painstakingly worked it through her hair until she had it ready to pin up. She'd often wished she'd been born male. Then she could just cut it all off and be done with it.

A loud knock nearly rattled the house.

She raced down the steps. Her heart beat hard, hoping. Being Saturday, it was possible. She'd dressed in one of her nicer dresses. Blue to offset her dark hair.

She flung the front door wide.

George stood there holding a bouquet of un-wilted daisies. She gaped at him in amazement. No longer in coveralls, he wore tan pants and a solid green cotton shirt. Most noticeably different, he had no hat. Though he lacked hair on the top of his head, the sides had enough of it that warranted slicking back—which he'd done efficiently.

"Hey, George," Beth said with a sigh. "Them for me?" She pointed to the daisies.

"Yep." He handed them to her.

Because it would be inappropriate to invite him in, she stepped outside. They stood, silently staring at each other.

George scratched the back of his head and cleared his throat. "You hungry?"

"Yes." She hadn't eaten breakfast and it was nearly dinner time.

"Can I t-take ya to eat?"

"I'd like that. Stay right here. I need to tell Henry I'm leavin'." She hurried back inside. Before closing the door she glanced one last time at George. He hadn't budged and gave her a timid smile. The nicest thing she'd seen lately.

She'd been making progress with her uncle. He hadn't had a drink for a week, and she intended to keep him sober. He'd finally started working again and had managed to complete some unfinished projects. It'd take some time for his business to get back into full swing, but she had him headed in the right direction.

She pushed through the swinging kitchen doors. Henry was at the table sipping a cup of coffee. He looked up as soon as she walked in, but she went straight to the cupboard for a drinking glass. She filled it with water, then put the daisies in it and set them at the center of the table.

Taking a step back, she placed her hands on her hips and stared at him.

He set down his coffee. "What'd I do?"

"Nothin'. *YET*." She looked him in the eye. "I'm goin' out. Can I trust you here alone?" She hadn't left him by himself since she'd arrived. The thought of what he might do churned her stomach, but she wasn't about to turn down a chance to eat with George.

"Where ya goin'?"

"If you hafta know, I'm havin' dinner with a man!"

Henry burst out laughing. "Heck! Miracles *do* happen!" He slapped himself on the leg. "That where them pitiful-lookin' flowers came from?"

She wouldn't let him ruin this for her and didn't care what he said. "I'm goin', an' you better not get into trouble while I'm gone. I'll be back this afternoon."

Turning, she headed for the door.

"Don't I get to meet 'im?" Henry asked, still chuckling.

"NO! Don't want you to scare him off!" She marched out of the kitchen and returned to the front stoop. Henry had met George before, but he'd likely tease her about him and make her even more miserable.

George hadn't moved an inch. "Everythin' all right, Miss Beth? I heard y-yellin'."

She moved toward his wagon. "Things is just fine. He's hard a hearin'. I *hafta* yell."

"Oh." He followed her.

She gestured with her head to the seat. Surely he'd help her up.

With a quivering hand, he reached out. She grabbed hold of it, then stepped onto the floorboards. He placed his other hand in the middle of her back and pushed as she hoisted herself up.

She settled onto the seat, while he climbed in beside her.

He took the reins and clicked to the team. One white horse and one black.

Her body jerked when the wagon moved and she grabbed hold of the seat to steady herself. She rolled her eyes, then looked his way to see if he'd noticed her fumble. Luckily he hadn't. He stared straight ahead, looking incredibly handsome manning the wagon. "You look real nice today, George."

He glanced her way. "S-So do you, Miss Beth."

"Why don't you just call me Beth? I don't consider it disrespectful. 'Specially comin' from you." She smoothed her skirt.

"All right, B-Beth." His eyes shifted her way, but his head didn't move. A slight red tint filled his cheeks. She'd never met a man so nervous around her. But then again, no man had ever truly given her the time of day.

He drove to Sylvia's, the place where they'd shared a meal when Claire had been in the hospital.

"Hope this is all right," he said, pulling the wagon to a stop. "We know the f-food's good."

Yes, it had been good, but the memory of Claire nearly spoiled her appetite. "This is fine, George." If she'd suggested another place to eat, she might have shattered his confidence. The last thing she wanted to do.

When they walked in, they found the place surprisingly empty. George gestured to a table by the window, then helped her take her seat.

His folks have taught him some manners.

"Thank you, George." She gave him her best smile.

His cheeks reddened just as they had before. "Welcome."

"Glad to have some business," the waitress said, approaching their table.

"Where is everyone?" Beth asked.

"Reckon folks are gettin' ready for that weddin'." The waitress frowned. "You two must not a been invited neither."

Huh?

"Weddin'?" Beth wrinkled her nose. "What weddin's that?"

The girl laughed. "Where y'all been? It's the talk a the town! Victoria O'Malley an' Doc Fletcher. Folks say it'll be the finest weddin' Mobile's ever seen. What with all the money her daddy's puttin' up for it."

Beth grunted. Oddly, her reaction prompted George to reach across the table and place his hand atop hers. She nearly lost her breath. Her frown melted into a smile. For George, of course.

Beth looked up at the waitress. "Dr. Fletcher ain't marryin' her, so how can there be a weddin'?"

"You sure?" The waitress knelt down beside the table. "Folks have been sayin' there's some big surprise. If you're right, maybe that's it. Reckon Victoria got stood up at the altar?"

Beth shrugged. The waitress bustled away without taking their order. Though Beth couldn't hear what was being said, the girl was whispering to another woman.

"Folks love to gossip," Beth said, then looked down at George's hand still perched on hers. She liked having it there. Heat rose into *her* cheeks this time. "Thank you, George. Somehow you knew I was upset. How'd you do that?"

"Don't know." He looked into her eyes. "I care 'bout you. Reckon that's how." He didn't stutter once.

Beth gulped, unable to utter a sound. Luckily the waitress returned and took their order.

Deciding to make the meal last, Beth took her time eating. George did, too. Seemed he had similar thoughts.

The waitress kept her distance, much to Beth's liking. She returned to their table to clear their plates and offer dessert.

"We have chess pie today," the girl said. "It's one a my favorites."

"M-Mine, too," George said. "Sounds good. Want some, Beth?"

She shook her head. As much as she loved chess pie, she needed to resist. "No, thank you."

"D-Don't ya like it?"

"Yes, but I shouldn't eat it."

"Why?"

She rolled her eyes and pointed to her belly. "I ain't like you, George. You can eat anythin' you want. But I eat it and it sticks to me like glue."

The waitress looked toward the ceiling.

George cleared his throat. "Two pieces," he said to the girl.

She walked away without saying a word.

"But—"

"B-Beth." George stopped her from objecting. "You said you like it. Don't never pass up on sumthin' good." He gave her hand a squeeze.

She squeezed back. "That's might fine advice, George." Her heart beat out of her chest.

The pie ended up being the best she'd ever put in her mouth. Maybe it had more to do with George than the pie. He made everything sweeter.

The somber ride home passed too quickly. They were silent for some time, but as they neared Henry's, George fidgeted.

"You okay, George?" She wished he'd held her hand again, but he'd kept both hands on the reins.

"I g-got sumthin' to ask ya." He didn't shift his gaze from the road.

Her heart thumped. A proposal seemed too soon. "Yes?"

"Do ya mind I'm so old?"

Not what she'd expected, but relief flooded her. "You ain't old. You got a *little* life left in you." She nudged him with her shoulder and chuckled.

A nervous laugh escaped him. "B-But am I too old for *you*?"

She stopped laughing. "I think you're just right." Even though his gaze hadn't left the road ahead, she could tell he was smiling. "Fact is, I like spendin' time with you. I don't care you're older, long as you don't mind my bein' younger."

He pulled the wagon to a stop in the middle of the road. Finally, he faced her. "So I can k-keep callin' on ya?"

"Any time you please." She blinked slowly and became lost in his brown eyes. They glistened with tears. With compassion, she reached out and placed her hand against his cheek. Her action caused him to look down and away from her. "Sorry. I didn't mean to upset you." She folded her hands in her lap.

"Ya didn't. I j-just ain't used to bein' touched."

"Then we'll go slow. But you should know it's all right to touch someone you care for." She tipped her head, studying him. "Actually, you already *do* know that. It's like when we was in the restaurant an' you put your hand on mine. You knew I was hurtin' an' you reached out to me." Smiling at him came easy, and she offered one of her best. "I like you, George. I want you to keep comin' 'round."

"I'm glad." He got the wagon moving again, and they were home much too soon for her liking.

Beth waited for him to help her down. He stood below her and held out his hand. She took it, but when her foot hit the ground, she stumbled into his arms. He kept her from falling, but it seemed he didn't want to let go. She certainly didn't mind.

"Thanks, George," she rasped. "I can be awful clumsy at times." They stared at each other, but then he released her.

Stumbling again might make him suspicious, though she considered it. "Reckon I better get inside an' check on Henry. I got rid of all the whiskey I could find, but he might have more hid."

"All right." George didn't move.

"Um . . ." This felt a little awkward. "I had a nice time today, George."

"I-I did, too." He still didn't move. "How 'bout I come back next Saturday?"

"I'd like that." Since he still hadn't budged, she decided to. She headed for the front door. "Bye, then!"

"Bye!" He gave a timid wave.

She went inside, then peeked out the living room window and found him staring at the closed door. She watched until he finally hopped back into the buggy and drove off.

She understood. Their time together hadn't lasted nearly long enough.

CHAPTER 13

Victoria O'Malley's wedding day.

More money had been spent on the happy occasion than most of Mobile had seen in a good year's time. But Victoria would settle for nothing less. It had to be perfect, just like the man she'd soon marry.

St. Mary's parish would likely draw a bigger crowd than on any regular Sunday.

The church was only a few years old and a brilliant setting for the affair. Made of pristine white brick, it matched her chosen colors. Everything had been decorated in bright red with white accents.

Victoria gazed upward at the tall steeple. They'd been given strict instructions to ring the bell at the precise moment of the wedding kiss. She giggled and grabbed hold of Penelope's hand. "Every man in Mobile will know what he lost out on. That bell will declare the exact moment I become Mrs. John Martin."

"Folks still think you're marryin' Dr. Fletcher," Penelope said, biting her lower lip.

Victoria had chosen her as maid of honor. Not wanting to have any attention drawn away from *herself*, she'd have preferred to have no attendants at all, but her mama had insisted on at least one.

"I know." Victoria giggled even harder. "Won't it be *fun* to see their faces when John comes out instead?"

Penelope frowned. "I don't know."

"Oh." Victoria huffed. "Let's go inside. You're depressin' me." She yanked on Penelope's hand and led her into the church.

"Where have you been?" Victoria's mama hurried toward them. "You need to get dressed! People are already arriving."

"Truly?" Victoria headed toward the sanctuary. "I want to see who's here."

Her mama grabbed her arm. "No! You'll see them soon enough." She shuffled her to the bride's room. Penelope traipsed behind.

"Miss Victoria, you'll be the death a me," Izzy fussed and fisted her hands on her enormous hips. "Get undressed, so we can put your weddin' dress on ya."

Dear Izzy. The only person she'd miss when she left Mobile. She'd wanted her to come along, but John insisted he had enough help. Besides, her daddy would've had a fit if Izzy had agreed to leave. He'd die of starvation if he had to live off her mama's Irish stew.

With Izzy's help, Victoria shed her day dress. She'd bought a new corset and chemise with plenty of lace for the special occasion. "Izzy, help with my corset—for old time's sake."

Izzy positioned the thing, then tugged on the strings. "Who's gonna hep ya when I ain't around?" She sniffled.

Is she cryin'?

"I suppose John will." Victoria turned her head and gave the woman a reassuring smile. "Pull it *real* tight now."

"I always do," Izzy mumbled. She tied off the strings, then stepped in front of Victoria. "Now, you listen. Once you're with child, don't even think a wearin' this thing. Hear me?"

"Course. I know better. Sides, it'll be a while 'fore I'm with child."

Izzy grunted. "I knows you." She leaned close. "Wouldn't s'prise me if you already *is* with child."

"Oh, Izzy." Victoria waved her hand, dismissing her.

"But I don't wanna wear a corset, Mrs. O'Malley," Penelope whined. "I never wear one."

Victoria rolled her eyes, then glared at her friend. "You'll wear one today. Your dress was designed for it. Like mine."

Izzy lowered Victoria's gown over her head and she wiggled into it. It plunged perfectly. Victoria pursed her lips and grinned. "You see? Without a corset I'd be droopy. By liftin' myself proper, I've assured that every eye in the church will be on me."

"So why do *I* need to bother?" Penelope droned. "If everyone's gonna be lookin' at you, no one will give me a second thought."

Victoria tipped her head, studying the girl. "Today might be the only opportunity you have of bein' noticed. All the important people in the city will be here. If you're lucky, an eligible man *might* see you."

"Here, dear," Victoria's mama said and extended the corset to Penelope. "She's right. You have a lovely figure. Why not let the men of Mobile see it?"

Grumbling, Penelope positioned her corset and let her mama tie it off.

Victoria watched in amazement. "Why, Penelope! You're endowed. Look at what the men have been missin'."

Penelope glanced down at herself wide-eyed, prompting another giggle from Victoria. Her mama then placed her bright red gown over the undergarments.

"I look like a harlot," Penelope said, looking at herself in a full-length mirror.

"You look lovely," Victoria's mama soothed. "Doesn't she, Victoria?"

Victoria nudged Penelope out of the way so she could get a good look at herself. "Yes, she does, but *I* look even better." Pulling her shoulders back, she turned from side to side and admired her rounded breasts. Then she dug into her satchel and removed the heart-shaped necklace Andrew had given her and fastened it around her neck.

"Why are you wearing that, my dear?" her mama asked.

"It's my sumthin' old." Victoria again peered into the mirror. The necklace rested in her cleavage. *Look what you're missin' out on, Andrew Fletcher.* She giggled. "'Sides, I don't like to take it off for long. It reminds me how easily men lie. I intend to keep John honest. He's nothin' like Andrew."

"You can say that again," Izzy mumbled. "Here." She handed Victoria a handkerchief. "Ya need sumthin' borrowed. Tuck it somewhere. You's gonna need it."

Victoria hesitated taking the thing.

"Land sakes, child," Izzy fussed. "I done washed it."

"Oh." Victoria took it and tucked it into her bosom. "Thank you, Izzy. With the blue satin ribbon on my bouquet, I'm ready. I'd like to get this ceremony over with so we can start our honeymoon."

Her mama frowned. "Don't be in such a hurry. You look lovely and your father spent a fortune on this wedding. You'd best enjoy it! The honeymoon can wait."

"But you an' Daddy made me wait for more than a week! It was silly, Daddy forbidding me from goin' with John to his hotel. You know full well he'd already had me, so why make me wait until the weddin'?" Victoria crossed her arms and pouted. Soon she'd be out from under the control of her parents. She couldn't wait to make her own decisions.

"You're wearing *white*, Victoria. You could *try* to act virtuous."

"I went to confession after we did it. I was forgiven." She cocked her head to the side and pursed her lips. "I'm as virtuous as the blessed Virgin."

Her mama quickly crossed herself. "Shame on you speaking sacrilege in this holy place."

Victoria rolled her eyes, then waved Izzy over to help with her veil. Once they had it positioned atop her long, red ringlets, Victoria added the final touch—a white silk scarf to hide the scar on her neck. Memories of John's lips gliding over it gave her chills. He'd taken away every ounce of shame she'd felt and turned everything to pleasure.

She wanted more.

"I wonder what John's doin' right now?" she said with a dreamy sigh. "He wasn't happy 'bout bein' kept from me either. But I intend to make it up to him."

Soon she'd remind him exactly why she was the greatest prize in Mobile. Perhaps in the entire country.

* * *

John smoothed the front of his suit jacket and gazed into the mirror.

God, I look good.

He was supposed to have been Andrew's best man, but he'd managed to once again outdo his son. Knowing he'd stolen Andrew's fiancée gave him more pleasure than should be allowed. Besting Victoria's father had been even more pleasurable.

Of course, if he wanted to dwell on *pleasure,* then Victoria herself should be at the top of the list. He'd bedded hundreds of women and none had been finer. But Victoria's youth made her even more desirable. Fresh and easily manipulated.

Her insatiable body certainly doesn't hurt.

He'd get at least a few good years out of her.

In the mirror he noticed Jake Parker peeking over his shoulder. With a slight turn of the head, John glared at him. "Do you require something?"

"N-No, sir," Jake muttered. "That is—I wanted to check my hair. Make sure I look all right."

The O'Malley's had asked the man to step in as best man at the last minute. Having a simple store clerk stand beside him wasn't John's idea of quality, but he had little choice. Besides, tomorrow he and Victoria would be on a train headed north and far away from Alabama. He had no intention of ever returning, so why worry about unimportant things?

"Does it truly matter?" John asked. "No one will be looking at you."

Jake took a few steps back, and John sighed with contentment.

Someone knocked on the door.

John shrugged and decided to open it himself. When he saw Shannon standing there, he was glad he did.

She gasped and fanned her face. "Oh, my, John." Yes, Victoria's mother had become enamored with him. He couldn't help the effect he had on women. "I see the tailor did a fine job of fitting you into Andrew's suit." Her Irish accent managed to fuel his own passion. She leaned close. "You're the most handsome man I've ever had the pleasure to know."

"Thank you, Shannon." He took her hand, then lifted it to his lips and kissed it. "You're a stunning woman." He glanced over his shoulder to be certain Jake was out of hearing. Even so, he kept his voice low. "If I wasn't about to marry your daughter, I'd show you what real pleasure is." He kissed her hand again, this time letting his lips linger.

"Oh, John . . ." She breathed heavily, breasts heaving. *An extremely satisfying view.*

It wasn't difficult reading her mind. Given the chance, she'd have gone with him willingly, even if only for one night's gratification. But considering where they were and what he was about to do, he decided it would be wise to change the course of the conversation.

He stood upright and adjusted his tie. "I don't believe I care for this red tie."

Shannon licked her lips and fingered the expensive silk. "'Tis fine. 'Twas Victoria's idea."

"Yes, I know. This whole affair was her idea. She's good at spending your husband's money, isn't she?"

The woman laughed. He could likely say anything and it wouldn't upset her. "Soon she'll be spending *your* money, John."

He didn't need the reminder. *I hope she's worth it.*

Patrick O'Malley appeared in the doorway and Shannon's demeanor instantly changed. "Who's talking about money?" he asked. "Me ears were burnin'."

"Oh," Shannon said. "I'm glad you're here, Patrick. I need to speak with you."

She shuffled him away. John enjoyed watching her leave. The view from the rear rivaled her exceptional bosom. To his good fortune, Victoria had inherited her mother's attributes.

He closed the door, but within moments another knock made him open it again.

The priest stood beside Victoria's father. O'Malley's brow beaded with sweat.

Let the games begin.

John grinned. "Father O'Meara, I presume?" He waved the men into the room.

"Yes, and you are . . .?"

Before John could answer, Patrick stepped forward. "Father, this is John Martin, Dr. Fletcher's father."

The priest looked quizzically around the room. "I'm pleased to meet you, but where is Dr. Fletcher?"

John smirked. "Andrew couldn't make it, so I'm taking his place."

"Excuse me?" The priest couldn't have looked more befuddled. "How can you—"

"What he means is . . ." Patrick threw his hands into the air. "Oh, hell! Father, we need to talk." He grabbed the man by the elbow and led him from the room.

"Damn," John said. "I wanted to hear what he had to say." He let out a laugh.

Jake began to chuckle, but then cowered again when John leered at him.

This time, the door opened and Patrick appeared by himself. "He's agreed to marry you."

"I'm flattered," John said dryly.

"He was upset because he'd spent weeks instructing Andrew in Catholicism. He asked if you're Catholic and I told him *no*. But he doesn't have to know you're a *Methodist*. I assured him Victoria's marrying you willingly. *And* I promised a large donation."

"Money has always had its influence in religion, hasn't it?"

O'Malley scowled. "You'd best be good to my little girl!" He shook his finger as though scolding a child.

John grabbed hold of it. "Your *little girl* will have exactly what she wants." He put on his best *friendly* smile, then smacked the man hard on the back. "C'mon now, Patrick. You're much too tense. I assure you, I'll make Victoria extremely happy. She won't want for anything."

"I'm counting on it." He nodded to Jake. "You ready? The organ has started to play."

Jake hurried to his side. "Yes, sir, Mr. O'Malley. An' I'm a might proud to be a part a this here weddin'. Can't thank ya enough for askin' me."

"Just don't drink too much," O'Malley warned. This time he directed his pointed finger at Jake.

"You servin' alcohol?" Jake brightened like a lovesick boy. At any moment John expected his tongue to dangle from the side of his mouth.

O'Malley grunted and walked out of the room.

It's going to be a long day.

* * *

May had never been horribly hot, but Victoria's body had become overheated beneath layers of silk and lace. Or maybe she'd just begun to feel the hot anticipation of the looming night's activities.

"I wish I had a full bouquet," Penelope pouted. "Then I could hide *this*." She gestured with her single red rose to her protruding bosom.

"Stop whining," Victoria scolded. "I'm almost sorry I asked you to be in my weddin'. You should be thankin' me."

Jake Parker came down the hallway toward them, ready to escort Penelope down the aisle. His eyes widened as he neared them.

Victoria pursed her lips and leaned toward him to give him a full view. *You're gonna miss me, Jake Parker.*

He grinned from ear to ear, but then at Izzy's forceful direction, extended his arm to Penelope. A hint of jealousy crept up Victoria's spine when Jake's eyes moved to *Penelope's* bosom.

Oh, well. I have sumthin' much better than Jake Parker waitin' for me.

Her thoughts were accompanied by Penelope's whimper. The girl didn't seem to appreciate Jake's attention.

As the pair walked down the aisle, Izzy bustled around behind Victoria straightening her long train. Tears streaked the woman's face. They didn't look like happy tears, but Victoria wouldn't let anything upset her today. Not even Izzy.

"My beautiful girl." Victoria's daddy kissed her on the cheek. "Loveliest bride ever there was."

"Oh, Daddy." She returned his kiss, then linked her arm through his.

The bridal anthem arose into a resounding forte. Everyone stood and faced the back of the sanctuary.

"Look, Daddy," Victoria bubbled. "They're standin' for *me*. And there's so many." It appeared everyone she'd invited had come. Every pew had been filled to capacity.

Izzy handed her the bridal bouquet. A dozen red roses intertwined with baby's breath. Victoria's heart beat hard and fast. The day she'd waited for since she was a little girl had finally arrived.

"I love you, Daddy," she whispered, clutching his arm.

"I love you, too." His smile warmed her, but then as they began to walk, her attention shifted to the man waiting for her.

She wished she'd been there to hear the comments when John stepped to the altar.

Step by step they took their time walking the long aisle. Victoria purposefully held her bouquet low enough so everyone could benefit from her gifted endowment. Hushed whispers arose throughout the sanctuary, but they only fueled Victoria's fire.

The women are jealous because their men want me.

She broadened her smile and stood even taller. Then she focused again on her groom.

Soon, John, soon . . .

* * *

Every eye had been on John until Victoria started down the aisle. He'd enjoyed the whispers. His favorite being, "That gorgeous man is even better lookin' than Dr. Fletcher."

John would leave Mobile talking about him for months. Maybe even years.

Hmm . . . A beautiful blonde.

Victoria's choice for maid of honor couldn't have pleased him more. Her beauty came close to that of his wife-to-be. Well put together and no doubt unspoiled.

He met her gaze as she neared the front and gave her a smile to remember him by. Her eyes widened and she looked away.

Why am I committing myself to one woman?

At least it wouldn't have to be forever.

And then, Victoria came nearer. Dressed in white, like a pure flower ready to be plucked.

And even though he'd already done his share of plucking, she had more to give. If luck happened to be on his side, her parents would die in short order. Maybe the fever would return to Mobile and wipe them all out.

Victoria would inherit a handsome sum.

He grinned, but kept from chuckling at the thought.

Victoria met his gaze and upon seeing him smile, lit up like the flames on the candles.

If she only knew what made me smile.

When they reached the front of the church, the music stopped. Patrick O'Malley placed Victoria's hand into John's, and he guided her to the altar.

They faced the priest side by side. The man's eyes nearly popped from his sockets looking at Victoria's breasts. He pulled out at a handkerchief and dabbed at his forehead, then looked John in the eye.

Much safer view, isn't it Father?

Being John's third wedding ceremony, he gave it little regard. His mind wandered through the humdrum message and instead thought about how luscious the maid of honor looked in her red satin dress. He fully intended to dance with her later.

"The ring, please," Father O'Meara said, bringing John out of his fantasies.

John turned to Jake, who fumbled with the thing and nearly dropped it. Finally, he placed it in John's palm.

Now, this is a moment to remember.

Victoria's breasts heaved, breathing harder than ever. She gaped at the ring he'd managed to find on short notice. Even though it had cost him dearly, he'd have never given her the one Andrew had intended to place on her finger. This one would be the envy of every female his wife encountered. Shaped like a queen's tiara and set with diamonds and pearls.

Victoria leaned close. "You *do* love me, don't you, John?" she whispered.

"With all my heart." He slid the thing on her finger and repeated the vows after the priest.

Catholic priests had always intrigued him. How could any man abstain from the one thing given to men for their utmost pleasure? Chastity seemed ungodly.

Another good reason to be a Methodist.

"You may kiss your bride," the man uttered and nodded.

Victoria passed her bouquet to her blond friend, then moistened her lips.

I'll show Mobile a real kiss.

After lifting her veil, he grabbed hold of her and wrapped his arms around her, then covered her plump lips with his own. She let out a delicious moan and he deepened the kiss. Not caring where they were, he let his hands wander freely, and so did she. When her fingers moved from his back further downward, the priest cleared his throat.

They released each other and looked at him, but then their eyes met again and prompted another kiss.

This time Father O'Meara cleared his throat so loud that a few women in the congregation tittered. John pulled away from Victoria. The bells rang out and they faced the crowded sanctuary. Women fanned themselves and the men groaned. John held Victoria's hand tight, claiming his new possession.

"Mr. and Mrs. John Martin," Father O'Meara bellowed.

The congregation applauded.

If marrying Victoria had been a mistake, he'd made it and couldn't turn back now. They had a legal document and hundreds of witnesses. Once he got back to Bridgeport he'd put her in her place. For now, he'd have some fun and see where it led.

As they paraded down the aisle toward the reception hall, he took in those in attendance. A multitude of questions lay behind every set of eyes.

Shannon positioned them in a receiving line. She took the place beside him and made her husband stand beside Victoria. The gorgeous maid of honor stood on the far end beside Jake. The poor girl had to endure the man. He looked as though he might dive into her cleavage at any moment.

It won't happen, Parker. She's too good for you.

John cast a friendly smile in her direction and received one in return. But then, Victoria tugged on his arm.

"Well, John, we did it! I'm your wife! Are you the happiest man on earth?" She bubbled over with adolescent excitement.

"I can't think of a time I've been happier," John lied and gave her a kiss. The simple peck didn't come close to how he'd kissed her in the sanctuary, and she pouted. "My dear," he said and traced his finger around her protruding lip. "There will be time for that later. Mind your guests. Show me you can be a proper hostess. It'll be required of you in Bridgeport."

Her dour expression disappeared, replaced by the lovely smile he adored. "I can't wait!" she exclaimed, then calmed. "I'll show you how good I can be."

As the guests filtered in, John put on his best front. In his element, he savored every smile and congratulations. Especially those from the ladies. They left the line giggling and whispering. The older women fanned themselves.

As for the men, they lined up to kiss the bride. He marveled at his wife and how she discerned which she'd allow to kiss her on the lips. He didn't mind when they did. Truthfully, he found it stimulating. They were helping with his foreplay.

She'll be more than ready for me tonight.

Because of the large number of people, a canopy had been set up in the church yard for the reception. Once the flow of attendees ended, John escorted Victoria outside.

Abundant food overflowed several tables. O'Malley had even hired a string quartet. Lavish decorations and floral bouquets dotted the grounds. Caterers bustled around and replenished the empty platters as plates were filled.

Not bad.

Shannon O'Malley knew how to entertain. Victoria may have asked for the elaborate wedding, but he knew her mother had orchestrated every detail. He'd be sure to praise her for her efforts.

Not yet feeling hungry, he watched everyone else eat. Crab cakes, shrimp, and crawfish. Fruits and vegetables had been placed elegantly around the main dishes. They'd even somehow managed several ice sculptures. A true feat in the south. John chuckled when he noticed Patrick shaking his head at the largest sculpture—an enormous swan that was already disintegrating into a puddle.

Your money's melting away.

Champagne flowed freely. Odd considering where they were.

Patrick walked over holding a plate of shrimp. He nodded toward the waiter who distributed the flutes of golden sin. "I reminded Father O'Meara that even Jesus turned water into wine for a wedding." He let out a laugh. "Victoria has grown rather fond of champagne."

Victoria clung to John's arm. "Yes, I have. And I intend to have my fair share before the night's over."

John stroked her cheek. "Not too much, my dear. I won't have you falling asleep on me."

She tittered and her father groaned.

More enjoyment than I deserve.

The quartet began to play "Beautiful Dreamer."

Patrick took Victoria by the hand. "'Tis time for our dance." He leaned toward John. "Before she starts drinking that champagne." He let out a laugh and led her to a clearing made specifically for dancing. Planked wood had been crafted on the lawn to make an efficient dancefloor. Others gathered around to watch.

For a few moments, John followed their movement, taking in how well she danced. Obviously schooled. Her knowledge of the art would serve him well in the future. But for now, he had others to attend to.

He crossed to Shannon and placed his hand against the back of her arm. She gasped and her eyes drew open wide, meeting his.

"Shall we?" he asked and nodded toward the dancefloor.

The woman didn't hesitate.

Her body quivered in his arms and he held her tight against him.

"At least we can hold each other," she rasped into his ear. "You feel remarkable."

She closed her eyes and rested her head on his shoulder. When Patrick gave him a questioning stare, John loosened his grasp on the woman. She whimpered and grabbed on tight. He'd heard the same childish sound from Victoria. *Like mother, like daughter.*

He stopped in the middle of the dancefloor. "I'm sorry, Shannon," he whispered. "You and I weren't meant to be." He pried himself from her grip and escorted her to her husband. They switched partners, much to Shannon's dismay. She frowned as Patrick waltzed her away.

"Mama likes you," Victoria said and wrenched his body close. "But you're mine."

"Your mother's a fine woman who only wants the best for *you*. She's intelligent enough to know that I'm it."

They continued dancing. He could finally show her his capable moves. When the song ended he dipped her low. His face hovered over her bulging breasts, but he refrained from kissing them. *Not here. Not now.*

As he pulled her upright, she seductively bit her lower lip. "I know what you're thinkin'."

"You're thinking it, too, my dear." He kissed her and the crowd around them cheered.

His wife ate up the attention. Her face held a radiant glow, but then out of nowhere, she became somber and frowned. "Look at Penelope. She's gonna ruin everythin'. The old sourpuss."

John gave the girl a onceover. She'd just pushed Jake Parker out of the way after he'd stumbled over her on the dancefloor. No doubt he'd been downing the champagne.

"Can you blame her for being glum? The poor girl had to dance with that store clerk."

Victoria let out a naughty giggle. "I can handle Jake Parker. Why don't you ask Penelope to dance? Maybe *you* can put a smile on her face."

Easier than I expected.

"You don't mind?" He lifted Victoria's hand and kissed it. "After all, I'm yours."

"Course I don't mind. Penelope's my best friend. 'Sides, I know whose bed you'll be in tonight."

With a sly grin, he left his bride and made his way to the buxom blonde.

When he asked her to dance, she shyly looked downward.

He raised her chin with the tip of his finger. "I believe you're a capable dancer. You just have to be with someone who knows what he's doing."

She looked him in the eye, lashes slowly batting. "All right."

Her body felt incredible in his arms. After several times around the floor, she'd relaxed. No longer glum, she displayed an enormous smile.

"You see," John said. "When you're with an experienced man, you can learn many things." He slid his fingers along her spine. "Do you enjoy learning?"

She swallowed hard. "I read."

He laughed. "Good girl. And what else do you like to do?" He tightened his hold, and her breath hitched.

"Dance," she muttered.

He spun her in a circle, then brought her back to him. "You look beautiful in that dress."

"I do?"

"Yes." He put his lips to her ear. "But you'd look even more beautiful out of it."

He could've sworn she stopped breathing. Dreadfully, the song ended and she backed away, no longer smiling. She hastened off to the food table.

"Damn." Maybe he'd said too much.

* * *

"Mr. Parker," Victoria tapped Jake on the shoulder. "I know you've had too much to drink. You should refrain from dancin'."

"Now, Miss O'Malley—"

"That would be *Mrs. Martin*," she corrected him with a proud grin.

"That's right!" Jake tugged on his suit jacket. "Mrs. Martin, I've not gotten my kiss."

Victoria tilted her head, taking him in. He'd never been what she considered *attractive*, but today he looked rather fine in his suit. He'd even shaved for the occasion. After all the years he'd admired her, on this special day she'd treat him to one tiny fantasy.

"All right," she said. "But only one." She puckered her lips.

He wasted no time and grabbed her arms, then yanked her close. His lips covered hers. In the midst of the kiss, he released his hold, and before she could stop him, he squeezed her breast. Alcohol must have emboldened the man. In his right mind, he'd have never laid a hand on her.

She gently pushed him away and chastised him with the shake of a finger. "Now, now, Mr. Parker. I said a kiss. It didn't include takin' liberties." Unoffended, she giggled. "Don't worry. I won't tell." She placed a single finger against her lips.

Proud and obviously satisfied, Jake tipsily walked away. He headed for the food table. Oddly, Penelope was there, looking as miserable as ever.

Victoria hastened to John's side. "What happened? I thought you were dancin' with Penelope."

"I was, but I'm afraid she's not feeling well."

"Oh. That explains her mood." Victoria cuddled into his arms. "I don't care. I'm not about to let her spoil our day."

He kissed her forehead. "Well then, let's cut the cake and be done with it. We have other things to do."

She rapidly nodded, already feeling a warm tingle creep into her lower body.

They ceremoniously fed each other a piece of the three-tiered cake. When John gave her a bite, a small amount fell into her cleavage. Without hesitation, he retrieved it with his mouth, then raised his head and licked his lips. Men chuckled and women gasped, but Victoria loved every second of it. She ate up the attention more so than the sweet morsel he'd placed in her mouth.

Before they left for the hotel, the photographer posed them outside for their wedding portrait. Victoria sat on a white stone bench with John standing behind her. She held the bouquet of roses at her waist, and sat fully upright. After the photo had been taken, she begged the man for one more. The traditional, stone-faced pose had made her feel old and ugly. Wanting to be unique, she had John sit, then sat on his lap. He wrapped his arms around her and tucked one hand under her bosom. Then they did something completely scandalous. They smiled.

Victoria's memorable wedding had been captured forever. But she had no doubt their upcoming wedding night would be ingrained in her mind even more so than the developed photograph. Without other folks around to limit their activity, they could do most anything. She intended to be incredibly naughty.

CHAPTER 14

"I remember this room!" Victoria giggled, then hiccupped. She quickly covered her mouth. "The champagne . . ."

"Yes, my dear. You had more than you should." John escorted her to the bed. She wavered in his arms before plopping down onto the mattress.

"But I feel so good!" She ran her hands along her body. "Help me out of this dress so I can feel even better."

He stared at her, shaking his head. "Our train leaves at 8:00 a.m. We'll need to get *some* rest." He jerked off his tie and threw it on the floor.

She pouted. Why did he have to spoil the fun? "John, I *need* you." She beckoned him with the curl of a single finger. The champagne flowed through her veins and heated her blood with a wonderful sensation. "Don't you want me?"

With a sinister smile, he lifted her to her feet. "More than you know." He devoured her with a hungering kiss. Exactly what she'd been waiting for.

"Yes!" She tugged at his shirt, then clumsily fumbled with the buttons.

"You'd better let me undress myself," he said. "But you first."

Facing her, he reached around and worked the buttons at the back of her gown. "You're a stunning bride. Every man at the wedding wanted to be in my shoes." He bent down and nuzzled her breasts.

She let out a moan, wanting more. "You think so?"

"I *know* so." His tongue danced across her skin, then glided upward toward her neck. "And if they knew *everything* about you, they'd be even more envious."

"What might that be?"

He circled her ear with his tongue. "You're an insatiable vixen." He kissed her again, harder and deeper this time, all the while unfastening every button.

He removed her scarf and tossed it aside. As he pushed her dress down and helped her step out of it, tiny grains of rice fell to the floor.

"Maybe we should save those for later," she said, giggling. "We might get hungry."

"I'm hungry *now*." Effortlessly, he picked her up and flung her onto the bed.

She fell back into the pillows, ready to play.

Even though she never dreamed of going out without a corset, at times like this it gave her grief. The silly thing took forever to unfasten.

John knelt on the bed beside her and started unhooking it. "These look good on women, but are damned inconvenient."

His proclamation made her titter. Her thoughts exactly.

He worked the laces as though he'd done it many times before. His skill intrigued her, but then again, at his age he'd probably undressed a handful of women. Once unbound, he tossed it to the side, then lifted her chemise over her head.

His eyes opened wider, then his hands returned to her body, this time touching bare flesh. She closed her eyes and relished the sensation, then gasped when his lips replaced his fingers. His gentle sucking sent her nearly over the edge of the bed. Lightheaded with alcohol and passion, she held his head against her breast and ran her fingers through his thick hair. "Yes, John . . ."

He'd set her body on fire.

"You want me?" he asked, laying her back. His hand moved across her stomach, then slid beneath the fabric of her undergarment.

"Yes," she groaned. "Hurry."

He stripped her bare, then stood, chuckling. "I don't like to hurry."

Lantern light pulsed through the room. Breathing hard, she pushed herself up onto the pillows to watch him undress. Though impatient, nothing could squelch the heat running through her.

His eyes remained affixed to her body as he shed his clothing. She marveled at the perfection of his form. *How does a man of his age stay in such fine condition?*

His toned muscles didn't show a trace of fat. Starting at the top of his head, she took him in, studying every detail. But then, when her eyes fell below his mid-section, they stopped. She couldn't shift them away from her favorite part. The part he used so proficiently.

She bit her lower lip and giggled. "I'm waitin', John. I can see you're ready." My, oh my, could she ever.

Wanting more than anything to feel him, she couldn't understand why he was taking his time. He walked casually to the bureau and removed something from one of the drawers. Then he fitted it over himself.

Though tipsy, she found it a little odd. "What are you doin'?"

He grinned. "Controlling the population."

"What's that supposed to mean? Why are you wearin' that . . . *thing?*"

He moved toward her. She gaped at the strange object covering her beloved body part.

With the wave of his hand, he motioned for her to move over. "You won't mind it. Trust me. None of the others have." He lay down beside her. "I don't intend to have any more children. This will see to it."

"But . . ." A knot twisted deep in her belly. "You didn't wear it the last time. I never knew such a thing existed. It's ungodly!" She scooted away. "I don't want that *thing* in me!"

"This *thing* cost me a great deal of money. You'd better never breathe a word of it to a soul. It's illegal in this country. Damn ridiculous if you ask me." She whimpered at his threat. He rose up and looked down at her. "It won't hurt you. It's made of rubber. My God, you're such a child!"

"I'm not a child! I just want it to be like the last time!"

He lifted his hand into the air and she cowered. Would he hit her?

A soft smile covered his face. "I was foolish before." His voice had calmed. Maybe she could talk some sense into him. "Hopefully we won't pay for that mistake. But if for

some reason I've already impregnated you, I know someone who can take care of it."

Take care of it?

He lay atop her, but she didn't want him there. She
pushed against him, struggling to be free of him. It seemed
to embolden him and made his smile broaden.

"John." Tears threatened. "I'm Catholic. I don't believe
in that sort of thing. And . . . I want children. How can
you not want any?"

"I've had my children," he growled. He wedged his knee
between her thighs, attempting to pry them open. "You've
never acted Catholic, and frankly, Victoria, you're spoiling
the mood. You wanted a husband and you got one. I *never*
promised children." He hovered over her, eyes glaring.
"Spread your legs or I'll remove this thing and we can both
go to sleep!"

Her chin quivered and tears spilled onto her cheeks. "I
may not act Catholic, but I believe in what I've been
taught. This is all wrong. My body was made to have babies."

"Your body was made for my *pleasure!*" He forced her
legs open and rammed himself into her.

After a single gasp, she fell silent. In her mind she'd returned to that horrid storage building behind Parker's.
John had just completed what the Negro had failed to do.

She'd believed John to be everything she'd dreamed of in
a man.

I thought I loved you.

But she'd confused love with something else. He didn't
love *her*. Of that she was certain.

With her thumb, she twisted the wedding ring around her finger. The glorious ring hadn't meant so much after all. Maybe it was simply a symbol of his ownership.

His lips had found their way to hers, but she couldn't bring herself to kiss him back.

He moved rhythmically within her. Though his flesh had felt better, the thing he wore caused no discomfort. Her body relaxed into the bedding. She closed her eyes and focused on the sensation, not the man creating it.

"You'll thank me one day," he whispered. He kept moving, perfectly in time. "Your body will remain flawless, as it is now." He groaned with pleasure. "You're a work of art, not to be changed."

Opening her eyes, she looked up at him and found him peering down at her. His lips formed into a sly smile. She couldn't deny that she loved the way he made her feel.

Alive.

Desirable.

Sensual.

She pulled him to her and kissed him deeply. Unable to help herself, she began to move with him. A pleasurable moan escaped her.

"Now that's my girl," he said. "I knew you'd like it."

She'd succumbed. Given in to desire and the heat of lovemaking. It wasn't the wedding night she'd imagined, but he was her husband and she belonged to him whether she liked it or not.

Until death do us part.

* * *

Claire lay in bed staring upward. "You've been quiet tonight, Andrew."

"Just thinking." He let out a long sigh.

She had, too. It hadn't been easy sleeping in the room where she'd nearly lost her life. Even though the man had been buried and could never hurt her again, thoughts of the incident remained. But she had no doubt where her husband's thoughts lay. "You're thinkin' 'bout Victoria, aren't you?"

He rose on one elbow and looked down at her. "Yes. How did you know?"

"Today was supposed to be your weddin' day. It only makes sense you'd think of her." Even knowing how much Andrew loved Claire, she worried she didn't measure up to his former fiancée.

"I wish I could've stopped her from marrying John. Don't misunderstand me. I didn't want her for myself. But she's made a horrible mistake. I've seen what he does to women."

"I know what he did to my mama," Claire whispered. "She died of a broken heart. It took many years, but he killed her just the same."

Andrew caressed her cheek. "I'm sorry."

"Why? It wasn't *your* fault."

"I'm still sorry. He not only hurt your mother, he hurt *you*." Andrew lay against the pillows and pulled her onto his chest, then gently rubbed her back. "We were *all* hurt by him." His hands moved up and glided through her hair. "We deserve happiness. Look what we've been through in such a short amount of time. Do you think we can put all this behind us and start fresh? Be *happy*?"

She cuddled into him. "I *know* we can." Feeling at ease in his arms, she let her fingers wander across his chest. "But we both know bad things can happen. That's part a life.

I'm just glad I have you to help me get through them." She dotted his skin with tiny kisses, suddenly feeling sensual. But then, just as quickly, something else came to mind. "With everythin' that's happened, I forgot 'bout Henry's horses. Did you find someone to help him?"

His body became rigid. "There's something I didn't tell you."

"I don't like the sound a that."

He climbed out of bed and went to the living room. When he came back, he lit the lantern on the bed stand, then handed her a letter.

"What's this?" A pit in her stomach rapidly grew.

"I've had it all week. I couldn't bring myself to give it to you. But if we're starting fresh, you need to know everything. I just hope you'll understand why I didn't give it to you sooner." He sat beside her on the edge of the bed.

She opened it and read it to herself. Beth's words cut deep and she couldn't stop tears from forming once again.

"Please don't cry." Andrew picked up the letter that she'd let slip out of her hand and onto the floor.

"I can't help it." She sniffled. "She was my dearest friend. I still love her, but she *hates* me. Can't believe she gave back the house. It was my gift to her when Gerald an' I got married. She loved it there."

He wiped away her tears. "In time, I believe you'll be given the chance to mend your friendship. At least we can be grateful she's helping Henry."

"But her bein' there only proves how much she despises me. She was furious with him—swore she'd never forgive him. She blamed him for Gerald's death. Reckon she's decided it was *my* fault." Claire lay back against the pillows and curled into a ball. "Maybe it was."

"You know that's not true." He put the letter back in the envelope, then set it on the bed stand. "Don't blame yourself. Gerald's death was an accident."

No matter what he said, she couldn't stop crying. She closed her eyes and wallowed in her misery.

Andrew lay down behind her and tucked his body into hers. "Remember when you told me not to blame myself for Mrs. Lewis's death? You helped me heal." He laced his fingers into her hair, soothing her with his touch. "I'm telling you the same thing. It wasn't your fault." He brushed his lips across her shoulders. "I swear, you're not to blame."

Slowly, she twisted her body around to face him. "We *will* start fresh, Andrew. You, an' me, an' Michael. That's what's most important. I'll just keep prayin' that someday she'll be back in my life." She raked her fingers through his hair. "God brought you an' me back together." Peace covered her, and her tears began to dry.

"Yes, He did," Andrew whispered. "I love you, Claire."

"I love you, too." She nestled into his body, comforted in his loving arms. Their hearts beat together as one, and they fell peacefully asleep.

CHAPTER 15

"What was that?"

Victoria flailed her arms, startled by an abrupt jolt from a deep sleep. She attempted to open her eyes.

"It's six-thirty," John mumbled. "The desk clerk knocked on our door to let us know."

"Oh." Victoria rolled over and closed her eyes. *Much too early to wake up.*

"Damn it, Victoria! Get out of bed!" John jerked the blankets off her body, then smacked her hard on her bare bottom.

"Ouch!" The slap stung. She rubbed the spot, then sat up. "Why'd you do that? I'm not a child."

"You *act* like a child. I found it appropriate." He fastened his trousers. "Get up and get dressed. We can't miss the train. I hired a buggy to pick us up at seven. You have thirty minutes."

She watched John finish dressing, doing her best to wake up. Once they arrived in Bridgeport she'd set her own hours.

"I'm going out to relieve myself," John said and headed for the door. "You have twenty-five more minutes."

As he shut the door, she stood from the bed and went to her trunk to select an appropriate dress. She almost wished she'd not previously told her folks goodbye. Strangely, she already missed them. But even more, being without Izzy had her heartsick. She spotted the handkerchief Izzy had loaned her lying on the floor beside her crumpled wedding gown.

"You were right, Izzy." She picked it up. "I'm gonna need this." Not wanting John to see her cry, she pushed down her tears.

Things are bound to get better.

Looking on the bright side would be wiser. Even though she had no idea what to expect, it had to be glorious. Parties, political affairs, fancy gowns—all the things she adored. What could be bad about that?

The train ride would take two full days. She'd never ridden a train for that length of time. That alone could prove to be a memorable adventure.

The door opened and her husband stepped into the room. "Why aren't you dressed?" He flipped his watch open. "Twenty minutes, Victoria."

He behaved like her daddy. Treated her like a little girl.

I have a daddy, I don't need another one.

He hadn't even told her *good morning.*

"John?" She decided to be bold. Maybe start a decent marital conversation. "Did you sleep well?"

"Not long enough," he grumbled, while stuffing items from the bureau into his trunk.

"I'm sure you can sleep on the train—if you're *that* tired." She spoke softly, trying to ease him.

"The sleeping car is nowhere near as comfortable as the bed in this room. Truthfully, I won't sleep well until I'm in my own bed and out of this *state*." He'd not looked at her once.

Crossing the room, she wrapped her arms around him and kissed his cheek. "I can't wait to try out *your* bed."

He whipped around to face her. "Victoria. In fifteen minutes we have to leave this room. We don't have time for this!"

He might as well have slapped her. He couldn't have crushed her more. With a doused spirit, she finished dressing. She kept her back to him so he wouldn't see the tears welling in her eyes.

She chose a comfortable day dress, uncertain what would be appropriate for train travel. Aside from lacing up her corset, John gave her no regard. Didn't even tell her she looked nice.

At five minutes to seven they were out the door, waiting for the hired buggy.

The man arrived right on time, much to John's approval. Victoria watched in amazement as John tipped the man two bits for his punctuality and effort. In addition to taking them to the train station, the man didn't complain about helping John load their large trunks and numerous bags.

John wasn't so gracious. He scowled at her. "Are you taking bricks to Bridgeport?"

"No. Just clothes and personal items. I know you want me to look nice."

He grunted, but at least he assisted her into the buggy.

On the way to the station she sat with her hands folded casually on her lap. John paid her no mind, so she passed the time wondering about him. He acted nothing like the man she'd first met. And yet he'd become her husband.

I married a stranger.

Sharing the man's bed had made them intimate and nothing more. She knew nothing of his principles or beliefs. Though, like her, he loved money. And, he knew important people. Maybe she'd meet some of them. Possibly even P.T. Barnum, one of the most prominent residents of Bridgeport. John had become acquainted with him, so why couldn't she?

They arrived at the train station plenty early.

Finally, John smiled. "Wonderful! Better early than late, I always say."

After confirming the train would be on time, he motioned to a bench. "I'm going for a walk. Sit here and wait for me."

"Yes, John." Being compliant seemed the only way to please him.

He studied her for a moment, then walked away.

She breathed a sigh of relief and took in her surroundings. The day promised to be beautiful. The sky held no clouds and painted itself in brilliant blue. She'd never truly appreciated it before, but maybe she'd begun to realize how much she loved it here. Mobile had always been her home.

I'm bein' silly. Bridgeport will have the same sky for pity sakes.

But then her eyes shifted, and she jumped to her feet. "Izzy!"

She ran to the woman and grabbed her so tight she made her groan. Victoria loosened her grip and giggled. "I can't believe you're here!"

Izzy chuckled, then patted her on the back. "Couldn't let you leave 'thout sayin' goodbye."

Victoria released her, but then grabbed her hand. "You came a long way. Did you walk?"

"Course I did. No other way for a poor colored woman to travel. Had to get up at five to get here, but I had to see my girl off."

Out of nowhere, Victoria erupted into tears. "Oh, Izzy . . ." She yanked the handkerchief from her bosom and dabbed at her damp cheeks.

Izzy's eyes narrowed. "What happened, baby? That man hurt ya already?" She led Victoria to the bench and they both sat.

Not wanting Izzy to know the truth, Victoria looked away. "Course not. I'm just sad 'bout leavin'." With a deep breath, she faced her friend. "Wish you could go with me."

"I does, too. But your mama an' daddy needs me. 'Sides, Mista Martin already has folks what tend 'im." Izzy stroked her arm. "We already been over this, baby girl. I can't go. Even if I could, that husband a yours don't like me none."

"He just doesn't know you like I do." Victoria embraced her again. "I love you, Izzy."

"Oh, baby. You know I loves you, too." Izzy leaned back and pointed a stern finger. One she'd seen many times before. "Promise you'll come home an' visit. 'Specially when you has a baby. I can't waits to see you holdin' that little un. May not like the man you married, but he *is* handsome. You'll have fine-lookin' children."

Victoria let her tears flow, harder than before. This time Izzy pulled *her* close and rocked back and forth. "Hush now. You's gonna be just fine."

"What's going on here?"

Victoria gasped and looked up at John hovering over them.

He glowered at her. "Victoria, you're making a spectacle of yourself!" He snarled at Izzy. "What are *you* doing here?"

Izzy huffed out a breath. "Why you talkin' to her like that? Can't ya see she's hurtin'?"

John wrenched a firm hand around Victoria's arm and jerked her to her feet. "What's wrong with you?" The hate in his eyes made her shrivel.

She lowered her head and looked away. "I-I was just sayin' goodbye. Izzy's my friend and she came to see me off."

"Izzy is your *servant*. Tell her to leave so we can go about our business."

"No!" Standing her ground, Victoria looked him in the eye. "She can stay if she wants to!"

A hard back-handed smack across the face stunned her. "Don't *ever* speak to me that way again."

Before Victoria could blink, Izzy was on her feet, grabbing his arm. "How dare you hit her!" Her head shook violently and anger blazed from her eyes. Then they softened, looking at *her* with pity. "Don't get on that train, Miss Victoria. Go home. He ain't got no right hittin' ya."

John's chest heaved. "Remove your hand from my arm, or I swear you'll regret it." He glared at Izzy until she let go.

He could destroy her. A colored woman didn't stand a chance against a white man. Especially an attorney.

She placed her hand to Izzy's face. "You best go. John's right. I shouldn't have crossed him." Unable to look at him, she focused on the ground. "I'm sorry, John."

He let out a satisfied grunt. "You heard her, go!" He flitted his hand toward Izzy, then wrapped his arm over

Victoria's shoulder and kissed the cheek he'd just struck. "I forgive you, my dear."

"Miss Victoria?" The pain in Izzy's voice broke her heart. "You shore you want this?" Izzy reached out to take her hand, but Victoria knew better than to grasp it. She gave Izzy a simple nod in reply.

With a frown, her dearest friend walked away.

John gestured to the train that had just come into the station and nudged Victoria in that direction. But after only a few steps, she slipped out of his grasp and fled back to Izzy. Not caring what John might say or do, Victoria embraced her.

"I'm sorry, Izzy," she whispered in her ear. "I love you, but he's my husband. I gotta go."

Tears streamed down Izzy's cheeks. "If'n he hurts ya, promise you'll come home." She spoke so low that Victoria had to bend down to hear her. "Remember who ya are. You's Victoria O'Malley, an' you's a fine woman. Don't let no man push ya 'round. Make him do right by ya."

"I will." Victoria kissed her cheek, then held out the handkerchief—her something borrowed.

"No. You keeps it. You's gonna need it."

With a sad smile, Victoria tucked it into her bosom, then walked back to John.

Like a vise, he clamped down on her arm and led her to the train. "I have a great deal to teach you about appropriate public behavior. A servant must be treated as such. You made a fool of yourself."

She didn't say a word.

Like a gentleman, he helped her aboard the train. He smiled and nodded to the porter. She'd never seen a Negro so sharply dressed. His crisp uniform fit him well and he held himself upright and proud. He tipped his hat and she smiled. Oddly, John didn't object.

"You're in a Pullman car," John said, escorting her behind the man. "One of the finest made. I spared no expense." Much to her relief, his demeanor had changed. "These cars have separate *enclosed* sleeping quarters." His brows wiggled and he grinned.

The porter waved his hand and nodded to an open door. "This is yours."

John placed something in the man's palm. Presumably money. "See to it that my wife and I aren't disturbed."

"Yessa. You and your *wife.*" The porter winked.

"Yes, she *is* my wife." He took Victoria's hand and showed him her wedding ring.

Proud he openly acknowledged their union, Victoria lifted her chin. "We were married yesterday." She gave the porter another smile.

"Congratulations," he said. "I'll see to it no one bothers ya. Let me know if there's anythin' else I can do for ya." He bowed low and left.

John shut the door. "You'll find that porters are a cut above the *standard* Negro."

"Oh." He'd likely just insulted Izzy, but she wasn't about to say it.

"So, tell me what you think." He waved his hands around the small room. He'd become *cheerful.* "I purchased the finest for you."

"It's lovely, John." She took it all in.

The seats were upholstered in fine, heavy dark fabric and trimmed with braided gold piping. The floor was carpeted in lavish red—her favorite color. Silver-trimmed oil lamps lined the walls and lit the car. Vibrant window dressings with scalloped edges and golden tassels draped the windows. *Luxurious.*

But when she looked at the *beds*, she could tell they were lacking. Two shelf-like bunks attached to one wall. She nodded to them. "They don't look comfortable."

John drew her in close. "As I told you, we won't get a good night's sleep until we're home in my bed."

The change in him was unusual to say the least. "I'm lookin' forward to that." She spoke cautiously, waiting for him to lash out again.

"I want to do more than lie in it," he whispered, eying the bunk, then began kissing her neck.

This was the man she desired. The one who desired her.

He glided his lips upward until he reached her mouth. Their first kiss of the day.

"Let's try out *this* bed," he said and moved her toward the lower bunk.

She timidly lay down, afraid to undress. Though they'd asked for privacy, she feared someone might walk in at any moment.

"Silly girl," John said, chuckling. "At least remove the dress. I don't want my wife *wrinkled.*"

She stood and he helped her. Then with a devious grin, he yanked down her undergarments. "Now you're ready." He motioned to the bed, seemingly unconcerned about her corset.

Bare from the waist down, she reclined on the bunk.

John removed his trousers, then fumbled around in his bag. She frowned when he produced the rubber thing and fit it in place. Obviously, from now on it would be the only way she could have him. She'd have to get used to it and the idea of never having children.

But, she didn't *want* to. For now, she'd do as he wished, but as Izzy had reminded her, she was Victoria O'Malley and Victoria always got what she wanted.

I'm young. Time's on my side.

With that pleasant thought, she gave in to her husband.

CHAPTER 16

It didn't take Victoria long to grow accustomed to the movement of the train. She rather enjoyed it. More than anything, she liked seeing John happy. Once they'd left the train station, he became a different person.

Having never been north of Mobile, she initially spent time looking out the window, but then found other things more entertaining.

John occupied his time in the parlor car playing poker. Very few women stayed there to watch, but *she* found it fascinating. The men talked about politics, while smoking cigars. John sounded like the most intelligent man in the room and managed to win most hands. She couldn't have been prouder.

Best of all, he boasted about *her*. She fixed herself up for all of the men to enjoy. The attention fueled her pride, making her feel more like herself.

"Your wife is exceptional," a gray-haired man boldly said to John.

"That she is." John nodded to her. "Come here, my dear."

She sauntered over. "Yes, John?"

"This gentleman paid you a compliment. You should thank him."

Donning her coyest smile, she bent low for the old man's pleasure. "Thank you, kind sir." She'd strategically dabbed a small amount of perfume between her breasts. As close as she was, he could probably smell it, nearly *taste* it.

He gaped at her rounded breasts. The sensation she received from the attention overwhelmed her. She craved gratification.

John chuckled. "As you said, *exceptional.*" He scooted his chair back. "If you'll excuse us, gentleman, my wife and I have business to attend to."

He took her hand and kissed it, then guided her toward the door. As they exited the smoke-filled car, she relished the comments following them. "I'd like to have some of that business myself," and "That's the luckiest man on earth," were two of her favorites.

Once alone, John quickly had her undressed and well on the way to satisfaction.

Their two-day journey required them to change trains more than once. Each offered a fresh room and new men for John to become acquainted with. She stayed by his side and ate up the attention they afforded her. Attention that fueled their passion.

By the time they arrived in Bridgeport, she could scarcely keep her eyes open. Already approaching evening, she didn't care what kind of bed John had as long as she could sleep in it.

Stepping off the train in Bridgeport, she shivered. Being May, she didn't think she'd need a covering, but cold air seeped through the fabric of her dress.

"You'll get used to it, my dear," John said, wrapping his arm around her. He then kissed her forehead. "Welcome to Bridgeport."

"Thank you." She was too tired to fully appreciate it.

Once in the buggy, she burrowed into his body. He radiated warmth. He held her like the lover he'd been on the train. Their marriage had certainly taken an upward turn.

They stopped in front of an enormous house. She sat bolt upright. "Is this it?" He'd described his home, but until she saw it for herself she honestly didn't know what to expect.

John laughed. "Yes, my dear."

He helped her down and paid the driver, who began unloading their belongings.

Already dusk, deep purple and navy clouds perched over the top of their home. It reminded her of a painting she'd seen in a book. Truly magnificent. Even in the dim light.

They walked past sculpted hedges. Spring flowers in assorted colors lined the walkway. The two-story brick home stood tall and grand. By far larger than the one she'd grown up in. Swirling wrought iron framed the windows with patterned glass that adorned their uppermost part.

Anxious to see the interior, she hastened toward the front door.

John gently took hold of her arm. "Wait, my love."

His terms of endearment warmed her. "Is sumthin' wrong?"

"Wrong? Heavens, no." He gave her hand a sweet kiss. "I'd like you to wait here for a moment. There's something I need to do. A *surprise*, you might say."

She placed a hand to her breast, overwhelmed. "I *love* surprises! Course I'll wait."

John positioned her on the fanned front porch. "Don't look inside. Not yet." He inched the door open, then slid in.

Excitement filled her. Maybe she'd misjudged him.

* * *

John closed the door just in time.

"Oh, John, I have missed you!"

Emilie leapt into his arms, then wrapped her long legs around him. She kissed him all over his face.

His French maid had exceptional qualities. Not necessarily in the line of housekeeping. Her talent had always been more of the *undercover* sort. The girl had introduced him to contraception as well as many other interesting things. It seemed the French were always ahead of the rest of the world concerning intimate matters.

He had to admit he'd missed her French accent and found it more appealing than Victoria's southern drawl. However, he'd left his bride shivering in the cool air and things needed to be taken care of quickly. His petite brunette status symbol would have to go.

Damn.

He didn't move, though he couldn't keep his eyes from admiring the bare flesh exposed beneath her open silk robe.

"What is wrong with you?" Emilie pouted. "Did you not miss me?"

He afforded her a slight smile and her eyes lit up.

"Yes," he said, emotionless. "I did *not* miss you."

She deflated and slowly let her legs drop to the floor. She rested her hand against his chest. "You are teasing me, no?"

"I didn't have time to miss you. I've been kept quite entertained." He found an evil pleasure in breaking women's hearts.

"Entertained? How? You went to see your son married, no?"

"Yes. However, he didn't get married. *I* did." He purposefully spoke with no feeling.

"You? Married? No! I do not believe you!" With every word, her voice grew in volume. Not wanting Victoria to hear, he took her firmly by the arm and led her to the parlor.

"Yes, I'm married and my wife is waiting outside. You need to leave." He'd likely have to throw her out.

The girl burst into tears. "You said you would marry *me*! You promised!"

"I promised no such thing." He looked directly into her eyes, not caring that he'd upset her. "You must have imagined it. I'd never lower myself to marry a mere servant. Victoria's more than you could ever be."

"I was your lover! We shared everything!" Her crying became sobbing.

God, I hate this part. Women blubbering like babies.

"I paid you for your services. Don't act as though I was the only man you spread your legs for. I know you serviced James as well. You did your job and now your duties have been reduced. If you'd like, you can continue to clean for me *and* my wife."

Her face contorted. His final words had to have cut deep. "James would *never* tell what we've done. How do you know this?"

"He's my business partner. We discuss *everything*. You should go to him. I believe he may actually care for you. I enjoyed you, but I have someone more gifted. And, she's legally mine. You know full well how much the law means to me." He stood a little taller and straightened his tie.

Breath hissed out her nose. Cursing in French, she rambled on and on. Then she shook her fist at him, spitting French expletives.

"Emilie. *Dear*. I've told you time and again to speak only English in my home. I can't understand what you're saying." He smirked. Inability to understand French hadn't kept him from reading into her gestures.

Her eyes widened. "You pig! Bastard! I hate you! I will *never* clean up after you *or* your wife! I'm leaving!"

"Good!" He delighted in yelling at her. "That's what I want! Consider yourself unemployed!" He yanked on her arm and led her toward the back door.

"You cannot throw me into the street this way! I need my clothes!" She jerked from his grasp and raced up the stairs.

He followed her into his bedroom. She'd folded her clothes neatly on his settee.

She tossed her robe to the floor and he enjoyed watching her for a final time. Though petite, she had delectable curves. If they'd had more time, he might have had a final go at her before dismissing her.

Taking his eyes off her, he finally realized what she'd done. A bottle of champagne rested in a bucket of ice. Lit candles dotted the room. The bedding had been pulled back and rose petals were scattered across the silk sheets.

"Thank you for this, Emilie," he said. "My bride will love it."

"Damn you!" She slapped his face. "I should go to her and tell her what kind of man you are!"

He smacked *her* as hard as he could, glaring. He took her arms in his hands and squeezed. "Don't go near my wife! You do and I'll have you deported! Understand?"

Staggered breath seeped from her lips. "I hate you!" She wrestled out of his grasp and fled from the room.

Knowing she'd take his threat to heart and go nowhere near Victoria, he listened until the back door slammed shut. Then he casually descended the stairway and went to the kitchen to speak to Jean-Pierre, his cook. No doubt the man had heard everything.

"Welcome home, monsieur," Jean-Pierre said.

"Thank you." John took a spoon and sampled the soup simmering on the stove. "Marvelous." He licked his lips. "I've missed *you*. That's for certain."

"Your new wife will not replace *me* as well?" Jean-Pierre grinned.

"Definitely not!" John leaned against the wall. "You'll meet her momentarily. I trust you'll keep what you've heard to yourself?"

"Of course, monsieur. I always do."

John gave him a satisfied nod, then went to retrieve Victoria.

He found her in the same spot. She shivered in the cold.

"My poor dear," he said, wrapping his arm around her shoulders. "Forgive me for taking so long. I hope you'll find what I've done worth the wait."

"It's c-cold."

He scooped her into his arms and she gasped. "What's wrong, Victoria? You should've known I'd carry you over the threshold."

She grinned and hugged his neck.

God, I'm good.

* * *

Victoria couldn't imagine what had taken John so long, but she was glad to finally be inside. The fact he'd swept her off her feet hadn't hurt. Her heart pattered, anticipating the surprise.

He set her gently down onto an ornate wood floor with a swirling floral design that spread out through the entryway until it met a grand staircase. Though wide at the bottom, the stairway narrowed as it ascended. The top of the stairs met a long hallway that overlooked the lower floor. Carved wooden rails lined the stairs and continued down the hallway.

"Our room is upstairs on the left," John said. "But first, I'd like to show you the rest of the house."

Overwhelmed, her heart thumped. "I don't know what to say. It's more than I dreamed of."

First, they went left of the stairway. The large entryway contained an enormous cloak room. Perfect for all the guests they'd likely entertain.

They walked into a ballroom, the full two-stories in height. Her breath caught. Never had she seen something so exquisite. Tall marble pillars reached to the ceiling, where multiple gold candelabras held flickering white tapered candles. A balcony from the upstairs hallway overlooked it, with wooden rails that matched those on the stairwell.

On the far end of the room was a bandstand on a raised platform. A magnificent grand piano sat to one side. Not far from the instrument was an enormous fireplace with an ornate mantel displaying a brilliant floral arrangement. Above hung a tall, gold-framed painting of a man and woman dancing.

Beautiful.

Appropriately positioned along the walls, were upholstered settees. *A place for weary dancers to rest.*

"Oh, my . . ." Victoria had difficulty finding the right words. "I can see it, John. The parties. The dancin'. You an' I movin' cross the dancefloor. It takes my breath."

He replied with a smile and guided her to another room.

"This one's my favorite," he said, opening the door. "The smoking parlor."

Numerous sets of tables and chairs dotted the floor. "Reminds me of the train." She worked her lower lip, remembering how she'd flirted with all the men.

"Somewhat. But you won't be coming in here, my dear."

"Why? Don't you want me to entertain your friends?"

He pulled her close and nuzzled her neck. "Not the way they're accustomed to being entertained in this room. This isn't a place for *proper* women."

"Oh." She shrugged it off and pointed across the room. "Do you serve alcohol there?"

"Yes. It's a full bar. I have only the finest. Mostly imports."

From there he took her past the only guestroom on the lower floor, then pointed out the room that he said was occupied by the cook, Jean-Pierre. It was conveniently located behind the kitchen.

Next, he showed her a fantastic bathing room. It held a claw foot tub that beckoned her. She envisioned many nights soaking there. The room had its own wood stove to heat water pumped in from an indoor pump. Brass pegs lined the walls for towels and clothing, and a large mirror hung on the wall over the tub.

"We'll have indoor plumbing soon," John proudly said. "Then we'll have no need for the outhouse, which, by the way, is out there." He pointed to a side door.

"I'm in awe." She'd never said anything truer.

"You'll certainly appreciate what's next."

She loved this side of him. If only he'd stay this way.

She inhaled an incredible aroma. *The kitchen.*

"Victoria," John said. "This is our cook, Jean-Pierre."

The man kissed her hand. "Welcome, madame." His French accent made her tingle, but his looks did little for her. He wore a white cook's hat and apron. His size indicated he enjoyed sampling what he cooked. *Like Izzy.* Victoria guessed he was about forty years old. "If you are hungry, I have prepared something light."

She liked him immediately. "Thank you."

The huge kitchen had two stoves with ovens, a large sink with an indoor pump, rows and rows of cupboards, and an oversized wooden countertop. Metal pegs on the walls held pots and pans, and large canisters sat here and there full of cooking utensils.

Izzy would just die.

She leaned over a simmering pot and inhaled. "Mmm . . ."

John led her away to a table for two set in front of a bay window. "Sit here and Jean-Pierre will bring you something unlike anything that has ever passed between your luscious lips." He sat across from her. "The formal dining room is through that door." He pointed behind him. "However, I rarely eat there. Unless we have a dinner party, the room gets little use."

"Madame." Jean-Pierre set a bowl in front of her. Then he placed a plate beside the bowl that held lettuce, but she didn't recognize what had been scooped atop it.

"Onion soup," John said. "And lobster mousse."

She wrinkled her nose. It didn't sound appetizing.

"Taste it," John said, nodding toward the bowl. He hadn't *demanded*. Truthfully, he looked *excited*.

She spooned some soup into her mouth, then followed it with a bite of mousse. "Oh, my." Her tongue experienced a bit of heaven. "Nothin' like Izzy's." Something that resembled bread rested beside the mousse. She broke off a piece and popped it into her mouth. Sweet and flaky. "Delicious."

"That's a croissant," John said. "And you're correct. None of this is like Izzy's. I'll show you many things you'll enjoy more than what you've experienced before. I'll teach you how to be a northerner."

"Don't expect me to *sound* like y'all." She laughed. "You're stuck with my southern talk even if you change my ways."

"We'll work on it." He patted her hand. "However, I know many men who will find you charming just as you are."

"Long as *you* find me charmin', that's all that matters." She leaned across the table and kissed him.

After they finished eating, she thanked Jean-Pierre, then followed John upstairs to their bedroom. Lit candles surrounded the bed, and he'd drawn back the bedding and sprinkled rose petals on the sheets.

In astonishment, she covered her mouth, then looked lovingly at her husband. "This was my surprise, wasn't it?"

He smiled and nodded.

"You *do* love me!" She wanted to cry, but kissed him instead.

"I hoped you'd like it. It took some doing to arrange it, but you're worth it." He shut the door, then returned to her and gave her another kiss. "Do you like our room?"

Much larger than her old bedroom. Truth be told, it was bigger than her old *living* room. The wood floors had been stained darker than those downstairs. The draperies were a deep lavish purple accented with violet. A Persian rug lay on the floor at the foot of the bed, in colors of turquoise and purple to match the drapery.

The bed had four tall, carved wood posts, stained dark like the floor. A sheer canopy covered the top. A thick white down-filled comforter had been folded at the end of the bed, and at the headboard were satin pillows in lavender and white. Their ornate purple patterns were an inviting lure. It reminded her of her own bed, but like everything else, much bigger.

Two tall windows were centered with a fireplace. Perfect to take away the night's chill. Though she doubted they'd need it tonight.

The room also held a large bureau and wardrobe as well as an oriental-printed changing screen and standing mirror. But what most captivated her was a full-length painting of John in his suit and top hat. His hands held his lapels and he looked incredibly dashing and distinguished. Below it was a settee that she immediately perched on. Maybe he'd commission a portrait of her to go beside his. Eventually, she'd ask him.

"I love it, John."

He lifted a bottle of champagne from a bucket on the nightstand. "One more surprise," he said and winked.

She jumped to her feet and hurried across the room to him. "I don't know what to say!"

"Then don't say anything. There's much more we can do." He covered her breast with his hand and gently squeezed. His lips brushed along her neck, then grazed her ear. "Let me show you my bed."

"I see it," she rasped.

"Yes, but you need to *feel* it." He started unbuttoning her dress.

I'm home.

CHAPTER 17

John couldn't wait to return to work. The time he'd spent away had been difficult, though to a certain degree, *enjoyable.* Yet nothing surpassed the thrill he received every time he entered the courthouse. It gave him a sense of power—something he relished.

Most of his cases involved civil disputes. He'd dabbled at criminal law, but found it to be less lucrative and potentially dangerous. Regardless of the type of law he practiced, he'd made enemies throughout the course of his career. He excelled at putting men behind bars and slid money under the table to keep them there.

Walking the streets of Bridgeport, he held his head high. People feared him. No one would dare cross John Martin.

He'd left Victoria naked and exhausted. Just the way he liked her. He'd shown her that even though he exceeded her in age, he could rival any man in bed. He'd taken her more times than he could count in the days since they'd arrived home. He needed a break.

She'd never find a more capable lover, even if she tried.

He chuckled. His wife wouldn't dare stray from him.

God help her if she does.

He'd built his office close to the courthouse and near the city square. The stylish brick building held a room for himself, another for his partner, James Stanley, and a large conference room they both used.

"Good morning, James," John said as he walked in. The man usually arrived first. He had little else to do. Overweight, nearly bald, and nothing special to look at, his social life had always been lacking. Unlike John's. But he was a capable attorney, and they frequently discussed their cases. John cared little about anything else the man had to say.

"John!" James jumped up from his chair and rushed toward him with an extended hand. "Thank you!"

John took his hand and the man pumped it so hard, he could've broken his bones. "What's this all about? Did you miss me that much?"

James stepped back, grinning. "No. That is . . . I missed having you here, and I *do* have some notes for you on several of your pending cases, but I'm thanking you for Emilie."

John lifted a single brow. "Emilie?" *She must have taken my advice.*

"Yes! She came to my door several nights ago and professed her love."

John feared if the man became any more excited, he might combust. "Did she, now?" He put on his best *astonished* face.

"Yes, she did. When you returned with your bride, Emilie told me she realized just how much she wanted to marry me." James' head bobbed up and down, emphasizing every word. "She said, *marriage means more to me than you could ever know.* And then, she told me she loves me."

Loves you? No, she wants a steady roof over her head without out the risk of being deported.

John patted him soundly on the back. "Congratulations!" He leaned in close. "You and I both know how pleasurable she can be."

Instantly, James deflated. He sulked his way back to his seat. "Would you mind so much not mentioning what happened between the two of you? I intend to marry her as soon as possible, and from this point on she's sworn to be faithful. She'll share my bed only."

"Of course. Truthfully, I meant it as a compliment. You're fortunate to have won her heart."

James sat a little more upright, then grabbed a pen and twisted it between his fingers. A nervous habit John had witnessed many times. "So," James said and tapped the pen on his desk. "Does your new wife like Bridgeport? I was thrilled when you sent the telegram stating you'd married, though I couldn't understand why you asked that I not mention it to Emilie."

"Yes, I realize it was an odd request, but I didn't want to hurt the poor girl. I'd thought she might have feelings for me and wanted to break it to her gently. But it seems I'd misjudged her. Obviously, she'd deceived me and hid her feelings for *you.* As for Victoria, she's not gotten out yet and can't make a judgment about our city." John let out a low chuckle. "I've kept her too busy *in*side."

The pen in James' hand tapped even harder. "I'm certain you have."

"What can I say? The girl's insatiable. However, I'll do all I can to keep her satisfied. Wait until you see her. She's more beautiful than any woman in Bridgeport. Perfect in *every* way."

James swallowed hard, then glanced around the small room. "I'd best get busy. Plenty to do. I left the notes on your desk. Let me know if you have questions."

"I will. And congratulations once again on your *achievement*. Emilie will be a fine wife. You've mourned your late wife long enough. It's high time you move on."

A shadow covered James' face. "Yes, high time," he whispered.

"Well then. Work beckons." John cast an enormous smile in James' direction, then sauntered to his office.

Everything sat neatly in place, just as he'd left it. He took a seat in his leather chair and shuffled through the stack of notes his partner had scribbled. The one on top was an offer from James to throw a wedding reception for him and Victoria, but he asked that it be held at John's own home. Why he'd written it rather than mention it in conversation seemed rather odd.

He carried the note back to James' office. "A reception?"

"Yes." James looked down, staring at his hands folded atop his desk. "I thought it appropriate. Especially since you married elsewhere. People will want to meet your new bride. If she's as lovely as you say, she'll make quite an impression."

More than you realize.

"Thank you. Your suggestion is considerate. Even if *I'll* be hosting the affair."

"Oh. *No.*" James waved his hands in the air. "I only suggested your home because mine isn't suited for entertaining. I'll take care of everything. I'll invite the guests and plan the menu. And I thought I'd hire a string quartet."

"Sounds splendid."

James twisted his mouth from side to side. "Do you suppose Jean-Pierre would mind cooking for it?"

John couldn't help but laugh. "You'll plan the menu, but my cook will prepare it?"

"Yes. Since it will be at your home and he's there, I just thought—"

"Say no more. Invite the guests and hire the musicians. I'll take care of the rest. My bride will be thrilled."

"Good!" James' demeanor had once again improved.

"I'll look forward to having her meet Emilie," John said with a sideways grin.

"Yes." The man's enthusiasm vanished. "I'll see to the guest list. Shall we say, a week from Friday?"

"Very well." John nodded and returned to his office. He'd had enough frivolity. The time had come for business.

Time to increase my fortune.

* * *

"Willie!" Victoria poked her head into the hallway. "Willie!"

Their new housekeeper was nothing like Izzy. Victoria still found it odd that John's former maid quit so suddenly. He'd had to hire a new one immediately. Victoria would never lower herself to do household chores.

The woman's name was Willeen, but Victoria didn't like it, so she'd adjusted it to something more suitable. John must have had pity on her. Willie was middle-aged, unattractive, *and* a widow. She had three young children to support.

My husband has such a big heart.
"Willie!" *Where is she?*

"Damn it, Victoria!" John came around the corner and grabbed her by the arm, then positioned her in the middle of the room. "Why are you yelling?"

She stood before him in her bloomers and chemise. She cocked her head to one side. "I need help with my corset. You want me to look nice for the party guests, don't you?"

"Of course. But I don't wish to hear you bellow like a foghorn! Willeen happens to be helping Jean-Pierre. She doesn't have time to tend you."

She pursed her lips. "Will *you* help me?" Lifting the corset from the bed, she held it in the air by her fingertips, then swayed it back and forth. "I know you like how it makes me look."

He stepped closer. "Yes, I do." He grabbed onto her and gave her a kiss that took her breath. "I'll help you tie it up tight. Then later, if you behave yourself at the party, I'll help you *un*tie it and do the things you've grown to love."

"Mmm. Sounds wonderful." She giggled and kissed him back.

He cinched her corset *extra* tight, then helped with her gown. Her royal blue dress sat just off her shoulders and plunged low. The corset bulged out her breasts and narrowed her waist. As long as she held her head high, she felt no pain.

"You, my dear, will make the women hate you and the men wish they were me," John said, nuzzling her neck. "I couldn't ask for anything more enjoyable."

"Except for what we'll do *after* the party." She ran her hand along his chest, then moved it lower to give him a taste of what was to come.

He moved away from her. "Not now, my dear. I must have my wits about me when we meet our guests. The time for play will come. You'll be meeting some important people. Speak when you're spoken to and refrain from excessive giggling."

He's startin' to sound like my daddy again. "I know how to act, John."

"I'm counting on it. Oh . . . and only *one* glass of champagne." He held up a single finger as if she didn't know how to count. "If you became tipsy, you could spoil everything."

"Just one?" she pouted.

"You can have more *after* the party. We'll bring some to our room."

She wrapped her arms around his body and rested her head against him. "Thank you." Lifting her head, she looked in his eyes. "I won't disappoint you. You'll see I can be the perfect wife. Maybe a senator's wife one day."

He caressed her cheek. "Yes. Hopefully, one day soon."

* * *

As the guests arrived, John and Victoria greeted them at the front door. She didn't let him down. He couldn't have been more pleased.

He knew she'd had training at a Catholic girl's school and it must have included etiquette. She held herself like a refined woman. And just as he'd predicted, the women gave her that *stare* that only females could exude. Not only were they jealous of her beauty, they'd have likely given anything to be standing by his side. The women in Bridgeport had gossiped about him endlessly. None of them expected him to marry. He'd certainly fooled them.

"Ah . . . James!" John greeted the man with excessive vigor, then turned to Victoria. "My dear, this is James Stanley, my business partner."

Victoria extended her white-gloved hand. "It's a pleasure meetin' you."

James gave her hand an appropriate kiss. "*My* pleasure." He looked at John. "Your description didn't do your wife justice. She's *exceedingly* beautiful."

Victoria placed her hand against the crest of her breast, drawing James' eye.

My dear, you are a devil.

"Why, thank you," she said, pursing her lips.

John forced himself not to chuckle. "Yes, thank you, James. But where is *your* lovely wife? I'd hoped we could celebrate *your* recent marriage as well."

"I regret to say her head is aching. She sends her best wishes."

I'm sure she does.

"I hope she feels better soon," Victoria said. The sympathetic look she gave was almost believable. This particular talent couldn't have been learned at a religious institution. She had to have mastered it on her own.

"Yes," John added. "Tell her I missed having her here."

James nodded, but frowned.

"Go have some fun," Victoria said and motioned to the ballroom. "I'll save you a dance."

With a rapid nod, James left.

"Pity 'bout his wife," Victoria said. "Hope it's nothin' serious."

John gave her hand a pat. "I doubt it is." The poor girl just needed time to get over him.

The evening progressed as he'd hoped. He paraded Victoria around the dancefloor, to the envy of every man present. His prize lit up the room, even more so than the multitude of candles.

I'm sure they'd like to see even more of you.

"What's that smile for, John?" Victoria asked as he spun her in a circle.

"For you, my dear. Only for you."

He'd come up with the perfect idea, and tomorrow he'd set his plan in motion. For tonight, he'd reward her with well-deserved passion. He'd coddle her and gain her trust.

Then she'll do whatever I ask.

CHAPTER 18

Oliver Stevens had been hard at work on the addition to their home, and Claire needed to get away from the hammering. The noise made it nearly impossible for Michael to take a decent nap. So she took him to Alicia's. She'd already been there several times over the past week.

During her visits, she'd often found Samuel perched on a stool in the corner facing the wall. She pitied the child, but Alicia's punishment seemed just. The boy kept running off.

It helped Claire forget her own troubles by worrying about him. She asked Alicia if she could hire him to help with the construction. Simple tasks to make him feel needed, not to mention teach him a trade. He'd shown no interest in farming.

After only a slight hesitation, Alicia agreed. But it brightened Claire's spirit even more seeing how excited Samuel was about the idea.

He started working the following Monday and didn't let her down. Every day he showed up bright and early and listened to Mr. Stevens. The man even said that Samuel was a better worker than some of his hired hands. He'd started him out simply, but after a few days, taught him how to measure wood and hammer nails.

She had a feeling he'd no longer occupy that stool in the corner.

In the afternoons they'd walk together to his mama's house and talk nonstop. She discovered he'd never learned to read, so she offered to teach him while Michael napped. Alicia loved the idea.

Her heart lifted, helping them, but then one afternoon while she returned home with Michael, her thoughts drifted to Beth. She missed her terribly, but couldn't dwell on it. Andrew deserved a happy wife. Thinking about Beth and their tattered friendship made her miserable. She had to believe that Andrew was right and one day they'd reconcile.

But now that she's at Henry's, my little house is empty.

Empty . . .

A brilliant idea struck her, and she couldn't wait to share it with Andrew.

"Well . . ." Andrew set his fork down. She'd shared her idea for a trip to the bay house over supper. "I don't have to work this weekend. I think it's a wonderful plan."

Excited energy filled her. "I'll get our things together after I clear the dishes. Then we can leave first thing in the mornin'."

Their eyes met. His held as much joy as she felt. "Perfect."

"I just wanna make sure the house is all right. Maybe it's silly, but I hate to think of it all alone."

He let out a soft laugh. "I understand. Besides, since we're starting fresh, what better way than to go back to where everything began?"

She closed her eyes envisioning what they'd done there, but then her thoughts dimmed, remembering the last time at the bay. It'd been the final place she'd seen Gerald alive and where he was buried. "Lots of memories there," she whispered. "Good *an'* bad. I wish I'd only remember the good."

"Unfortunately, our memories don't work that way. So let's go and make more *good* memories."

"I'd like that." She'd finished eating, so she started clearing the table. "Reckon I could ask Samuel to come by an' milk Rosie. She'll need to be tended while we're away."

"Samuel? I thought he claimed it was *women's* work." Andrew looked up at her and grinned.

"He did. But he's still capable. Maybe Jenny can help. We can go by and ask Alicia." Thinking of Samuel brightened her mood. "He's done real well helpin' the men. When I left him this afternoon he said he couldn't wait till Monday. I'm real proud of him."

Andrew beckoned her with a slight jerk of his head, then reached out his hand. The smile on his face drew her in and she took it. "I married a smart woman. You're good with children." He nodded to Michael, who sat in his high-chair eating. "Look how happy Michael is."

"It's because *we're* happy. He feels it." She took a deep breath. "Andrew?"

He scooted his chair back and patted his lap. "What's wrong?"

She gladly sat. "I want another child."

"I do, too." He studied her face. "Don't worry. It'll happen."

"Can't help but worry. I'm not gettin' any younger." She stared at her fingers, twisting them into knots.

He covered her hands with his. "I don't mind working on it." Grinning, he nuzzled her neck. "This weekend we should have time. We can work extra hard and give it our best effort."

"Can we start tonight?" She bit her lower lip and raked her fingers through his hair. "An efficient worker gets right on the job." She gave him a thorough kiss.

Giggling, Michael clapped his hands and pulled them from their play. Once she put him down for the night, she'd show his daddy just how proficient she could be.

* * *

The weather cooperated for a pleasant ride to the coast. Andrew hoped it would turn out as he'd planned. After Claire had made the suggestion, his mind spun thinking of how he could ease her. Wash away all her guilt. Her emotions had been as up and down as the distant sun.

Arriving at her house, it appeared unchanged, though her garden had already become overgrown. Claire looked away as they passed it and hurried toward the front door. He drew the key from his pocket to unlock it, then she pushed it open.

She peeked inside and placed one foot across the threshold. "I'm not sure if this was a good idea." Her sad eyes blinked slowly.

He put his arm around her and guided her in. Michael wasn't so timid and walked past them. He looked under the sofa and then moved around the living room. Abruptly he stopped in the middle of the floor and let out a squall. Claire rushed to his side.

"Here, baby, take your bunny." She placed it in his outstretched hands. "Your other toys are at home."

Satisfied and no longer crying, he plopped down on the floor and clutched the toy close. He looked at Andrew as if wondering what was next.

I'm not quite sure.

Andrew wandered into the bedroom and sat down on the edge of the bed. It had been neatly made. Everything in the house seemed to have been left where Claire had put it. As far as he could remember. The last time he'd been here, his mind had been focused on Claire. Just like now.

She stood in the doorway staring at him.

"Claire." He patted the spot beside him and she came right over. She sat and laid her head on his shoulder.

"I have an idea," he said, then took her hand in his and caressed it. "Let's retrace our steps. We could start at the beach where we first met, then go to the fishing hole. And after we put Michael down for the night, I could douse you with water and pretend we just came in out of the storm."

She gave him a reprimanding grin and he wiggled his brows.

"I admit," he went on. "I enjoyed seeing you all wet."

"Andrew Fletcher!" Laughing, she playfully smacked his chest. "Shame on you!"

"I'm serious!" He'd never forget how her wet dress had clung to her curves. Laughing along with her, he laid her back against the bed. Their laughter subsided. Heat pumped through his veins. "You took my breath away." He stroked her cheek. "You still do."

They became lost in each other and entwined in a passionate kiss.

"Mama!" Michael hit his hands against the side of the bed. "Dada!"

Sitting up, they sighed in unison.

Claire lifted Michael onto her lap and grinned at Andrew. "Let's do what you suggested. All of it. Though I don't wanna be doused. All right?"

"Are you sure? I really hoped to see that again."

She pursed her lips. "You'll see plenty after Michael's asleep." She giggled and stood with him perched on her hip.

You're so beautiful.

She'd started behaving more like the woman he remembered. Playful. At ease. Witty. And hearing her laugh made coming here worth it. Even if they didn't do another thing.

Once on the beach, they let Michael put his toes in the cool water. Claire kept a tight hold on his little hand. Knowing what had happened here, Andrew understood.

She became somber. A complete change in her mood.

"That's where it happened," she whispered and pointed out to sea. "There's a drop-off. Gerald couldn't swim." She swallowed so hard, Andrew heard it.

He looked from where she'd pointed and faced her. Tears pooled in her eyes. Her chest heaved. He gripped her hand and stroked it with his thumb.

"Why?" She sucked in air. "Why does it hafta hurt so bad?" Tears trickled down her face.

"It hasn't been long enough. It's still fresh in your memory."

She shifted her body toward him. "How do you do it? You're always so calm 'bout my feelin's for Gerald. Doesn't it bother you knowin' I was with another man? That I shared his bed?"

He couldn't look at her, so he focused on the sand and made patterns in it with his feet. He struggled with what to say. A fight between truth and not wanting to hurt her. "I understand why you went to him, and that's what keeps me sane. I would've thought less of you if you hadn't learned to love him and did all you could to make your marriage work. You made a difficult choice, and I know you did it for Michael."

He raised his head and looked her in the eyes. "If I think about you in his arms, yes, it hurts. So I choose not to think about it. I know you love me, and we're together now. That's all that matters. I want you to be happy, because when you are, so am I." He couldn't stop his own tears from forming. A solitary drop ran down his cheek.

Claire wiped it away. "I *do* love you. I want you to be happy, too. I'm glad we came here. Talkin' 'bout this helps."

They started walking again, each holding one of Michael's hands.

"Andrew?" Claire looked straight ahead. "Do you ever wish you could change the way things happened?"

"Sometimes. But I trust they happened for a reason. I'm glad we're together now. Nothing will change that. *Ever.*" He swung Michael up into one arm and draped his free arm over Claire's shoulders. They walked along silently.

* * *

Claire tucked her legs up under her and watched her *men* throw rocks into the pond at the fishing hole. Between

Michael's innocent giggles and Andrew's heartfelt words, she'd warmed from the inside out.

They didn't stay long—mainly because she worried about snakes. Not so much for her, because she was used to them, but her baby would never survive a snake bite.

Luckily, Beth had left behind some canned goods, so she threw together a light supper. And just like they'd done on that stormy night, they shared a meal at her kitchen table. Of course, Andrew belonged here now. Back then, they'd done something highly inappropriate.

Desire couldn't be swept aside then, and for all accounts had multiplied since they'd reunited. She wanted him more than ever.

Michael let out a loud yawn. He rubbed his eyes and whimpered.

Andrew stood and went to their bedroom, then returned with one of the dresser drawers. Something tugged at her heart as he folded a blanket inside and prepared Michael's bed. It brought back even more memories.

Lifting Michael onto his shoulder, he nodded for her to join them on the front porch. He took a seat and began rocking their son to sleep.

She stood beside them and gazed across the bay. The very reason why she loved it here so much. The sun had started to set. The sky swirled in red and orange, with small wispy clouds. The water sparkled under the fading light.

Breathing deeply, she inhaled the sea air. Content, she smiled.

She cupped her hand over Michael's tiny head. "I'll be back soon, all right?"

Andrew looked up and nodded, though the concern in his eyes affirmed he wasn't so sure. But he didn't try to stop her.

The night sky held enough light for her to return to the beach. She went back to the place Gerald had died. She sat on the sand, stared at the water, and allowed herself to cry. Then she lifted her face to the heavens.

"Lord, please help me let go. I love Andrew. You know I do. Forgive me for rushin' things." She closed her eyes and moistened her dry lips. "I don't wanna hurt him. He deserves a good wife. Not one who cries all the time. Help me heal. And Lord, if you see fit, help Beth understand. I miss her."

Tears streamed out beneath her closed lids. When she opened her eyes, she realized that darkness was setting in. So she pushed herself up off the sand.

Even in the warm air, a cold chill ran down her spine.

She shuddered. "Gerald?"

Somehow his presence surrounded her. She glanced from side to side expecting to see him, then smiled recalling his goodness. "I need to say goodbye, Gerald. I never got to. Please, let me go. Let me know it's okay to love Andrew."

Warmth permeated her body and her heart lifted. The vision she'd had of Gerald became replaced by one of Andrew hopping around on the hot sand. She laughed, recalling how she'd started loving him at that very moment. Even in all the time she'd been with Gerald, she'd never stopped loving Andrew.

"I *am* where I belong!"

She waded into the water in her pink cotton dress and kept walking until the waves reached her neck. The lightweight fabric clung to her skin.

Looking down, she grinned. She'd give Andrew exactly what he'd asked for.

Excitement filled her, anticipating his reaction. Because of her love for him, she wanted to please him however she could.

She returned to the shoreline and wrung the excess water from her skirt. Then she gazed out to sea one last time.

"Goodbye, Gerald." She blew a kiss to the wind, then headed for home.

* * *

Maybe I should go after her.

Andrew paced beside Michael's slumbering body. Claire had been gone too long.

In her eyes, he'd recognized the need for privacy, so he'd let her go without a single objection. But he feared he'd made a poor judgment.

She could be hurt.

Though she'd lived here all her life and likely knew every inch of the surroundings, he couldn't help but worry.

The door creaked open and he spun around. Claire took his breath. Her soaked dress clung to her like a second layer of skin. Desire coursed through his body. His heart pumped hard.

She met his gaze with a coy smile, then shut the door and walked past him into the bedroom. He'd wanted to run to her, but could tell she had something else in mind. So he stood frozen to the floor, listening to the beat of his heart reverberating in his ears.

She came out holding two towels. "Here," she whispered and handed him one.

"What's this for?" He wasn't the one dripping water on the floor.

"It's *your* turn. Take off your shirt and drape the towel over your shoulders. If we're recreatin' that night, you need to look the way *I* remember *you*."

My Claire. Playful. Sensual.

If he was going to comply, he'd have to avert his eyes from her breasts. Did she realize how much she tortured him?

He kept them safely on her face while he unbuttoned his shirt, then tossed it on the sofa. Once he'd bared his chest, her brows rose to her hairline and she nibbled her lower lip.

Let me nibble it for you.

He steadied his heart and draped the towel as she'd requested. "Is this what you remember?"

"Mmm . . . Yes." She eliminated the space between them and brushed her hand across his naked flesh, causing him to tremble. "I'll never tire of lookin' at your bare chest."

"Then you and I have something else in common." He unfastened the buttons on her dress, then peeled it from her skin and let it drop to the floor. *Her* body quivered when he stripped away her undergarments. They, too, were completely soaked. "Much wetter than the last time."

She giggled and handed him the other towel. "Use this."

She closed her eyes as he dried her body, following each dab of the towel with a tender kiss. Her breasts heaved with every heavy breath she took.

He pulled the pins from her hair and let it fall onto her shoulders. Then he buried his face into the honey-sweet scent.

"I made sure I didn't get it wet," she rasped. "I know how much you like the smell."

Her hands roamed over his body. He couldn't take it any longer. He picked her up and carried her to the bed, then laid her down gently.

He rapidly removed the rest of his clothing, then climbed onto the bed and knelt between her legs.

"Just like before," he said, then bent and kissed her. Though craving gratification, he slowed down and rose up, looking at her. Then he ran his hands over her skin, feeling every part of her.

She shivered.

"You trembled the first time, too," he whispered and began to lower himself onto her.

"It's *like* the first time." Her voice shook. "I want it to *always* be like the first time." She wrapped her legs around him, then slid her hands down his back until she reached his bottom. Taking hold of it, she jerked him tight against her.

"You didn't do *that* the first time," he said, nearly losing control.

She blinked ever so slowly. "I was scared. Afraid it would hurt."

"I promised you I'd never hurt you." He bent to kiss her again, then after tasting her lips, moved his mouth to her neck.

"You never have. All you've ever done is make me want you more." She took his face in her hands and kissed him. "I love you so much. I don't ever wanna lose you."

The fear of loss dwelt in her eyes. Sadly, she knew it well. "You never will. I'm your husband. Your lover. I'll always be with you."

Her legs grasped him even tighter and their bodies joined.

Even with no storm raging outside, in their tiny room lightning flashed and thunder rolled. But no rain fell. Their tears had dried. They'd started over and allowed themselves pleasure.

CHAPTER 19

With Michael in the house, Claire didn't need a rooster. She reluctantly climbed out of bed and donned a robe, then went to the living room. She found him sitting upright in the drawer, crying. He could've easily climbed out of it. His tears had likely formed from utter confusion.

"It's all right. Mama's here." She lifted him into her arms, instantly calming him.

Andrew walked in and gave both of them kisses. Still bare-chested, he took her breath. Last night had been more than lovemaking. They'd truly taken a step forward.

No chickens meant no eggs. Canned peaches and rolled oats would have to suffice for breakfast. They'd be returning home, so she'd cook them a decent meal when they got there.

After locking things up again, Andrew followed her outside, holding Michael.

"Can you give me a minute?" she asked and gestured to the graves.

"I'll wait for you."

"Would you mind so much comin' with me? Just stand by me?"

His face warmed with a smile. "Of course."

She picked some wildflowers to place on the graves, then knelt beside her mama's and set half of them there. "Mama, I followed my heart. I'm married to Andrew now. You know I always loved him. He's a good man, an' he's takin' care of us. You don't hafta worry 'bout me ever again."

After kissing her fingers and touching the headstone, she shifted and faced Gerald's grave. Shriveled daisies lay atop it, probably put there by Beth. She replaced them with the remaining wildflowers. "Thank you for lettin' me go. And for bein' so good to me while you were here." She touched the wooden cross marking his grave. "Goodbye, Gerald."

Andrew helped her to her feet, then guided her toward the buggy. "Are you all right?"

"Better than ever." She burrowed against him. "Can we make one more stop before we go back?"

"Church?"

She rapidly shook her head. It might be Sunday, but she wasn't ready for that. "I'd like to see Mrs. Sandborn. By the time we get to the boardin' house, she should be home from services."

"I'd like that. You've said so much about her."

"It's high time she meets you." She tickled Michael under the chin. "An' she's gonna love seein' *you* again."

He giggled. "More."

"Not sure if he means more ticklin' or more food. Maybe both."

By the time Claire knocked on Mrs. Sandborn's door, she'd started having second thoughts. "Reckon she's not home," she said and turned to leave.

"Give her a minute," Andrew said. He nodded toward the door. "I think I hear someone."

Oh, fiddle.

Too late to run. The door swung open.

"Oh, my!" Mrs. Sandborn held her hands against her cheeks. "Look who's at my door!" She grabbed Claire and hugged her tight. Reminiscent of the hugs she used to get from Beth. "Come inside!"

Her enthusiastic welcome relieved Claire. She walked in with Andrew and Michael behind her.

"Feared I'd never see ya again," Mrs. Sandborn said and led them to the kitchen.

"It hasn't been that long," Claire said. "Not even a month."

"Feels like forever." It seemed the woman had purposefully avoided acknowledging Andrew, but then she stepped closer to him and the baby. "Look at you." She took Michael's hand. "You've grown."

Claire's heart pounded. What would she say to Andrew?

Mrs. Sandborn's head tilted upward, taking him in. "You must be Dr. Fletcher."

"Yes, ma'am. But please, call me Andrew."

To Claire's relief, Mrs. Sandborn smiled. "Andrew it is. Are ya hungry? Just took a peach cobbler outta the oven."

"More!" Michael chirped.

Laughter filled the small kitchen.

"That sounds wonderful," Andrew said. "Thank you."

More peaches?

Claire had married the most gracious man in the country. Though likely already full of the fruit, he'd never say a word.

They sat at the large oak table. Once Mrs. Sandborn had four portions of cobbler dished up, she took a seat, too.

Claire swirled her spoon through the dessert. "Reckon Beth told you 'bout us."

Mrs. Sandborn leaned back in her chair and folded her hands across her belly. "Yep. She did. Left here real upset. Ain't never seen her that way. *Bitter.*"

"She hates me, doesn't she?"

"Don't say that. You an' Beth go way back. She'll come 'round. She just don't understand, and frankly—no offense to y'all—but I don't neither." Her usual cheerful disposition had been replaced by a questioning frown.

Claire glanced at Andrew, who gave her a nod of encouragement. "Mrs. Sandborn, will you let me explain?"

"Course I will. I *wanna* hear what you have to say."

If only Beth had said the same thing.

Claire told everything and Mrs. Sandborn listened without interrupting.

"So, you see," Claire said. "I've always loved Andrew. Even when I was with Gerald. But I loved him, too. Maybe it's wrong, but it's how I feel. Andrew's Michael's daddy. We belong together."

Andrew took hold of Claire's hand. "I love her, ma'am. We wanted Beth to know the truth, but she didn't give us the chance."

Mrs. Sandborn stood, then opened a drawer and withdrew a dish cloth. She sniffled and wiped her eyes with it. "Well, if that ain't the saddest story I ever heard. Two folks in love who thought they'd done wrong, only to find out it was always right." She blew her nose on the cloth and sat back down.

"Claire? How'd ya do it? If I'd been you, I'd never been able to keep that locked inside me. And you . . ." She jerked her head toward Andrew. "Knowin' the woman you loved was with someone else? You two have been through enough. Love don't come easy in this world. When ya find it, ya gotta hold onto it." She waved the dish cloth like a proclamation. "I had my Leonard, an' I still miss him. Now, don't get me wrong. I loved Gerald like my own son an' never woulda wanted to see him done wrong. But I can look at the two a ya an' see real love."

Claire turned toward Andrew, heart pounding. "We *do* love each other."

"Yes, ma'am," Andrew added. "We do."

"Beth's wrong 'bout you, Claire," Mrs. Sandborn said. "She thinks you lied. But I *know* you loved Gerald. I saw that, too. 'Sides, where's it written a woman can't love more than one man in her lifetime? Lotsa women lost their men in the war, and they're married again. It may look like the two a ya rushed things a might, but folks don't realize you've been lovin' far longer than they know." Shaking her head, she let out a long breath. "I *do* understand. You have my blessin'. You go on an' love each other an' don't let no one come between ya."

Despite her desire to jump in the air and shout, Claire kept her composure. She scooted her chair back and went around to Mrs. Sandborn, then knelt down and hugged her. "Thank you. You don't know how much that means to me."

The woman patted her on the cheek. "Oh, honey. Reckon I do."

"Mmm!" All eyes turned to Michael. He held his cobbler-covered hand in the air, then formed it into a fist and shoved it in his mouth. Once he pulled his hand out, he stuck his sticky fingers into his hair.

"Michael's always loved your cookin'," Claire said with a laugh.

"I do, too," Andrew said. He twirled his finger around the inside of his bowl, then licked it clean.

"Well," Mrs. Sandborn said. "How 'bout some more?"

"More!" Michael shouted, then pushed his empty bowl toward her.

The last bit of heaviness lifted from Claire's heart. Mrs. Sandborn's acceptance and understanding meant everything. Maybe because she knew every party involved, her opinion mattered even more to Claire than those from acquaintances she'd met through Andrew.

They stayed and talked for several hours. Before heading home, Claire asked her to look after her house. She gave her the key and offered to pay her for her trouble, but Mrs. Sandborn refused. All she required of them was a promise to come and visit often.

"It'll be our little getaway," Claire said. "I'll feel better knowin' you're tendin' it."

"I'm happy to. An' if Beth comes to see me, I'll tell her she needs to give you a chance to explain. She owes you that."

"No. I owe *her* that."

Mrs. Sandborn walked to the buggy with them. "Oh, Claire? Do you remember that farmhand a Martha's?"

"George?"

"Yep. He carried Beth to Mobile. Took her to Henry's. Seems to be a might sweet on her."

"I'm happy for her. He's a good man. *Quiet*, but good."

Mrs. Sandborn chuckled. "Beth can make up for him bein' quiet."

They said their final goodbyes and drove away. Claire was ready to get on with her life.

* * *

Andrew returned to work Monday morning with a little more bounce in his step. The weekend had proved to be exactly what they'd needed.

But then, his spirit dampened when he was summoned to see Mr. Schultz. After all this time, it shouldn't faze him, but the man could be extremely unpredictable.

Deciding to set the appropriate mood, he entered the man's office with a smile. "You asked to see me?" Andrew froze and nearly swallowed his words mid-sentence.

"If you'll excuse me," Mr. Schultz said and passed by him, then closed the door leaving Andrew alone with Patrick O'Malley.

The last time he'd been alone in this room with the man, he'd orchestrated his life. Planned his marriage to Victoria without giving Andrew any say.

The animosity he felt toward O'Malley hadn't diminished. But being a gentleman, Andrew wouldn't be rude.

"Thought you'd never see me again, didn't you, lad?" O'Malley chortled, seeming to find pleasure in the frigid air between them.

"Hello, sir," Andrew said, undaunted.

O'Malley took a seat at Mr. Schultz's desk. "You can sit, Doctor."

Andrew sat in a chair on the far side of the room. "Why are you here? Is everything all right?"

"Aye! Couldn't be better!"

Andrew folded his arms over his chest. Putting up a barrier seemed like a good idea. The man liked to play games, and he wasn't about to be a part of one. "Then why did you ask me here?"

"Relax, lad. I came to thank you."

"Thank me?" *I don't trust you.*

"Aye! The missus and I just received a telegram from Victoria. Seems she's happier than she ever dreamed. Quite the house your father lives in from what she tells." He produced a cigar from his pocket and lit it, then leaned back and blew a puff of smoke into the air.

"He moved after I left. I've never seen his home."

"Victoria describes it like a palace. Me daughter is where she should be. And that's why I want to thank you. For bringing him into her life. I had me doubts at first, but she's happy. And me daughter's happiness is all that matters." After another puff on his cigar, he extended an envelope. "Here, take it."

"What is it?"

"Open it and see."

With a wary glance at the man, Andrew cautiously opened the envelope. Inside he found a large sum of money. "I don't understand. What's this for?"

"The ring. The one I made you purchase for her. John bought her another. One she finds more to her liking." O'Malley rested his cigar in a glass dish on the desk. He laced his fingers behind his head and leaned back. "I made Jake take back the one you bought. This is a reimbursement for what you already paid. And I spoke to Klaus, so he'll no longer take money from your salary. I'm afraid I couldn't return *all* the money you paid. Jake argued that Victoria had been wearing the thing, so it was used. Strictly business, of course."

Andrew stared at the money, overwhelmed. "I don't know what to say."

"You tried to do right by me daughter. And from what I've been told, you have a family now and can use this money. That woman—the one who occupied so much of your time—she's your wife now?"

"Yes, sir. She is. Her name's Claire." Why did talking to him about her make his stomach churn?

O'Malley sat upright and retrieved his cigar. He took a long drag. "Am I to understand she's John's daughter?"

"Yes." Andrew swallowed the rock in his throat. Distrust had put it there.

"You married your sister?" O'Malley laughed. "Seems ungodly. But rumor is that you aren't John's son. Strange things happen in this world."

"We've not done anything illegal *or* ungodly. We made certain of that." *Time to leave.* "Is there anything else you need from me?"

"No, but I have a wedding gift for *you*." O'Malley stood and crossed the room, then hovered over him. "I've told my people to leave you alone." He hissed out a breath. "You know exactly what I mean. I heard you had some trouble at your home. Another filthy Negra messing with a white woman. When will you learn you don't belong there?"

Andrew tried to stand, but O'Malley pushed him down again. "I don't approve of what you do in Shanty Town, but your new wife is kin to me daughter. Your child, too.

You'll have my protection for now. If you have any sense at all, you'll move away from those animals. Start acting like a white man."

Rigidly, Andrew rose to his feet, forcing O'Malley to take a step back. "I'll take care of my family. There are good people in the shanties that need me. Claire wasn't hurt, and she wants to stay there. She understands what I'm trying to do for them. I'll *never* stop my work there, and it doesn't interfere with what I do in the city. So it shouldn't matter to you or anyone else what I do for the people in the shanties."

"You'll take care of your wife? Bah! You did a lousy job of taking care of her!" O'Malley pressed his finger into Andrew's chest. "You should've learned from what happened to Victoria! Whites and coloreds aren't meant to live together. They should've been sent back to where they came from!"

"And what about you? You're Irish. Why don't *you* go back where you came from?" Andrew had had enough. He moved toward the door.

"It's a blessing you didn't marry Victoria!" O'Malley snarled. "I never liked your mixed blood from the first time I saw you!"

"Thank you for returning my money," Andrew said coldly and walked out.

"Damn half-breed!" O'Malley screamed after him, then slammed the door shut.

CHAPTER 20

Melissa Montgomery couldn't stop the turmoil in her belly. Truth be told, every part of her ached, but nothing more than her heart.

If not for her sister, Mary, she'd never have agreed to come here. Riding in a wagon for months wasn't her idea of a pleasant time. But she had nowhere else to go.

"Is that it, Pa?" Her nephew, J.J., stood behind her in the wagon, pointing over her shoulder. His hand quivered with excitement and she feared he'd fall out. The over-active boy had a tendency to hurt himself.

"Yep. That's it. My old stompin' grounds." Thomas, her brother-in-law, had his arm around her sister and gave her a squeeze. "Mama ain't gonna know what to say when she sees us."

Melissa wished he would've telegrammed the poor woman. After all, she'd not seen her sons in years.

Sons.

The thought made tears form, but she quickly wiped them away. Only one son had returned home.

Melissa stared at the old farmhouse as the overloaded wagon drew closer. They'd brought as many belongings as they could. The four-horse team had had difficulty with the long haul. A mare had even died on the way and had to be replaced. Sometimes she wished *she'd* died along with it.

The heat smothered her. So unlike Montana. But they couldn't stay there. Not after what happened.

Dust rose from beneath the wheels as Thomas pulled the wagon to a stop. No sooner than he had, and a heavy-set old woman came running toward them. She'd lifted her skirt and exposed . . .

Men's boots?

Odd thing for a woman to wear.

"Thomas!" the woman yelled. "Oh, good Lord!"

He jumped from the wagon and picked her up off the ground. *Not an easy task.* "I'm home, Mama!" He swung her in a circle, then set her down.

Tears streamed down his mother's face, but then she turned her head and spit. Melissa gaped at her cheek full of chaw. She hadn't been prepared for the likes of Martha Montgomery.

"Is that all ya have to say?" Martha asked, fisting her hands on her hips. "I'm home, Mama? Like you'd only been gone a short spell? Why ain't ya wrote? Did ya forget you *had* a mama?"

Thomas bellowed with laughter. "You haven't changed a bit, have ya?" He gave her another hug. "I missed you, too!"

Gripping him so hard he groaned, Martha rocked him back and forth. "You best not be tryin' to give me heart failure. I ain't ready to give up the farm just yet!" She let him go and took a step back, then wiped away tears with the corner of her dress. This time she lifted her skirt so high she exposed her bloomers. Maybe they didn't teach modesty in the south. "Can't believe you're here. Look at ya. You're roundin' out like me." She patted his large belly.

Thomas laughed again, then waved them over. Mary stepped down first and helped Fran to the ground. Melissa's niece had been the one thing that kept her going on the long journey. The little girl had a heart of gold and always managed to lift her spirits when she felt gloomy.

Melissa slowly got out and stood beside Mary. This wouldn't be easy. Soon, her brother-in-law wouldn't be laughing.

"Mama," Thomas said, taking Mary's hand. "This here's Mary, my wife, and the taller one there is her sister, Melissa."

The old woman's face crinkled. She squinted. "I can tell. Ya look just alike. Nice to meet ya."

They used to be mistaken for twins. Their long dark hair and freckles matched as well as their high cheekbones. Truthfully, Melissa had liked being compared to Mary, who was five years younger than her. But sorrow had aged Melissa. That mistake would never be made again.

J.J. hopped out of the wagon and stepped in front of Thomas.

"Mama," Thomas said. "This is J.J. Your grandson." He shoved the boy toward her. "Give your gramma a hug, boy."

"Do I hafta?" he whined.

Martha winced. "No need to force the boy. He don't know me from Adam."

J.J. grinned, no doubt relieved.

"The little one here is Francis, but she likes to be called *Fran*."

Martha's head drew back, studying her. Then the woman smiled broadly, displaying a large gap from a missing tooth. *Likely from the chewing tobacco.*

Fran walked up to her grandma and peered into her face. "You waitin' for your teeth to come in, too?" She pointed to the space in her own mouth.

Martha bent down so the two were eye to eye. "'Fraid not. Mine ain't comin' back." She waved her finger in the air. "Here's my first advice as your gramma. Don't chew tobacca."

"That's good advice, Mrs. Montgomery," Mary said.

"I try." Martha scratched her head. "So. Now I know who everyone is, but are ya gonna tell my why you decided to come see me after all these years?"

How would he say it? Melissa let out a sigh, waiting.

"Why don't we go inside an' talk?" Thomas said, motioning to the house.

"Fine by me," Martha said. "It's hot as Hades out here."

They followed her inside. Melissa remained silent, listening to Fran cheerfully ask her mother what Hades was. If only she could have the innocent joy of a child.

I've been in Hades.

The scent of bacon filled the house. The wood floors were dotted here and there with what looked like dried tobacco. *Does she spit on the floor?* The furnishings were old and in need of a good cleaning. Aside from that, the house was tidy.

Not big enough for all of us, though.

After having them sit in the living room, Martha brought out glasses of sweet tea punch, as she called it.

Sweet didn't do it justice. She had to have filled the pitcher with sugar and added a *bit* of water. *Maybe* some tea. But Melissa wouldn't complain. She was thirsty after being on the long, hot road for so long.

Martha plopped down in an overstuffed chair. Thomas and Mary sat on a long sofa with the children beside them. Melissa tried to get comfortable in a wooden chair that Thomas had brought out from the kitchen.

No one spoke. Thomas fidgeted with his drinking glass.

"Thomas," Martha huffed. "You're makin' me nervous. Tell me what's on your mind, or I'm gonna take away your tea."

The glass went still between his fingers. "Mama." He swallowed hard. "We left Montana."

She threw her hands in the air. "Do I look that dumb? Tell me sumthin' I *don't* know!"

"Well . . ." He set his punch on a table beside the sofa. "We'd like to stay with you for a while. Move in."

"Would ya now?" Martha's eyes opened so wide, Melissa feared they'd pop from her head. Then her face twisted into something uglier than it already was. "Ya don't write. Ya don't bother to come for a visit! Did ya even happen to notice your daddy's nowhere to be seen? He died a few years after ya left! Did ya bother to find out 'bout that? No!" She turned her head and spit on the floor. "An' now I find out ya have a wife! I didn't even know I had granbabies!" She folded her arms firmly over her large, sagging breasts. "Ya think you can just show up here an' move back in?" Fire burned in the woman's eyes, which were squinting and shooting daggers.

Fran tugged on her mother's sleeve. "I'm not a baby. I'm seven."

"Shh . . ." Mary patted her leg.

"An' if that weren't enough to break an old woman's heart, ya not only brung your wife, but her sister, too!" Martha glared at Melissa, then returned her angry stare to Thomas. "You take up polygamy out west?"

"What's pigamy, Ma?" Fran asked.

"Hush, Francis," Mary whispered. She briefly met Melissa's gaze with an apologetic look. It did no good. Martha's words couldn't be erased.

"Fran, not Francis!" Her niece corrected, then pouted. The poor child had no idea what had actually just been said.

"Mama." Thomas leaned forward, meeting her wretched frown. "Melissa is your daughter-in-law, too. But she's not my wife. She was Joe's."

Martha leered at Melissa. "What do ya mean, *was*? You leave my boy?"

Her accusation snapped Melissa's heartstrings. She couldn't take another minute in the same room with the woman. She stood and rushed out the door, no longer able to hold back tears.

Damn her.

A swing hung from the ceiling of the front porch, so she sat and wallowed in her memories. Thomas was likely telling his mother everything. Even as hateful as the woman had been, no mother deserved to be told her son was dead.

Mother's should never have to bury their children.

At least Martha didn't have to be there to witness it. Unlike Melissa, she could sleep at night without seeing his blood-covered face and the children . . .

She shook her head. *No, I won't think about them.* The nightmares were bad enough.

Thomas came out the front door and sat in the swing beside her. "You all right?"

"It hurts."

He put his arm around her shoulder and pulled her against him. She let her tears fall and burrowed into his body.

He was younger than Joe, but they had similar features. Somehow even smelled the same. Both had let their beards grow long. But he wasn't Joe. There'd never be another Joe.

The squeaky door opened again, and Melissa looked up.

With a tear-streaked face of her own, Martha walked over. "Honey? I'm sorry. Had no idea. Can you forgive an old fool?" She extended her hand.

Melissa studied the shattered woman. Old and ornery, but they shared the love of the same man. And, she *had* to feel the loss of the grandchildren she would never know. She stood and embraced her, and Martha stroked her hair with motherly affection. They cried in each other's arms, mourning their loss. Maybe she'd misjudged her.

"I'm glad ya came," Martha whispered. "You're welcome here."

For the first time, in the body of a tobacco-chewing, feisty old woman, Melissa held a gleam of hope.

Martha released her hold, but took one of Melissa's hands. "Sometimes food can ease more than hunger. Reckon them children are hungry. Why don't I make us all a good ol' southern meal? You ever had one?"

"Joe tried to show me once how you fried chicken, but he burned it." Melissa wiped away the remaining moisture on her face.

"Sounds like my boy." Martha shook her head, chuckling. "An' that's how I aim to remember him. You should, too."

The old woman peered deeply into her eyes. This gaze was nothing like the one she'd given her earlier. Love lay there now. And she was right. Melissa needed to remember the good things, not how he'd died.

She nodded, and Martha led her inside.

In no time at all, Martha had the kitchen smelling wonderful. Frying chicken overtook the aroma of bacon. "Now this is how ya do it," Martha muttered as she flipped it in the wrought iron skillet.

Melissa leaned over her shoulder. "Perfectly golden-brown." She and Mary had been given the task of preparing green beans and rolling out biscuits.

"Yep. I ain't never burned a bird," Martha said, puffing out her chest. "Don't never intend to, neither."

While they cooked, Thomas and J.J., along with Martha's farmhand, George, unloaded the wagon. Martha told her the man was shy, so Melissa didn't meet him. Not everyone felt comfortable talking to strangers. Unlike Martha. Maybe the old woman was exactly what Melissa needed. Someone who spoke their mind and would talk to her about what had happened. But not now. It was still too fresh.

The meal tasted delicious and everyone had seconds. Even Melissa had found her appetite.

As the evening waned, Martha assigned their rooms. With only three bedrooms, Melissa didn't have one to sleep in. Unless she wanted to share Martha's bed, and that didn't appeal to her. The bed was small, and Martha wasn't.

So she made herself comfortable on the living room sofa. Her belongings were put in Martha's room.

"It'll be tight quarters," Martha said. "But I wouldn't have it any other way. There's nothin' like family!"

Before they turned in for the night, they all gathered again in the living room. Martha served slices of apple pie with fresh whipped cream. A milk cow was a luxury they'd not had for some time.

They'd taken the same seats. It seemed they already knew their places.

"Yep," Martha said, shoveling in a large bite of pie. "Lots happened since you been gone. Claire married herself a doctor. They got a little boy just a might over a year."

"A doctor?" Thomas sat up a little taller. "That could come in handy. J.J.'s a bit accident-prone."

The boy rolled his eyes.

"Where on earth did ya come up with a name like J.J.?" Martha asked. "What's it stand for?"

Thomas laughed, but then instantly sobered. "His real name's Clarence. After Daddy. But he doesn't like it."

"Well, I reckon not every boy would like to wear a name like that, but how in the *hell* did ya get J.J. outta Clarence?"

Melissa's breath caught. Not only did her mother-in-law spit, she cursed.

Fran's eyes popped wide.

Martha's mouth screwed together, then twisted from side to side. She glared at the girl. "I meant, *heck*."

Fran settled back into the sofa and raised her chin in the air with a satisfied expression befitting an adult.

"Hmph," Martha grunted. "Can't believe I'm bein' scolded by a seven-year-old."

"I didn't scold ya, Gramma. I just looked at you."

"Same thing!" Martha's brows danced up and down. "Where'd ya learn to do that anyways?"

"I think she has a bit of you in her, Mama," Thomas said, grinning. "As for J.J., it stands for *Just Junior*. Reckon it might sound silly, but a couple years back he asked why we named him Clarence. Said other kids teased him. I told him he was named after his granddaddy. Almost like he was a Clarence *Junior*."

J.J. had perked up. The boy had always liked being the center of attention. "So I told my pa I didn't like bein' called Clarence and said, if you don't mind, just Junior. Right, Pa?'

"Yep." Thomas ruffled J.J.'s hair. "We teased him an' called him Just Junior for a time, but eventually it became J.J."

Martha's eyes shifted from Thomas to J.J. and back again. "Dumbest thing I ever heard. But if the boy don't wanna be called Clarence, I reckon J.J. ain't so bad." She pointed a single finger at him. "I'll have ya know, your granddaddy was a good man. He'd a been proud to know you was named after him. Maybe when ya get a little older, you'll change it back again."

"But I like J.J.!" J.J. gave Martha a scornful look, similar to ones she'd been giving out earlier.

"Fine!" Martha huffed. "But don't get mad if I call ya Clarence every now an' then just to try it out for size."

J.J. rolled his eyes and slumped down on the sofa.

Melissa felt a tug on her heart. He looked so much like her boy, Steven.

Don't think about it.

Soon she'd be lying down to sleep, and she needed her mind free of the memory.

After cleaning up the dessert dishes, they all readied themselves for bed. Fortunately for Melissa, the sofa was well-stuffed and comfortable. But even the walls between them offered little privacy. She could hear everything being said in the children's room. Mary was in the room with them, tucking them into bed. Melissa closed her eyes and silently listened.

"Ma?" Even Fran's small voice carried.

"Yes, dear?"

"Pa says I'm like Gramma. Does that mean when I get old like her, I'll be ugly, too?"

Melissa's heartbeat increased its speed. She'd thought the same of the woman until she saw into her heart.

"Sweetie," Mary said. "Your grandma isn't ugly. Look at her a bit closer the next time you talk to her. You'll see a beautiful person."

You said it perfectly. You're such a good mother.

"It's kinda like that story you told us 'bout the ugly duckling." Fran's voice rose a little louder. "Guess Gramma done it backward."

Melissa covered her mouth to hold in laughter.

"Ma?" Fran's chipper voice softened again. "I'm glad we came here. I was 'fraid of the Indians."

Melissa gasped, as if she'd been punched in the stomach.

Don't think about it, Franny. Don't . . .

"You don't have to be afraid anymore," Mary said. Her soothing words likely eased Fran, but Melissa's body had become drenched in sweat. "Now, go to sleep."

A soft shuffling affirmed her sister had stood. Melissa tried to steady her breathing.

"No!" J.J. fussed. "I'm too big for a goodnight kiss!"

"You'll never be too big for my kisses," Mary said.

"Am I always gonna hafta share a bed with Fran? She wiggles too much."

"Do not!" Fran protested.

"Hush," Mary whispered. "In time, we'll get you your own bed, J.J. For now, we should be thankful we have a roof over our heads. Time to close your eyes and go to sleep."

Melissa's eyes were shut, but she doubted sleep would come.

CHAPTER 21

Beth paced on Henry's front porch. She'd gotten used to George's visits and he'd always come around the same time every Saturday. But it was nearly suppertime and there was no sign of him.

I musta done sumthin' wrong.

She racked her brain trying to think what that *something* might have been. Nothing came to mind. She thought things had been going well. Hoped a marriage proposal would be coming.

Her head jerked up to the sound of an approaching wagon. "Thank goodness," she mumbled, then smoothed her skirt and primped her hair. She'd fixed it up on her head beneath a stylish hat. Uncle Henry had told her all the fine ladies in town were wearing them.

George pulled to a stop directly in front of her. He got down, but lacked the energy she'd seen in him every Saturday prior. His shoulders slumped and he wasn't smiling.

She rushed to his side. "George? You all right?"

He scratched at the little patch of hair above his right ear. "Yep. You ready to go?"

He couldn't have sounded more depressed. She didn't believe him. Something had happened and she aimed to find out.

After helping her into the wagon, he grabbed the reins, then looked sideways at her. "How 'bout we g-go to the shore an' walk?"

"Huh?" Not their usual routine. She hadn't eaten, waiting to have dinner with him. "Aren't you hungry?"

"Nope. Don't feel like eatin'."

He had to be sick. Even though he was the smallest-framed man she'd ever known, he could put away food like no one else.

He raised his arms to snap the reins, but Beth grabbed his elbow to stop him. "Wait! I don't wanna go nowhere till you tell me what's wrong."

Slowly, he lowered his arms. His shoulders dropped right along with them. "H-How do ya know sumthin's wrong?"

"Cuz I *know* you. When you don't want food an' you look like your cat just died, sumthin's wrong. So, what is it?"

He sat motionless without uttering a sound.

"C'mon, George." She softened her voice. "You can tell me anythin'."

He stared at his hands, gripping the reins. "Miss Martha let me g-go. I d-don't have a job no more."

Instant heat coursed through Beth's body. "She did what?" she yelled and stood upright in the wagon. "After all the hours you worked for her sweatin' and slavin' away? I never did like that woman!"

"N-No," George shook his head and tugged on her skirt, making her sit again. "D-Don't say that. She's a good woman. She d-didn't wanna let me go. B-But her son came home with his family. They're helpin' her now. With all the extra mouths to f-feed, she c-couldn't afford to k-keep me, too."

He finally looked at her and attempted a smile, though he couldn't hide the heartbreak that shadowed his face. She knew him well enough to understand most all of his expressions. "I'm sorry. I just get riled up sometimes without thinkin'."

He grinned. A real honest-to-goodness grin. "That's what I like 'bout you. Never know what you might s-say."

Compelled to touch him, she took his hand. It had taken some time for him to get used to her touch, but he didn't pull away anymore. "My words get me in trouble. Mama always said we should think 'fore we speak. Reckon it was good advice."

His eyes were glued to their joined hands. "Beth?" *He sounds so sad.* "Don't know what I'm gonna do. I need a j-job. Someday I'd like to be able to support a larger family." He gave her hand a little squeeze.

Oh, my.

She knew what he meant. Her heart thumped so hard she had to fan herself. And then her mind tumbled, finally coming to a sensible place. The thought struck her like an abrupt slap. "George! I know what you can do!"

Her outburst caused him to jerk away. "You do?"

"Yep!" She slapped her knee. "You can work for Uncle Henry. You need a job an' he needs a reliable partner. Ain't no one more reliable than you." She took a firm hold of both of his hands. "Best of all, you'd be here every day. We'd see each other all the time an' I could cook for you when you're here." She'd hidden him from her uncle long enough.

His eyes blinked slowly and the brown in them seemed to darken. "But . . . I don't know nothin' 'bout b-black-smithin'."

She shrugged. "Neither did Gerald when he started workin' for Uncle Henry. Henry had him shoein' in no time." She scooted a little closer to him. "You can do it, George. Let's go talk to Henry."

"But . . ." The man cowered. A little like the old George.

Beth jumped out of the wagon. "C'mon. He don't bite."

Looking a bit like a rabbit trembling in front of a fox, George inched out of the wagon. "What if he d-don't like me?"

"What's not to like?" She linked her arm with his, at-tempting to boost his confidence. "Don't be so shy."

He allowed her to lead him through the front door and into the living room, where Henry sat reading a book.

"He's taken to readin' since I got him off the bottle," Beth whispered. "Says it keeps his mind off the whiskey. Oh, an' remember, he don't hear good, so talk real loud."

She tugged him across the floor and positioned him in front of her uncle. "Uncle Henry!"

The man jumped and dropped the book. "Dang, woman! Don't sneak up on me like that!" He cast a leery eye at George.

"This here's GEORGE!" she yelled and pointed.

Henry eyed him up and down.

"P-Pleased to m-meet ya!" George managed to get out, much to Beth's relief.

Henry's lip curled and he turned his attention to her. "He always this nervous?"

"He has a STUTTER! It's not YOU!"

"I can tell," Henry muttered, then his eyes squinted tight. "Don't you work for Martha Montgomery?"

George's mouth fell wide open. The rabbit was ready to bolt.

"Henry!" Beth stomped her foot. "Martha had to let him go! He needs a JOB! I want you to HIRE HIM!"

Henry glared at her. "I hire my own hands. Don't need no woman tellin' me what to do!"

George's eyes widened and he gulped. She turned him around, away from Henry. "George, give me a minute alone with him. All right?"

"Glad to," George mumbled, then hurried across the floor and out the door.

Beth whipped around and scowled at her uncle. "Dog gone it, Henry! I've been workin' my fingers to the bone for you! It's 'bout high time you help me! George is a good worker and I know you can teach him what to do. He takes care a his folks, an' needs the money. He can help you get your business back to where it was before Gerald left. Please Henry? Do this for me."

He squirmed and ran his feet back and forth across the floor. She felt certain he'd understood every word. He'd been watching her lips the entire time. "Why do you care whether or not he has a job?" He jerked his head toward the front porch. "Does he mean that much to ya? Seems kinda old. Looks my age."

She hissed out a long breath. "Don't go talkin' to me 'bout age! I know good an' well you fancy younger women!"

For an instant he turned away, then looked her in the eyes. "I'll give him a try. But only that. If he don't have the gift for it, I won't keep him on. Understand?"

"Yep. But you gotta promise me you'll try hard." She shook her finger at him, making her point. "Teach him everythin' you can." She took a step back, lowering her hand. "I have a feelin' you won't be disappointed. He's a capable man." Thinking of him, she smiled. "He means a lot to me. Truth be told, I might be fallin' in love with him." Her hand flew to her mouth. Had she truly said it aloud?

"Damn! That's the last thing I need in this house!"

"We won't be in the HOUSE!" she yelled and stomped her foot. "'Cept to eat dinner. George is a gentleman. He knows we can't be alone inside."

"See to it! He crosses the line an' he's out the door!"

Henry grabbed his cane and stood, then went to the kitchen and left her standing alone.

Long ago, her uncle wasn't so bitter. But he'd lost so much, and she understood why he acted this way.

Probably still pinin' over Claire.

The simple thought made her tighten her hands into fists. She had to stop thinking about her or she wouldn't be any good to George.

She'd never had a better plan. George had a calming way about him that might help Henry. He'd work for her uncle Monday through Friday and while he was there she'd show him her skills at cooking and keeping house. He'd see exactly what kind of wife she could be. And then, it was just a matter of time.

CHAPTER 22

After returning from the bay, Claire felt reborn. The weight she'd carried for so many months had finally lifted. She'd hold onto Gerald's memories, but managed to let *him* go. Her heart had become devoted to Andrew and Michael, but something was missing.

Mr. Stevens had finished their house and even crafted two new oak beds for the added bedrooms, as well as a much larger one for her and Andrew. They planned to move the bed they'd been sleeping on into the loft.

Best of all, the man had replaced the bloodstained floorboards. The other reminder of that horrible day would never be completely gone. *The scar over Michael's eye.* At least he wouldn't remember how it got there.

Upon completion of the house, the only unhappy person was Samuel. He'd moped around so much that Alicia shared her concerns.

Andrew suggested they keep him employed three days a week. They always had plenty for him to do. And on the days he didn't work, he promised to help Clay in the fields and *not* run off.

So with everything coming together so well, why did Claire want to cry?

She tugged the blankets into place on their bed, then smoothed it straight. A beautiful Sunday morning, and one she shared for the most part with Andrew. On the weekends he didn't have to go to the hospital, he went to the shanties to check on folks.

"Claire?"

She jumped, shaken from her thoughts. "Yes?"

Andrew stepped closer. "I didn't mean to scare you, but I wanted to know if you'd go with me today?"

"To the shanties?" Truthfully, she didn't feel comfortable going.

He nodded. "There's something I want you to hear."

"Hear?" He'd piqued her curiosity.

"Yes. So, will you?"

His eager eyes took away her trepidation. "All right. I'll get Michael ready."

As she dressed the baby, she couldn't stop wondering what Andrew meant. And would the patients they visited accept her as they had Andrew?

I'm no nurse.

Trusting her husband, she climbed into the buggy.

The sun had already risen high in the sky. Summer heat was upon them. She fanned herself and the baby trying to stay cool.

She'd never been this far down the road. Her heart sank seeing the simple wood structures these folks called *home*. Alicia's house was small, but finer than the ones before her. Oddly, no one was about.

"Where is everyone, Andrew?"

"It's Sunday." He smiled broadly.

"Church?"

He nodded.

Church. Her last experience at her hometown church had been horrid. Ever since, she'd felt separated from God. She'd *fallen from grace*, as her mama used to call it. Though Alicia had assured her of God's forgiveness, Claire wasn't convinced.

Andrew slowed the buggy. The clip-clop of the horse's hooves ceased and another sound filled the air.

Singing.

He stopped completely outside a white wood church, similar to the one she'd attended back home. She closed her eyes and listened to the incredible voices. "It's so beautiful."

"They know how to sing, don't they?"

Not only were they singing, they were clapping their hands. Claire didn't recognize the song, but she'd never heard such joy. As the song ended, shouts of "Alleluia" and "Praise the Lord" resounded.

Andrew leaned close. "You know, they're *Baptists.*"

"Truly?" Her mouth dropped open wide.

"Yes." He chuckled and shook his head. "Are they so different from what you think Baptists should be?"

"Well . . . folks at my church weren't quite so loud. Someone might have said an *amen* every now an' then, but not with so much feelin'." Claire tipped her head. "They sound so *alive.*"

"Want to go in?"

He can't be serious. "What? No. I couldn't. There's just colored folks in there. They wouldn't want *me* there."

"You might be surprised. They're worshipping. I doubt they check color at the door."

She studied his face. *Completely serious.* He wasn't teasing. "Don't reckon I'm ready yet. I'm takin' baby steps here. You hafta remember where I came from."

"I understand. But I knew this would mean something to you. Alicia's here every Sunday with her family. Maybe one day you'll be ready to go in with her. For now, we can wait until they all come out, then we'll go see my patients." He wrapped his arm over her shoulders. "I won't make you do anything you don't want to."

Another song started, and Michael clapped his hands along with it.

Claire let out a laugh. "He likes it, too."

Before the service ended, Andrew drove the buggy further up the road. "Less conspicuous this way," he said, grinning. But then his face fell. "Are you all right?"

She'd tried to hide it. If he hadn't been so eager for her to come with him, she'd have gladly stayed home. Unfortunately, the sharp pain she'd just felt hadn't gone unnoticed. "It hurts a bit." She placed her hands over her stomach.

"I'm sorry. I didn't realize. Shall I take you home?"

"No. I'm not sick. It's . . . my cycle. Came this mornin'."

He scooted over and drew her close, then kissed her forehead. "I know what you're thinking. Don't worry. It'll happen. I know it will."

"But why's it takin' so long? Last time it happened right away. What if there's sumthin' wrong with me?"

"There's nothing wrong with you. You're perfect." He kissed her. This time on the lips. "It's taking longer, but I assure you, it'll happen. That is, as long as we keep doing our part."

"Oh, you . . ." She smacked him playfully on the chest, then Michael did, too.

"Dada."

He lifted their son off her lap and onto his own. "You'll have a baby brother or sister someday."

Claire certainly hoped so.

Once the service ended, Andrew drove to check on his first patient. They saw everything from a woman he treated for poison ivy, to a young child who'd broken her wrist. Andrew had set it weeks prior and found it healing properly.

Everyone welcomed Claire with smiles and kindness. Something she'd not expected. And when the rounds were finished, they'd been blessed with two chickens, one rabbit, and three loaves of bread.

"I have something else to show you," Andrew said. He stopped the buggy again by the church, then helped her down.

He led her to a small cemetery set behind it, then pointed to a grave. "He's buried there."

She nodded, with a sigh. *Jeremiah Lewis.* Somehow Andrew knew she needed to see this.

She held Michael close. "He can't hurt us anymore, baby." She smoothed her fingers over his scar. His sweet face held so much joy—proof that the terrible man hadn't touched his heart.

When they got back into the buggy, she thanked her husband with a silent kiss.

Andrew almost snapped the reins, but then turned to face her. "Since we're already out, would you like to pay Martha a visit? If you're feeling up to it?"

"I'd like that. I've managed these pains for a long time. Seein' her will keep my mind off it."

He lit up with a bright smile and started down the road. Martha would be surprised to see them.

A large jolt nearly sent her over the side of the buggy. She grabbed onto Andrew. "What happened?"

"We hit a rut. I'll check the wheel when we get to Martha's. It might need to be tightened."

They stopped in front of Martha's just in time. The loosened wheel had nearly come off.

"You should take Michael inside and get out of this heat," Andrew said. "I'll go to the barn and see if I can find something to tighten the bolts."

"All right. I'll bring you some sweet tea punch." She grinned, then kissed him on the cheek.

They went their separate ways. She hurried to the front door, holding Michael. No longer her home, she knocked. Out of the corner of her eye, she noticed children's clothes hanging on Martha's clothesline.

Odd.

The door swung open. "May I help you?"

Claire faced a woman with long brown hair and freckles. A complete stranger. "I . . . um. Where's Martha?"

The woman smiled. "I'm sorry. You have no idea who I am. Are you Claire?"

"Yes. But how do you know me?"

"Please. Come in. Get out of this heat!" She took her by the arm and pulled her inside. "What a sweet baby. Martha's been talking up a storm about you."

Claire couldn't have been more dumbfounded. She felt out of place in a house she'd once considered *home*.

The woman kept smiling like they should be old friends.

"I'm Mary, Mrs. Montgomery's daughter-in-law. I married Thomas."

Claire gaped at her. "You're Tom's wife? Is he here?"

"Yes. He's in the barn doing some work. The children are with him, too. Martha stepped out to tend to personal matters, but should be right back."

Claire hadn't seen Tom in years. He'd headed west during the war. Tired of fighting, he and his brother, Joe, had said they wanted more out of their lives.

She set Michael down and he went straight to Mary, holding up his hands.

"He's friendly," she said. "May I hold him?"

"Course you can. He knows good people when he sees them." Mary had a kind face and sweet disposition. Claire liked her immediately. "My husband's outside checkin' on one of the buggy wheels. We hit a rut and it came loose."

"Why don't I get Tom to help him?" Mary bounced Michael in her arms, prompting him to giggle.

Claire was about to answer when a loud commotion stopped her. Someone was yelling.

Andrew?

They rushed to the window and peered out. Tom had Andrew in a headlock.

"What's going on?" Mary asked.

"C'mon." Claire headed out the door with Mary on her heels, still holding Michael.

Claire lifted her skirt and ran across the yard. "Tom! What are you doin' to my husband?" She grabbed Tom's arm and yanked, trying to pull him away.

Michael started bawling.

Tom released Andrew and took a few steps back. His lips curled into an ugly snarl. Not the man she remembered. "Your *husband*? You married a damn Injun?"

"Don't call him that!" Claire fumed. "He's a fine man, an' a doctor, too!" She took her place beside Andrew and held his arm. The heat of his anger seeped through his clothing.

Martha ran toward them, waving her arms. "Land sakes! Calm down! We're all family here!" She took Michael from Mary. He hadn't stopped squalling.

Tom glared at Andrew. "He ain't *my* family! Don't want him near me or my children! He scared the fire outta Francis! She's just gotten over her nightmares. Cuz a him they'll be startin' again!"

Andrew's chest heaved. "How could I have scared her? She walked up on me and I merely said *hello*."

"Then how come she came runnin' to me cryin'?" Tom took a step closer to Andrew, then pushed against his chest. "I *know* you hurt her!"

"I didn't touch her!"

"Thomas?" Mary took his arm, and pulled him back. A hint of disappointed anger came out in the way she'd said his name. "Where's Franny now?"

"Told her to wait in the barn with J.J. I promised I'd make *him* leave." Tom's hands formed into fists. "So, leave!"

"Thomas!" Martha yelled. "You'd best calm down! Doc would never hurt Franny. He's a good man."

"He's a filthy Injun!" Tom spat on the ground at Andrew's feet.

Claire stroked Andrew's arm. "Let's go home." She looked at Martha. "I don't understand what happened, but Andrew doesn't deserve this."

Martha crossed to them, holding Michael. His little face crinkled with tears, and his lip trembled. He reached for Andrew, who instantly took him.

"Don't leave," Martha said. "If everyone calms down we can talk 'bout this. See, Indians out west killed my boy, Joseph. His family, too. 'Cept his wife. She's in the house restin' a spell. Thomas is a might sensitive 'bout Indians."

"Don't sugar coat it, Mama!" Tom yelled. "Injuns *butchered* Joe's family! An' *he's* one of 'em!" He pointed at Andrew. "I could kill him with my bare hands!"

With a huff, Martha slapped Tom hard. "Shame on ya! He didn't kill your brother! An' I'd bet my life he didn't touch a hair on Franny's head. Stop this crazy talk!"

Still fuming, Tom stomped his way to the house. The front door slammed so hard, Claire thought he'd broken it from the hinges.

Mary looked as though she might cry. "I'm sorry," she muttered, and followed him inside

Martha laid her hand on Andrew's shoulder. "He's angry 'bout losin' his brother. Give him time to get to know ya. I'll try to make him understand."

"Some people *never* understand. It's easier to hate." He took a large breath. "I need to fix my wheel. Do you have a wrench I can use?"

"Course, but—"

"Once I fix it, we'll leave. We won't come back." Michael cuddled into Andrew's body. "I won't have my son around people who treat us this way."

Martha's face fell. For the first time Claire had ever known, at a loss for words.

"Martha . . ." Claire reached out to her. "I'm sorry 'bout Joe. Can't believe he's dead. And to have Tom home—well —you must be glad a that."

"I was. Till now. Thomas was outta line. I swear I'll set him straight. As for Joseph . . . thought I lost him long time ago. Strange as it may seem, it don't hurt so bad. But I lost three granbabies I never knew. That hurts a whole lot. The way they died gives a grown woman nightmares." Martha's eyes closed and her head bowed low.

It broke Claire's heart. She hugged Martha tight, then kissed her cheek.

Slowly, Martha lifted her head, then looked between her and Andrew. "Hate this happened. I'd a much ruther had a nice visit. Some other time I reckon."

She motioned toward the barn and they followed her. No one in sight. Tom had obviously retrieved the children.

Once Andrew fixed the wheel, they told Martha good-bye and left for home. He remained quiet for the entire ride, and Claire let him be. Unable to comprehend what he must be feeling, she tried to console him by rubbing his leg. He offered her a weak smile, then silently faced for-ward.

CHAPTER 23

Friday night parties became a normal occurrence in the Martin home, and Victoria anticipated each one with even more excitement than the previous. She never wore the same dress. *Heaven's no.* To her good fortune, John didn't complain.

She'd acquainted herself with the finest boutiques and was a favorite customer at all of them. That is, all except the one owned by that nasty Mrs. Beauchamp. Victoria much preferred the shops owned by men.

Willie wasn't very good company, so flitting around town and talking to the locals, better suited her. Besides, strutting down the sidewalks of Bridgeport boosted her esteem. She'd already established a reputation.

Men love me, women hate me.

Rainy days offered boredom. She'd spend some of her time attempting conversation with Jean-Pierre, but he'd only talk about food. Once he'd made all her favorites, he became dull.

So she would wait for John to come home, hoping *he'd* spice things up, but he'd been arriving later and later.

Sometimes after dark. He'd be too tired to do much of anything.

This happened to be one of those horrible, rainy days. She sat at the grand piano plunking on the keys.

"Victoria!"

John!

She hopped off the bench and hurried to the front entrance, then ran into his arms.

Laughing, he picked her up off the floor and swung her around.

"You're in a fine mood tonight," she said. "What's the occasion?"

He gave her a sly smile. "Am I normally that ill-tempered?"

Without replying, she pursed her lips until he kissed them. His hands glided down her back and rested below her bustle.

"I have a surprise for you," he said with a low growl.

"Where?" She coyly bit her bottom lip, tipping her head.

"It's not something to be found."

"Don't tease me!" She smacked his chest. "Tell me."

He led her to the chaise and they sat. "I've commissioned an artist to do your portrait."

She let out a shriek. "Oh, John! Just like I'd asked you to." She could hardly sit still. "Is it the same artist who did yours?"

"No. But he's one of the finest. He's painted some of the most beautiful women in the world. He's in high demand and it was difficult acquiring him, but I want the best for you. He's Italian and speaks very little English, but that shouldn't matter. He'll pose you. Speaking isn't necessary."

She held her hand to her breast in attempt to still her racing heart. Her throat had become painfully dry. "I'm overwhelmed. Thank you!" She kissed him, but it didn't seem near enough.

"He'll be here in the morning, so you'd best turn in early. You'll need your rest. I won't have you all droopy-eyed for your portrait. This painting will capture your beauty for all time."

"In the mornin'?" Her mind whirled. "What shall I wear?"

He took her hand and kissed her knuckles. "Anything you wish. You have a closetful." He winked.

He'd not acted this charming since she'd first met him.

"While you're spinning that around in your sweet little head," John said, "you should know that a portrait of this size and quality will take several days. But I assure you, he'll make certain you're comfortable."

"Will it be as large as yours? One we can hang beside it?"

"Yes, it will be similar in size. Possibly even larger." He grinned. "But I have another place in mind for it."

"Oh." If it was going to be *that* large, maybe he'd hang it in the ballroom for everyone to see. "Where?"

"That's part of the surprise, my dear. Now, have your dinner, then off to bed. I don't want to distract from your beauty sleep, so I won't be joining you tonight."

"But, I'll miss you."

"It's for the best." He kissed the tip of her nose, then swatted her behind and sent her on her way.

Excited beyond words, she doubted she *could* sleep.

* * *

A loud rap on Victoria's door woke her.

"He's here," John said. "Get dressed."

True to his word, John hadn't slept in their bed. She assumed he stayed in the guestroom. "Aren't you goin' to work?"

"I told Signor Gaspari I'd help him bring in his supplies. Once he has you settled, I'll leave."

"Is Willie here to help me dress?"

"No. I gave her a few days off. With pay, of course. I didn't want her creating any disturbance, but I won't have her children starving."

"You're so thoughtful." Sometimes his actions truly surprised her. "Will *you* help me with my corset?"

"You won't need it. As I told you, this could take days. I'd never ask you to endure such torture." He started to leave.

"But—"

"Signor Gaspari is waiting. We're setting up in the guest room with the long cream drapery. You'll be positioned on the chaise beneath the window." He removed his pocket watch and flipped it open. "You have thirty minutes." He snapped the thing shut and walked out.

Thirty minutes?

How could he expect her to prepare in such a short span of time. Not only did she have to dress, but her hair had gotten tousled in the night.

"Oh, Izzy. I wish you were here."

Victoria chose her red velvet gown. She'd been told she looked like royalty in it. Her breasts wouldn't look right without the corset, but sitting bound for days on end didn't appeal to her, so she'd have to make do. If this artist was as gifted as John claimed, he could probably enhance them to make them look right.

She ran a brush through her hair and by John's request, left it down. Lastly, she donned the heart necklace Andrew had given her. Her permanent reminder of the lies he'd told.

"Victoria!" John strode into the room. "The man's waiting!"

"Sorry. I had no idea. You should've come for me."

"I assumed you would watch the clock." He jerked his head toward the hallway.

"How do I look?" She spun in a circle.

"Ravishing," he replied, almost coldly. Taking her by the wrist, he practically drug her toward the guestroom.

Why must he get so uptight?

"What 'bout my shoes?"

"You won't need them."

The second she saw Signor Gaspari sitting at his easel with a brush in hand, her heart began its excited thump. No wonder it would take days. The canvas was life-sized, but strangely positioned horizontally.

She nodded to him as she passed. "Thank you for doin' this, Signor Gaspari." She tried to say it as John had. Hopefully she'd not offended the man with her attempt at an Italian pronunciation.

He returned a polite smile and nod. "Call me Alberto."

"Oh. I like that. *Alberto.*" She said it in a way that lifted his brow. Proud of herself, she batted her eyes.

She found his small stature surprising, but his dark wavy hair and well-groomed mustache made him appear the way she assumed Italians looked. *Alberto* was the first *real* Italian she'd ever met.

She crossed the room and positioned herself on the green velvet chaise. Pulling her shoulders back, she folded her hands on her lap, then cast one of her best smiles. "How's this, Alberto?"

The man's eyes narrowed and he scowled. Then he stood erect and whipped around, facing John. "What is this?" he yelled, then rattled off something presumably Italian. Whatever it was didn't sound happy.

What happened?

She looked down at herself. Everything appeared to be in place.

John set his hand on Alberto's shoulder. "I'll speak to her."

With a pronounced nod, Alberto sat.

John crossed the room and lifted her to her feet.

"He's angry, isn't he? Did I do sumthin' wrong?"

John put his mouth to her ear. "Take off your dress."

"What? Doesn't he like this one?"

"Just take it off. Take *everything* off." John spoke with no emotion.

"Don't tease me." She looked him in the eye.

He said nothing. Just stood there staring at her, breathing hard.

He's serious.

"No! I won't do it! How could you ask me to?" She took a step away from him intending to return to her room, but he grabbed hold of her arm and held on tight.

He wrenched her body against his. "I'm your husband." He hissed the words into her ear. "It's what I want. You have the most perfect body I've ever seen. I told you I want to capture your beauty for all time. I want to remember how it is now, so when you're old and wrinkled I'll have something pleasant to look at."

"You'll be *dead* by then!" Anger boiled out of her and she tried to jerk away.

John's free hand flew upward, ready to strike. She cowered and closed her eyes. But when the sting didn't come, she opened them again. Her husband obviously had thought better than to hit her with a prominent witness present. He'd lowered his hand.

"You will remove your dress, or I'll remove it for you." He'd kept his voice low. She doubted Alberto could hear him, but the man looked as though he was losing his patience. He twirled his paintbrush through his fingers, watching them.

"I paid good money to bring him here," John whispered. His soft voice didn't hide his anger. "Your portrait will be the finest work of art he's ever done. He only paints beautiful women. When I described you and told him of your red hair, he wanted to paint you right away. He canceled another sitting for you." John's grip became even tighter. "Don't embarrass me, Victoria."

"Embarrass *you*?" she huffed. "*I'll* be the one sittin' here naked!"

"You won't be sitting. He wants you to lie down. He'll position you. You *will* let him touch you. Understand me?"

Ashamed, she looked away. Why would he want another man to see her bare?

John grabbed her chin and made her look at him. "Don't act like you don't want this. I know you. You like the attention. You *want* men to look. With this painting, they can *all* look, but only *I* will have you."

Alberto walked out of the room.

"See what you've done?" John yelled and shook her. "You've upset him!"

"Upset *him*? What 'bout me? This isn't what I wanted!"

"Why is it always about you? You never consider what *I* want? Stop being selfish, Victoria!" His fire-filled eyes suddenly softened, and he released her. "I promise you," he whispered, no longer spiteful. "The painting won't leave this house. Please, sweetheart, do this for me." He lightly brushed her cheek with his hand, then pulled her against him and covered her lips with his own. His passion melted her into his body. "I love you, Victoria. I love you so much." He kissed her again.

She gazed deeply into his eyes and believed him. He could be unpredictable, but his boldness and strength appealed to her. "I love you, too, John." It took an enormous breath to give her the courage she needed. "If this is what you truly want, and it'll make you happy, then . . . I'll do it."

He stroked her hair. "That's my girl. You won't regret this. Soon, you'll be immortalized."

He helped her remove her dress and her undergarments. She lay down on the chaise on her side, then John left to find Alberto.

The frigid air in the room made her tremble. Or maybe it had something to do with her nerves. Strange as it was, she found something about this exhilarating.

When John returned with Alberto, Victoria instinctively tried to cover herself.

Albert rushed across the room and yanked her hands away. "No! Do not!"

She tried to smile, but her lips quivered. His eyes moved over her body, taking in every last inch. Then he stepped back and pressed a single finger to his chin.

Until now, John had been the only man who'd ever seen her nude this way. Aside from Andrew. But he'd viewed her body solely in a medical capacity.

Maybe if he'd seen me like this, he woulda wanted me.

She scowled. *The only woman Andrew ever wanted was Claire.*

"No! Do not frown!" Alberto stepped close and touched her lips.

She pursed them, then smiled.

"*Bello!*"

"What?"

"Beautiful!"

Exactly what she wanted to hear. She licked her lips and gave him an even better smile.

He ran his hand along her shoulder, then cascaded it down her body. She swallowed hard and glanced at John. Her husband displayed no offense by Alberto's familiarity. He watched them with a sly grin.

He finds this stimulatin'.

She expected a pleasant reward later.

Alberto had her sit upright, then placed two satin pillows at the head of the chaise longue.

"Lay down," he said, pointing. His English was better than she'd expected.

She obliged him, lying on her right side. He gently pushed her shoulders back, angling her body. The large pillows gave her support. She wiggled around just enough to get comfortable, and realized he was chuckling. *Amused?* Or maybe he simply delighted in watching her move.

Once she'd settled, he drew his fingers through her hair and brought some of it forward across her breast. Then, with a lone finger, he pushed it over, leaving her breasts completely exposed.

Concern dipped his brows and he touched her scar, then carefully covered it with some of her hair. Oddly, he followed his action with a tender pat on her cheek. The man had compassion. His gentleness eased her, and her heart rested.

His touch no longer bothered her. He placed her left arm along her side, with her hand forward across her hip. Her tiara-shaped wedding ring glistened in the well-lit room.

He brought her right arm up toward her head and bent her elbow. Her hand rested on the pillow beneath her, close to her cheek.

He left her legs extended, but bent her lower leg slightly at the knee.

"*Capolavoro*," he muttered and again took a step back, studying her.

"What's that mean?" she asked, but didn't move.

"Masterpiece."

She closed her eyes and reveled in his compliment.

He fingered her heart necklace, popping her eyes open.

"Want me to take it off?" She hoped he'd say *no*.

"No."

She smiled, relieved. John had *his* reasons for wanting her to bare herself, but she had her own reasons for keeping the necklace on.

She quivered just slightly when Alberto positioned the heart at the center of her breasts.

"Now," he said. "Look at me as you would your lover."

That she could easily do. She'd learned the art of seduction well. The look she gave him made him wipe his brow.

"*Bello!*" He kissed the tips of his fingers, then shook his fists in the air.

John left his place on the far side of the room and approached them. "You *are* beautiful, Victoria. Never be ashamed of your body. It's perfect."

Alberto vigorously nodded his agreement.

"I have to go now, my dear," John said. "You be a good girl and do what he tells you. Don't let me down."

"I won't. I love you, John."

He turned and left and she shifted her attention to Alberto. They'd made her *feel* beautiful, and she trusted John. He'd promised the portrait wouldn't leave their home. Besides, she wanted to please him. She'd do most anything for him.

* * *

By day three, Victoria was nearly spent. She found it odd that lying down could make her weary, but she wanted this over with. She worried she'd catch cold, but even worse, Alberto wouldn't show her his progress. He wouldn't even let *John* near it.

She feared he'd made her ugly.

So along with a tired back and aching bones, she spun worry through her mind like a web.

The day Alberto proclaimed it finished, she jumped up, then stumbled because her legs had fallen asleep. But she picked herself up again and quickly crossed the room. "Show me!"

"No!"

"Why?"

"We wait for your husband." He shooed her out of the room.

She dressed and paced. Lucky for her, he came home early for a change. "He's done, John!" she shouted, the second she saw him, then grabbed his hand and yanked him toward the stairs.

Seemingly as excited as she was, he didn't resist.

They composed themselves before entering the guestroom. Alberto stood by the painting, which still faced the wall. He motioned for them to go to the middle of the room.

Victoria's heart pumped harder and harder. She'd never had to wait so long for gratification.

John put his arm around her. "If he captures even *part* of your beauty, it will be a fine work of art."

She kissed his cheek. "You're so good to me."

Alberto puffed out his chest, then slowly rotated the easel. He waved a single hand in front of his work.

Victoria gasped. "I can't believe it." Unable to control herself, she started to cry.

Alberto's brows wove and he shook his head. "You do not like it?"

"No!" she exclaimed. "It's wonderful!" She turned to John, who hadn't made a sound. "Am I truly that pretty?"

Pride covered his face. "Did you doubt it?" He cocked his head to one side. "I've seen you gaze at yourself in the mirror. You *know* you're beautiful." He gave her a kiss on the forehead, then crossed the room to Alberto.

He shook the man's hand. "You've more than earned your pay. I can't thank you enough."

"*Grazie*! *Grazie*! I thank *you*. Your beautiful Victoria made my work . . . *joy*!"

Victoria moved closer to her likeness. He'd captured her image in rich-colored oils. His delicate brush strokes enhanced every curve of her form. Detailed and precise, right down to the green of her eyes.

Astonished, she placed a hand to her mouth. "Look at my eyes, John. It's as though I'm lookin' at you." She moved to the right. "My eyes move with the picture. I don't know how he did it. Somehow I'm lookin' at everyone in the room at the same time."

John rubbed his chin, studying the painting. "I doubt many people will be looking at your *eyes*, Victoria. But I'm happy you're pleased."

She hugged him. "I am. Thank you. And thank *you*, Alberto, for makin' me beautiful."

"*God* made you beautiful, not Alberto." He bowed low, then began packing his supplies. John helped carry them out, while Victoria remained in the room admiring herself.

She pulled her shoulders back and stood tall.

John was right. I'm perfect.

* * *

John had the life-sized portrait framed and hung it over the bar in the smoking parlor. Their female guests never stepped foot in there, but every man that came to their home did. John could gloat over his prize, while having a friendly game of poker.

"John," Victoria pleaded. "Please don't leave it there. The men will see me. I won't be able to show my face!"

"Of course they'll see you. I *want* them to. That's why I had the painting made. They'll see what a ravenous beauty you are."

"But they'll know what I'm like *everywhere*. I did it for *you*. Not for your friends."

He drew her close and raked his fingers through her hair. "In their minds, they've already pictured you this way. The painting shows them what's real. It's nothing to be ashamed of, so stop acting like a child. You're a grown woman. *Exactly* what men want to see."

"But after they see it, how will I look them in the eye? Or carry on a civilized conversation?"

"You, my dear, will hold your head high and look at them as you always have with that wonderful smile and charm you possess. You're my wife and the envy of all of theirs. Be proud. Every woman wishes she looked like you. Never forget that." He hugged her, then gave her a kiss on the tip of her nose. Though she lacked the enthusiasm he had for the placement of her image, he didn't care. She'd never change his mind.

She stared at the floor, so he lifted her chin. "I have some men coming over for a game of poker. Go on up to our room. I'll be up later." He patted her behind to get her moving, but she didn't budge.

She stood there, pouting.

"Be a good girl, now," he said and gave her another *firmer* pat.

"Yes, John." With her shoulders slumped, she left the parlor.

John clapped his hands together, then lit a cigar and gazed at the likeness of his voluptuous wife. "The envy of all. And only *I* can bed her."

He draped a cloth over the portrait so he could unveil her at the appropriate moment.

Soon his guests arrived. He ushered them into the parlor and offered drinks. He'd hinted at something more from the evening, and several complained when he hadn't provided female company. In the past he'd brought in prostitutes, but no longer. If he was to become a senator, he had to start acting *somewhat* respectable.

After several hands and numerous drinks, John drew their attention to the draped painting.

"As you know, I recently married. Some of you have had the pleasure of meeting my wife."

"Not as much pleasure as you've had!" Charles Oglesby shouted from the back of the room.

"Granted," John said with a laugh. "I'm blessed with an insatiable young wife. And it's my pride in her that made me want to share her with you."

"What?"

"Not that way, Oglesby." John shook his finger at the inebriated man. "In that respect, she's mine alone. But every work of art deserves to be seen, even if it's not *touched*." With a single pull, he yanked the cloth and exposed the painting.

Gasps in the room were followed by applause and uproarious cheers.

"My God!", "Fantastic!", and "I wish I was John!" were some of his favorite remarks. He'd accomplished exactly what he'd set out to do.

Oglesby slapped him on the back. "My wife looks nothing like that. Never has." His words were slurred, but even so, John believed him. "Mind if I *think* of her tonight?"

"Thoughts are permissible. Just don't tell your wife." John laughed and served him another drink.

He sent the men home to their unattractive dour wives, then went up the stairs to claim the object of their desires. The idea alone gave him great satisfaction and a firm arousal.

After fitting his protection, he climbed into bed and pressed his naked body behind hers. He'd instructed her to always sleep bare. As her husband, he wanted her readily available. She'd learned to obey.

His hands glided over her breasts, delighting in her soft skin.

"Victoria," he whispered. "They all want you. *I* want you." He dotted her neck with kisses. "I love you."

She rolled onto her back and looked up at him. "Truly, John?"

"More than anything."

"Will you move the paintin' to our room?"

"No. It's where I want it."

She faced away from him. *Cold.*

"You're so *selfish,* Victoria." A spoiled child he should turn over his knee. "I've made you into something you never would've become without me. You're immortalized." Still aroused, he was determined to have her, no matter her mood. He slid his hand along her waist and over her bottom, then slipped it between her legs, hoping to entice her.

"I don't want to be remembered that way," she said, then sniffled.

Crying? Damn her.

"But you *will* be remembered." He jerked her onto her back and climbed atop her. "No man will ever forget that painting." Forcing her legs open, he slyly grinned. "My perfect wife. My beauty."

A tiny whimper escaped her as he entered. But eventually, she responded as he'd wished. He took what no other man would ever have.

His prize.

His Victoria.

CHAPTER 24

It had taken Andrew some time to recover from his anger over the incident at Martha's. But he focused on his family and let it go, though it troubled him that Claire had been separated from *her* family.

She'd assured him that he and Michael were all that was important to her, but he knew she missed her aunt. Hopefully someday they could reconcile, though as he'd told her, he'd *never* return to Martha's.

It had been two years since he and Claire first met. The longest years in his life. Wanting to make things better, he decided to do something special for her.

He looked all over Mobile for a locket, but couldn't find what he had in mind. Begrudgingly, he pushed open the door to Parker's Mercantile. Another place he'd sworn he would never return.

"Well!" Jake Parker exclaimed. "If it ain't Doc Fletcher! What brings *you* in here?"

"Necessity," Andrew said flatly. "I couldn't find what I wanted elsewhere."

Jake smirked. "You forget I got the best place in town?" He grabbed hold of his collar and puffed out his chest.

Spare me the pride.

"I need a locket for my wife. Please show me what you have."

"Wife, huh? Heard you got hitched. Was told ya married Mrs. Alexander. I seen her in here before." Jake raised his brows, then had the gall to wiggle them. "She's a fine-lookin' woman."

No doubt Jake was trying to upset him, but Andrew wouldn't give him the satisfaction. "Yes, I married Claire. I'm fortunate. She's an *exceptional* woman."

Jake produced a case of assorted jewelry from beneath the counter. "Seen her son with her, too." He looked Andrew in the eyes. "Always wondered 'bout that boy. Looked nothin' like his daddy. Fact is, he looks a might like *you*."

Andrew ignored him and pointed to a gold locket in the case. "I'll take that one." The oval locket had a winding leaf pattern and tiny roses at the center. *Perfect.*

"Want it in a box?"

"Yes. Thank you." Apparently Jake would let the subject drop, so Andrew decided to be civil. "I've been meaning to thank you for returning the money I paid for Victoria's ring. It was good of you."

"O'Malley insisted." Jake shrugged. "Didn't have no choice."

Nothing more needed to be said. Andrew paid him and turned to leave. With the gift in his pocket, he headed for the door.

"About that boy," Jake said, stopping him. "You poke that pretty little thing before her dead husband?" He erupted into laughter.

Heat coursed through Andrew's veins. He spun around to face the vile man. "What did you say?"

"Reckon ya didn't understand me." Jake smirked. "Did ya *have* that pretty gal before Gerald Alexander? That boy looks just like ya."

Andrew glared at him. "Don't speak about my wife that way. She's not some cheap piece of gossip you can throw around like trash!" He wanted to grab Jake by the throat and strangle the life out of him. But the truth of his words kept him from doing it.

Chuckling, Jake stepped out from behind the counter. "Knew I was right. It's the quiet ones always surprise ya. But I don't hafta tell *you* that, do I Doc?" He moved directly in front of Andrew. "Ya missed a fine weddin'. Your daddy got himself a *real* woman. Reckon he's havin' himself a good time. That Victoria makes your little wife look like a hag."

Andrew had heard enough. Fury driving him, he grabbed Jake's collar. "I never liked you, Jake." Their faces nearly touched. "You're a sorry little man with nothing better to do with your life than try to make other people miserable. You're a disgrace to our city. I won't come in here again. *Ever.*" He shoved Jake hard into a display of canned goods, sending them tumbling to the floor. Then he headed for the exit, wishing he'd never come in. He'd just given Jake more gossip.

"Hope she likes the locket!" Jake yelled. He got to his feet and brushed off his pants. "Maybe she'll thank ya *real* good!"

Andrew wished he'd not been watching the man. Along with laughing, Jake thrust his hips to accentuate his words.

Disgusted, Andrew walked out. Jake belittled the love he had for Claire. She deserved respect. But a man like Jake Parker would never know how to respect a woman. His own wife had left him years ago, taking their children with her.

Probably the smartest thing she ever did.

Jake had earned his lonely, miserable life.

Deciding not to waste another ounce of energy on him, Andrew set his mind on Claire. Her loving arms were waiting.

I'm the fortunate one.

* * *

With the fried chicken nearly ready, Claire checked on her baking-powder biscuits. She'd decided to fix the same meal she'd made for Andrew on their first outing.

She'd taken Michael to Alicia's for the evening, with plans to pick him up at bedtime. They didn't like to have him gone all night.

She'd bathed in bath salts and put on the dress she'd worn that special night.

The door swung open.

"Perfect timin'!" she chimed and raced into Andrew's arms.

He swayed with her pressed against him, then kissed her. "Do I have time to wash?"

"Course you do. I left some water in the tub." Her favorite part of the remodeling. A bathing room with a cast iron tub set permanently in one place.

"Wonderful." He kissed her again.

"I'll have everythin' on the table when you're done."

She bustled around the kitchen while he bathed, finalizing their meal. She'd just set the filled plates down when he came in wearing only pajama bottoms.

He pulled out a chair and sat. "This looks delicious."

With a pattering heart, she walked around behind him, then rubbed her hands down his bare chest. "*You* look delicious."

He shifted in the seat and brought her down onto his lap. "Happy anniversary." His arms entwined around her and they kissed.

Drawing back, she held his face in her hands. "Happy anniversary." Another kiss. This time, *she* initiated it. "A lot has happened in two years."

"Most importantly, we're together. I love you, Claire."

"I love you, too." They froze, simply staring each another. Love hung in the air between them. Stronger than ever. "We'd better eat before it gets cold." At this rate, they'd likely skip supper and go directly to the bedroom.

"Good idea." After helping her to her feet, he patted her on the bottom.

She hesitated; tempted to take his hand and lead him away from the table.

They ate without speaking a word, gazing at each other between bites.

Is your heart beatin' as hard as mine?

"I made dessert," she said, breaking the silence. "Mrs. Sandborn's cobbler."

"Mmm." He licked his lips, and she had to stop herself from rushing to him and capturing his tongue with her mouth.

You're torturin' me, Andrew Fletcher.

When she set down his bowl of cobbler, he pushed a small box toward her.

"What's this?" she asked, pointing.

"An anniversary gift."

"But I didn't get *you* anythin'."

"Yes, you did. You prepared a fantastic meal. *You're* my gift, Claire. Now, open the box."

Her eyes filled with tears. She'd married the most wonderful man on earth. She sat down, then did as he asked.

A locket.

"Oh, Andrew. It's so beautiful."

"I thought the design matched your ring."

She laughed. "That's exactly what I just thought." Her misty eyes blurred her vision, so she wiped at them with her sleeve. "Thank you."

"It opens and there's room for two photographs. I thought about having a picture of you and me made to fit, but maybe you'd rather have one of Michael on one side, and—"

"Our child-to-be on the other?"

"If that's what you want."

"Yes." She held it against her breast. "It's kinda excitin' wonderin' what face will go on the other side. A boy or a girl? Which would you prefer?"

"It doesn't matter. It will be ours regardless. Someone we create." He stood and lifted her to her feet. "So, how about we clear away these dishes and do some creating?"

"Will you put the locket on me first?" Her heart thumped. His essence overwhelmed her and his bare skin tantalized her.

"You want to wear it while we—"

"Yes. And *only* it." She glided her fingertips over his chest. "Hurry."

He quickly fastened the locket around her neck, then she nodded toward the table. "The dishes can wait. We have better things to do with our time."

She led him to their bedroom.

They'd been there many times, but something seemed different tonight.

They took their time. Peeled away clothing amidst tender caresses, and when they'd bared themselves, made love until the sun set and the moon rose high in the sky. They savored every touch and relished each kiss.

Maybe they'd created that new life. If not, in time their love would bring them another child.

Claire prayed for that miracle.

CHAPTER 25

The sweltering summer heat wouldn't let up, and it drained Andrew's energy. Still, he was determined to enjoy his meal break at his favorite table in the corner of Sylvia's Pantry. He'd read the newspaper and eat a quick bite before returning to the hospital, allowing him time to gather his thoughts.

Why am I drinking coffee on such a hot day?

He stared at the cup in his hands. Coffee tended to perk him up, but it certainly didn't cool him down.

Unfortunately, John Martin came to mind.

Please be good to Victoria.

In time she'd see the real man. *If she survives him.*

Realizing he'd been staring at the same sentence in the paper for a great deal of time, he shook his head. He needed to finish eating and return to work.

"Ya ain't gonna find better food in town!"

Andrew dipped the newspaper to see who'd spoken, though he already knew.

Martha.

Mary and her little girl followed Martha in, along with another woman who looked a lot like Mary.

Must be her sister. At least Thomas isn't with them.

Not wanting a confrontation, he kept the newspaper high, shielding himself from their view.

They sat on the far side of the café.

"You got sammiches?" the little girl asked the waitress.

"Yes, we do."

"Could you fix her one with just a slice of cheese on it, please?" Mary asked. "She's particular about what she eats. Oh, and do you have dill pickles?"

"Yes'm."

Andrew focused on the same article he'd read five times. The ladies ordered their meals and he needed to leave. But leaving would mean they'd see him.

You're being foolish!

Scolding himself didn't help. He didn't budge.

Be a man.

With a deep breath, he folded the newspaper and laid it down. He'd tried not to draw attention to himself, but the waitress came right over.

"Need anythin' else, Dr. Fletcher?"

Of course she'd have to call him by name.

He shifted his gaze and met Martha's. She smiled, almost apologetically. Mary also looked his way. She patted Martha's arm and stood, then walked toward him. *Why?*

"Where ya goin', Ma?" the little girl asked.

"Don't talk with your mouth full, Francis," the other woman scolded. "Your mother will be right back."

"It's Fran!" Francis fussed, still munching on her food.

"Mind your aunt." Martha added her own reprimand. "Don't talk back."

"Yes, Gramma." Francis pouted, but kept eating.

The interchange had caused Mary to momentarily stop, but she moved closer as soon as it ended.

"May I sit?" she asked him. The waitress stepped aside.

"Of course," he said. The woman appeared as uncomfortable as him. He likely should have stood out of respect, but their shared discomfort kept him in his seat.

While taking the chair across from him, she kept her eyes on the table. Then slowly, she lifted her head and met his gaze. "I'm sorry about what happened. My husband has been through a horrible ordeal. I'm afraid he doesn't trust your kind."

Up until her last few words, Andrew had a good feeling about her. "My kind? You mean, *doctors*?"

With wide eyes, she blinked several times. "I meant no disrespect, but you can't deny your blood."

"No, I can't. However, I was raised in a fine home in Connecticut, not a teepee in the plains. I hold high regard for my ancestry, but it's not who I am. Until the encounter with your husband, I'd never experienced such prejudice. I've seen it all around me, but never felt it personally until that day."

She stared at him.

"I came here," he went on, "because I want to help the Negros. They're surrounded by bigotry due to the color of their skin. Like me, they didn't choose their heritage. None of us do. But, being human, we need to learn to live together regardless of color. I help them because they're people in need. Not out of pity or shame, but out of human kindness. I wish your family could treat me with the same consideration. Especially for Claire's sake and that of our son."

Mary held her hand to her breast. "I truly am sorry."

"Thank you." Sincerity lay in her eyes. "I doubt your husband feels the same."

"I'll try to talk to him." Her lips quivered, attempting a smile.

Andrew scooted his chair back and stood. "I need to return to work. I appreciate your apology, however *you* weren't at fault. I could tell you didn't agree with your husband's actions."

Martha bounded across the restaurant. "Doc! I'm glad we run into ya!" She grabbed him tight.

He couldn't help but laugh. "Thank you, Martha. Truthfully, I'm glad, too. I wish Claire was here. She's been quite upset over what happened."

Martha released all but his hand. "Tell her you saw us, ya hear? Let her know I aim to talk some sense into my boy. Thanksgivin' an' Christmas will be here 'fore ya know it. Family needs to be together." She yanked on his hand and nodded to her table. "I want ya to meet someone."

When Andrew reached them, the little girl lowered her eyes.

What did you tell your father? Likely an untruth.

"Missy, this here's Claire's husband, Andrew. Course, *I* call 'im Doc." Martha addressed the other woman at the table. Though similar in features, she appeared timid and frail.

"Ma'am," Andrew said. "I'm sorry about your family. I can't imagine what you must feel."

"Thank you," she whispered. "I'm actually Melissa. *They* call me Missy." She gestured to her family.

Martha clapped her hands. "Now there's a good start!"

Andrew decided to ease the little girl. "How's that dill pickle?"

She raised her eyes. "Good. Want a bite?" She extended it toward him.

"Thank you, but I'm full." He patted his stomach and smiled.

A broad grin assured him he'd made amends.

"I really must go," he said to Martha. "But I'm glad to have seen you."

The woman latched on to him again, nearly squeezing his dinner from him. "I figgered ya might be here," she whispered in his ear. "Glad I was right." She let him go and stepped away. "Now don't ya forget to tell Claire you seen us. Tell her I love her."

"I will." He nodded to Mary and Melissa. "Ladies, have a good day."

"What 'bout me?" Francis asked.

"You, too." He patted her on the head.

He walked outside more refreshed than when he'd entered the café.

Martha planned this.

Smiling, he went the short distance to the hospital. He couldn't wait to finish his day and return home to Claire. He'd give her hope.

* * *

Melissa had a hard time believing that the kind doctor had been the one Thomas had fought with. Martha had told her how he'd saved Claire's life. And she'd heard every word he'd said to Mary.

He's a good man.

She picked at her food. Though it tasted good, she had no appetite. Her back ached from sleeping on the sofa and if she didn't find an alternative soon, she'd be even more miserable.

The answer lay in finding employment. Then she could rent a room at a local boarding house.

The busy café gave her an idea. Being an accomplished cook, perhaps they needed extra help. She couldn't ask now. Not in front of Martha. But she'd come back and talk to the owner. If hired, she'd break it gently to her mother-in-law.

She managed to steal away from Martha's a few days later with an excuse of needing time to herself. No one argued.

As she entered Sylvia's, her stomach churned. Nerves unlike any she'd had in some time.

When she didn't take a seat, the waitress approached. "Sit anywhere ya like."

"I didn't come to eat. Is the owner available?"

The young girl grinned. "Yep. I'll get her."

Melissa wrung her hands and took deep breaths, trying to stay calm.

A tall, plump woman came out of the kitchen, drying her hands on her apron. "Hear you're lookin' for me." Her heavy accent rivaled Martha's.

"Are you the owner?"

"Yep. Sylvia Watson. How can I help ya?"

"Well . . . I need a job. I hoped maybe you could use some help."

Sylvia shook her head. "Nope. Don't need none. Your husband outta work?"

"I . . ." Melissa fumbled with the words. "I'm a widow."

Taking Melissa's hand, Sylvia huffed out a long breath. "Me, too. Let's sit down an' talk a spell."

After several minutes of conversation, Melissa managed to talk without stumbling. She shared her story with Sylvia, who listened without interrupting.

"You've been through hell," Sylvia said, shaking her head. "Reckon I could find sumthin' for you to do couple days a week. Long as you can cook an' clean."

"Thank you!" Though compelled to hug the woman, Melissa remained seated. "I won't let you down. I'm an excellent cook and a hard worker. I just need to be given the chance."

"Then you can start next Monday. Be here at 5:00 a.m. I get lotsa folks what want a good hot breakfast."

"I'll be here. Thank you!"

With Sylvia's gentle chuckles following her out the door, Melissa left, nearly dancing.

She'd passed a boarding house earlier, so she stopped to inquire about a room. She had enough money to pay a few months of rent in advance, which pleased the owner.

I pray Martha understands.

Melissa needed to find her own way. Though thirty-eight years old, her life had just started over. She felt like a baby bird jumping from the nest. An *enormous* baby bird with broken wings.

I hope I can fly.

CHAPTER 26

Summer turned rapidly to fall. The temperatures in Connecticut didn't appeal to Victoria in the least. She'd always hated wearing coats, but here they were necessary.

Nearly bored to tears, she decided to venture out, hoping to stumble across something entertaining. Bundling up in a heavy green velvet dress covered with a wool coat, she gazed at herself in the mirror.

"Victoria," she mumbled, "you're too young to be actin' like an old married woman." She positioned a matching green hat.

By day, she could be herself and make her own choices as to what to do. By night, she was under John's thumb, doing his bidding. She needed to make the most of her time.

She unbuttoned the coat enough to display her cleavage. The scarf around her neck would keep her warm enough.

Walking out the front door, she headed for Seaside Park. Quite a distance away, but she didn't care. The walk would be good for her. Besides, she had nothing better to do.

When John first mentioned P.T. Barnum and his acquaintance with him, she'd been envious. Mr. Barnum was the toast of Bridgeport, and she'd been told Seaside Park was his pride and joy. He'd funded the project and was known to stroll there on occasion. Maybe she'd run into him.

The park was beside Long Island Sound. A different kind of body of water from what she'd been used to. The cold Atlantic Ocean pounded against the shore, unlike the warm water of Mobile Bay.

She strolled casually, smiling at others as she passed them. The men tipped their hats, and the women who accompanied them pulled them in a little closer. Their actions made her giggle.

As temperamental as John could be, she had to admit he'd been right about most things. Women envied her, and men wanted her. So with justifiable pride, she walked tall with her shoulders back and gave everyone in Bridgeport what they wanted. A vision of perfect beauty.

I'm Mrs. John Martin. But more importantly, I'm Victoria O'Malley.

Because of who she was, she'd always gotten everything she wanted.

There's no one as wonderful as me.

Positioning herself pristinely on a wooden park bench, she admired the trees. Their leaves had just started to turn color. *Nothin' like the moss-covered trees back home.* But like the ocean, these trees added a unique beauty to her surroundings.

She drummed her fingers on the bench, wishing she had someone to talk to. Even Penelope would be a pleasant change.

A young woman approached, pushing a baby carriage.
Baby . . .

Victoria's heart thumped.

"Mind if I join you?" the woman asked, nodding to the vacant spot.

"Not at all."

After pulling the carriage in front of them, the woman sat.

Victoria shivered and buttoned up her coat. No need to display herself to this young mother. "It's so cold."

"You're southern, aren't you?" The woman's smile confirmed she'd not said it to be hateful.

"Yes." Victoria laughed. "My accent give me away?"

"Yes. It's nice. Where are you from?"

"Mobile, Alabama. It's much warmer there."

"Oh, this is nothing." The woman held onto the carriage and moved it back and forth. "Wait until it snows."

"Snow?" Something she'd not considered. "I can't recall the last time I saw a snowflake."

"You'll see more than flakes here. More like *inches*." The woman let out a pleasant, soft laugh.

"Oh, my. I'm not sure I'll care for that. I won't be walkin' much then." *Snowed in with nowhere to go. What'll I do with myself?*

"Have you been here long?"

Time to impress. Victoria readjusted herself and faced her. "I've been here since May. Married an attorney. *John Martin.*" Surely she'd know him. As far as she knew, everyone in Bridgeport talked about her husband.

"I see. I'm afraid I'm not familiar with him. But Bridgeport's a large city."

"Yes, it is." Even though she'd not enthralled the woman, conversation felt incredibly good.

The baby whimpered, so the woman reached into the carriage and pulled it out. She secured a blanket tightly around it, then held it over her shoulder. Patting its back, she whispered words Victoria couldn't hear.

"Your baby's sweet," Victoria said. "Boy or girl?"

"Boy. His name's Daniel. He's my first. My husband and I want at least five. How many children would you like to have?"

Why'd she have to ask?

Victoria's heartbeat became rapid. "I'm not sure. We've not been married long. Haven't discussed it much."

"As pretty as you are, you'll have lovely children." This stranger couldn't have been sweeter, or sound more sincere.

Heat warmed Victoria's cheeks. *So odd havin' a woman compliment me.* "Thank you."

"Would you like to hold him? He's real good. Rarely cries." She shifted Daniel in her arms and extended him toward her.

Without a second thought, Victoria took him and held him close. His tiny form nestled into her. A sweet, warm little bundle. She kissed the top of his precious head. "He's such a treasure," she said and swayed with him in her arms.

"I assume you have experience with babies," his mama said, smiling. "I can see you know what you're doing."

"Truthfully, no. I'm an only child. No nieces. No nephews. Your baby's the first I've ever held."

"You have a mother's instinct." Daniel started to whimper. "I think he's getting hungry."

"Well, then. You'd better take him." She reluctantly returned him.

"I'd best be going." The woman tucked him into the carriage. "I need to feed him and I can't do it here." She accompanied a modest grin with a soft giggle. "I'm Angela by the way. Maybe I'll see you here again sometime."

"I'm Victoria. I'm glad I met *both* of you."

"Have a good day, Victoria," Angela said as she walked away.

Victoria watched them go, then turned her attention to the waves crashing against the shoreline.

Little Daniel had felt wonderful in her arms. He felt *right.*

I want a child.

The only thing she wasn't allowed to have. Somehow she'd have to convince John otherwise. However, if he couldn't be swayed, she'd find another way.

I'll have a baby. With or without him.

* * *

John adjusted his tie, then tried on the black mask. This party would be the most important one he'd hosted to date. His Halloween masquerade ball had always been well attended, but this year's promised to be the best ever.

The guest list included several senators with their wives, a judge, and a well-known actor. Edward Olmstead was held in high regard by every respectable theater attendee in Bridgeport. Known for his exceptional Shakespearean dramas, he'd promised to perform a scene from *Macbeth.*

The guests would love the entertainment, but John's interest lay elsewhere. James' assurance that Emilie would be attending had John reminiscing about their creative sexual encounters. Last year she'd worn a revealing gown that had him tearing it away before the end of the party. She'd likely not tempt him this year, but his curiosity about her had his blood pumping.

"Do you like my mask, John?" Victoria inched toward him displaying the thing.

She'd claimed to be a cat, but the only thing resembling the creature was the long whiskers extending from the corners by her cheekbones. It had been decorated with glittering stones and covered her eyes and nose. She looked sweet. *And* sensuous.

"I'll make you purr after the party," he said, then proceeded to scratch her behind the ears.

"Oh, John!" She giggled. "You can scratch my *belly* later."

"I'll do more than that, you fabulous feline." He swatted her bottom, then escorted her down the stairs to greet their guests.

They were quite the pair. John in his three-piece black suit, and his feline wife dressed in a form-fitting black gown that sparkled with sequins to match her mask.

He brushed kisses across her bare shoulders. "Won't you be cold, my dear?"

"No. Once I start dancin' I'll be plenty warm. 'Sides, my scarf keeps my neck warm."

Yes, her ever-present scarf.

Seemed she'd never overcome the shame of the scar that lay beneath it. But no scarf could take away her beauty. His prize had brought him even more notoriety with every important man in the city.

As the guests arrived, they greeted them graciously, then directed them to the cloak room. He'd hired a man to take their coats, then point them to the ballroom.

Jean-Pierre had outdone himself. Multiple tables of food lined the walls, but left a great deal of room for dancing. Along with French pastries, their guests would find other foods they could eat with their fingers, with a gourmet flare that only Jean-Pierre could master.

John had given Willeen extra pay to serve the guests. She'd been told to fill their glasses, clear away empty plates, and keep enough clean dishes available for everyone in attendance. Dressed in a plain gray uniform with an apron and no mask, John felt certain their guests would recognize her as hired help and keep her busy.

A knock on the door brought the very one John had anticipated. He found himself staring into Emilie's eyes. His throat dried. *Exquisite.*

James removed her cloak, revealing a floor-length silver gown, gathered up on one side, exposing her long, shapely legs. The square neckline of the dress revealed her slender neck and smooth skin. Her white mask was adorned with peacock feathers. It shone with silver flecks.

John couldn't take his eyes off her.

"I'll take this to the cloak room," James said and left.

"John?" Victoria tugged on his arm. "Why don't you introduce us?"

"Oh . . . yes," he stammered. He needed to regain his composure or his wife would likely see into his thoughts. *Not wise.* "Victoria, I'd like you to meet Emilie, James' wife. Emilie, this is Victoria. *My* wife."

"I'm glad to finally meet you," Victoria said.

Emilie tipped her head. "You are lovely. I am not surprised. Even with a mask." Her French accent fueled John's fire. He'd forgotten how seductive her simple words could be.

"Thank you," Victoria said. "Your dress is breath-takin'. Isn't it, John?" She batted her eyes at him, but nothing she did could compare to Emilie. She'd mesmerized him.

"Yes, it is." He returned his attention to his former maid.

"*Merci beaucoup*, John," Emilie said and licked her lips. Even through their masks, their eyes locked.

You know what speaking French does to me, you luscious temptress.

They'd begun a game he intended to finish.

James returned and escorted her away, but John followed them with his eyes until they were out of sight.

"John!" Victoria yanked on his arm.

"What is it?" he snapped. Her southern drawl had begun to grate on him.

"You like her, don't you?" Victoria's lip protruded in a spoiled pout.

He'd not done well hiding his feelings. "She's the wife of my business partner. Of course I like her."

"No, you *like* her. I can tell."

He let out a dismissive laugh. "Are you jealous?"

"Should I be?" She crossed her arms, squeezing her breasts into even larger mounds. Even *they* did nothing for him.

"My dear . . ." He drew her in close. "I'll share a bed with only you tonight. However, I'm still a man. It's hard not to appreciate a woman who looks like Emilie." *Very hard.*

"She's French. I've heard things 'bout French women." Her pout hadn't disappeared.

"Have you now? Well, I don't know what you've heard, but she's James' wife. You need not worry." He gave her a quick peck on the lips.

"Promise me you won't dance with her?"

"I promise. *Pussycat.*" He tapped the tip of her nose. "Now, no more pouting. It doesn't become you. Besides, if anyone should be jealous, it should be me. That necklace you wear . . ." He released her, then lifted the gold heart from her bosom and held it in his fingertips. "Andrew gave it to you, didn't he?"

"Yes. We've discussed this before. I told you why I wear it." She took it from his hand and let it drop back into place.

"Oh, yes. As a reminder that men lie." *And some of us are more gifted at it than others.* "I often wonder if it's because you want to be reminded of *him.*" He'd succeeded in changing the subject.

"I married you, John. Andrew was nothin' like you. I know you'll never lie to me. Will you?"

He took her hand and gave it a kiss. "Never. I'll always tell you the truth."

"Then don't worry 'bout my necklace. If anythin', it should remind you that you won. *You* have me. Andrew doesn't."

That alone gave him almost as much pleasure as thoughts of Emilie. "Let's set all this seriousness aside and enjoy ourselves tonight." He playfully jiggled his finger in her face. "Don't worry about *anything.*"

Another knock on the door took their attention. Soon, all of the guests had arrived and gathered in the ballroom. The large space filled with laughter and dancing.

People will be talking about this for months.

He made a point of speaking to the senators, and knowing the judge as he did, escorted him to the parlor for a look at the painting. It didn't take long before many of the men found an excuse to visit the smoking room. Men had many vices. Their favorite being the one displayed for their pleasure over the bar.

They'd return to their wives smelling of smoke and whiskey, and feeling more amorous than before they'd left. John believed he'd not only done the men of Bridgeport a favor, but their wives as well.

Victoria behaved as he'd trained her, much to his relief. He waltzed her across the dancefloor to the ooh's and ah's from their guests.

"I can't wait to hear that young actor!" she chirped as he spun her in a circle. "I've been told he's been asked to entertain Queen Victoria! Did you know I was named after her?"

"No, I didn't. Now I do." He gave her a believable smile. *That actor has given me prime opportunity.* The waltz came to an end and he dipped her low, then lifted her with a gentleman's kiss.

Applause resounded through the ballroom.

John bowed low and Victoria curtsied, with a coy tilt of her head. He positioned her in front of the stage, then stepped up onto the band platform. "Our musicians will be taking a well-needed break, but I'm pleased to introduce one of the finest actors of all time. I expect you'll give him more applause than you bestowed on me and my lovely wife. Ladies and gentlemen, Edward Olmstead!" He waved his arm and the man hopped onto the stage in appropriate Shakespearean garb.

John gave him a polite nod, then stepped down. No longer being the center of attention, the time had come to take care of personal business.

"Victoria, I'm getting a drink."

"Fine." She barely glanced at him. Her eyes were on the stage. *Just like everyone else's.*

Except for Emilie's. He'd already caught her eye more than once. They hadn't danced together, so he'd not broken his promise to Victoria. But this was something he had to do.

Before going to the stage, he'd taken notice of where she stood. So he wormed his way through the crowd and passed by her, meeting her gaze as he did. She'd know where to go.

The spare room beside the parlor had often been used for this purpose. For guests anyway. He and Emilie had taken advantage of every room in the house at one time or another. This particular guestroom had double locks. Once inside, it would take a battering ram for an uninvited party to enter.

John went in first, then stood off to the side of the door until she came in.

She stepped to the center of the room and he fastened both locks.

They removed their masks and just stood there. The rise and fall of her breasts told him she wanted this as much as he did. Their heavy breathing overshadowed the muffled sounds from the ballroom.

"Oh, John." She rushed into his arms.

Their lips locked together. He tasted her as if he never had before. How could he have so easily forgotten her essence? "Talk to me, Emilie. I need to hear you."

His hands roamed her body, remembering where they'd once been. His mouth searched her flesh, moving from her lips to her neck and downward.

"I knew you would miss me," she rasped. She tipped her head back. "James is nothing like you. I always wanted *you*. Not him."

Her accent set him on fire. He'd been aroused just hearing her earlier, but *feeling* her had him out of control. His hands roamed freely. They didn't have much time, and he intended to make the most of it.

He knelt down and reached under her dress, then jerked away her undergarments. The silky fabric of her gown easily lifted up and over her waist. "Hold onto it," he said and pushed the folds of material into her hand.

Within seconds, he bared his lower body. He picked Emilie up off the floor and she wrapped her lithe legs around him. He glanced at the bed, then chuckled. He'd not break *that* promise either.

Carrying her across the room, he pressed her body into the wall and entered her with heated force.

"Oh, John!" She gripped him tight. Not only with her hands, but with her capable legs. "Do you know how pleased I am you still want me?"

"Of course I want you. Now hush, so I can show you *real* pleasure."

He ravished her and devoured her with hungering kisses. He cupped her firm, bare bottom with his hands and held her to him, able to move without breaking their connection. "Yes," he groaned, and kept going, harder and faster.

His heart pounded. Knowing their spouses were none-the-wiser multiplied his desire.

"John," she panted. "What are we to do?" She moaned. The pleasurable sound she'd make just before ...

She's close.

"We're doing it," he said and thrust harder, still pinning her to the wall.

"Oh!" Her exclamation of satisfaction, though loud, wouldn't be heard. At the moment, no one in the other room cared about anything but Shakespeare.

Her tightened muscles sent him over the edge. Flesh against flesh, just as he preferred. Then he, too, cried out with his own release. The feeling he craved and could never get enough of.

He gripped her buttocks even tighter and held her there until every last throb had dulled. Their breathing steadied.

"I never stopped wanting you," he said. "But Victoria can't know." He kissed her. A sweet sincere kiss to seal her silence.

"Am I to be your mistress?" She held onto him as if she'd die without him.

"Yes. If you'll have me." He winked. "But what of James?" He glided his tongue along her neck and she shivered.

"He will not know. No one will know." She placed her hands on his cheeks and made him look at her. "If this is the only way I can have you, then so be it."

"So be it," he whispered, then kissed her pouting lips.

She'd not untangled herself from him, and he'd become rigid again and ready for more. If only there'd been more time. "If we don't stop now, we'll be missed," he said with an appropriate sigh.

She whimpered. "*Oui*, John. For now." She let her legs slide down his body and onto the floor, and they separated.

He grabbed the pants he'd laid neatly across the bed and got dressed, then delighted in watching her. She removed a small bottle of cologne from her satchel and sprayed some between her legs.

She grinned. "No one will know."

"*We* will know," he said and bent to kiss her a final time. "You go first. I'll come later."

"*Oui*, John. Isn't that how we *always* do it?" With a naughty lick of her lips, she ran her hand down his chest, then gave him a gentle squeeze where she knew he'd like it best.

Yes, you know me well.

Once she'd left, he straightened his tie and positioned his mask. Satisfaction from two women suited him. What more could a man ask for? Besides, he was no ordinary man. He'd just ravished a woman whom he'd sent away belittled only a few months prior.

He paused to check his appearance in the mirror beside the door. "You're good."

After giving himself enough time for his lower extremities to calm, with a sense of accomplishment, he paraded back to the ballroom and wound his way to Victoria.

The crowd applauded as Edward finished his piece and took a bow.

"Wasn't it wonderful?" Victoria exclaimed, beaming.

"Yes, it was," he said and joined in on the applause.

She didn't even realize I'd been gone.

He glanced to the far side of the room. Emilie had taken her place beside James. John nodded to her. She tipped her head and smiled, then clutched her husband's arm.

She'll keep our secret.

Once all the guests had gone, John escorted Victoria to their bedroom. She teetered, and he assumed she'd had more than one glass of champagne. Tonight he'd let her misbehavior go unpunished.

He sat down and watched her strip away her clothes, giggling all the while. It made him chuckle.

"Don't laugh, John," she scolded, but her playful grin told him she had other things in mind. "I may not let you pet me." She'd not removed her mask and lay down on the bed. The only thing remaining on her body was the blasted necklace.

Still thinking of Emilie, he undressed and joined his wife. "You *want* me to pet you, pussycat." He considered ripping the necklace from her body, but left it alone. He lifted the mask from her face so he could look into her eyes.

Blinking slowly, she met his gaze. "Thank you for not dancin' with Emilie. I *was* jealous."

"I told you I wouldn't. I also said that you'd be the one I'd go to bed with tonight, and here we are." He laced his fingers through her hair, then kissed her.

"You kept your word. Can you forgive me for bein' jealous? She's so pretty and—"

"Shh . . . She's nothing like you, my dear. You're the woman I want. My wife. There's no need to be envious of anyone else." He stared deeply into her eyes. "I forgive you."

"Thank you, John." Her supple body began to writhe.

He toyed with the necklace. "You don't need this. I'll always be true to you." Reaching behind her neck he unfastened the thing.

He wanted to laugh aloud at his cleverness, but focused on the flesh squirming beneath him.

"You're right," she rasped, breasts heaving. "I don't need it. I know you love me and won't lie to me."

Nearly forgetting the most important thing, he stood from the bed to retrieve his protection.

"Must you use that?" she asked, reaching for him.

"Yes." He fitted the thing and joined her again on the bed. "But you've never seemed to mind it."

She whimpered but didn't hesitate opening her legs.

He hadn't bedded two women in one night in a very long time. Satisfying them both took great skill. A task he gladly took on. He wanted both of them, so why not? He'd continue as long as he possibly could.

Is James bedding Emilie now?

The obese man could never measure up to *his* standards.

Poor girl, having to look at that. At least Victoria is pleasing to the eye.

It was unlikely James would suspect anything.

He trusts me.

Besides, John had sent her to him. They'd shared her for a long time. Why not continue?

CHAPTER 27

Beth bustled about the kitchen preparing breakfast for Henry. She stopped and stared out the window when she realized she'd been humming.

With a smile, she started moving again.

For a time, she thought she wouldn't be happy ever again, but things had finally started looking up. Henry had gotten off the bottle and with George's help Alexander's Blacksmith Shop had regained most of its customers.

It had taken some time for Henry to get used to George's stutter. He'd complained that he couldn't read his lips. But after a while, they got comfortable with each other and as Beth had assumed, George took to blacksmithing like he'd been born to it.

The back door opened and Henry walked in, mumbling.

"You ALL RIGHT, Uncle Henry?" She hadn't been able to make out his words.

"No!" He sat down hard in a chair at the kitchen table. *What now?*

She bent down and looked him in the eye. "Wake up on the WRONG side a the bed?"

He scowled. "No!"

Taking a step back, she fisted her hands on her hips. "Then what's the problem?"

"It's November fourth! My birthday!"

She let out a laugh. The man grumbled over the silliest things. "Why are you MAD 'bout it? You ain't right!" With a huff, she went to the stove and spooned out a bowl of oats for him, then set it on the table. "HAPPY BIRTH-DAY!"

After glaring at her, he poured milk on the cereal and began to eat. "Used to like havin' birthdays." He grumbled his words with a full mouth of food.

Beth dished up her own bowl, then sat across from him and fixed it to her liking. She patted his hand to get his attention. "Be thankful you're still livin'!"

"I ain't *that* old!" His eyes dropped from her face to his bowl. He shoveled in several more bites. "Sarah used to fix me a cake. She'd make a real nice supper, too. Made everythin' special."

"Henry." Since he wasn't looking at her, she had to pat his hand again. "I know you miss her. Kinda like I miss Gerald. But don't think your life's over. Never know what's 'round the corner."

He dismissed her with the wave of his hand. "You say that cuz you got a beau now. I'm happy for ya, but it don't help *my* bein' lonely."

"It's your own fault! If you got out some, you might find a woman who's just as lonely as you. Lotsa women lost their men in the war."

"Don't talk 'bout the war."

Once again, she'd let her mouth get ahead of good sense. She stood and poured them both some coffee. When George knocked on the back door, she got excited and almost spilled it.

With a grin, she carefully set the cups on the table, then opened the door. George always came by for coffee before starting work. Their new daily routine.

"Mornin', Beth," he said and removed his hat. He stepped inside and nodded to Henry. "M-MORNIN', HENRY!"

Henry grumbled and waved him away.

George questioned Beth with his eyes.

"I'll tell you later," she whispered, then motioned for him to sit. She poured him a cup and set it down.

Most days, Henry and George took this time to discuss what they'd do for the day, but today Henry's mood kept him silent. It kept *everyone* silent.

Henry pushed his empty bowl to the center of the table. "You two *lovebirds* behave. I'm goin' to the shop." He stood and grabbed his cane, then hobbled out the back door.

"I-I best hurry up," George stammered. His discomfort stood out like a redbird in a flock of pigeons.

"Drink your coffee, George. It ain't gonna hurt us to be alone for five minutes." She reached across the table and took his hand.

He held it, but trembled all the while. "I c-can't stay here."

After five months of courting, he should be used to her. "Henry's ill cuz today's his birthday. He's feelin' kinda down. Reckon we could take him to town for dinner?"

"Oh. S'pose so. Where'd ya have in mind?"

"Henry don't like nothin' fancy. Thought Sylvia's would be good." She leaned her head to one side, grinning. Sylvia's held special memories for them. Besides, Henry liked her good southern cooking.

"How will we g-get him to g-go?"

"Reckon I'll just *forget* to cook dinner. Then, if he wants to eat, he'll *hafta* go."

With a rapid nod, George agreed, then sped out the door.

Someday, George Barnhardt, I'll get you alone for good.

Their plan worked, but Henry fussed the entire way. Beth knew he'd rarely set foot in the city since her aunt had died, but her determination to set him straight and get him living again pushed her on. Regardless of how much he complained.

Knowing Dr. Fletcher frequented Sylvia's didn't help. She had no idea what she'd do if he came in. So she said a little prayer. Whether or not it was right to ask God to keep someone away, she did it anyway.

Henry fidgeted with his silverware.

"Uncle Henry!" Beth scolded. "Stop doin' that! You're actin' like a child!"

He slammed the fork onto the table. "I ain't no child! What if I don't like the food?"

The waitress approached them, arms crossed. Beth had never seen her before. Obviously having heard him, she didn't look happy.

"If you don't like the food," the woman said. "Then maybe you'd like to cook it yourself."

Henry looked up, then cupped his hand to his ear. "Huh? I didn't hear ya."

"I said, you can COOK IT YOURSELF!"

Beth's eyes popped wide at the outspoken waitress.

Definitely not from 'round here. She talks funny.

Henry leaned back in his chair, grinning. "You always this pleasant?"

"Yes," the woman said sharply, then let out a slow breath and seemed to relax a bit. "What would you like to eat?"

With the scowl removed from her face, the woman looked pretty. And from Henry's expression, he must have thought so, too. His head moved up and down.

He's dissectin' her.

The waitress took a step back. "Sir, I am not on the menu!"

Henry let out a laugh. "Your husband mind ya workin'?"

"Not at all." She soundly tapped her foot. "Are you going to order, or should I come back?"

"Bring me a surprise," Henry said. His brows rose to his hairline. "Sumthin' good. I'll let *you* decide. See, today's my birthday."

"Well, happy birthday," she said, emotionless.

Beth was silent throughout the interchange. A few times she'd looked to George for help, but his eyes were on the table. *More uncomfortable than ever.*

"Ma'am," Beth said. "I'm his niece."

"I'm sorry," the woman said. Her sarcasm wasn't polite. *Why'd Sylvia hire her?*

"If you got some cake," Beth went on, choosing to ignore her remark, "we'd like some for dessert. You know, for his birthday an' all."

"We don't have cake, but we have pie. Would that do?"

"Birthday *pie*?" Henry sat up rigidly. "Ain't never had birthday *pie*."

"It's sweet. Isn't that all that matters?" She smiled. One of the fakest smiles Beth had ever seen.

"I *do* like sweet things," Henry said and winked at the woman.

Beth gasped. She grabbed hold of Henry's hand and forced him to look at her. "Henry! Mind your manners!" She turned to the waitress. "Sorry. He don't get out much."

"It's all right. I've met men like him before. I know how to handle him."

The woman must have understood Henry's bad hearing, because she'd turned her back to him while speaking to Beth.

"What was that?" Henry asked. He craned his neck trying to get a look at the waitress's face.

She smiled at Beth. This time it looked sincere. "I'll keep him guessing."

She took their orders, then left the table.

"What's gotten into you, Henry?" Beth asked.

He waved his hand at her and didn't answer. His eyes remained fixed on the tall, dark-haired waitress.

He likes her.

But the last thing they needed was for him to get involved with some married woman. If her husband had seen the way Henry had behaved, he'd probably hunt him down with a shotgun.

Henry's surprise meal turned out to be meatloaf. He ate every bite and didn't complain once.

For dessert they had apple pie.

"Birthday pie," he chuckled and devoured it.

"Ma'am!" Henry waved the waitress over to the table.

With a sigh, she came, looking as though she expected a reprimand.

"Ya done good," Henry said. "I liked all the food ya brung. Even the pie."

"I'm glad." The waitress sighed and looked directly at Henry. "I made it myself. You see, I normally cook here. Sylvia was short-handed today and asked me to take orders, too. I'm sorry I was rude. I shouldn't have taken out my poor mood on you."

"Rude? You wasn't rude! Now Beth here . . ." Henry patted Beth's hand. "She knows how to be rude!"

Beth sat upright and glared at him. "I ain't!" She turned to George. "Am I?"

"Well, n-no. You ain't r-rude at all." He gave her the sweetest smile.

The waitress laughed and shook her head. "I don't know how you do it, Miss. Is your uncle always so ornery?" Once again, she'd turned her back to Henry.

"Yes, he is," Beth said. She jerked her head toward her uncle. "You *do* know how to handle him, don't you?"

"Hey!" Henry yelled. "Look at me when ya talk! Ya know I can't hear!"

The waitress turned abruptly toward him. "Lucky for you!" She again shifted her body, looking at Beth. "Be thankful your husband is so polite." She nodded to George, then walked away. Beth had no time to correct her assumption.

George's cheeks turned red as cherries. "Pay it no mind, George," Beth said. "She doesn't know." She liked being called his wife. And since Henry hadn't heard her, he couldn't tease them about it.

She sure put him in his place.

George paid for the meal and thanked the woman for her service.

Henry held tight to his cane, but also managed to hold the door for them as they walked out. Beth watched him nod to the waitress a final time before following her and George to the buggy.

"Damn woman!" Henry fussed as he climbed in. "Thinks she can talk behind my back!"

"She wasn't behind your back, Henry!" Beth laughed. "She just wasn't lookin' at you!" He might be grumbling, but she knew he liked her. "Too bad she's MARRIED!"

"Huh? What difference does it make if she's married?" Henry motioned for George to get going, so he snapped the reins.

Beth saw no need to answer. He knew full well what she meant. He continued to fuss and complain, mumbling all the way home about *birthday pie* and *that ornery waitress.*

* * *

Melissa watched the ornery man limp out the door, leaning on a cane. He seemed much too young to need it.

Looking beyond his constant complaints and his behavior, she found him appealing. *Attractive.* But someone she'd keep her distance from. If she didn't work in a professional manner, she'd likely be dismissed. She needed the job.

There's only one man I should be thinking about.

However, thoughts of her late husband only brought pain.

"Melissa!" Sylvia waved her into the kitchen. "You know who that man was, don't ya?"

"No. I've never met him before."

"That was Henry Alexander. Owns a blacksmith shop. The other man—the quiet one—is George Barnhardt. Used to be Martha's farmhand. Surprised ya didn't recognize 'im."

"No, I never met him. Martha said he was shy. He kept his distance. And then she let him go because Thomas started helping her with the farm."

"Hmm. I figgered you'd know 'im. But it don't matter none. Heard he's workin' for Henry now. As for Henry, he's well off. Has more money than most folks 'round here." *Why is she telling me this?* "You got more in common with that man than ya realize. He lost his family, too."

With a sad smile, Sylvia walked to the stove and began stirring the contents in the pot.

Melissa considered what she'd said.

I shouldn't have been so rude.

Multiple questions spun through her mind, yet she didn't want to ask Sylvia. If she did, the woman might get the impression she was interested in him.

He looked to be older than her, but far from being an *old man.*

Maybe I'll see him again.

She just couldn't understand why she wanted to.

* * *

Beth found herself humming again. Though Henry had fussed all the way home, George had popped his head into the kitchen and told her that Henry had been dancing around the shop.

Hard to do with a cane.

Proud she'd gotten him out of the house, she'd begun thinking of other things. Like why George had never tried to kiss her.

The man's so nervous I'll probably hafta do it myself.

"Hey, B-Beth." George slowly pushed the kitchen door open. "I c-came to say goodbye."

The day had flown by. "Bye, George. See you t'morra."

He inched his way inside. "Miss Beth, Thanksgivin' is c-comin' and . . . I'd like ya to come to my p-place for din-ner." He sucked in an enormous amount of air. "It's t-time for you to m-meet Mama an' Daddy."

Heart racing, she gaped at him. "You want me to meet your folks?" She grabbed hold of him, making him gasp. "Oh, George!" She knew exactly what it meant.

With his arms straight at his sides, he stood locked in her embrace. "That mean y-yes?"

"Course it does!" She laughed and released him. "Can Henry come, too?"

"Yep."

"Then tell your folks we'll be there!" She could hardly stand still. "What should I bring?"

"N-Nothin'. Just you. An' Henry." He gingerly reached for her hand, then stepped closer and looked into her eyes. "I had a nice time today, Beth." He didn't stutter.

His thumb began to move in a gentle caress. Hardly able to breathe, she swallowed hard. "Me, too." The ten-derness of his touch sent her heart thumping. Compelled to follow her desire, she leaned in and kissed him on the cheek.

George gulped. Releasing her hand, he touched the spot she'd just kissed. "I'll tell Mama."

"That I kissed you?"

"No!" His head shook violently. "That you're c-comin' to dinner." With a brisk nod, he jerked the door open and walked out.

"See you t'morra, George!" She yelled after him.

I'm gonna get me a husband.

CHAPTER 28

Of all Mr. Steven's additions, aside from the new bathing room, Claire's favorite was the new porch. It wrapped around the front of the house. He'd also hung a swing, similar to the one at Martha's.

On the other side of the porch, were two rocking chairs. Plenty of room for everyone to sit. But on days like today, she and Samuel liked to sit in the swing and work on his reading lessons while Michael napped.

"Miss Claire?" Samuel asked. "You an' Doc gonna have more babies?"

The question came out of nowhere. "I hope so." Every month brought more disappointment.

"Oh." His eyes went back to the book in his lap. "Reckon Mama an' Daddy woulda had more babies if Daddy hadn't hung."

His words made her heart ache. The poor boy had never spoken about his daddy's death before. "I'm sure you're right." What else could she say?

"I . . . I didn't get to tell him goodbye."

She shifted in the swing to face him and took his hand. "I'm sorry."

"That night I was so scared. I knew them men was outside." His chin vibrated and his chest rapidly rose and fell. "He told Clay to take care a Mama, but din't say nothin' to me. I wanted to say, *I love you, Daddy,* but I couldn't move."

"Oh, Samuel." She gripped his hand tight.

"Michael's lucky. He gots a mama *and* a daddy."

She prayed she'd say the right thing. "Samuel, your daddy loved you very much. *You're* lucky because you have a wonderful mama. I'm sorry your daddy died. I wish I'd known him."

Samuel grinned. "He was big. *Real* big. He made me mind. I hope when I grows up I'll be as big as him. If I'm strong, maybe no one will hurt me."

"You won't be hurt, Samuel."

He blinked slowly. Fear shadowed his face.

She searched his eyes hoping to find a trace of acceptance. "What happened to your daddy was wrong. It won't happen to you."

He looked at the ground. "It's why I runned away. I hid in a secret place."

"You don't hafta hide ever again. If you get scared, come here. Andrew an' I will always be here for you."

He latched onto her and erupted into heavy sobs. She held him and let him cry until no more tears came. He'd probably never mourned his daddy.

"Miss Claire?" He sniffled and wiped his eyes on his shirt sleeve. "Don't tell Mama I cried."

"If that's what you want. But it's good to let her know you miss your daddy. She misses him, too."

He nodded. "She cries sometimes at night. It ain't fair what happened."

"No, it's not. But sometimes things happen we can't control. That's why we have friends. To help us through." She smiled and ran her hand over his head.

"You my friend, Miss Claire?"

"Course I am!" She gave his hand a squeeze, then tipped her head and drew her brows together. "I'm also your employer and we have work to do." Hopefully getting him busy would help him feel better. Still holding his hand, she led him inside.

Michael stirred in his crib.

"I'll get 'im," Samuel said. He picked him up, then laid him down to change him. His face scrunched together. "He needs a bath, Miss Claire."

Samuel's expression was all she needed to see. She began preparing the water while he entertained Michael.

"Miss Claire?" Since Samuel had become his old self, talking almost nonstop, she believed crying had done him a world of good.

"Yes?"

"I don't care you're white."

"I'm glad. That's sumthin' I can't help. And I don't mind you bein' colored."

He laughed. "Can't change that neither." His laughter stopped. "Some a the boys at church call me names cuz I come here. I don't like it, but I'm gonna keep comin' anyways."

She scooped Michael up to get him ready for his bath. "Calling you names isn't nice. They just don't understand. Maybe someday color won't matter anymore."

"Hope so. Name callin' ain't good."

While she bathed Michael, Samuel swept the floor. He'd become quiet again.

She hoped she was right. Too much pain had come into her life because of prejudice.

Michael giggled and splashed in the water.

I want a better life for you.

She kissed his cheek and said a prayer.

* * *

It was rare for Andrew and Dr. Mitchell to have simultaneous time away from the hospital. But since another doctor had been hired, they both had a Sunday free. Claire would finally meet Margaret Mitchell. Andrew didn't know who was more nervous. Claire or himself.

"She's wonderful, Claire. I'm sure you'll love her."

Claire twisted her gloved fingers together. "I hope she likes me. You sure she knows our situation?"

"I'm certain Harvey told her about us. Don't give it a second thought." He'd been doing enough of that for both of them.

Harvey greeted them at the door, along with incredible smells from whatever Margaret had cooked. "Finally," he said, laughing. "Come in!"

Claire held Michael so tight he squirmed. "I'll take him." Andrew lifted him out of her arms.

"Such a handsome boy," Harvey said. "Now come and meet my family."

Andrew had been there a number of times, but he enjoyed watching Claire take in their surroundings. Harvey Mitchell's home boasted many fine things. Furniture from overseas, along with tapestries and paintings.

"Nothing like our home," he whispered in her ear.

"No," she whispered back. "But I love our home." She linked her arm through his and smiled, seemingly more relaxed.

They were led directly to the dining room. The ornate table settings looked like something that would be used for a formal dinner party.

"I believe we've underdressed," Andrew said to Harvey.

They'd come wearing typical daywear.

"You're fine." Harvey leaned close. "The girls wanted to do this. They like to impress."

"*I'm* impressed," Claire said.

Margaret Mitchell entered the room with her girls following. Rachel, the eldest, had recently become engaged. Elizabeth, however, had yet to find a beau. She was approaching nineteen and Harvey had told him she feared becoming an old maid. *Unlikely.* The girl was beautiful.

One by one, Harvey introduced his family to Claire.

Elizabeth looked directly at Andrew, then shot a scowl in Claire's direction.

Not a good way to start the affair.

He hoped she hadn't noticed.

"Oh, he's so cute!" Constance exclaimed, rushing toward Michael. "Mama, isn't he adorable?" At twelve, the youngest Mitchell daughter seemed to find more interest in children than men. Much to Andrew's relief.

At one time, both Rachel and Elizabeth had set their sights on him. With Elizabeth's watchful eye covering him like a fog, his discomfort grew.

Michael giggled and reached for Constance, so Andrew released him.

They were assigned seats and everyone sat, except for Margaret who kept bringing in food from the kitchen. She placed a baked ham at the center of the table, then brought out bowls holding mashed potatoes, carrots, beans, and biscuits. Two smaller bowls held fruit preserves.

"I made custard for dessert," Margaret said, taking her seat. "I know you like it."

"Yes," Andrew said. "Thank you."

Food was passed from hand to hand. With Claire beside him, Andrew held the bowls while she dipped out her portion. She looked up at him with a timid smile.

I love you, he mouthed silently to her.

"So," Elizabeth said, interrupting their moment. "How old's your baby?"

Did Rachel just giggle?

Claire cleared her throat. "Eighteen months."

"But weren't you just married this past May?" Elizabeth asked. She twisted her mouth into a satisfied pucker.

"Elizabeth!" Harvey scolded.

"What, Daddy? I'm simply curious. Michael looks just like Andrew, but how could that be?" She returned her attention to Claire. "You were married to someone else, weren't you?"

Harvey stood, fuming. He pointed out of the dining area. "Go to your room, Elizabeth! I'll not have this at our table."

"Why should I? I've not said anything rude." She took a bite of food and didn't budge from her chair.

"I don't understand," Constance said. "Isn't Michael Dr. Fletcher's son?"

"Yes, he is," Rachel said. The room heated with every word spoken.

Andrew loosened the buttons at his neck. "Yes, he's my son. And I'm proud to be his father."

He looked sideways at Claire and found her staring downward.

"Elizabeth," Andrew said. He'd slipped his hand beneath the table and rested it on Claire's leg, gently caressing. "You're well aware of our situation. Some things don't need to be spoken. I love my wife, and I expected more from you."

She frowned, then scooted her chair back. "And I expected more from *you*! I looked up to you! I thought you and I . . ." Her hand flew over her mouth and she stood. "I don't wish to be in the same room with you!" Whipping around, she sped away.

Margaret hung her head low, and Harvey inched slowly back down into his chair. "Forgive my daughter," he said. "That was uncalled for."

Rachel threw her napkin on the table and followed her sister.

"Why are they mad?" Constance asked.

"Excuse me," Claire said. She, too, pushed her chair away from the table. When Andrew looked up at her, his heart wrenched. Tears streamed down her cheeks. She fled the room before he could speak.

But where would she go?

"Mama!" Michael cried out. He'd been placed in an old highchair Harvey had brought in for him.

Andrew got to his feet and picked up his son. "I need to go after my wife. I'm afraid we'll not stay for dessert."

"Please, Andrew," Harvey said. "Don't go. I'll speak to my girls later, but for now, you're still our guests."

"I—"

"Let me talk to her," Margaret said, rising. "Please, finish your meal." The pain in her eyes made him comply.

The Mitchell's had always been good to him. Choosing another woman over their daughters shouldn't end a longtime friendship.

"Thank you," Andrew said. He positioned Michael on his lap and let him eat from his plate. Manners didn't appear to be important at the moment.

* * *

Claire wanted to run, but had no idea where to go. She wouldn't take the buggy and leave Andrew and Michael behind. But she couldn't stay in that room.

She didn't need their self-righteous judgement.

Glancing around the large room she'd entered, she felt foolish. She had no business parading around a stranger's home.

They must think I'm horrid.

"Claire?"

She quickly wiped her eyes, then turned to face Margaret Mitchell. Another beautiful redhead with two lovely, eligible daughters who had their sights set on Andrew.

My husband.

Feeling sorry for herself only made things worse, but she couldn't help it. No longer welcome at Martha's, and obviously not welcome here, the only place she was tolerated was in the shanties.

My world's upside down.

Deep in thought, she stared at the woman.

"Claire? Are you all right?"

She shook her head from side to side. "No. Forgive me for spoilin' the meal."

Margaret moved closer. "You didn't. My daughters did. I'm ashamed of how they behaved. Harvey and I raised them to have better character than they displayed."

"So, your daughter Elizabeth had her eyes on Andrew? You know his mama's name was Elizabeth."

"Yes, he told us. The first time we had him here for supper."

"Oh." How many times had he eaten here? *It doesn't matter.* What he did prior to their marriage needed to remain in the past. "Are you ashamed to have *me* here?"

"What?"

"I'm no saint. I don't know how much your husband told you 'bout me an' Andrew. But know this, I love him with all my heart. Our baby, too. But I don't wanna be 'round folks who insinuate ugly things. I know Andrew respects your husband, and I'd never do anythin' to harm his position at the hospital. But we shouldn't a come here."

Margaret waved her hands in the air, then motioned toward a sofa. "Please, sit."

Reluctantly, Claire complied.

Margaret glanced over her shoulder, then sat beside Claire and leaned close. "I don't tell this to many people, but Harvey and I were familiar before we married. My girls don't know, and I don't want them to. But you don't have to explain yourself to me. I understand. When you love a man, sometimes things just . . . *happen.*" She took Claire's hand. "You and Andrew have been through such an ordeal. I can tell he loves you. As for Elizabeth, she's accustomed to getting what she wants. I admit we've spoiled her. But that doesn't give her the right to be cruel."

Confiding something so personal took courage. *Trust.* "Thank you for tellin' me. Reckon I'm a might sensitive 'bout certain things. I've been torturin' myself over my mistakes for years."

"You and Andrew aren't a mistake. So if you're referring to *that*, you need to let it go." Her warm smile touched Claire's heart.

"Thank you again." She managed a smile of her own. "Reckon we should go back to our men?"

"I do." Margaret stood and extended her hand. "Besides, you *must* try my custard."

Claire set her hand into Margaret's and followed her back to the dining room. Andrew's face lit up the second he saw them.

"I had a hankerin' for some custard," Claire said and took her seat. "How 'bout you, Michael, would you like some?" She tickled his belly.

"More!" He patted his hands on the table, causing everyone to laugh.

Andrew leaned close. "Are you all right?" he whispered.

"I'm fine." Claire faced him straight on. "I love you." Tempted to kiss his lips, she settled on his cheek. She'd answer his questioning eyes later. Looking across the table at Margaret, she received another warm smile. *A new friend.*

Just like she'd told Samuel, she needed friends to help her through the tough times.

Please Lord, ease up on us a might.

CHAPTER 29

Beth's stomach churned. Not from hunger, but utter terror.

"What's wrong with ya?" Henry asked. "You look like ya swallowed a goat. You sick?"

"Yes!" She flew out the back door, then braced her hands against her thighs and bent over to heave. Nothing came up, but she kept her position, waiting.

Henry patted her on the back. "You pregnant?"

Rigidly, she stood upright and scowled at him. "How dare you say such a thing! George ain't never even kissed me!"

Henry burst out laughing. "What's wrong with that boy?"

"Nothin'!" She pointed a finger in his face. "And you'd best not say anythin' bad 'bout him. I LOVE him! I'm just nervous 'bout meetin' his folks."

Thanksgiving had come and eating was the last thing on her mind. If his folks didn't like her, he might not propose.

"You're bein' damn silly." He poked her with his cane. "Get yourself together, cuz we need to go. I'm fetchin' the buggy now." He walked away.

Breathing deeply through her nose, she managed to follow him. She'd already put on her finest blue cotton dress. She'd piled her hair high on her head, but not wanting to mess it up, wore no hat. Hopefully the wind wouldn't blow and ruin everything.

Henry had also dressed up. He looked might fine in his three-piece suit. She just wished he would've worn a tie.

He brought the buggy around, then hopped down to help her up. They rode silently for a short distance. She fidgeted with her skirt, until Henry popped her hand.

"Stop doin' that," he fussed. "You ain't got nothin' to worry 'bout. We're havin' dinner. Nothin' else."

George had given Henry directions to his home, but even so, she worried they wouldn't find it in time. If they showed up late, she'd make a horrible first impression. She let out an overly loud sigh that drew her uncle's attention.

"What now?" he asked, shaking his head.

"What if they don't LIKE me?"

"Then, to hell with 'em!"

She gaped at him wide-eyed. "Henry Alexander! PROMISE me you won't CURSE in front of the BARN-HARDTS!" *That's all I need.*

He chuckled. "I promise. I'll behave myself. I'm just havin' some fun with ya."

When they arrived, they found George waiting on the front porch. The small wood house looked barely big enough for a bachelor, let alone three people.

A broad grin covered George's face as he lifted his hand to help her down. "Ya l-look real nice B-Beth."

"So do you, George. I like your suit." Like Henry, he'd dressed in a handsome, dark suit, but unlike Henry, George was wearing a string tie. She cast a sideways glance at her uncle. "See, I told you. You shoulda worn a TIE!"

Henry shrugged, then they followed George inside. A wonderful aroma filled the air around them. A woman she assumed to be his mama was placing a nicely browned turkey at the center of a long table.

Henry nudged Beth. "Thank goodness it's turkey. Thought for sure it'd be some confounded German food." He'd mumbled the words into her ear, and she prayed George's mama hadn't heard.

The woman crossed to them, smiling. "I'm Mrs. Barnhardt." She was tiny. Much shorter than Beth and small framed. Her silver hair had been tied into a bun at the top of her head. She wore a gray cotton dress, mostly covered by a white apron.

Knowing how hard it would be for George to make the introductions, Beth dipped her head. "I'm Beth, an' this here's my uncle Henry." She yanked him forward. "Henry, this is MRS. BARNHARDT, George's mama!" She grinned at the woman. "He's hard a hearin'."

"Oh," Mrs. Barnhardt said, then nodded at Henry. "I'm glad you came today."

"Thank ya, ma'am. My pleasure."

For a moment, Beth's nerves calmed. They'd gotten through half the introductions. George stood close by saying nothing, but he held an unending smile.

She glanced around the tiny house, looking for George's daddy. It didn't take long to find him. The man sat in an easy chair about ten feet away. The crowded living room held two chairs and a sofa, perched around a fireplace. Two doorways were at the far end of the small room.

Must be the bedrooms.

Though little, the house was tidy. The table took up most of the kitchen. Mrs. Barnhardt bustled around it, going from the stove to the table, adding more food.

"Come m-meet my daddy," George said, nodding to the other room.

Beth did her best to curtsy. "Hello, Mr. Barnhardt. I'm Beth."

The old man grinned, then winked at his son. She liked him instantly. "Pleasure to meet you. And your uncle, too."

Henry bobbed his head, but said nothing.

Mrs. Barnhardt announced that dinner was ready, so George helped his daddy to his feet. He struggled to move, but George stayed right by his side. His arthritis had to be horribly painful. The man groaned with every step.

Henry tapped along right beside them, leaning on his cane.

Once they were all seated, Mr. Barnhardt said a short blessing. Henry clapped his hands together with a loud *amen*. Beth wanted to crawl into a hole. She sent him a reprimanding glare, only to receive a shrug in reply.

As they ate, Beth managed to relax again. Unable to keep her eyes off George, every time their eyes met, a tingle crept down her spine. Did he feel it, too?

"You know," Beth said. "George is doin' might fine work for Uncle Henry."

Mr. Barnhardt beamed. "I'm proud of my boy taking on something new at his age."

George's smile vanished, and he stared at the table.

"George ain't old at all," Beth said. "He has a lot a life left in him. I'm proud a him, too. Knew all along he'd do well for my uncle."

Slowly, George's head lifted with a renewed smile.

Following dinner, Beth helped Mrs. Barnhardt clear away the dishes, then set about washing them. The woman excused herself and walked away, taking George with her.

That's odd.

Beth continued scrubbing.

Moments later, Mrs. Barnhardt returned and tapped her on the shoulder. "I'll finish up. George needs to see you on the front porch."

"Oh." Beth dried her hands on a towel, then passed by Henry and Mr. Barnhardt, who were still at the table having seconds on pie. Something had happened, and she had no idea what. Hopefully George would shed some light.

She pushed open the squeaky front door and found him pacing, mumbling to himself. The door slammed behind her and she jumped. "Did I do that?"

"Nope." He stopped pacing and gulped. "Does it all the time b-by itself."

"Oh." She twisted her mouth together, uncertain what else to say.

George gestured to a rocking chair, and she sat. Then he started pacing again.

Her stomach knotted, and her throat dried, but then she grew dizzy watching George go back and forth across the wood planks.

"Dang, George! Can't you sit down?"

He froze. "Sorry. M-Maybe I should."

He took his place in a rocker next to her, then got it moving with his feet. Faster and faster.

She grabbed hold of it and jerked it to a stop. "George. I can't take much more a this."

He puckered his lips and blew out a long breath. "B-Beth."

"Yes?" Her heart skipped a beat.

"I." He wrung his hands. "I . . ."

"Yes, George?"

"I'd like ya to b-be." He gulped. If his face got any redder, she feared he might explode.

"Yes?" *Just say it.*

"I'd like ya to b-be. M-My w-wife." He stared at her without blinking.

It took her a second to fully grasp it. But then she jumped from her chair and nearly knocked him over. "Oh, yes, George!" She hugged him so tight he coughed.

"N-Now, Beth." He gently pushed her away. "M-Mama an' Daddy are inside."

"I know!" Nothing he could do or say would douse her enthusiasm. "Let's go tell 'em!" She grabbed his hand and yanked him out of the chair. They flew into the kitchen with the front door slamming behind them.

"I said YES!" she exclaimed.

Henry looked up from his pie. "What was the question?"

Beth cocked her head. "Very funny, Uncle Henry!" She swatted his arm. "George an' I are gettin' married!"

Mrs. Barnhardt held her hand to her breast, then approached Beth. "I'm very happy. Do you like the ring?"

Beth wrinkled her nose. "Ring? What ring?"

The woman looked at her son, perplexed. "Didn't you give it to her?"

"I d-didn't have a chance, Mama. She b-brought me inside 'fore I could d-do it." He reached into his pocket and pulled out a small box.

Beth almost fell on the floor, shaking. "You mean you have a ring, too? Oh, my! I need to sit."

George helped her into one of the chairs at the kitchen table, then placed the box in her trembling hand. With a sheepish grin, he nodded for her to open it.

Inside, she found a simple gold band and slipped it on her finger. Though snug, it fit. "Oh, my!" she cried out again, this time nearly breathless. She fanned herself, hoping it would help.

"Do ya like it?" George asked. "It was my g-grandmother's."

Beth burst into tears. "It's perfect." She sniffled. "I'm so happy!"

Henry shook his head. "Don't look happy."

"I know those tears," Mrs. Barnhardt said. "She's happy."

"So, when's the wedding?" Mr. Barnhardt asked.

Instantly, Beth's tears dried and she sat up straight. "Oh! We have so much to do! We need to pick a date, an' I'd like to have it at my old church, an'—an' I'll need a dress! Oh, my!"

"There ain't gonna be no livin' with her like this," Henry mumbled, then put his head in his hands.

George cleared his throat. "B-Beth. There's sumthin' else we gotta t-talk 'bout." He gestured again to the front porch.

"All right." She stood and followed him out. Again, her belly churned. George's smile had disappeared.

They didn't sit, but remained standing, facing each other. "What's wrong, George? I've never been happier."

"Well . . ." He squared his jaw. "After we're married, are ya willin' to live here with Mama an' Daddy?"

Her heart fell into her shoes. "Here? There's not much room."

"I know. But . . . they need me. Daddy can hardly get around. Mama relies on me to k-keep things up." He stepped closer. "I know she likes ya, an' you'd be a b-big help to her, too." He took her hand. "Please? I love you, ya know."

Time stopped. She couldn't take her eyes from his face. He'd just said the words she'd longed to hear, and never once stumbled over them. Tears puddled in her eyes. "I love you, too. I have for a long time."

But what would become of Henry if she left him? She'd never forgive herself if he took to drinking again. But since George would be working with him every day, he could keep watch. Still, did she want to live in such a tiny house with his family?

He stood motionless with a tight grip on her hand. His eyes remained on her face.

He loves me.

Love for the man moved her to speak. "Yes. I'll do it."

He drew her hand toward his chest, and her body followed. Then he released his grasp and moved his shaking hands to the sides of her face. He inched closer and closer, then bent forward and pressed his lips to hers. She gasped, breaking the contact, but then she grabbed hold of him and kissed him thoroughly.

When they separated, his wide eyes said everything.

Heat rose into her cheeks. "That was nice, George."

"Yep." His breaths came out in rapid bursts. "I do love ya, an' I won't never hurt ya." Like hers, his eyes filled with tears. "You've made me a happy man."

She let out a laugh, then dabbed at his eyes with the sleeve of her dress. "Looks like we both know how to shed happy tears."

They returned inside to make wedding plans. Even though they had less than a month, they chose December 20th, the Saturday before Christmas. But when she began thinking about the ceremony, the church, and everything that went along with it, she thought about Claire. Had things been different she would've been the first person she'd tell, and Claire would've been by her side at the altar. All that changed when Claire deceived her.

Not wanting to ruin the perfect day, Beth set aside thoughts of her former friend. No matter how much she missed her, that woman was long gone. Dead and buried with Gerald.

* * *

Claire bustled around the kitchen putting the finishing touches on the meal. They'd invited Alicia and her children for the holiday. She'd not felt this happy in a long time.

Her cycle was a week late, but she didn't want to tell Andrew. Until she was absolutely sure, she wouldn't get his hopes up.

Jenny had come over early to help with the meal. Almost thirteen, she'd started blossoming into a young woman. Beautiful, just like her mama.

"There's a boy at church," Jenny said, beaming. "He's handsome. I reckon he's noticed me, too."

"Don't rush things." Claire handed her the utensils to set on the table. "You have plenty a time to find a husband."

"One a my friends is already married. She's fifteen. That's old nuff."

"Fifteen? That's much too young. I was twenty-five 'fore *I* got married. There's other things you should think 'bout first."

"What kinda things?"

"Well . . . Growin' up, I reckon."

"Then what?"

Claire let out a laugh. "Gettin' married."

"Knew I's right." A satisfied grin lit up Jenny's face.

Every girl dreamed of the perfect marriage, and of course, they needed the perfect man. They didn't come along often, but Claire had been blessed with two.

Gerald.

She'd not thought about him in some time, but being Thanksgiving, she needed to give thanks for all her blessings. He'd been one of them.

The house soon filled with laughter as everyone arrived. The children entertained Michael until the food was ready, then everyone ate their fill. Andrew had even brought home a turkey that he'd received for services rendered. Alicia contributed the pies.

After the meal, Andrew took Clay and Samuel outside to chop wood to keep the fire blazing. The rest of the children remained indoors, playing in the living room.

Alicia helped Claire clean up. She stopped amid scrubbing a plate and smiled. "You're with child, ain't ya?"

"Maybe." Claire kept one eye on the door, waiting for Andrew's return. "I'm only a week late. But I hope I am."

Alicia took her hand and gave it a pat. "I say you is. I seen it in your eyes."

"I want this so much. Andrew does, too."

"Well, I won't say nothin'. But it couldn't happen to finer folks."

By the time Andrew returned, they'd finished the cleanup. The afternoon had flown by and darkness was setting in. Andrew offered to carry them home in the wagon.

While they were gone, Claire got Michael ready for bed. With a full belly, he yawned and stretched, and she rocked him to sleep.

Thoughts of those she loved came to mind. Gerald. Beth. And even Henry. Aunt Martha hovered at the top of the list. Even though she'd said some kind things to Andrew when he saw her at Sylvia's, it didn't erase all the hurt. Besides, how could they ever get together as a family again with so much hate coming from Tom?

After lighting the lantern beside the bed, she slipped under the covers to wait for Andrew. He'd caught her eye several times throughout the day. At one point, he'd mouthed the words *I love you,* across the dinner table. She'd returned them with a rapidly beating heart.

Her love for him ran deep. They had something special.

She rubbed her belly. *Is another life growin' inside me?*

The front door opened, then closed. She sat a little taller in the bed, nestling into the pillows behind her.

Without speaking, Andrew walked in. Their eyes met. He smiled as he undressed, dimmed the lantern, then took his place beside her.

He raked his fingers through her hair and pulled her body to his. Their lips met, and their eyes closed. They breathed in unison. Separating, he glided his mouth along her neck. The warmth from his breath covered her. She trembled with anticipation as his hand ran up along her leg, lifting her gown.

He kissed her again. Stronger and deeper. Then, their love took control.

CHAPTER 30

"Hurry up, Victoria!" John yelled up the stairs.

Damn woman doesn't understand the importance of punctuality.

He smoothed his clothing, then crossed to the hallway mirror. With a low chuckle, he admired his reflection.

When they'd received the invitation from James to join him and Emilie for Thanksgiving dinner, John had to read it twice. James claimed Emilie could cook. Something John never knew. The girl could clean, but it had been her exceptional performance in the bedroom that had kept her employed.

"John!" Victoria's shriek made him shudder. "Come help with my corset!"

He grunted and proceeded up the stairs.

Victoria stood with her back to him, motioning to the dangling strings. He took hold of them and yanked.

"Pull extra hard," Victoria said, holding tight to the bedpost.

"If I pull any harder, I'll break a rib. Is that what you want?"

"No. Course not. I simply don't want to look fat."

He tied off the strings. "There's not an ounce of fat on your body. If there was, I'd be the first to tell you." He gave her a hard smack on the rear. "Now put on your dress, so we won't be late. The buggy arrives at three."

With a huff, he walked out and returned downstairs to the entryway. A sly smile worked its way to his lips. No matter how hard Victoria tried, she'd never rival Emilie. He only married her to prove something to Andrew. The money she'd inherit didn't hurt, but besting his self-right-eous son had made it worthwhile.

Emilie had whined about marriage herself, but he couldn't bind himself to a simple housemaid. Not where matrimony was concerned.

It's a great deal more pleasurable playing with her from time to time.

He grinned. She enjoyed being *bound* every once in a while.

A swish of fabric turned his head. Victoria glided down the stairway in a red velvet dress. A white silk scarf encir-cled her neck, and then, as always, the heart necklace centered her bosom. He hated the thing.

"Well?" she said. "Do I look fine?" She paused for a mo-ment and posed.

"Yes, my dear. As always." He forced a smile, and she continued down the steps until she reached him.

"Thank you," she said and kissed his cheek. "I left my hair down to keep me warm. This weather might be the death of me."

That would be convenient.

Only seven months into their marriage and he'd already grown weary of her. Granted, he enjoyed her physically, but otherwise she grated on him. At least he had Emilie to look forward to. It kept his mind off the torment of his married life.

He helped her with her coat, then led her outside to the waiting buggy. Right on time.

Victoria nestled into his body once they settled themselves in the seat. She blew out a long blast of air. "I can see my breath."

"Nothing like Mobile, is it my dear?"

"No. I don't like the cold. Least I have you to keep me warm." She ran her hand over his chest, then put her lips to his ear. "Too bad we're not in an enclosed carriage. We could make the ride much more enjoyable."

"Hush. Behave yourself."

Her lips drew into a pout, but she listened to him and remained quiet for the rest of the ride.

It wasn't far to James' home. They could've easily walked, but John wouldn't consider it in the cold. After instructing the driver to pick them up at eight, he escorted Victoria to the front door.

He lifted his hand to knock, but she grabbed it.

"What's wrong with you?" His patience had run thin.

"Do I look all right?"

That again?

"Victoria. You're one of the most beautiful women in the world." *And you're mine.* Even with the unpleasantness of marriage, he had to admit he enjoyed showing her off.

A timid smile from her took some of the chill from the air. *Why is she so nervous?*

John rapped hard on the door and James swung it open.

"Welcome!" he chimed. "Please come in!"

Victoria stepped inside and James helped her remove her coat. "You look lovely, Victoria," he said, smiling.

"Thank you." She coyly batted her eyes, then once again linked her arm with John's and held on tight. *Always the flirt.* If she ever followed through, she'd have hell to pay.

"Emilie's in the kitchen," James said over his shoulder, while hanging Victoria's coat on a peg. "She's been cooking since daybreak. Wants to make a good impression. I think you'll be pleased."

His pride couldn't be more obvious. If he puffed out his chest a little more, he'd likely pop some buttons. "I'm certain we will," John said. She'd pleased him in every other manner possible. "Is there something Victoria could do to help her?"

Victoria gaped at him, wide-eyed. "Help her?"

"Oh, no." James chuckled. "Everything's ready. She was waiting for you to get here so she could put the food on the table. Shall we go to the dining room?"

John released a laugh of his own, watching relief flood across Victoria's pretty face. But as lovely as his wife might be, he couldn't wait to see what Emilie had chosen to wear.

Though not as fine as in his own home, James had quality furnishings. Spotlessly clean, of course. The dining room table had been lavishly set with ornate china and sparkling crystal.

James opened a bottle of wine and filled a goblet for each of them. "Might as well start things properly," he said with a grin, then handed Victoria a glass.

Her head whipped around, asking John's approval with her eyes. "Go ahead," he said. "But only one. You know how you get."

After handing John his wine, James took a sip of his own. "Emilie's the same. More than one glass and she's not herself."

John smiled inwardly. He'd witnessed the effect. They'd shared an entire bottle one night with memorable results. *Maybe not herself, but more fun than any man deserves.*

"What are you saying about me, James?" Emilie floated into the room. Dressed in a simple blue gown with a floral-printed apron, she couldn't be plainer. She'd piled her hair high on her head, but a small strand had fallen down and framed her face. Heat coursed through John's body, recalling their tryst on Halloween. Her arms entwined around her husband, but her eyes locked with his.

"That you can't handle wine," James said and kissed her cheek.

"I'll show you," she said, returning the peck. She took the glass from his hand and downed it in one swig. "You see. I handle it well."

John laughed. "It's good the food is ready. If she keeps that up, she'll be *under* the table, not eating from it."

Emilie tipped her head to one side, grinning. "You would like to see that, wouldn't you, John?"

Only if I could be under there with you. Her thick accent warmed the room even more. He raised his glass to her in a silent salute, then followed her example and drank down the wine.

Victoria latched onto him. "Don't tease her, John. She's worked hard. Just look at her and you can tell." She primly pursed her lips.

"*Bonjour*, Victoria," Emilie said. "*Oui*, I have worked very hard. I hope you will like it." She had James direct them to their seats, then began bringing out food.

As each dish was laid on the table, John stared in astonishment. "I had no idea you could cook like this."

Lifting her chin, Emilie pointed to the browned turkey. "It has a crust of Dijon mustard and herbs. The potatoes are au gratin, and of course the beans are *French* cut." She winked. "But save room for dessert. I made pumpkin brioche bread pudding."

"James," John chortled. "You've been keeping this a secret. You should've had us for dinner much sooner." He met Emilie's gaze. "*Quite* the secret."

"*Merci*, John." Emilie nodded politely.

He enjoyed every tasty morsel, and while they ate, he managed to catch Emilie's eye on several occasions. More importantly, he watched her mouth and the way it moved as she chewed her food.

Incredible mouth.

He should have realized sooner how special she was.

His skin began to heat, so he downed more wine.

Victoria scooted her chair back. "Excuse me, but could you direct me to your facilities?"

Emilie started to stand, but James motioned for her to remain seated. "Please stay. You've worked hard. *I'll* show her the way." He rapidly shook his head. "That is, I'll direct her there. I won't go with her." His face turned crimson.

Emilie cast a disgustingly lovely smile at the man, then the two walked away. John wasted no time. He glanced over his shoulder to make certain they were alone, then went around the table to Emilie.

"I've missed you," he whispered, while massaging her shoulders. Her body trembled beneath his touch. "When can we meet again?"

She stood and faced him. "James is going out of town for a few days." She gasped when he started nibbling her neck. "Please . . . don't."

"I can't help myself. You amaze me. I had no idea you could do so many things." He ran his hands down her body, then let them linger on her breasts. "I'll come to you when he leaves. This time I want to take my time. Not like before. I want to make it last." He intensified his caress and she let out a low moan.

"John . . . please. Stop. We can't be found. It's much too dangerous." She moved out of his grasp and began clearing away dishes.

John followed her into the kitchen.

* * *

Not only is she beautiful, she can cook!

Victoria needed to get out of that room. Emilie's coy little attitude had become unbearable.

She'd quickly taken care of personal business, but decided to wander around the house before returning to the dining room and her husband's gushing praise of the French girl.

She gasped when James tugged on her arm. "James! You startled me."

"I need to speak privately with you."

Odd.

Even so, she allowed him to lead her down the hall. But then he guided her through a door into a bedroom.

I shouldn't have flirted so much.

She cast her eyes nervously around the room. If John discovered them, he'd be furious.

James pushed the door shut.

Oh, my.

He had to have seen the horror in her eyes, because he waved his hands and shook his head. "It's not as it seems. I came to our bedroom because I know they won't look for us here."

She gave him a wary stare.

"I'm certain John has told you about Emilie and her former employment with him."

What? She had no idea what he was talking about, but she masked her surprise and let him continue.

"You see . . ." James wrung his hands. "My wife is sensitive where her former stature is concerned. I'd like you to be sympathetic to her feelings and not mention it. She's more to me than a simple housemaid. She's become a lady and I'm proud to call her my wife." He took Victoria's hand. "Unlike you, she wasn't raised in a sophisticated home. She's learning how to fit into society. Please, be gentle with her."

John's been keepin' secrets.

She gave James' hand a loving squeeze. "I won't say a thing. She's a lovely girl and I can tell how much you adore her. I wouldn't dream of sayin' a hurtful word to her." Offering a warm smile along with another squeeze of the man's hand, Victoria held her anger inside.

Time to turn the tables. "James . . ." She petted the back of his hand like she was stroking a cat. "May I ask *you* sumthin'?"

He gulped hard. "Of course."

"Have you seen my portrait?"

His cheeks flushed, then he looked at the floor. She waited patiently for his answer. She much preferred being the one in control.

"Y-Yes, I have," he stammered, then raised his head.

Using the art of seduction she'd learned well, she gazed into his eyes. "What did you think of it?"

"Well . . ." He cleared his throat, then coughed. "You have nothing to be ashamed of. You're beautiful. The painting captured you well."

Standing a little taller, she pulled her shoulders back. "Thank you." She rested her hand on his cheek and didn't break their eye contact. "I was simply curious." She wrinkled her nose and grinned. The same expression her daddy loved. "I suppose we should go back to the others."

"Y-Yes. We should." He whipped around and opened the door. Before going out, he peered in both directions. Then, without waiting for her, he bustled into the hallway.

Victoria tittered. She could've easily enticed him into bed, but the unattractive man didn't appeal to her. She merely wanted to prove her capability. If John had secrets, why not have some of her own?

By the time she reached the dining room, James was already there, clearing away plates.

"*I'll* help," she said, and purposefully bent down in front of him. The wicked smile she cast caused him to trip and drop a dish. It shattered on the floor.

Emilie rushed in. "James, let me take care of this." She began sweeping up the broken fragments. Perfectly in her place with a broom.

That little housemaid is no match for me.

Knowing the little wench was at the bottom of the social scale improved the day tenfold.

"Thank you, my love," James sheepishly said. "I'm so sorry."

Without a word, Emilie smiled and finished the task.

"Why don't we go to the living room for more wine?" James asked, then motioned down the hall.

John came in from the kitchen. Victoria had wondered where he'd gone off to. "I'd love more wine," he said, then winked at her. "I've grown rather thirsty."

Victoria took his hand. "You look parched. Did Emilie have you in there washin' dishes?"

He chuckled. "Certainly not. My hands weren't made for menial tasks." He laughed again and swatted her behind.

With a satisfied grin, she met Emilie's gaze. Then they followed James into the living room.

John allowed Victoria another glass of wine since she'd eaten a good meal. But conversation had become strained and uneasy. No one seemed to know what to say. So when the buggy arrived, she couldn't have been more relieved.

As they rode home, John held her a little closer. A few snowflakes drifted down and landed on her face. She shivered and he pulled her in tighter. Had it not been for her suspicions, she would've found their ride romantic.

He lifted her chin, then kissed her. A kiss indicating he wanted more. The wine had softened her mood, so she gave in.

They rushed up the stairs to their bedroom as soon as they arrived home.

Feeling light-headed, Victoria let him remove her clothing. He nearly ripped the fabric from her body. What had made him so amorous?

She watched him frantically undress. He fumbled with his protection.

"Leave it off," she said, waving the thing away.

"No. As much as I want you, I can't." He finally managed to fit it on himself, then took her fiercely.

He kept his eyes closed and she couldn't help but wonder what or *who* he was thinking about. But, no matter. She tossed aside all thoughts of Emilie and the other secrets John might have. When the time was right, she'd confront him.

For now, with the warmth from the wine, she intended to enjoy the moment.

* * *

The instant John stepped out of bed, he began fussing, and Victoria wondered if the long holiday weekend had been a bad idea. Since they'd been married, he'd never taken so many days off in a row.

"I'll have to work late tonight," he grumbled, heading for the door. "I'm behind on my work."

She followed at his heels. "Is James behind as well?"

He scowled, then wrapped a scarf around his neck. "How should I know? We have different schedules."

"Hmm." She sighed. "I wonder if Emilie gets as lonely as I do when he works late?" It seemed an appropriate time to bring up his former housemaid.

"I don't know! Now stop this idle chatter and let me be on my way!" He reached for the doorknob.

"John . . ." Having grown used to his ill moods, she wouldn't let up. "Why didn't you tell me Emilie used to be your servant?"

He froze, then spun around to face her. "Did James tell you?"

She'd struck a nerve. "Yes. He feared I might say sumthin' that would hurt her feelin's. Make her feel less important than the rest of us."

"What else did he tell you?"

"Oh—that the two of you were lovers." She spoke without emotion, looking for a reaction.

"He said what?" John yelled and clenched his fists.

Perhaps her jest had been inappropriate. "I'm teasin', John." She let out a laugh.

He grabbed her arms and cinched them tight. "James is my business partner and Emilie is his wife. Never make light of it! You should be ashamed of yourself!" He shook her, then let go.

She stared at the floor. "I'm sorry. I just don't understand why you never told me." Expecting to be slapped, she cowered.

Unexpectedly, with a gentle finger, he lifted her chin. "I kept it from you because the poor girl is ashamed of what she'd once been. I thought it best not to mention it. She's found happiness with James and that's all that matters."

What he said made sense. "Was she a good maid?"

"As a matter of fact, she was. *Very* good. However, she's much better suited in society, don't you agree?"

"Yes, I do. She's lovely. Someone like her shouldn't be scrubbin' floors."

A warm smile transformed John's demeanor. He pulled her close and kissed her. "Remember, I'll be late. Don't wait up."

"Why don't you wake me when you get home?"

"Perhaps. If I'm not too tired." He tapped her nose with the tip of his finger and left.

With a contented sigh, she strolled to the kitchen to see what Jean-Pierre had made for breakfast.

* * *

The brisk walk to work cleared John's head.

Thank God James didn't tell her everything.

If Victoria knew Emilie had been more than a mere maid, she'd have complained every time they were near each other. Though he could've eased her by telling her that had happened before he avowed himself to her.

And why would I ever break a vow?

What Victoria didn't know, couldn't hurt.

James had left by train that morning to meet a client in Rhode Island. Just as Emilie had indicated, James told him he'd be gone for several days. Before leaving, the man had asked him to look in on her to make certain she was all right.

He'd played right into John's hand. If anyone happened to see him go into their home, he had good reason.

She'll be better than all right.

He rescheduled an afternoon appointment, then walked nonchalantly down the street to her home. Anticipation of their time together had already begun its effect.

He casually rapped on the door, then grinned when it only opened a crack and revealed little more than the fluttering of her lashes.

Quickly he stepped inside and pushed the door shut. Wearing a simple, sheer nightgown, Emilie smothered him with kisses. He hadn't even had time to remove his coat.

"John, I knew you loved me."

Love?

Oh well, what does it hurt for her to believe it?

"Slow down," he chuckled. "We have all day."

"I don't want to waste one minute!" She jerked his coat off, then took hold of his scarf and drug him toward the bedroom.

He always admired an eager woman.

Once inside the room, she closed the door, then stepped away from him and backed toward the bed.

He flung the scarf on the floor and took her in. The buds of her breasts poked firmly against the sheer fabric. Though not endowed like Victoria, her body beckoned him.

He crossed to her and circled her pert nipples with his fingertips. Though the silk felt good against his skin, he wanted bare flesh. He grabbed the bottom of her gown and lifted it over her head, then pulled her naked body against him.

She smelled remarkable. A hint of lavender mixed with roses. He buried his face in her hair, while his hands glided down her back and came to rest on her bottom, squeezing and feeling.

"Mmm," she moaned.

He silenced her with a deep kiss. Their tongues moved together in a familiar dance.

She broke free and moved catlike to the bed, then lay down on her back. They'd done this many times. The girl loved watching him undress. So he took his time, teasing her with his eyes.

With each second, his heartrate increased. They locked eyes as he pushed his pants to the floor. She licked her lips. Her incredible mouth could do so much more.

"John, you're taking too long." She reached out. "Please, I'm dying for you."

He removed his protection from his coat pocket and began fitting it into place.

"No, John. There is no need."

He paused. "What? Of course there's a need. I should've worn it the last time, but as you're well aware, we didn't have time."

She stood and moved to him, then took it from his hand. "No. Do not wear it. James and I want a baby."

"You want a baby?" Gaping, he stepped away. "What is it with you women?" Anger erupted from him and doused his desire. "It's always the same! Eventually you all want *babies*!"

His anger didn't faze her. She tipped her head to one side, bit her bottom lip, and eliminated the space between them. Her hand enticed him. "Don't be angry. Be happy. You can feel my flesh without anything between us. It's best this way. I know I feel good to you." She placed his hand over her breast, then drew him in close and kissed him.

Her skill won him over. It not only calmed his anger, but revived his arousal. "What if I'm the one who impregnates you? Not James. Doesn't that matter?"

"I *want* it to be you." She nipped his bottom lip, then grinned. "You're more handsome than James. I want a beautiful baby."

She lured him back to the bed, then pushed him down and straddled him. She'd taken control and took him into herself. "Do you love me, John?" Her lithe body moved skillfully upon him.

How did I lose control?

Even so, he enjoyed watching her. "No, I don't love you, but I *want* you. Does it matter so much?" Knowing she wanted to bear his child forced him to speak truthfully.

She frowned, but continued moving. "It hurts my heart, but I still have James to love me."

How dare she speak his name now?

He grabbed hold of her waist and flung her onto her back. Her eyes flew open wide. "What are you doing?" Her voice trembled with fear.

"If you want my seed, I'll decide how to give it to you!" He pinned her down, forced her legs apart and took her hard. He'd intended to go slow, but rage changed everything. No woman would best him. It was his place to be in control.

In one aspect he agreed with her. Bare flesh felt redeeming. It didn't take long before he gave her what she wanted and burst his seed inside her.

He took her more than once, as the afternoon turned into evening, and the evening darkened into night. At two a.m., he woke from a brief rest and headed for the door.

Emilie followed him. "I know you don't love me, but I still love you. You can have me again, whenever you please. But James must never know."

Their lovemaking had improved through the course of the evening. Once she'd learned her place. So her offer had its appeal. He ran his hand a final time over her body, then stopped it on her stomach. "I'll have you until you swell with a child. Then I'll never touch you again. Understand?"

"*Oui.* I do." She lowered her eyes, then looked away.

He walked out and returned to his wife. He found her sleeping soundly, but decided to undress and lay beside her.

He cupped her large breast in his hand, then kissed her neck. Her body immediately started to writhe.

"Oh, yes, John," she rasped.

He had full control over this one. She'd never disappoint him and bear a child.

His night was far from over.

CHAPTER 31

Since Samuel wasn't there, Claire decided to take advantage of Michael's naptime and sneak one in for herself. She reclined on the sofa and in no time at all fell asleep.

A loud knock on the door startled her. She woke with a jerk, followed by a pounding heart. The last time she'd had an unexpected visitor, it had been Jeremiah Lewis.

You're bein' silly.

Even so, her heart kept thumping as she walked across the room to open the door.

"Aunt Martha!" She flung her arms around the woman.

Martha chuckled. "Well, I swanee, Claire Belle. I missed you, too."

"Come inside!" She couldn't hide her joy. She'd missed her terribly. "How'd you find me?"

With the cold weather, Claire had a roaring fire crackling in the fireplace. Martha bustled across the room and stood in front of it. "I been by the hospital. That husband a yours told me how to get here. He acted happy to see me, too. Makes me feel kinda special."

"You *are* special. I've missed you so much."

Martha's face twitched as she looked around the room. "Nice place." She let out a huff. "Ah, hell. I shoulda come sooner. Can you forgive me?"

"There's nothin' to forgive. You're here now. That's what matters."

"Well, with Christmas comin', figgered I should bring your presents."

"You didn't hafta get us a thing. Seein' you is all we want." Claire hesitated. "I take it you won't be comin' here for Christmas?"

"Nope. Still can't talk no sense into Thomas. Damn him. He's stubborn as a mule. Gets that from Clarence, ya know?" Martha turned her head and Claire feared she'd spit on the floor. But then she scurried across the room, opened the door, and spat outside. When she came back in, she sat down on the sofa. "Always forget my spittoon."

"I'm just glad you're here." Sitting beside her, Claire nestled against her shoulder.

"Did I wake ya?" She took Claire's chin in her hand and studied her face. "Ya look kinda tired."

Claire grinned.

Martha slapped her knee. "Oh, lawdy! You're with child again, ain't ya?"

"Yes, I am. Isn't it wonderful?"

"You sound a might different than the last time it happened." Martha shook her head, chuckling. "I'm happy for ya. Bet Doc's just fit to be tied."

"He doesn't know. I wanted to be sure before I said anything. His birthday's next week. I plan to tell him then."

"He ain't much of a doctor if he can't see it for himself. I could tell just by lookin' in your eyes."

Claire snuggled down again next to her aunt. "He's been kinda preoccupied with other things. It was almost a year ago that Elijah died. Andrew doesn't like talkin' 'bout it, but I know he's still havin' a hard time with it. It happened on his birthday, so I thought maybe I could change the memory and give him something happy to think 'bout."

"Hope he's not still blamin' himself for what happened. Doc's a good man." Martha's body deflated beneath Claire. "Wish Thomas could see it."

Claire sat up and gazed into the fire. "Yes, Andrew's the best. I'm fortunate. I've seen what he does for folks here. If Tom knew, do you reckon he'd see him differently?"

"It'll take an act a God to get my boy to change his way a thinkin'. *I* surely can't." Martha softly chortled. "Bad as things are, I feel right blessed. I love my granbabies. 'Specially that little Franny. She's a handful, but she's my girl. J.J.'s hard-headed like his daddy. Still, I'm glad they came. If only they'd done right by you an' Doc."

Claire took hold of Martha's hand. "I'm glad they came for you, too. Are you gettin' along with the women? Mary seemed nice, but I didn't meet her sister."

"I like Mary better than Thomas, if that tells ya anythin'." Martha rolled her eyes. "As for Missy, she moved out a while back. I don't blame her. She needed her own space. She's got her a room in town and works over at Sylvia's. She visits every Sunday. Brings home all the town gossip an' might fine apple pie!"

"Andrew mentioned he'd seen her workin' there. *She* doesn't seem to have a problem with him. You'd think she could tell Tom he's bein' unreasonable. After all, it was her husband who died, an' children, too. If she can be civil to Andrew, why can't he?"

Martha stood and put her back to the fire. A mixture of frustration and pain covered her face. "Reckon Thomas has it in his head that if he gives in, he'll betray his brother. It's a *man* thing." Her lip curled. "Damn men!" She hurried across the room, spit out the door, then returned to the same spot. Her brow wove with a different type of concern. "I heard sumthin' what might interest you. Beth's gettin' married."

The second she said her name, Claire's heart wrenched. "To George?"

"Yep." Martha said it almost apologetically. "I know things ain't right between ya, but I also know you still care 'bout her. They're gettin' married on the twentieth. Just 'fore Christmas. Havin' the weddin' in the same church you an' Gerald was married in. Figgered you'd wanna know."

"Yes, I'm glad you told me." *How can something be both painful and wonderful?* "I hope she'll be happy. She deserves it." She meant it. "If you see her, tell her I miss her."

"I will. George invited me to the weddin'. Made my day. Figgered he was mad at me for lettin' him go. But I had no choice once Thomas came home. Did ya know George is workin' for Henry Alexander?"

Expressionless, Claire shook her head. Another painful memory. Not wanting to make Martha feel even worse, she hid her feelings.

"Yep," Martha said. "Seems he's doin' real well. Ain't it odd how things work out?"

Claire stared at her hands, digesting it all. She wished she could be by Beth's side.

"Claire Belle?"

"Huh?" She met her aunt's gaze. "Sorry. I was just thinkin'. You'll hafta come back an' tell me all 'bout the weddin'. I hope for Beth's sake Lucy Beecham isn't there."

"Who's she?"

"A troublemaker." Claire left it at that.

They continued talking and getting caught up on everything that had happened since their last visit. Then Michael woke up and added to Martha's joy. He promptly yanked on her nose, so Martha pulled on *his* nose and made him giggle.

Before leaving, Martha brought in some homemade preserves and a wrapped gift for Michael to be placed under the tree. A tree that hadn't even been put up yet. Too much to do. First things first, Andrew's birthday.

Martha gave her a hug. "I can tell you're happy, Claire. I know I was hard on ya at first, but you an' Doc was meant to be. I love ya."

"I love you, too, Martha." Claire had Michael perched on her hip and he reached out for her.

Martha took him into her arms and squeezed him tight. He yanked her nose a final time.

With laughter filling the air, Martha drove away. Even though some of the things they'd discussed had been painful, Claire needed this, and she believed Martha did, too. Maybe one day, she'd mend her friendship with Beth and they could sit and talk like old friends.

Least she'll have someone to love her.

Maybe George could melt Beth's heart.

* * *

Rain steadily fell, dampening Andrew's already dismal mood. It was his birthday, yet thoughts of Elijah filled his mind and replaced any thought of celebrating.

Alicia had invited them for supper and a graveside memorial. Of course they'd accepted the invitation, but why'd it have to rain?

Claire had Michael clutched against her as they rode the short distance in the buggy. Not feeling like talking, Andrew gave her a sad smile when she affectionately rubbed his leg. Her sorrow-filled eyes displayed her shared grief.

"I wish I'd known him," she whispered, then remained silent the rest of the way.

Alicia greeted them at the door wearing her Sunday church clothes. The children were also sharply dressed. But even fine clothing couldn't cover their pain. Alicia's puffy eyes indicated she'd shed many tears.

Andrew gave her a hug, as did Claire. Even Michael seemed to sense the darkness of the day and remained quiet and still.

"I wish the rain woulda held out," Alicia said, sighing. "No matter. I'm goin' to the grave."

"We'll go with you," Andrew said. "Maybe it'll let up."

Alicia bobbed her head, then gestured to the kitchen table. "I made stew. Don't feel much like eatin', but come sit an' have ya some."

They complied, but like Alicia, Andrew had no appetite. He managed a few bites, but they were insignificant. Silence hung heavy in the tiny house.

As they made their way to the grave, the rain eased to a light sprinkle. Grass had grown up around the mound of earth, but it was dry and brown. Everything looked dead and barren. The oak tree hovered over them like a large hideous beast. The wind blew, chilling their damp skin.

Andrew held Michael in one arm, with his other around Claire. He drew her closer to him as they stood facing Alicia on the opposite side of the grave. The children huddled close to their mother, with the exception of Samuel. Looking completely distraught, the boy stood alone, leaning against the tree.

"Lijah," Alicia said, looking upward into the rain. Her voice came out strong, even through her pain. "I knows you're in Heaven, an' I'm shore it's beautiful. But I miss ya sumthin' awful. So does our children."

She closed her eyes, but kept her face lifted to the sky. "Lord, please bless us all. Hep me take care a my children. Give me strength to be a good mama. I thanks ya for the friends you brought to me. I don't understan' why you took Lijah so soon, but I's doin' the best I can 'thout him. You blessed us with fine children. Hep me raise 'em right." Opening her eyes, she smiled at each child in turn, but then whipped her head around, searching.

She just noticed Samuel's absence.

Claire's breath hitched and Andrew gave her a little squeeze.

Leaving the four children at the grave, Alicia went to Samuel. "Sam? You all right, boy?"

He stared at the ground, then Alicia took his face in her hands and made him look at her. "I knows you miss your daddy. Come to the graveside. Tell him how you feel."

"No, Mama." Samuel's chin quivered. "Daddy din't tell me goodbye. I don't *wanna* talk to 'im."

"Oh, baby. Your daddy left us in a horrible way. We was all scared that night. He done what he could."

"But Mama . . . he told Clay to take care a you. Then, when Jenny tried to run out the door to him, he yelled at her an' told her he'd see her in Heaven. But he din't say nothin' to *me*! Why?" Tears streamed down the boy's face.

Claire sniffled, then wiped away her own tears. Andrew lovingly rubbed her arm, then kissed her on the forehead.

Sobbing, Alicia pulled Samuel into an embrace. "Your daddy loved you!" She regained her composure but didn't release the boy. "'Lijah always said you reminded him a hisself when he was young. Thought you'd grow up to look just like 'im." She held him at arm's length, gazing into his eyes. "He walked outta our house that night so the rest a us could live. Gave his life for us. Ain't no greater love. Reckon he din't wanna tell you goodbye, cuz he still had hope. But I's shore if he coulda, he woulda held you one last time."

Samuel's face twisted, taking in everything she'd said. His breaths came out in rapid bursts. "You think I'll look like Daddy one day?" He drew his arm across his face, wiping his eyes.

"You already does, my handsome boy." Alicia stroked his cheek, then kissed it. "Now, come tell your daddy you love him." With her arm over his shoulder, they walked back to the grave.

Samuel dropped to his knees. "Daddy ... I's sorry I was mad at you. I blamed ya for leavin'. Thought for shore if you'd a stayed inside I wouldn't a lost ya." His shoulders shook and he broke out crying. "I love ya, Daddy!"

Clay crossed behind him and placed a hand on his shoulder. Then the rest of the children gathered around.

Alicia lifted her hands upward. "*Amazing grace, how sweet the sound . . .*" Her lovely voice started softly singing, then Claire joined in, and soon they all added their voices to the familiar song.

As they ended the verse, the black clouds overhead darkened even more and burst wide, pouring rain down in torrents.

God's crying, too.

They rushed the children inside. Alicia grabbed a stack of towels and handed them out, then helped the little ones change into dry clothes. Andrew did his best to dry off Michael.

They needed to get home. Even though they wore coats, the rain had soaked through. "Alicia," he said. "I hate to leave, but I need to get them home."

"I understan'." Alicia narrowed her eyes. "You takes care a Claire, hear me?"

"Of course." The intensity on her face seemed a little harsh. Why'd she feel the need to remind him to take care of his wife? "Will you be all right?"

She glanced over her shoulder at her children. Samuel lit up with a bright smile. "I shore will. Gots some wonderful children to look after me." Shaking her head, she looked at the ceiling. "We done good, Lijah!"

Her faith and love never ceased to amaze Andrew.

They hurried home. He stopped the buggy at their front door and helped Claire inside. Then he took it to the barn.

When he returned to the house, she'd already put on dry clothes and changed Michael.

"Get outta your wet things," she said. "I'll make us some hot cider."

"Perfect." He went to their bedroom and peeled out of his drenched clothing. After patting dry and redressing, he joined his family in the living room. Michael didn't seem at all bothered by the rain. He sat in the middle of the rug by the fireplace and played with some buttons Claire had strung together.

Andrew took a seat on the sofa and watched him. Thoughts of Samuel filled his mind.

Maybe now he can heal.

Since Andrew had become a part of Michael's life, he couldn't imagine his son having to grow up without him. But nothing in life was guaranteed.

"Andrew?" Claire sat beside him and handed him a steaming cup. "Happy birthday."

"Yes, it's my birthday, isn't it?" He hadn't realized that enough time had passed to heat the cider. The spicy aroma started to soothe him. "Not so happy, though."

"I'm sorry." She caressed his leg. "Sorry you'll always remember that horrible time on a day you should enjoy. I feel kinda bad that I didn't plan sumthin', but I didn't think you'd wanna celebrate. Still, I have a present for you."

"I don't need a present. I have everything I want right here in front of me."

"Well," she sighed. "I hope you'll want this. It's sumthin' I can't return."

He took her hand and raised it to his lips. "I'll love anything you give me."

"You sorta gave this to *me*. We made it together."

He froze, staring into her unblinking eyes. Alicia's words came rushing back. *Take care of her.*

His heart thumped and his eyes misted over. "Are you saying what I think?"

She rapidly nodded. "Yes. We're gonna have a baby." Tears trickling down her cheeks matched his.

He couldn't take his eyes from her beautiful face. "How long have you known? I mean . . . are you certain?"

"Well, *Dr. Fletcher,* my cycle is more than a month late. Aside from that, I just know." She searched his face, brows weaving.

Unable to hold back, Andrew kissed her to wipe away every trace of concern. "Do you know how happy I am?" He kissed her again, longer and stronger, to prove his point.

Giggling, she drew back. "Reckon I do. I'm happy, too."

"Baby," Michael said, clapping his hands.

Andrew scooped him off the floor. "Yes, your mama is going to have a baby. You'll have a little brother or sister." He gave him a squeeze, then set him down again to play.

Taking it all in, Andrew stood and wandered toward the fire, raking his fingers back through his hair. Then, he returned to the sofa. "I missed so much with Michael." Grabbing hold of Claire's hands, he ran his thumbs along her skin. "I don't want to miss anything this time. No matter what, I'll be with you when it's born." He pulled her against him. "We're going to have a baby."

By far the best birthday gift he'd ever been given. Because of their love, their family was about to grow.

Chapter 32

Beth paced, trying to keep from shivering. She'd likely wear a hole in the floor of the Baptist church. Maybe a December wedding had been a bad idea.

What's keepin' Mrs. Sandborn?

The woman had agreed to stand up with her *and* make their cake. George had wanted his daddy to stand up with him, but the poor man couldn't stay on his feet for any length of time, so Henry had agreed to do it. Hopefully, *they* were ready.

"Right cold outside!" Mrs. Sandborn exclaimed. She walked in the room wearing a blue cotton dress and shivered even more than Beth. She looked a little odd without her ever-present white apron.

"Oh, my!" Relieved, Beth rushed across the small room and hugged her. "Feared you wasn't gonna make it."

Mrs. Sandborn burst out laughing. "It's an hour 'fore you walk down that aisle!" She guided Beth to a chair. "Sit down and try to keep calm. You look like you're ready to bust—an' not in a good way."

"I don't wanna sit. I might wrinkle my dress." Though simple, her white wedding gown was the finest dress she'd ever owned. Pacing seemed safer. While she paced, she wrung her hands, wishing George's grandmother's ring was already on her finger and the entire ordeal was over.

"Beth." Mrs. Sandborn grabbed her by the arm. "It ain't gonna hurt your dress to sit. You're makin' *me* nervous."

With a heavy sigh, Beth obeyed, carefully tucking her dress beneath her.

"Much better," Mrs. Sandborn said.

"No it ain't. Think I'm gonna be sick." Beth doubled over and put her head between her knees.

Mrs. Sandborn glided her hand in slow circles over Beth's back. "Honey, you'll be all right. George is a good, kind man. He'll make a fine husband."

"I know." Beth spoke into the fabric of her dress, but then, feeling light-headed, sat upright. "But we can't even go on a honeymoon. His folks need his help every single night a the week. We can't get away. Not even for one night." With her cheeks heating, she dropped back down against her knees.

Mrs. Sandborn tapped her on the shoulder. "No private time, huh?"

"Nope." With a huff, Beth sat up again. "That ain't even the worst of it."

"Go on . . ." Mrs. Sandborn scooted a chair next to Beth's and sat.

"Well . . ." Nervously, Beth chewed her lower lip. How would she say this? "I don't know what to do. Remember when you told me things would work themselves out. Natural-like?"

"Yep."

"George ain't very romantic. Truth be told, he's only kissed me once. It was nice. But I don't reckon he knows how to do them *other* things."

With a shake of her head, Mrs. Sandborn took Beth's hand and gave it a pat. "I have a feelin' George knows more than you're givin' him credit for. The man's worked on a farm all his days. He's probably seen them animals—"

"Hush!" Beth held up her hand. "Don't talk 'bout that."

"But that's what we *was* talkin' 'bout."

Beth fanned her heated face. "Reckon so." She screwed her lips together, deciding whether to push on with this discussion. *I gotta know.* "Since I'm kinda scared neither of us knows how, is it possible to do it *wrong*?"

The woman laughed, but then quickly covered her mouth. *Good thing.* It hadn't been easy asking.

"If anyone *has*," Mrs. Sandborn said. "They'd never tell." She took Beth's hand again and held it firmly. "Stop thinkin' 'bout all that an' think on what a nice weddin' you're gonna have. There's a stack a presents already waitin'." With a smile, she looked Beth in the eyes. "When you an' George are alone, you'll know what to do."

Mrs. Sandborn stood and clapped her hands together. "I'm goin' to check on George an' Henry. Make sure they're ready. You sit here and *breathe*. I love ya, Beth."

"Love you, too."

Mrs. Sandborn walked away and Beth did all she could to stop thinking. But she'd been born to worry. What if no one came to the wedding? Of course, Mrs. Sandborn had just said there were presents, so she could cross that worry off the list. *Unless they just dropped the gifts by an' left.*

Oh, God, I feel sick.

Taking deep breaths through her nose, she tried to ease her out-of-control nerves.

Deciding pacing was easier than sitting, she stood. Mrs. Sandborn was taking much too long getting back.

What if sumthin's wrong with George? Or Henry? Or Mr. Barnhardt?

Tears came.

Perfect. Now I'm gonna look a sight.

Mrs. Sandborn walked in, and Beth quickly wiped away her tears. Unfortunately, the woman noticed. "Oh, honey. Have you been cryin'? Everythin's fine. The church looks wonderful. They decorated it with green boughs and pretty red ribbons, an' your future in-laws are sittin' on the front pew."

Beth erupted into a heavy bawl. "Gerald's weddin' was beautiful! But it was all a lie!" She dropped down into the chair, not caring any longer about how she looked.

"Don't be thinkin' those things today. Think 'bout the man you're gonna marry."

"But . . ." Beth sniffled. "I don't understand why I'm feelin' like this. As much as I hate her, I miss Claire. Always figgered she'd be here with me—if I ever got married."

Mrs. Sandborn sat and wrapped an arm over Beth's shoulder. "Maybe it's time to set things right. Least you could talk to her. I know there's more to what happened than ya think."

Beth gaped at the woman. "You seen her, haven't you? Was *he* with her?"

"Yes, he was. They care 'bout you. I know Claire misses ya."

I don't wanna hear it.

Not wanting to risk reprimand, Beth didn't voice her feelings. Instead, she stood and walked toward the door. "We'd best go. I got me a husband to marry."

From that point on, numbness set in. It seemed the only way she could keep from thinking about Claire and *her* new husband.

In a fog, Beth walked down the aisle to George. Music played. Lots of folks filled the small church, and she should be grateful, but her mind wasn't right.

Shaking her head, she focused on George, and when she reached him, she linked her arm into his and held on tight.

"I ain't never lettin' you go, George," she whispered in his ear.

His bright smile eased her troubles.

The ceremony went as planned. Reverend Brown had agreed to shorten George's vows so he'd only have to say, "I do." He barely whispered it.

When Beth's turn came, she said her vows loud and clear. And when they were proclaimed Mr. and Mrs. George Barnhardt, Beth thought she'd die right there on the spot.

George managed a timid wedding kiss, and she couldn't be prouder of the man she now legally called *husband.*

As they walked away from the altar together and proceeded down the aisle, she caught Lucy Beecham's eye.

Why'd she hafta come?

She cradled a tiny baby in one arm. Another dirty-faced boy, or possibly a girl. Hard to tell under all that filth.

Someone should teach that woman how to properly bathe her children. Especially for special occasions.

Beth and George reached the end of the aisle and headed toward the fellowship hall. Unfortunately, Lucy followed.

"Beth!" Lucy shifted the baby onto her shoulder and patted its back. "Where's Claire? I figgered the two a you was joined at the hip."

I won't let her get under my skin. Not today. "Hey, Lucy. Claire couldn't be here."

"Heard she got married again. Your brother ain't been in the ground long."

Beth kept walking, practically dragging George along with her. Though Lucy's words sickened her, she chose not to answer.

"How's that nephew a yours?" Lucy hollered. Everyone in the congregation likely heard her.

Beth jerked away from George and faced the horrid woman. "He *ain't* my nephew!" She spewed it out, but immediately regretted it.

George took her hand. "You all right, Beth?"

"Oh, she's fine," Lucy said, stepping closer. "But sometimes when the truth comes out 'bout things, it don't feel too good."

Beth's hand flew into the air, ready to smack the wretched girl like she'd done before. Before she could, George stepped between them. "Ma'am," he said to Lucy. "You're upsettin' my wife. P-Please don't. It's our weddin' an' I want her to b-be happy. P-Please don't be ugly no more."

With a huff, Lucy walked away.

George put his arm around Beth. "You all right n-now?"

Tears puddled in Beth's eyes. Her wonderful husband had defended her. "Right as rain, George."

In a tender gesture, he dabbed at her tears with his shirt-sleeve. "Want some w-weddin' cake?"

"Yep."

They went on to the reception.

After cutting the cake, it dawned on Beth that Henry was nowhere in sight.

"What happened to Uncle Henry?" she asked George.

"He w-walked out the door after the weddin'. Wasn't himself. Seemed a might glum."

Just as she'd feared.

Henry had told her he'd get used to her living elsewhere, but she didn't believe him. "Hope he doesn't hit the bottle again."

George grasped her hands. "You've done all you c-could. He's a g-grown man."

Before she could respond, she sensed a presence over her shoulder and turned around. *Martha Montgomery.* Lucy had made Beth angry, but seeing Martha brought entirely new feelings.

She'd grown fond of the ornery old woman when they'd stayed by Claire's side in the hospital. Even so, she didn't want to be around anyone related to Claire.

"George," Martha said, taking his hand. "I'm happy for ya." She cleared her throat. Hopefully she wouldn't spit. "Happy for *both* a ya." She nodded to Beth.

"Thank ya for b-bein' here," George said.

Beth looked the other direction.

"Beth?" Martha had never said her name so quietly. "Don't know if this is the right place to say this, but Claire misses ya. She woulda loved to be here. I hope someday you can find it in your heart to forgive her."

No.

Hoping Martha would leave, Beth buried her face into George's shoulder.

"All right then," Martha whispered. "I best be goin'."

"Thank ya, again, Martha," George said.

Beth didn't budge until she knew for certain Martha was gone. When she finally raised her head and looked at George, his eyes were filled with love and understanding.

He cupped his hand to her face. "You'll be fine, Mrs. Barnhardt. T-Time makes everythin' b-better. Just wait an' see."

She kissed his cheek.

George's mama walked up to them. "Are you about ready to go? Karl is starting to hurt." She nodded toward the far wall.

Mr. Barnhardt was sitting in a chair with his eyes closed and his head leaning back against the wall. "Yes'm," Beth said. "We can go."

George helped his daddy into the wagon, then in turn helped his mama. Once he'd settled Beth, he hopped up himself.

After being showered with rice, they headed down the road.

The last thing Beth heard was Mrs. Sandborn yelling out that everything would be fine.

Fine?

How could it be when her heart ached and her stomach had resident butterflies?

George handed her a blanket. "Put this over you an' my folks. Don't want ya g-gettin' cold."

She tucked one end of the quilt around her knees, then handed the other end to Mrs. Barnhardt. She placed it around herself and her husband. Every now and then Beth noticed him wince.

What've I gotten myself into? Would she be comfortable living with them?

"Beth . . ." Mrs. Barnhardt patted her knee, then leaned close. "I changed the sheets on George's bed this morning."

Beth gaped at her.

"I wanted them to be fresh for you."

"Thank you," Beth whispered.

The reality set deep. His folks knew they'd be sharing a bed.

Course they knew.

Familiar heat rose into Beth's cheeks. Hopefully George's mama would think the red hue had been caused by the cold.

As the tiny farmhouse came into view, Beth's nerves once again got the best of her. What would George expect from her tonight? Worse yet, what would his folks think?

She considered bolting back to Henry's.

George jumped down and extended his hand. Tentatively, she took it. Once on the ground, he lifted her into his arms with a grunt.

"What are you doin'?" Beth feared he'd break his back. After all, she was no small girl.

George continued on to the house as if she weighed next to nothing. "I'm c-carryin' ya over the threshold." He pushed the squeaky door open, and she folded her body closer into his. "Welcome home, B-Beth." He set her down, gave her a quick peck on the cheek, then went back outside to help his folks.

When his mama came in, she hastened to the kitchen. "I'll fix some stew." She cast a smile at Beth, then bustled around gathering things for supper.

Beth probably should've helped, but she couldn't move from where George had put her.

George guided his daddy to his favorite chair, then crossed to her. "Why d-don't ya go unpack your things?"

Uncle Henry had dropped off her trunk that morning. "All right." She pointed to the room she thought was theirs and George nodded.

Swallowing hard, she went in. It couldn't have been plainer.

Good thing George is small. That bed ain't very big.

It had a simple wood headboard and footboard. Nothing fancy. The only other furniture in the room was a wooden chair, small bureau, and a tall wardrobe. He'd placed her trunk at the foot of the bed.

Opening the wardrobe, she found that he'd pushed his clothes to one side. So she hung up some of her clothing. Then she placed her other things in a bureau drawer that had been emptied. He'd been considerate giving her some of his space, but they'd need another bureau. She set some of her personal belongings on top of it and left things she had no room for inside the trunk.

The only bright thing in view was the multi-colored quilt covering the bed. It would be easy to improve the looks of the room. She'd start by making a colorful drapery over the single window to replace the ugly brown one currently there.

Definitely a man's room.

She sucked in air. *Oh, dear Lord, I'm in a man's room.*

Needing to change, she shut the door, then took off her wedding dress and put on a day dress. Then she sat on the edge of the bed, getting a feel for it.

Soft, but not too soft. *Should be comfortable.*

The door opened and Mrs. Barnhardt poked her head into the room. "Supper's ready."

Beth jumped to her feet, cheeks flushing. *Why didn't she knock?* Would they have no privacy whatsoever? "Thank you." She smoothed her dress and walked out of the room, passing by her mother-in-law.

George beamed and pulled out a chair at the table for Beth.

Timidly, she sat. Heavy snoring caught her ear.

"Daddy's sleepin'," George said, grinning.

"He tires easily," Mrs. Barnhardt added. "I'll keep the soup warm for him." She ladled bowlfuls for the three of them.

Beth pushed the vegetables around inside the bowl with her spoon, then sipped at the soup. *Should I apologize for not helpin' with supper?*

She looked across the table at George, who grinned and lapped up the contents of his bowl. Seemed nothing was wrong with *his* appetite. He ate heartily, all the while grinning between bites.

After eating, they joined Mr. Barnhardt in the living room. Of course, they didn't have to go far. The man hadn't moved, but continued to snore.

Beth and George sat side by side on the sofa. Mrs. Barnhardt sat across from them in another chair. Aside from the noise from Mr. Barnhardt, the house was quiet. No one seemed to know what to say. Odd for Beth who'd never been at a loss for words.

Until now.

Mrs. Barnhardt picked up a book from a small side table. She brightened the lantern beside her and began to silently read.

George looked at Beth. "Ya tired?"

"Uh-uh. Not really." She folded her hands in her lap and stared at the wall. A clock on the mantel over the fireplace caught her eye, then she noticed its loud ticking. With nothing else to do, she watched the hands move.

Snore.

Tick. Tick.

Snore.

Tick. Tick.

She sighed.

"Beth?" George cleared his throat. "Ya sure you ain't t-tired?"

"Reckon I am a might." The ticking of the clock had started to lull her.

"We should go to bed then." He patted his legs as if making a grand proclamation.

"All right." *Oh, Lordy . . .*

They both stood rigidly from the sofa.

"Need some help g-gettin' Daddy into bed, Mama?" George asked.

"Not tonight. He's so peaceful I don't want to disturb him. You go on to bed." She smiled at both of them in turn. With a sigh, she bent her head down and continued reading.

George cleared his throat. "Well, then . . . n-night, Mama."

"Good night, George," the woman replied, then lifted her head and gave Beth another smile. "Good night, Beth."

"Night, Mrs. Barnhardt." Beth's mouth twitched into a smile for her mother-in-law, then she grabbed George's arm. "I need to use the outhouse."

Without waiting around for a reply, she scurried out the door. Even in the cold dark, she stayed there longer than necessary. Her heart thumped.

Once she returned inside, she'd have to go to *their* room and *their* bed.

Stop bein' so foolish!

She scolded herself and stomped her foot.

I'm a married woman. I'm goin' back in that house to my husband!

She followed her feet back inside.

After washing at the kitchen sink, she gave Mrs. Barnhardt a friendly nod and went to the bedroom.

George rushed past her. "My turn."

He looked a might nervous himself.

We'll never get through this night.

She shut the bedroom door and locked it this time, then changed into a nightgown. As she climbed into bed, the doorknob jiggled.

"Beth?" George rapped at the door. "It's locked. I c-can't get in."

She jumped up and opened it. When he stepped inside, he closed it again, then stared at her in her nightclothes.

"Ya look b-beautiful," he stammered and kept his distance.

"Thank you." She pulled back the blankets for both of them, then sat on the edge of the bed. When she put her weight down, it made a small sound. Not a *creak*, but a noise nonetheless.

George froze, wide-eyed. "Shh!"

"What? I didn't do nothin'."

He stepped closer. "They'll know you're in the b-bed," he whispered.

"Course they'll know I'm in the bed. I'm s'posed to be in the bed. That's what you do when you go to bed. You get *in* the bed!"

"Shh!" He waved his hands at her.

Plum silly.

Tiptoeing, he crept across the floor and stood beside her. "I d-don't want them to think we're d-doin' sumthin' in the bed."

"We *ain't*." She spoke in a loud whisper.

He looked over his shoulder at the door, then back at her again. "Just t-try to be as quiet as ya can."

"Fine." He acted more nervous than her. The man needed to calm down and stop being so ridiculous. "Why don't you get in bed, George?"

With a nod, he started removing his clothing. Overwhelmed, Beth turned her head. He climbed in beside her and she glanced his way. Wearing long underwear that covered his entire body, he lay back and yanked the blankets up to his neck.

She shifted on her side to face him.

"Shh!" he scolded.

"Heaven's sake, George. This is silly. I've gotta be able to move. Everyone turns about in their sleep."

He looked down and sighed. "Sorry. I just d-don't know what to do."

I knew I was right.

Mrs. Sandborn was wrong. They were in for a heap of trouble if neither of them knew what to do.

"Well," Beth said. "We could go to sleep. If you're tired an' all."

"I am." He smiled, looking relieved. "It's been a long d-day."

She worked her bottom lip. "Anythin' *else* you wanna do?"

The intensity of his breathing grew noticeably stronger. "Reckon so. But I c-can't. Not with Mama an' Daddy right on the other s-side a that d-door."

"I understand." Boy, oh boy did she ever. "Can I at least kiss you?"

"I'd like that."

She scooted closer to him, then rose up on her elbow. Their lips met in an affectionate kiss. "I love you, George. I can wait for *other* things till you're comfortable."

He gave her a peck on the cheek. "G'night."

"Night." She rolled onto her side, facing away from him.

How long would it take him to get comfortable? Truth be told, she wasn't ready either. Still, someday she'd like to know what it was like to make love. He probably did, too. But even more than that, she'd like to have a baby.

I ain't gettin' any younger.

If they had to wait until his folks weren't on the other side of the door, it could be years.

Oh, Lordy . . .

She closed her eyes.

Might as well sleep. There ain't nothin' else to do.

CHAPTER 33

Beth and George easily developed a daily routine. He'd get up early to tend the livestock. By the time he came inside, she and Mrs. Barnhardt would have breakfast waiting. He'd eat a hearty meal, then head for Henry's.

Beth packed his dinner with enough for Henry, too.

Fortunately, her worries about her uncle had been unfounded. George told her he was doing fine and working hard. He also appreciated the food she sent.

As for her relationship with her in-laws, it improved day by day. Mrs. Barnhardt thanked her frequently for the help around the house and farm. Mr. Barnhardt rarely spoke. His English wasn't as good as his wife's. But he smiled most of the time.

Every day when George got home from work, Beth had supper on the table. She'd greet him at the door with a kiss.

At times, his mama looked uncomfortable with their affection. George told her that his folks had never been openly physical with each other, so seeing them kiss was odd. No wonder George had such a hard time showing affection. Not only were his parents unaffectionate toward each other, they never showed George any either. Until she'd come along, he'd probably never even been hugged.

It's a wonder there's a George at all.

So, they kept their physical contact to a minimum. Their nightly routine remained the same as it had been on their wedding night. Even behind closed doors, George was uncomfortable. Less than a week into their marriage and Beth already felt like an inadequate wife. Even so, George didn't complain.

Christmas arrived quickly with little festivity. Luckily, Beth had sense to make gifts for everyone before the wedding. She'd knitted Mr. Barnhardt some socks and a sweater for her mother-in-law. For George, she'd sewed a pair of coveralls.

George surprised her with a store-bought dress. Blue— her favorite color—with tiny white flowers. The sleeves were trimmed in lace. It was the most beautiful thing she'd ever seen, and she nearly hugged him. Instead, she thanked him with a simple peck on the cheek, afraid to do much more.

Henry came for Christmas dinner, but left quickly after. He claimed he didn't want to intrude.

Then, that evening, they gathered in the living room just like any other day of the week.

Nothin' feels right 'bout this holiday.

Recalling the good times she'd had on Christmas with Claire and Gerald, she became even more depressed.

She got into her nightclothes, then climbed into bed and waited for George.

As always, he shut the door, took off his outer clothes, and got in bed wearing his long underwear.

"G'night Beth," he whispered.

Her body deflated. "George, I don't wanna go to sleep just yet."

"Ain't ya tired?"

She shifted to face him. "No." She moistened her lips. "Will you hold me? Please? I promise to be quiet. I just wanna be close to you."

"All right. Reckon we can do that."

With such a small bed, she found it easier to face away from him. She turned over, then inched her body into his. Normally, they each kept to their own side with a large gap between them. Not easy in such a tiny space.

She could've sworn he trembled. His warm breath covered her neck.

"This is nice," she whispered. He draped his arm over her waist, so she took his hand and kissed his fingers.

His breathing grew heavier. "Beth," he rasped. "I d-don't think I can do this. I w-want ya too much."

His words warmed her from the inside out. "Then take me. I'm your wife." She shifted onto her back. As she did so, his hand brushed across her breast. He jerked it to himself.

"N-No. I c-can't." He turned over and faced the other direction.

Tears pooled in her eyes. "Merry Christmas, George."

"Merry Christmas."

His body stilled.

She stared into the darkness. She knew he loved her, but fear kept him from showing it. Not knowing anything about lovemaking, she didn't have the confidence to make the first move. *Whatever that might be.* She worried if they waited too long, it'd never happen.

Having a husband wasn't what she'd expected. Her list of worries had grown by leaps and bounds.

With a sigh, she closed her eyes.

* * *

Claire hadn't laughed so much in a long time. With a child growing inside her, happiness filled her heart.

Alicia had invited them for Christmas dinner, and they'd all eaten their fill. The children talked endlessly about the pageant they'd soon be attending at the Baptist church. Jenny had been chosen to play the part of Mary in the presentation of the nativity story. Samuel would also be in the production as a shepherd.

"I'm still not certain 'bout attendin' your church," Claire said as Alicia poured her a cup of coffee.

"Now, Miss Claire," Alicia said. "We all worship the same God. White or colored, He don't care."

"That's right," Andrew said. "No one will mind our being there. Many of them have already met you—"

"An' everyone loves *Doc*," Alicia said, jumping in. "So stop worryin'. Mind that baby inside ya."

Claire rubbed her hands over her flat stomach. The child had barely begun to grow, but it was there. And already loved.

Andrew had become overly attentive since she'd told him the news. He'd always charmed her, but now even more so. Sharing this with him felt wonderful.

"Are you warm enough?" he asked as he helped her into the wagon. He followed his question by draping a heavy quilt over her lap.

"I'm fine." Christmas cheer kept her smiling.

He passed Michael into her arms. He held a candy stick in his tiny hand that had fortunately not yet made its way to his mouth. Otherwise he'd be a sticky mess. He seemed more interested in the bright color of the thing.

Alicia's children settled down into the back of the wagon —all but Betsy, who Alicia held on her lap. They sat to one side of Claire and Andrew hopped up on the other.

Betsy tried to grab Michael's candy stick.

"No child," Alicia said. "That ain't yours."

"Mine," Michael said and pulled it against him. His little face scrunched together as he shifted his body away from Betsy.

Claire couldn't help but laugh. "He knows so few words. Funny which ones mean so much to a child."

Alicia chuckled. "Don't fret. When you has your new baby, he'll learn out how to share."

It would be one of the many lessons she'd have to teach them. *Them.* She cuddled into Andrew, happier than anyone should be allowed.

Approaching the small church, music filled the air.

"Are we late?" Claire asked.

"No," Alicia replied. "Some a the folks comes early to sing. Nice, ain't it?"

"It's beautiful."

After parking the wagon, Andrew took Michael, then helped Claire down.

Her hand instantly shot to her mouth, and an old habit kicked in.

"I thought you stopped doing that," Andrew said. Unfortunately, he'd noticed her nail biting.

With a gulp, she folded her hands in front of herself. "I did. But, I've not felt this nervous in some time. They love *you*, but they scarcely know me."

"You're my family. They'll love you, too." With Michael in one arm, he draped the other over her shoulder. "Merry Christmas, Claire."

"Merry Christmas." Safe in his arms, she smiled.

He winked.

Excited laughter surrounded them as the children raced into the church. Jenny and Samuel ran off to get ready for their play.

As Claire and Andrew walked in, several folks wished them "Merry Christmas." Met by smiles and accepting nods, Claire's fears vanished.

They sat near the middle of the crowded church. In many ways, it reminded her of her church back home on the bay. Simple wood pews. A large cross at the front over a small wooden altar. And rows of windows that lined the walls. It even smelled the same. Earthy and fresh.

The minister came out and greeted everyone, then offered up prayer. They prayed to the same God and read from the same Bible.

Alicia had been right, the color of their skin made no difference to God. They celebrated the birth of Jesus, and joy covered Claire.

Thank you, God.

The play started and the congregation fell silent, attentive to the children. Jenny was a lovely Mary, and the young boy who played the part of Joseph seemed genuinely fond of her. There seemed to be a spark between them— not just acting.

"Mmm, mmm," Alicia mumbled, shaking her head.

"Jenny's growin' up," Claire whispered, leaning into her.

"Not shore I likes it. Worse yet, look at Clay." Alicia jerked her head to the side.

The boy was sitting with a group of young adults. He sat up tall and proud with a girl to each side. His broad grin showed how much he was enjoying their attention.

"He's just like his daddy," Alicia whispered.

Andrew leaned over the top of Claire. "I heard you," he softly said with a smile. "You should be proud of Clay. I know Elijah would be."

"I am," Alicia said. "Just wish the boy wadn't such a charmer. Lijah charmed me, an' I knows where it can lead."

With a grin, Andrew sat back.

Applause filled the church as the play ended and the children took their bows. Jenny held little baby Jesus—an infant one of the young mothers had bravely offered for the occasion. It didn't cry or even whimper throughout the performance.

Joshua stood and pointed. "Baby Jesus done real good, Mama!" He yelled so loud, everyone heard and broke into laughter.

Befuddled, Joshua looked around the congregation. "Well, he did!" The laughter grew even stronger, and the boy puffed up, seemingly having realized he'd made an impression.

Alicia pulled him onto her lap, then kissed his cheek. "Yes, he did. An' you be shore an' tell your brother an' sister they done good, too."

"I will, Mama." His grin reminded Claire of Clay's. Bright and beautiful.

The lanterns around the perimeter of the church were dimmed. A large woman stepped forward in front of the altar holding a single flickering candle. After taking a large breath, she began to sing "Silent Night."

Everyone joined in. Love blanketed the small building and all the folks in it.

"Her voice is lovely," Claire whispered to Andrew.

He nodded. "I know her. I'll introduce you when the service is over."

On the final verse, the woman walked slowly down the aisle toward the door. Everyone followed her, and the service ended.

Once outside, more Christmas greetings were shared. Then the woman who'd sung bustled over to them and hugged Andrew.

"Doc! It's good to see ya!"

"You, too, Izzy!"

Claire had Michael in her arms and took her place beside her husband. She smiled at the enthusiastic woman.

Andrew beamed. "Izzy, this is my wife, Claire, and Michael . . ." He swallowed hard as though suddenly uncomfortable. "My son."

Izzy stared at them, but not in a rude way. "It's might fine to meet you, Miss Claire." She brushed Michael's cheek. "I can tell he's yours, Doc. Looks just like ya."

Her brows started to weave. She, too, looked ill at ease.

Andrew cleared his throat. "So . . . have you heard from Victoria?"

Claire finally made the connection. No wonder she seemed uneasy. Andrew's revelation of a son had to have upset the entire family.

Izzy looked at the ground. "Ain't heard from her in some time. She sent a telegram a ways back. Said she was fine. Seems your daddy has a nice big house." She huffed. "Figgered she'd come home for Christmas. Don't know when she be comin' home."

"I know you miss her," Andrew said. "I'm sure she'll visit soon. Her parents must miss her, too."

"They does. Things ain't the same with her gone." Izzy's joyful spirit disappeared.

Claire decided to change the subject. "Miss Izzy, you have a lovely voice."

"Thank ya." She lifted her head. "Was a real nice service, wadn't it?"

"Yes, very nice," Andrew said.

Claire nodded her agreement.

Izzy grinned. "First time in a colored church?"

Claire laughed. "Yes. How'd you know?"

Without answering, Izzy kept grinning and shook her head. "Hope you come back again. Merry Christmas."

Claire instantly liked her. "Merry Christmas, Izzy."

She walked away with her head held high. Seemed her Christmas spirit had returned.

Andrew gave Claire a squeeze. "You were gracious. Thank you."

"Why wouldn't I be? She's a kind woman. 'Specially the way she reacted to Michael. She didn't judge us."

He kissed her forehead, then brushed a hand over Michael's head. "No one judged us here."

Claire gazed at the beautiful little church. She had a feeling she'd be back.

"You get your tail in that wagon!" Alicia yelled, drawing their attention.

With his head hung low, Clay raced past them with his mama on his heels.

Alicia came to a stop beside them with a huff. "Now I gots even more to worry 'bout."

"What happened?" Andrew asked.

"That boy . . ." Eyes blazing with anger, Alicia shook her finger at his long-gone figure. "I couldn't find 'im. Looked everywhere. Know where he was?" Her eyes widened. "Behind the church with one a them girls!"

"I see," Andrew said in his calm doctor mode. Claire nearly busted.

"I see? That all you has to say?"

"Well, you said it earlier. He's like Elijah. Knows how to charm them."

"He was charmin' with his lips!" She fisted her hands on her hips.

"Well—"

"Don't you say it, Doc! Not one word. You's a man. Don't defend my boy."

Claire covered her mouth to keep from laughing. Between Alicia's overly animated gestures and the dumbfounded look covering Andrew's face, it was hard not to.

Mumbling, Alicia walked away. They followed her to the wagon and found the rest of the children waiting. Little Betsy was sound asleep in Jenny's arms.

"Mama?" Clay stood up behind Alicia, who'd taken her seat at the front of the wagon.

"Not one word," Alicia said, holding up her hand.

"But she's real nice, Mama."

Alicia whipped around to face him. "Nice? Nice girls don't sneak off with boys behind a church!"

Jenny giggled and received her own reprimanding look.

"What's so funny?" Samuel asked. "An' why are ya mad, Mama?"

"I's mad cuz your brother done sumthin' he shouldn't."

"What'd he do?"

"Never you mind. Just don't you grow up. Hear me?"

Samuel shrugged and said no more.

Claire had remained quiet. She squeezed Andrew's arm and he grinned. Feeling the need to once again lighten the mood, she began singing "Jingle Bells." Everyone joined in except Alicia and Clay. It took them until the third time through before they added their voices. By the time they arrived at their house, everyone was smiling again.

Michael had discovered the real purpose of his candy stick on the way home, so Claire had to wash all the stickiness off him before putting him to bed. When she and Andrew finally snuggled together beneath the quilts in their own bed, she felt completely at peace.

Andrew rubbed his hand over her belly.

"That feels wonderful," she said.

"*You* feel wonderful." He circled her stomach with his finger. "I'm glad you enjoyed tonight. I thought you would."

"I truly did. It reminded me of my old church." She giggled. "Alicia's gonna have a time with Clay, isn't she?"

"He's becoming a man. Eventually, we all do. Us *men*." His low chuckle heated the air around them.

"I'm glad a that." She gasped when his hand moved further up her body, then melted into a contented sigh. "Would you like your other present, Andrew?"

"Hmm . . . I have another one?"

Her breath hitched. His fingers had begun to tease.

"I think you found it." She grasped him tight and kissed him deeply. "I love you, Andrew. I've never been happier."

"Me, too. Merry Christmas."

"Merry Christmas."

He took full possession of the gift she'd readily give him on *any* day of the year.

CHAPTER 34

John brushed a light dusting of snow from his shoulders before entering the house.

He'd left work early for two reasons. One, it allowed a brief romp with Emilie before heading home, and two, he needed to arrive at his own residence in plenty of time to prepare for their guests. Their annual Christmas party rivaled the Halloween Ball. And, with any luck, he'd find a way to sneak off with Emilie again. He couldn't seem to get enough of her.

Even with James in town, they'd managed to continue their affair. In many ways, it intensified their passion. Fear of being caught always made ones blood pump a little harder.

He chuckled. *Emilie likes it pumping hard.*

However, even more important than dallying with his former maid, his guest list included someone he needed to impress. Not another love-smitten female, but a businessman with deep pockets. Raymond Wilson owned a large shipping yard, and John intended to approach the man in regard to financially backing him on his quest for the senate. Wilson had two sons interested in studying law. Offering to apprentice them could be the key to attaining some of the money he needed.

Winning a senate seat in Connecticut oftentimes required putting a bit of *influence* into the hands of members of the General Assembly. Ultimately, they elected the senators. Aside from money, Raymond Wilson had friends in high places.

The thought cast away every trace of the chill that had covered him moments ago. A sly smile covered his lips.

Money.

Power.

Women.

What more could he want from life?

"John! You're home!" Victoria floated across the room, still in a simple day dress. "Want some cocoa? Jean-Pierre made the best I've ever tasted."

"Hello, Victoria." He gave her a peck on the cheek. "No cocoa. I believe I'd rather have a brandy." He headed for the parlor, and his wife stayed at his heels. "Shouldn't you be getting dressed?"

"I'll need help with my corset. Willie went home early since she has to come back to work tonight."

He poured a brandy at the bar, then raised it in silent salute to the masterpiece on the wall, ignoring the one behind him. He drank it down, then leaned closer to the painting. After studying it for a few moments, he looked at his wife and grinned.

"Why are you lookin' at me like that?"

"You *were* cold that day, weren't you?"

She tipped her head to one side and got that innocent confusion on her face that had charmed him when he'd first met her. "Y-es."

"It's obvious." He gestured to the fine work of art. "Such a gifted painter. Signor Gaspari captured you right down to every *pointed* detail." He smirked and refilled his glass.

Victoria smacked his arm. "That's not funny."

"Oh, simmer down. You know you love the attention. I enjoy looking at you. It should make you happy I've not tired of you yet."

Her lower lip protruded. "Stop teasin' me. We've only been married seven months. You'd best not be tired of me."

"None of that now," he said, tapping her mouth. "Go and get ready. I know how long it takes you."

Her expression instantly changed to that of a well-trained seductress. Thanks to his lessons, of course. She batted her eyes. "Why don't you come up to our room and help me undress?"

He pulled his watch from his pocket. "Not enough time for play, my dear."

"Not even sumthin' quick?" She ran her hand over his chest, then glided her lips along his neck.

"No." He drew her close and kissed her. The least he could do. "We'd end up hot and sweaty. I need you fresh and beautiful tonight. If all goes as I've planned, our future will be secured."

"Fine. But I'll expect you to ravish me after the party." She blinked a few times, then sighed. "I'll go now. Come up in a few minutes to help with my corset."

He nodded, then gave her a heavy-handed smack on her rump as she walked away. She looked over her shoulder and twirled her tongue around her lips. The girl had developed impeccable talent.

Most men would be satisfied bedding only her, but he prided himself in being nothing like ordinary men. His insatiable appetite had to be fed, and he needed variety.

* * *

Though disappointed that John dismissed her advances, Victoria had a plan, and he'd already gotten a good start on making it happen. He'd begun to drink. If the night went as she hoped, he'd be drunk enough to forget his ungodly rubber device, and sober enough to do the necessary deed.

And if for some reason she conceived, how could he fault her? Especially if they'd both been partaking of the fine beverages and got a little out of hand.

Passion knows no bounds.

Conceiving a child would be her Christmas present.

John helped her with her corset and left the room. She then dressed in a red and green velvet gown, appropriate for the holiday. After tying a red bow around her neck and fluffing the large green bustle, she giggled at herself in the mirror.

I look like a Christmas present. John will enjoy unwrapping me.

Earlier, while Jean-Pierre was preparing her cocoa, she'd helped herself to a small bottle of vanilla. She dabbed a bit in her cleavage and around her neck. John loved the smell. She'd tried it out on a previous occasion and he'd told her she smelled good enough to eat.

She grinned. Hopefully tonight it would work its magic.

Ready to face their guests, she glided down the stairway. John was waiting at the bottom. He extended his hand, looking dashing in his black suit. He even wore a red string tie.

"We make quite the pair, don't we, John?" She batted her eyes and took his hand.

"Quite." He gave her a simple kiss on the cheek. "You look exquisite. Remember to behave yourself tonight."

"I always do." She bit her lower lip. "Except with *you*."

He cast an expression she'd grown to love. One that promised more to come.

I'll get my Christmas present one way or another.

The thought increased her excitement. This could turn out to be the best night of her life.

Lovely music filtered in from the ballroom. They'd hired a pianist for the party. The grand piano had never sounded better.

As their guests arrived, they greeted them at the door. They'd had so many parties, this had become a routine she looked forward to. It excited her to no end, being the center of attention.

Her exhilaration slumped when they opened the door for Emilie and James. Partly due to the way John lit up like the Christmas tree they'd erected in the ballroom. He eyed Emilie like he'd never seen her before.

Snowflakes graced her dark hair, then melted in the warmth of the room. James removed her coat, and Victoria waited eagerly wondering what lay beneath it.

Her jealousy flared. Emilie's crushed velvet green gown was dotted with a white snowflake pattern and fit her petite body like a glove. With her hair cascading down around her shoulders, she looked elegant. *Too* elegant for Victoria's liking.

"I see you have your hair down as well," Emilie said in her annoying French accent. "To keep you warm, no?"

"Yes," Victoria said, forcing her best smile. "I haven't gotten used to the cold weather. Especially the snow. We didn't have it in Mobile." She glanced at her husband, whose eyes covered Emilie like a cloak. Victoria linked her arm into his. "Of course, I have John to keep me warm every night."

He raised a single brow. "Yes, Victoria, you have me." He patted her hand like a child, then shifted his eyes again to his former housemaid.

James placed his arm around Emilie's shoulders. "Are you cold, my dear?"

"Not now." Emilie cuddled close to him. "Shall we go get even warmer by the fire?"

"That would suit me." James nodded politely to John, then smiled at Victoria. "We'll see you both later. Thank you for having us. You always throw a splendid party."

"We're *happy* to have you," John said, looking at Emilie.

Victoria wanted to slap him, but remained calm. There were other ways to lash out. "Emilie, you must try some of Jean-Pierre's pastries. You could use more meat on your bones."

John's brows dipped low. "Emilie is small-framed. I think she looks marvelous."

Not what Victoria wanted to hear. "Maybe so. However, I believe she looks rather thin." She cocked her head to one side, smiling all the while at the girl. "No offense, but I don't believe it's healthy bein' so small. I'm simply lookin' out for you."

Emilie met her gaze. "*You* obviously love Jean-Pierre's food, no?"

"Yes, I do."

"It shows." Emilie smiled broader than she had since she arrived. She then took James' hand and led him away.

Fuming, Victoria jerked on John's arm. "Did she insinuate that I'm fat?"

John laughed. "Perhaps. But I believe she was defending herself." He lifted her hand and gave it a kiss. "Emilie's not as endowed as you are, my dear."

Victoria looked down at her exceptional bosom. He was right. More than likely, Emilie was jealous of *her*. "But, I'm not *fat*, am I?"

"No. Now, let it go and enjoy yourself. Forget about Emilie."

She did just that. She avoided the woman and focused on their other guests.

Throughout the evening, she pranced around the ball-room and entertained nearly every man in attendance. The desire in their eyes proved there was nothing wrong with her body. Desire turned to raw lust after they visited the parlor. *Imagine that.*

Along with an abundance of food, alcohol flowed aplenty. She'd grown fond of champagne. When John wasn't looking, she'd indulge. She limited herself to three glasses, but should've stopped at two.

She stumbled into John. He wrenched her arm tight and forced her to the side of the room.

"Do I have to remind you that there are important people here tonight?" he hissed in a whisper. "Don't make a fool of yourself."

"I'm sorry. I had a bit too much to drink."

"Go to the kitchen and have Jean-Pierre make you some coffee. Sit there until your head clears." He shook her arm, his anger burning into her. "Do you understand me?"

"Yes."

He jerked his head toward the kitchen and walked away.

I know. I'm goin'.

Dizzy, she had to force herself to remain upright. But she managed to make it to the kitchen and found Jean-Pierre hard at work.

"Coffee?" she said, plopping down into a chair by the small table at the window.

Without saying a word, he grinned and began preparing the pot.

She stared outside into pitch darkness.

I wonder what Mama an' Daddy are doin' right now.

They'd always made Christmas special. Aside from the numerous presents under the tree, she loved going to Christmas Mass.

Feeling a little homesick, she sighed.

Emilie walked in, taking her from her memories. Victoria sat as rigidly upright as she could.

Unfortunately, the girl crossed the room to her. "Victoria, I'm sorry if I upset you earlier."

What?

Sincerity filled the girl's large eyes. Maybe she'd misjudged her. Being jealous hadn't benefited Victoria. It only made her stomach ill. "It's all right. I shouldn't have said what I did."

"Think nothing of it." Emilie smiled, then glanced around the room. "I came for some water."

Jean-Pierre stopped what he was doing and poured her a glass.

"*Merci.*" After a few sips, Emilie turned to Victoria. "Why are *you* in here? You should be out enjoying the party."

Victoria looked away. "I had too much champagne. John told me to rest a spell and have some coffee."

"Oh. *I* cannot drink champagne. I . . ."

"Yes?" Victoria watched her, newly intrigued.

"I shouldn't say, but . . ." Emilie placed her hands over her tiny belly. "James and I are trying to have a baby. If I'm with child, alcohol would not be good for it."

Victoria now had reason to be genuinely jealous. Emilie would have what *she* wanted. She pushed a smile onto her lips. "I understand. That's . . . *wonderful.*"

"*Merci.* I hope by this time next year, I will have a baby." Emilie's hands encircled the invisible infant. "Maybe soon you and John will start *your* family."

Victoria moistened her lips. "Yes. Soon."

Emilie drank down the remaining water in her glass and handed it to Jean-Pierre. "*Merci*, Jean-Pierre." The two exchanged an interesting glance. One Victoria couldn't decipher. "I am sorry you had to listen to women's conversation."

Before walking out, Emilie nodded to Victoria, who remained seated, unmoving. Their conversation had a sobering effect and her head started to clear.

Why should a simple housemaid get what I deserve?

Her plan had to work. Otherwise, she'd have to take drastic measures.

* * *

John guided Raymond Wilson into the parlor. In the short time he'd known the man, he was certain he'd appreciate Victoria's painting.

Though Raymond was younger than John and had kept himself fit, his wife, Charlotte, was anything but. The woman had premature wrinkles and because of her fondness for pastries had become twice the size of her husband. By all accounts she was jovial, but not someone John would want in *his* bed.

The man stared at the portrait. "Doesn't it bother you having other men see your wife this way?"

John let out a laugh, then opened a box of cigars. He offered one to Raymond, who gladly took it. After lighting it for him, John lit up his own. He took a long drag, then blew the smoke out toward the painting. "It pleases me to share her. *Visually,* that is." He cast a quick glance at Raymond. *I know what you're thinking.* "I'd never allow her to be shared physically. I keep *that* to myself."

"You're an interesting man, John," Raymond said. His eyes remained focused on the portrait. "A man of your character and intellect would be a great benefit to the senate. Would you seriously consider it?"

The small hint John had made earlier paid off. Now, he needed to seal the deal. "Yes, I would. But as you know, it takes ties and money to get a man into politics. *And,* we both know you're a successful and *connected* man."

Raymond's head slowly rotated to face him. "Say no more. I have a proposition for you."

"I'm listening." This was turning out even better than he'd planned. The man would believe this to be *his* idea. John motioned to two leather chairs in the corner of the room. "Why don't we get comfortable?"

They sat and John leaned back in his chair, feigning calm. His heart beat hard and his palms sweat, anticipating the amount of money the man could bestow on him.

Raymond also eased into a chair, casually blowing smoke from his cigar. "As you know, my sons are studying law. Randall will finish his classes in the spring and hopes to pass his exams. However, he's been preoccupied with a young woman. His head hasn't been in his *books*." Raymond nodded toward Victoria's painting. "No need to further explain." He inhaled deeply. "Fine cigar by the way. Thank you."

John chuckled. "I understand perfectly. And, you're welcome. I'm glad you're enjoying it."

"So . . ." Raymond leaned forward. "Here's my proposition. Take my son into your law firm as an apprentice. Teach him what he needs to know so he can pass the bar. Do that and I'll give you what you need."

A game had never been so easily played.

Raymond's eyes narrowed. "Buckingham's term will be up in seventy-five. We need a good Republican to take his place." He leaned back, but then jerked upright again. "There's one other thing."

"Yes?"

"My younger son, Robert, has two more years of school. I'd like you to employ him over the summer. I have high hopes for him. His head is much clearer than his brother's." He let out a long breath. "So, what do you say?"

John extended his hand. "I'd say we have a deal."

They vigorously shook hands in a gentleman's agreement.

Raymond stood. "I'd best get back to my wife. She'll be missing me by now. I'm sure I'll find her at the food table."

With a heavy sigh, he walked closer to the painting. "You're a fortunate man, John. I wish my wife looked like *her.*"

John stood beside him. "Trust me. I know I'm fortunate. Even more so than you could imagine."

"We'll need good fortune when it's time for the elections." He patted John hard on the back. "I'll be in touch regarding my sons. Randall will be picking us up this evening. I'll be sure to introduce you." He extinguished his cigar and left the parlor.

Elated, John pounded his fist on the bar. "Yes!"

He'd gotten everything tonight he'd hoped for, except the tryst with Emilie. But since he'd already had her once today, he let it go. The deal he'd just made would get him into the proper channels for his senate bid. He'd wanted this for years. He'd follow in Lincoln's footsteps, possibly all the way to the White House.

Tall and proud, he returned to the ballroom. He spotted Emilie leaning against the piano. *Stunning.* Her new stature as an attorney's wife suited her. Oddly, he was glad she'd married James. It had changed her. Made her even more desirable.

I'll have you again soon.

"John . . ." Victoria whispered in his ear, startling him from his carnal thoughts. She'd come up behind him and wrapped her arms around his waist. "I'm much better now. Forgive me?"

He shifted around to face her. *My beautiful wife.* The woman every man wanted. "Yes. I forgive you. Nothing can ruin this evening. Even you." He kissed the tip of her nose.

"What's that supposed to mean?"

"I'll tell you later. I have fabulous news. For now, tend to our guests. I believe I could use a drink. I'm in the mood!" He swatted her behind and returned to the parlor.

* * *

Victoria tittered.

Yes, John, drink plenty.

She had two things going for her. Not only was he consuming alcohol, but she hadn't seen him so happy in quite a while. He'd even forgiven her for indulging too much. Tonight's success looked promising.

As the evening drew to a close, she and John returned to the front door to bid everyone goodnight. With the New Year approaching, John had 1874 calendars made for their guests. He'd said he wanted everyone to leave with a favorable impression.

When James and Emilie left, not only did they get a calendar, but John also gave Emilie a look that reignited a tinge of jealousy.

Why is he so enthralled with her? I'm more woman than she'll ever be.

She'd show him soon enough.

Oh, my. There's that woman who tried to eat all *of the food.*

She'd met Charlotte Wilson earlier, but hadn't been impressed and spent almost no time with her. Her husband, on the other hand, had whisked Victoria around the floor more than once.

"Thank you so much for the splendid party," Charlotte said, cackling. "I'd love to steal your cook. He's exceptional!"

"You're more than welcome, Mrs. Wilson," Victoria said in her most charming voice. "I hope you'll come to our next affair."

"With pleasure. And please, call me *Charlotte*."

"Of course. *Charlotte*."

John draped his arm over Victoria's shoulders. "We're grateful you came tonight."

"If our son doesn't arrive soon," Mr. Wilson said, "we may have to spend the night." He chuckled, then motioned to their large grandfather clock. "I thought I'd taught him to be punctual."

Knock. Knock.

John opened the door to the timely rap.

Victoria's heart thumped. A tall, dark-haired handsome man stood in their doorway. Someone closer in age to her than anyone she'd seen all night.

He looks a bit like Andrew.

"Robert?" Mr. Wilson said, frowning. "I thought Randall was coming. I wanted to introduce him to Mr. Martin."

"No," Robert said. "We were playing poker and I lost a bet. So, *I* had to come. Sorry, Father."

Mr. Wilson huffed. "My boys. Always betting on one thing or another." He shook his head, then motioned Robert inside. "John, this is my younger son, Robert. His mother's pride and joy." He gestured to his son. "Robert, this is Mr. Martin, the attorney I spoke to you about."

"Call me John." He extended his hand. "Seems we'll be working together this summer."

Robert pumped his hand hard. "I see. So I take it Father has spoken to you about me." The young man's smile lit up the room and sent shocks of electricity through every inch of Victoria's body.

"Yes," John said. "He's told me how capable you are. I can teach you many things if you're willing to listen and learn."

Capable? I'm sure he is.

She licked her lips only to find Robert watching her. She cleared her throat.

"Oh, forgive me darling," John said. He took her hand and gently pulled her forward. Right in front of their gorgeous guest. "This is my wife, Victoria."

She extended her hand and Robert took it. She had to concentrate to steady the rate of her breathing.

"I'm pleased to meet you, ma'am." He shook her hand. Not like he'd done John's, but she'd expected something else. Their eyes momentarily locked.

"Your first lesson," John said. "When you make the acquaintance of a fine woman such as my wife, it's customary to *kiss* her hand." Robert's cheeks glowed red. "Perhaps the next time you meet."

"Shame on you, John," Victoria teased. "You shouldn't embarrass him. I'm happy to meet you, Robert." *More than you realize.*

"Well, then . . ." Raymond said. "We'd best be going. I believe my wife's tired."

With a loud yawn, Charlotte nodded.

As they walked away, Robert looked over his shoulder, and once again met Victoria's gaze. Heat rushed through her veins. The kind she used to feel with John.

John pushed the door shut, then grabbed her and lifted her off the ground. "I'm a happy man!" She giggled as he spun her in a circle. "Raymond Wilson is one of the wealthiest men in Bridgeport! Do you know what that means?"

He slowly lowered her to the floor. "No, I don't." Swept up in his elation, she laughed at his enthusiasm.

"My dear, your husband is going to be a senator!" He wrenched her tight against him, then kissed her deeply. The kiss lasted a great length of time, and his hands started to wander.

"John . . ." She came up for air. "Why don't we have some champagne and toast your good fortune?"

With an explosive laugh, he picked her up and carried her to the ballroom. After grabbing an open bottle, he headed for the stairs. "Let's take it to our room."

He flung her onto the bed, then downed a large portion of champagne directly from the bottle. "Who needs glasses?" he said, wiggling the bottle in front of her. "Have at it, my dear!"

She complied and took a large drink. "But, you know how I get."

"Yes, I do." He sat on the edge of the bed. "Since we're alone, drink your fill. I'll watch." Smiling slyly, he jiggled his brows.

She swallowed more, but not as much as before. She had to keep her wits. "Here. You have some." She handed it to him, then began to undress.

I need to get him where I want him.

"It's been a fine Christmas, hasn't it John?" She enticed him with her eyes, then forced his gaze downward. She showed him what Emilie never could.

"Getting finer all the time," he groaned. He set the bottle on the night stand, then started taking his clothes off. He appeared to be in a hurry.

His body wavered, and he stumbled while removing his trousers, then flopped down onto the bed, laughing.

Good.

Free of everything but what God had given them, she climbed atop him. In his condition, he needed all the help he could get. She kissed him with urgent need, and received the response she desired. He entered her free of the wretched device.

She moved with skill, hoping to make his release quick.

"Oh, yes, John," she rasped. "You feel so good." The instant she said the words, his entire body went rigid.

The champagne had made her loose-lipped. Why hadn't she just kept her mouth shut?

He shoved her to the side. "What have you done?" he screamed. "You purposely did this! Thank God I didn't finish!"

She reached for him. "I'd never do such a thing. Can't we just once do it this way? It's so much better."

He slapped her hard across the face. "How dare you!"

She hadn't seen it coming. The sting erased every ounce of passion. It brought tears to her eyes. "I'm sorry." Unable to help herself, she cried.

Showing no sign of mercy, he stood and threw on his clothes. "I'm going out. I can't even look at you right now!" He stormed from the room.

The front door slammed and she jumped.

He'll never forgive me.

Sobbing, she lay her head down on the pillow and cried herself to sleep.

* * *

Damn Victoria.

John tightened the scarf around his neck. The cold night air stung his face and the snow fell heavily around him.

The night had been perfect and then she had to ruin it.

He couldn't go to Emilie. She and James were likely hard at it.

And she's probably thinking about me.

He grinned at the thought. At least Emilie knew her place.

Luckily, he knew who'd see him. Someone who undoubtedly needed a little Christmas cheer. He walked briskly to the brothel. This time of night he had no worries of being seen going in. Nellie Flannigan would be waiting. And if for some reason she had a customer, he'd throw him out in the snow.

She'll be mine for the night.

He'd had her many times. Aside from being a paid whore, the woman had similarities to his wife. Irish, with long red hair, and a hunger for physical gratification. She claimed he was her favorite.

He'd rather spend the remainder of the holiday with a woman who appreciated him, than with one who'd betrayed him.

He intended to pay her well.

CHAPTER 35

Victoria awoke with a headache and an empty bed. No husband. No one.

Where could he have gone on Christmas night? The thought troubled her.

He'd been so angry—not to mention *intoxicated*—that she feared for him. He could be lying in a ditch somewhere.

Her thoughts turned to her dreams. They were as unclear as her mind had been when she'd fallen asleep, but one image remained. *Robert Wilson.*

Knowing she had to cast all thoughts of him aside, she set her mind on her husband. The sun had been up for hours. Maybe he'd slept in one of their other rooms.

She put on a gown and robe, then wandered down the hallway. The empty rooms glared back at her. With a sigh, she went down the stairs to the kitchen.

"*Bonjour, madame*," Jean-Pierre said. "What would you like to eat?"

"Nothin' right now."

"Coffee?"

"All right." She sat at the little table and waited. In no time at all, he placed a cup in front of her.

"Cream and sugar, just as you like it." He smiled, then returned to the stove.

She sipped at the drink, but honestly hated it. She only drank it because John told her it was appropriate. "Jean-Pierre, I'd rather have cocoa."

"Very well."

The front door slammed. "Never mind," Victoria said and rushed to the entryway.

John stood there, emotionless, dusting snow from his shoulders.

"John! I was so worried." She embraced him, but he didn't move. Anger seeped from his body into hers.

Releasing him, she stepped away. "I'm—I'm sorry for what I did. I just wanted you so badly . . ." Tears returned. She couldn't stop them.

He blinked slowly several times, his body as stiff as ever. "What you did was shameful. I trusted you, and you be-trayed me. I'll *never* trust you again."

No.

"John, I swear to you, it won't happen again. You can trust me." She stared into his eyes, pleading.

He grunted. "I don't take kindly to trickery. You knew exactly what you were doing. I shan't have you again until I believe you deserve my attention." His nostrils flared, and he glared at her.

"But—"

He held up his hand. "Not another word." He pushed past her and headed toward the kitchen. "I'm hungry," he mumbled and disappeared from view.

Heartsick and broken, Victoria trudged up the stairs. Once in her room, she shut the door and lay down on the bed. With the tips of her fingers, she massaged her temples, attempting to ease the pain. But nothing could erase the ache in her heart.

She'd been jealous of Emilie for all the wrong reasons. James obviously loved her. He doted on her and looked at her with utter devotion. James wasn't handsome like John, but he knew how to love.

Maybe that's what I should've been lookin' for.

Could that be what Andrew had constantly tried to tell her?

Even if it had been wrong, she'd made her choice. She couldn't change it. She'd have to endure John and pray for forgiveness. From this point forward, she'd do her best to be the kind of wife he expected her to be.

That night when she got ready for bed, John passed by her and headed to one of the spare rooms. Thankfully he hadn't asked her to leave.

Six weeks passed. The miserable weather kept her from going outside, so she roamed the lonely house. Neither Willie nor Jean-Pierre were good at conversation. She tinkered at the piano, but even that offered little pleasure. So, she read a few books.

Loneliness became unbearable.

She missed her parents and Izzy. Writing a letter to them was out of the question. She didn't want to lie. If she said she was miserable she'd have to endure Izzy's *I told you so.*

Things *had* to get better.

Sitting at the table in the kitchen, she gazed out the window. She loved this spot. Their courtyard looked lovely covered in fluffy white snow.

But the pit in her stomach grew. In six days she'd be twenty. Unlikely John would recognize her birthday.

"Good morning, darling," John said and kissed her on the cheek.

She gasped, and when she looked at Jean-Pierre, he, too, appeared surprised.

Victoria swallowed hard. "Good mornin'." She cowered, fearing to be struck.

He bent down and embraced her, then dotted her neck with tiny kisses. "I believe I'll join you in bed this evening. It's time." Releasing her, he took the seat across from her. "Jean-Pierre, I'd love some coffee."

"*Oui, monsieur.*" Jean-Pierre dipped his head.

Victoria found it difficult to breathe. She tentatively watched her husband, waiting for him to lash out.

He folded his hands atop the table. "You seem uptight, my dear. Are you unwell?"

She looked into his eyes. *No malice.* He acted as if nothing had happened. "You haven't spoken to me in weeks. Why now?"

"Did you miss me?"

"Course I missed you. I've been lonely." Thinking she might cry again, she inhaled deeply.

"Good. My intention was to teach you a lesson." He spoke down to her like a child.

"So . . . you forgive me?'

"Of course. You're my wife, and I love you." He leaned across the table, then took her chin in his hand and kissed her.

All she could afford him was a weak smile. "Thank you, John."

He sat back. "Now. No more tears. We need to plan a birthday party." He patted both of his hands on the table. "Jean-Pierre, could you throw something together with only a week to plan?"

"*Oui*. I would love to."

Could it be true? "A party for me? Oh, John!" She jumped from her chair, wrapped her arms around him, and kissed his cheek. "Thank you!"

"You're welcome, my dear. Only the best for you." He smiled warmly.

He truly does love me.

She'd been wrong to deceive him.

True to his word, he joined her in bed that night after properly placing his protection. She didn't complain.

To her delight, he ravished her for hours.

Feeling loved again, her heart rested.

CHAPTER 36

Valentine's Day.

Ugh.

Beth rested her elbow on the kitchen table, then leaned her cheek against her hand and sighed.

Her mother-in-law sat across from her, sipping coffee. George was busy outside chopping wood. Being Saturday, he didn't have to go to Henry's.

"What's wrong, Beth?" Mrs. Barnhardt asked. Her brows dipped with worry.

Beth wasn't about to tell the woman what was on her mind, so she stared at the table, preparing to lie. "I'm fine."

"Perhaps what I'm seeing is boredom. Am I right?"

In many ways she was, but would it upset her if she said so? "Maybe a *might*." She cautiously looked up.

Mrs. Barnhardt grinned. "All you need is a child to occupy your time. When that happens, you'll long for days like this."

Beth burst into tears. Blubbered like the out-of-control child she'd never have. She'd worried herself sick over what she and George *weren't* doing. This simply pushed her over the edge.

Mrs. Barnhardt moved her chair closer. "I'm sorry if I said something that upset you."

Sniffling, Beth looked at her. "You don't understand. I *can't* have a child!"

"Oh." The woman drew back. "Forgive me. George never mentioned you had a medical problem."

Beth cried even harder. Her loud sobs exceeded Mr. Barnhardt's snoring. Her mother-in-law patted her on the back. Odd, since she never touched *anyone*. "Have you seen a doctor?"

Beth breathed in short rasps, fighting the tears. "A doctor can't fix this. I can't have a child cuz we ain't done what we hafta to make one." Her tears turned into a heated flush. *I'm likely glowin' red.* She laid her head on the table, no longer able to look at the woman beside her.

"Oh, my," Mrs. Barnhardt whispered. "I see."

Having bared her soul with the ugly truth, Beth sobered and finally sat upright. "Mrs. Barnhardt, you know your son better than anyone. You know how nervous he gets." *Oh, Lordy. Just say it.* "With you and your husband in the next room, it ain't never gonna happen."

The woman's face changed color. A nice Valentine crimson to match Beth's own. "Then you and George need to get away. At least for one night." Her head dropped downward. "It's difficult to think of my son with a woman. But, you *are* his wife, and it's as God intended. It's his duty as your husband."

Duty?

Beth had never considered it that way. "I hope he *wants* to. I'm sure he loves me. Ain't he supposed to *want* to?"

Mrs. Barnhardt fanned her face. "Yes," she choked out.

The discomfort in the room made them both squirm in their chairs. But Beth had to push on. "I don't reckon George feels right 'bout leavin' y'all. Even for one night. I'd never convince him to go anywhere."

"Do you have somewhere you *could* go?"

It took Beth no time at all to think of the perfect place. Though it didn't belong to her any longer, she assumed it would be empty. "Yep. It'd take a few hours to get there from here."

"Then, it's settled. Go pack your things. Whatever you think you might need. When George comes in, I'll have a talk with him. I'll insist you go." Mrs. Barnhardt bobbed her head in a firm nod, solidifying her point.

Beth wiped her tear-streaked face with the sleeve of her dress. "Thank you . . . *Mama.*"

The woman's face brightened, no longer embarrassed, but happy. George had suggested it would be appropriate to call her that, but until now Beth hadn't felt compelled to do so.

She went to their bedroom and folded her nightclothes into a travel bag, as well as a small bottle of cologne. Her hands shook. Could she really make this happen?

She held her breath the instant the front door squeaked.

"Whew!" George exclaimed. "It's cold out there!" Wood clunked onto the floor.

Beth froze. She could hear everything going on in the other room. Inching closer to the door, she put her back to the wall beside it. She could listen without being seen.

Mr. Barnhardt grumbled when the wood hit the floor, but then immediately started snoring again. The man slept almost all the time.

"S-Sorry, Mama," George said. He spoke quieter than normal, but in the small house, his voice carried.

"George," his mama said. "We need to talk."

"Sumthin' wrong?"

"Yes. I believe you forgot today is Valentine's Day. You should do something nice for Beth."

Please, oh please.

Beth's heart pumped hard.

"Dang!" George exclaimed. She'd never heard him curse before. With wide eyes, Beth covered her mouth to keep from making a sound. "What should I do?"

"Take her on a honeymoon. You're long overdue. I told her the same thing."

"Ya did?"

"Yes. She's packing now."

And I'm fixin' to have heart failure.

"B-B-But what 'bout you an' D-Daddy?" George sounded more nervous than ever.

Is he that scared a bein' alone with me?

"We'll be fine," his mama said. *Good.* "Just come back tomorrow. We can survive for one night without you."

George's footsteps approached their room, so Beth whipped around and pretended to be packing.

He tapped her on the shoulder. "Happy Valentine's Day." *Not one single stammer.*

She turned to find his arms wide open. Moving into them, she nestled close. "Happy Valentine's Day." Safe in his embrace, his warm body gave her comfort.

"Mama says we should go away for a n-night."

"We need to, George. I just finished packin' an' I know where we can go." She lifted her head to look into his eyes.

"Let's go to the bay house where I used to live. No one will be there. We'll be all alone."

His body trembled. "All right." He gulped so hard his Adam's apple bobbed. "If that's what ya want."

She could swear she felt his heart beating against her. Thumping hard and fast. She placed a hand to his chest. "I promise it'll be all right." She raised her face for a kiss, and he obliged.

"All right, then," he said. "We'll go." He breathed so hard, she thought he'd burst. But despite his tremors, longing lay behind his eyes.

They took extra blankets and climbed into the wagon for the ride to the shore. Caught up in a mixture of excitement and worry, Beth barely spoke a word. Neither did George. He kept his eyes forward and frequently she noticed him gulp, and then cough.

It could be a very long night.

They arrived at the little house by midday. It didn't seem right opening the lock. Though she'd sent a key to Claire, she'd kept one for herself. Just in case she forgot something inside. Or maybe it was because she hadn't wanted to let it go.

She pushed the door open. "I don't care much for Claire no more, but I don't reckon she'd mind us usin' the house."

"Nope." George followed her in. He stopped and stared in the direction of the bedroom.

"I'll put our things in there," she said, and pointed to the room.

"Yep." He sat on the sofa, but then hopped right up again. "How 'bout I start a fire?"

"Why don't we take a walk on the beach first?"

"All right." He walked rigidly to the door.

Somehow, she had to make him relax.

They walked hand in hand to the place where her brother had died. The cold air stung her bare cheeks, adding to the pain of the fresh memory. She pointed to where it had happened and told George the horrible story.

As she spoke, he drew her in close. Tears welled in her eyes.

"George, I thought I'd die alone. Thought I'd lost everyone I loved. Then *you* came into my life. I don't feel alone no more." She blinked and a single tear fell down her face.

"You'll never be alone. I love ya." He kissed her. It took her breath. Then he did it again. Longer. Harder. Deeper.

"Oh, my," she rasped, coming up for air. She swallowed hard. "Let's go back to the house."

With arms around each other's waists, they walked the long pathway home.

When they got inside and closed the door, Beth pulled the window dressings shut. Light still shone through. "Wish it was dark already."

"Why?"

"I-I can't do it in the light. I don't want you to see me. It's embarrassin'."

He studied her for a brief second, then smiled. Understanding filled his eyes.

I've never been loved so much.

"Why don't I make a fire?" he asked.

She rapidly nodded, and he left to get wood.

Her stomach rumbled, reminding her they needed to eat. There were still canned goods in the pantry. Enough for her to make soup and biscuits. Bustling around in the kitchen, she finally felt like a real wife.

If only we could stay here forever.

Impossible. Mrs. Barnhardt could cope with her husband for one night, but any more than that would wear her down.

After eating, they went to the front porch and rocked. "This is nice," Beth said. Hopefully the sun would set soon.

"Yep. Real nice." He looked sideways at her and smiled.

Simply biding time.

She excused herself to the outhouse, then on the way back stopped by the graves.

How different would her life be if she'd saved Gerald instead of Claire?

I probably woulda never met George.

The thought wrenched her heart. Her mama had always told her that things happen for a reason, but having Gerald die so she could meet her husband didn't seem right. Nearly a year had passed since it happened. Searching her heart, anger was gone, replaced by hurt.

Don't think 'bout it now.

She hurried back to her husband, not wanting anything to spoil their time together.

They returned inside and she boiled water so they could wash. While George took care of his personal business, she stole away to the bedroom and retrieved the bottle of cologne from her bag. She lightly dabbed some behind her ears.

When she came out of the room, she found him gaping at her, then a look of relief flooded over him. Maybe he thought she was going to change into her bedclothes.

"You all right, George?"

"Uh-huh." He started nervously rubbing the top of his head.

She giggled. "Least you can't rub the hair off. It's already gone."

"N-Not all of it." He folded his hands in front of himself.

Bless your heart.

She crossed to him. The house had become darker. "George. Neither of us has done this before, so we're gonna learn how together. I'm nervous, too."

He closed his eyes and shook his head. "But . . . look at me." He splayed his arms wide. "I'm over forty years old, an' I ain't never had a woman. What kinda man am I?"

She put her arms around him. "One who was waitin' for me. I'm right glad you ain't never had a woman. I don't hafta worry 'bout bein' jealous. You don't have nothin' to compare me to."

His face drew tight. "What should I do?"

He'd hardly stammered at all since they'd arrived. Somehow, this was helping him in more ways than one. "Tell you what. Wait here. I'll go in the bedroom an' get ready. When I am, I'll call you in. Then . . . reckon we'll just see what happens." She turned to go, but stopped. "Oh, an' George . . . we don't hafta be quiet." She grinned.

With a pounding heart, she pulled back the covers on the bed, then undressed. Completely bare, she climbed beneath the cold sheets. She shivered and covered herself quickly with the heavy quilts. "I'm ready, George!"

Silence.

Did he leave?

"George?"

"I'm . . . I'm comin'!"

The house was completely dark. Heart thumping, she waited.

"Ouch!" George fussed. "Stubbed my toe."

She suppressed a giggle.

"Ah!" George hollered, stumbled, and fell down on top of her.

Grunting, her eyes popped wide. "Dang, George. Reckon you *are* anxious!"

She burst out laughing and he did, too. He awkwardly slid off of her and stood, then felt his way around the bed till he reached the other side. "You said we didn't hafta be quiet."

"Nope." Still giggling, she waited for the inevitable, listening to him undress. Soon, another bare body would join her.

She continued to giggle nervously. He lifted the covers and lay flat on his back.

"I'm scared," they said in unison, then both laughed uncomfortably. Their laughter died into silence, until heavy breathing overtook it.

George shifted, and Beth gasped when he rolled onto his side. So close she could feel the warmth from his body.

His hand brushed down her bare arm. "If I do anythin' that hurts, tell me."

"All right." She held her breath.

He climbed atop her.

Flesh on flesh.

Oh, Lord . . . this is really gonna happen.

It seemed he was trying to keep from putting his full weight on her. "It's fine, George. I'm a big girl. You're not hurtin' me."

His body relaxed into hers, but then he trembled, so she caressed his back to ease him.

He bent to kiss her, gasping amid his attempt. She intensified the pressure on his back, and he kissed her deeply. The movement of her hands produced a low moan from somewhere inside of him. The sensual sound affected her in a way she didn't understand, but definitely wanted more of.

"Oh, Beth," he groaned. He buried his face into her neck. "You smell good."

An' you feel amazin'.

His lips glided along her cheek, until they reached her mouth. Then he kissed her the way he had on the beach. Sparks flew.

They breathed harder and harder, until something incredible happened.

Just as Mrs. Sandborn promised, nature took hold.

Their bodies knew exactly what to do. Shaking from fear, excitement, and utter love, she opened to him. She closed her eyes, fearing pain, but it didn't happen. Just the opposite. George moved gently. Lovingly.

They let go. No longer afraid, they made sounds previously foreign to her.

He's happy.

She was beyond joy. No longer speaking, they simply felt each other. His hands roamed her body freely, and she made no objections. They were man and wife, and finally, they'd become lovers.

* * *

Beth straightened the bed, smoothing the quilt over the top and fluffing the pillows. Memories of what had happened made her heart flutter. She smiled recalling the tender way George had touched her.

They'd made love.

Love.

She touched her hand to her heart, struck with an entirely new thought.

This must be where Claire an' Dr. Fletcher made love.

Likely the very place Michael had been conceived. What if Claire really loved him?

No.

She didn't want to think about it. Claire was supposed to be in love with Gerald. She couldn't forgive her for what she'd done.

She hastily finished tidying up the house, then locked the door. George helped her into the wagon. His smile shone brighter than ever.

Their eyes locked for a brief second. It'd been a night they'd cherish forever.

They'd overslept, so it was too late to go to Sunday services, but Beth had another idea. "Let's go say hey to Mrs. Sandborn. I'd really like to see her."

"Sounds like a fine idea." George spoke smoothly and without a single hesitation.

Beth sat up tall in the seat. *I made my husband into a new man.*

Mrs. Sandborn was fit to be tied when she opened the door and saw them standing there. She shrieked with delight, then invited them in for dessert.

The scent of fresh-baked apple cobbler drifted through the air. Until that moment, Beth hadn't even thought about food. "You always did make the best cobbler in Alabama," Beth said. George pulled out a chair for her at the kitchen table. "Thank you." As she sat, she ran her hand along his arm.

He beamed and took his own seat.

"Hmm," Mrs. Sandborn said. She placed a bowl of cobbler in front of each of them. "You two seem to be doin' well. Ya look happy."

Beth looked sideways at George and grinned. "Yep. Things couldn't be better." Worried there might be other boarders within hearing, she glanced around the room. "Mrs. Sandborn," she whispered. "We finally had a honeymoon. Stayed at Claire's house last night." She gave the woman a knowing nod.

Mrs. Sandborn grabbed her hands and gave them a squeeze. "Good for you."

"This here cobbler is might fine, Mrs. Sandborn," George said. He waved his spoon in the air.

"Glad ya like it. You two are welcome anytime. An' I'm sure Claire wouldn't mind ya usin' her house. She an' Andrew asked me to watch over it. I go out there from time to time to check on things."

Beth winced. She could've gone all day without hearing their names spoken aloud.

"Beth," Mrs. Sandborn said. "One day you're gonna hafta go an' see her. *Talk* to her. Give her a chance."

"Maybe," Beth said. "But not today. Or t'morra."

Unable to look at Mrs. Sandborn's admonishing eyes, she shifted her gaze to her husband. He smiled, but concern lay behind *his* eyes. Couldn't anyone understand *why* she didn't want to talk to Claire?

Mrs. Sandborn finally sat, though she didn't eat. Luckily, she didn't bring up Claire again. Instead, they talked about Henry and how well the blacksmith shop was doing since George had started working there.

He kept pretty quiet, but Beth didn't mind. She'd always done most of the talking. Even so, things had changed. She suspected his thoughts had taken quite a turn. While munching on cobbler he was likely thinking of how he'd nibbled on *her* last night.

She giggled.

"Beth?"

She shook her head, staring at Mrs. Sandborn. "Huh?"

"Never mind. You was somewhere else right now."

George reached under the table and patted Beth's leg.

"We best be goin', Mrs. Sandborn," Beth said, standing. "Thank you for the cobbler."

After George thanked her as well, they returned to the wagon and headed for home. She snuggled close to him the entire way. Several times she caressed his leg, to let him know she was still there. He'd turn his head and grin.

You're thinkin' what I'm thinkin', I know you are . . .

Mrs. Barnhardt was waiting on the front stoop when they pulled up. "I'm glad you're home!"

George helped Beth down, but his face lost its joy. "What's wrong?"

"Karl had a terrible night. He's in a lot of pain. I'll need help getting him into the bathing tub. A good hot soak is what he needs."

"Yes, Mama." George cupped his hand over Beth's cheek. "Go on inside outta the cold. I'll settle the horses, then I'll come help with Daddy."

She gave him a sweet kiss. "I love you, George." She followed her mother-in-law into the house.

Mrs. Barnhardt had stew simmering on the stove. They quietly ate their supper, then while Beth cleaned up the dishes, George helped his mama prepare the bath.

A sense of calm swept over her. This wasn't so bad. They truly were needed here. And besides, she *belonged* here. They were her family, and this was her home.

"Thank you, Beth," Mrs. Barnhardt said, while Beth finished wiping down the table.

"I'm happy to help." They exchanged a silent smile, saying more than simple words.

When Mr. Barnhardt's water began to cool, George helped him out of the tub and into pajamas.

"I won't go away again, Daddy," George said. "But I hope ya understand. It was good we went."

"I do." The man grinned. "I was young once. A man remembers those things." He tapped a single finger to his forehead.

Beth turned away so they wouldn't see the color of her cheeks.

George helped his daddy into bed, then joined her in the living room. And like so many nights before, his mama sat across from them in a chair, reading a book.

With a heavy sigh, Beth stood from the sofa. "I'm gonna get ready for bed."

"All right," George said, and remained seated.

She couldn't help but frown as she removed her clothes and put on her gown. She got into bed and waited for her husband. Soon he'd come in and tell her goodnight, then they'd go to sleep as they always had.

It just ain't fair.

Several minutes passed. Finally, George came in, shut the door, and removed his clothing. *All* of it.

He climbed into bed beside her. "Beth?"

"Yes, George?" Her heart raced.

He pulled her to him with a passionate kiss.

"Oh, yes, George," she rasped.

Their nightly ritual had taken a very sharp turn.

CHAPTER 37

Melissa stared at the plate of perfectly cooked eggs.

"I don't see anything wrong with them," she said to April, the young waitress who'd brought them back to the kitchen because of a customer's complaint.

April's mouth twisted. "The man said they ain't done right. Said they was supposed to be over-easy. Told me to tell you, you cooked 'em too hard and he wants new eggs."

Luckily, no other orders were pressing, so Melissa took the plate from the girl and headed out to confront the customer. The second she saw him sitting at the table in the far corner of the café, she understood.

Henry Alexander. The ornery man *liked* to complain. However, after what Sylvia had told her about him, she'd decided not to be too hard on him. Still, she wouldn't have him challenging her ability to cook a proper egg.

She squared her jaw and crossed to his table, then set the plate down in front of him.

He looked up as if he was about to grin, but quickly turned it into a scowl.

So much for being nice.

"Them the same eggs I just sent back?" he asked, sneering.

With a plastered-on smile, she politely nodded.

"I don't want 'em," he grumbled. "They ain't done right."

"Have you tried them?"

"No. Don't like the way they look. I like 'em runny."

She kept her composure. "If you poke a hole in the top, I think you'll find that the centers *are* runny." She scooted the plate under his nose.

He pushed it away.

She shoved it back again.

"Fine!" He pierced the top of one of the eggs with his fork. Yellow yolk trickled from it. He chuckled and grinned.

Proud of herself for being right, she smirked. "You see? Sometimes they have to be poked to find out what they're really like."

The grin on his face grew into something slightly sinister. And then she realized what she'd said, and her face heated. *Oh, God, I want to crawl into a hole somewhere.*

Henry cleared his throat. "You *are* talkin' 'bout the eggs, ain't ya?"

"Of course I'm talking about the eggs!" Hoping to regain even an ounce of her dignity, she inhaled deeply. "If you'll excuse me, I have food to cook." She spun on her heels and hastened to the kitchen.

The nerve of that man!

He had no business flirting with her, and that's exactly what he'd just done. Flirting with someone single was one thing, but she'd led him to believe she was married. He'd stepped *way* over the line.

And why does he have to be so dad-blamed good-looking?

She shouldn't be attracted to *any* man. *No* widow should.

She plunged a long wooden spoon into the pot of oats. Taking out her frustration, she nearly stirred them to death.

April tapped her on the shoulder. "Missy," she said, rolling her eyes. "That man wants a word with ya."

Great. "More complaints about the food?"

"Don't know."

Melissa set down the spoon, then grabbed a towel and wiped her sweaty hands. With a huff, she went to Henry's table. "Yes?"

The man leaned back in his chair and comfortably locked his hands behind his head. *Some nerve.* "I was just wonderin' 'bout sumthin'."

His ease only made her more nervous. "What?" She shifted her legs back and forth, then started tapping her right foot.

He looked her over from head to toe. "You all right?"

"I'm fine. What do you want to know?"

"I'm curious as to what kind a man would let his wife work so much. I seen you in here often. A woman should be home takin' care of her family. It's a man's job to provide."

She studied his face. No foolery this time. Even his tone sounded sincere. But what would she say? *Just tell him the truth.* "Mr. Alexander? That is your name, isn't it?"

"Yes'm. But you can call me Henry."

"*Henry.* I'm afraid I misled you before. I had a husband, but he died. I don't have a family any longer—that is—I *do* have a sister and *her* family, but I lost mine. So no, there isn't anyone who would mind my working so much. I *have* to." She blew out a long breath. Saying those things hadn't been easy.

He sat forward and rested his hands on the table, then tilted his head and looked her in the eyes. "Then I reckon you an' I have more in common than I ever thought. I lost my family, too. Heck, even my niece—the one you met before—well, she moved out. She an' George got married. That's why I've been comin' in here more. I get kinda lonely."

For the briefest moment, he looked pitiful. Not the ornery, yet confident man she believed him to be. He seemed genuinely heartbroken.

"I'm sorry." She doubted he'd want pity, so she painted a smile on her face, determined to say something *chipper*. "It's wonderful she got married. Honestly, I thought they were married when I met them."

"Nope. They was just lovebirds back then." He scratched his head. "Them eggs was good. Glad ya made me try 'em."

"I'm happy you liked them, Henry." She took his plate and headed for the kitchen. Her refuge. Before she got there, she glanced over her shoulder. The smile he gave her made her walk a little faster.

* * *

Someone was following her.

Melissa quickened her pace toward the boarding house. At least they were in broad daylight. That helped a little. A wagon remained a short distance behind her. When she slowed, it slowed, and since she'd practically started running, the driver had eased the horse into a slow trot.

Every time she turned to get a look at the man holding the reins, he quickly faced the other direction.

What am I doing?

If the man actually was following her, the last thing she needed to do was show him where she lived.

Don't be so nervous! You're not in Montana anymore!

She scolded herself, but it did no good. Her heart still beat out of her chest.

Deal with it head-on.

She stopped abruptly, and the man yanked on the reins, halting his horse.

He looked down and away from her, but then, she recognized his shirt. *Why, you . . .*

"HENRY ALEXANDER!" she screamed with her hands on her hips.

His head shot up and he stared at her, wide-eyed. "What you yellin' for?"

Fuming, she marched over to his wagon. "You scared the FIRE out of me! Why are you following me?"

"Followin' you?" *Did he just grin?* "I ain't followin' you. I'm goin' to the mercantile."

She defiantly crossed her arms. "You know darn well you were following me!" She stepped closer and shook her finger in his face. "I'm not some young girl who doesn't understand men! I've known men like you Henry Alexander!" She lifted her chin high in the air. "You'd best be telling me you're sorry!"

He placed his hands on his thighs and leaned down toward her. "You've known men like me, huh? Don't reckon you have. There ain't no man like me. Know sumthin' else? I don't even know your name. Mrs.? . . ."

"Montgomery. It's Mrs. Montgomery." Anger had replaced fear, and she managed to calm down. Though she hated to admit it, as much as he bothered her, there was something about him she liked.

"Montgomery?" He gulped, looking oddly befuddled. "You ain't kin to Martha, are ya?"

"As a matter of fact, I am." This was the hard part. "Her son was my husband."

"I see." Henry climbed out of the wagon and stood beside her, leaning on his cane.

They were about the same height. Having him so close, set off a new kind of discomfort.

"Afraid Martha don't think much a me," he said. His voice had softened a great deal. "We kinda had a *family* problem."

"Family problem? I don't understand."

His eyes narrowed. "My nephew was married to Martha's niece, Claire. But, he died. It's a long story. One I don't care to talk 'bout right now. I just figgered you needed to know that Martha don't care for me."

This made no sense. "But, Claire's married to Dr. Fletcher. They have a child. I didn't know she was married before."

"Yep. Ask Martha 'bout it. I'm sure she'll tell ya. Then, if you wanna talk to me again, I'll be at Sylvia's next Saturday."

Unsure what to say, Melissa just stared at him.

"Sorry I troubled you," he said, nodding to her. "Mrs. *Montgomery.*"

"It's all right. And, you can call me Melissa." She looked directly at him, knowing his impairment.

He took his place in the wagon and grabbed the reins. Before driving off, he gave her a sad smile.

His behavior had changed after she told him who she was. Hopefully Martha could shed some light.

* * *

That Sunday, Melissa made her regular visit to Martha's. She took along a freshly baked apple pie.

After their usual family time—sharing mostly stories about J.J.'s antics and Franny's silliness—Melissa managed to pull Martha away for some private conversation.

The instant Melissa uttered Henry's name, Martha spit. A habit Melissa still had difficulty coping with.

"Damn that man," Martha fussed. Her eyes squinted nearly shut. "Stay away from him. He ain't nothin' but trouble."

"He seems harmless enough—"

"No!" Martha pointed a stiff finger in Melissa's face. "You don't know what he done."

"So, tell me." Did she really want to hear it?

"Fine. But bundle up. We'll talk on the porch." Martha's eyes shifted around the interior of the house as if speaking about Henry would taint it.

Melissa obliged her and put on her coat and mittens to keep her hands warm. Martha simply grabbed a quilt off her bed and nodded to the front door. Melissa sat on the porch swing. After winding the heavy blanket around her body, Martha took the spot beside her.

"That *man*," Martha growled, then spit again. "Tried havin' his way with Claire."

No.

"I can see by the look on your face, you don't believe it."
Martha's lips screwed together. "I aim to tell you everythin'.
It's a long story, so you'd best get comfortable."

Melissa had never been one to judge by the word of
someone else alone. She'd always believed in giving someone the benefit of the doubt and made a point to listen to
the other side of the story. However, the intricate details
Martha was literally *spitting* out of her mouth had her horribly concerned.

Henry had flirted when he'd thought she was married.
Was he the kind of man who enjoyed wooing married
women?

Or was he simply out of his mind from loneliness?

She knew better than most anyone how it felt to lose a
spouse. *And children.*

Martha kept rambling on, and Melissa turned her head
to wipe away a tear. Hopefully the woman hadn't noticed.

"I love ya," Martha said, firmly squeezing Melissa's leg.
"Don't wanna see ya hurt."

Melissa rested her head on Martha's shoulder. "I love
you, too. And I appreciate your candor." Confused as to
what to do next, Melissa sat upright and looked directly at
her. "I promise to be careful."

"That's my girl." Martha patted her cheek. "Now, let's
get back inside 'fore we freeze our tails off."

Shaking her head, Melissa followed the outspoken
woman into the house.

* * *

The following Saturday, Melissa's heart thumped when
April brought her the order for eggs over-easy. Of course,
many people ordered them that way. But when April rolled

her eyes and said, "It's that man again," Melissa knew Henry had stayed true to his word and came back.

She fixed the eggs. *Perfectly.*

When she handed the plate to April, the girl wrinkled her nose at the creative arrangement. "Why'd ya do that?"

"He'll understand," Melissa said. "Just take them to him."

"All right." The girl shrugged and walked out of the kitchen.

A small window at the center of the swinging kitchen door allowed those entering and exiting to see whether or not someone might be on the other side. Melissa peered out the glass, hoping to get a glimpse of Henry's expression when April delivered his order.

He looked like he'd taken even greater care in grooming himself today. Or maybe she imagined it, wanting to trust her instincts and believe he was truly a good man. No matter what he'd done, she doubted it had been in his usual character. Yes, it was *wrong*, but he deserved a chance to explain.

He studied the contents of his plate, then lifted his head as if searching.

For me?

Of course for her. Who else would've poked holes in both of his eggs, then drawn the yolk along the bottom of the plate to make it look like a large smile?

His head slightly bobbed, then his lips rose into a warm smile. Nearly as big as the one on his plate.

Though she could see him, she couldn't hear what he said to April.

Melissa stepped to the side of the door and waited.

April came into the kitchen. "He said to tell you, thank you."

"Did you tell him I did it?"

"No. First he thought I done it, but I told him it was you. I thought he was gonna get mad." She shrugged. "Seemed he liked it. Now he wants some grits an' toast, too. Whatever you done gave him an appetite. That man never orders so much food."

With a smile of her own, Melissa turned away from the girl to prepare the rest of Henry's meal.

* * *

I miss you so much . . .

Melissa let her tears flow. She shivered even though the air had warmed. The breeze blowing across Mobile Bay did little to refresh her. It stung against the moisture on her face.

She thought she'd started to heal. She'd even managed to smile more. But this date stabbed a jolt of pain deep into her heart. A year had passed, but it seemed like an eternity since she'd held her children and shared her husband's bed.

As she walked along the beach, she untied her bonnet and let her long hair fly freely. A bird cried out overhead, so she stopped to watch it. Entranced, she stared out to sea. Beautiful, yet too much grief kept her from fully appreciating it.

She startled when someone touched her arm. Defensively, she whipped around and gasped. "Henry? What are you doing here?" Embarrassed by the way she must look, she turned away.

Again he touched her arm, and shifted her to look at him. "I had to come. Went to Sylvia's hopin' to see ya. Said she gave ya the day off and told me why you wasn't workin'."

It hadn't been Sylvia's place to tell him. Melissa started to speak, but Henry held up his hand.

"Don't be angry with 'er. She cares 'bout you. I do, too. Reckon you could use a friend."

Melissa trembled and erupted into a heavy bawl. Henry opened his arms, and she moved into them without giving it a second thought. She buried her head into his neck and sobbed.

"Go on an' let it out," Henry whispered and stroked her hair. "I'll hold ya long as ya need me."

His warm arms gave her the comfort she needed. She'd tried to hold in her feelings for too long. "It's so hard . . ." She struggled to speak, but his gentle hand began to calm her.

Without saying a word, she stepped out of his embrace and nodded to the shore. Weak from crying, she stumbled, and Henry wrapped an arm around her waist, while steadying himself against his cane.

It couldn't have been easy for him walking through the sand to reach her. The poor man had difficulty on regular ground. Fortunately, she spotted a bench facing the water and pointed to it.

They sat silently for some time.

Her throat had become horribly dry, so she swallowed hard. She patted Henry's leg to get his attention. "How'd you find me?"

"Went to that boardin' house where you live. They told me you like to walk down here."

"Seems there's no privacy whatsoever in Mobile, Alabama." She gave him a timid smile.

"Nope. Folks like to know what everyone's doin'. Don't always benefit them bein' talked 'bout."

He didn't have to explain. He'd likely been the topic of gossip for some time.

"Henry?" He'd looked away, so she tapped him lightly. "How did your family die?" She sniffled. Had she been too forward?

His head drew back, then his shoulders dropped. "My boys . . . died in the war. My wife, Sarah, died after." He stared at his hands. His pain added to hers. "She didn't do well copin' with their deaths. Went *mad*. I took her to a hospital. They was s'posed to help her. Thought I was doin' right, but she died there." Slowly, his head rose and he looked her in the eyes. "They didn't help."

She grasped his hands. "I'm so sorry, Henry."

"It was 'bout eight years ago. Seems like yesterday." He readjusted in the seat and stared out toward the water. He kept hold of one of her hands.

"It's been a year for me," she whispered.

Henry gave no reaction, but then turned his head. "You say sumthin'?"

His eyes were on her lips. "It's been a year. Since I lost *my* family." It felt right to tell him, so she sucked in air and closed her eyes. The visions came instantly, like it was all happening in front of her. "Indians killed them. Even my youngest, Caroline. She was only eight." Tears spilled from her closed lids.

Henry released her hand and wrapped his arm over her shoulders, pulling her close. "Ya don't hafta talk 'bout it. Unless you want to."

She looked intently into his eyes. "I *need* to. But . . . you know what's the hardest thing of all?"

He shook his head.

"When I see them in my mind, I see how they looked when I found them. Covered in blood. I want to see them the way they were *before* they died. My little girl in her pretty dresses running through the fields. And my boys, Jeremy and Steven, climbing trees and laughing." Her heart raced, her breathing quickened. "But all I see when I close my eyes is . . . blood."

Her head dropped down, but then she jerked it up again. Thoughts and memories tumbled through her head. Horrid, ugly reminders.

She grabbed Henry's arm and hung on tight. "And Joe —Oh, God, Joe—they took his scalp. That's what I see, Henry! It gives me nightmares!"

In a fit of sobs, she buried her face into his shoulder.

His fingers drew through her hair. "Shh . . . You're safe here. I promise." He held her close and once again let her cry.

Aside from Thomas, no one else knew the horrific way her family had died. Neither of them would let Mary go near the house. Just knowing that Indians had killed her cousins gave Fran nightmares. If she'd seen what they'd done . . .

"I feel so guilty at times," Melissa said. "I'd be dead, too, if I hadn't gone to see my sister."

Henry yanked a handkerchief from his pocket and dabbed at her eyes. "I understand. I've felt like that many times. Guilty for livin'."

He placed the cotton hankie into her hands. She used it to wipe her nose. "Martha told me to stay away from you."

He bobbed his head. "Don't surprise me none. Reckon she told you 'bout Claire."

Reluctantly, Melissa nodded. She'd dried her tears, but now Henry's eyes misted over.

"I know what I done was wrong." His voice cracked. "Been livin' with so much guilt, I hate myself. If I could, I'd take it all back. But them kind a things can't be undone."

Knowing that he, too, needed to talk about hurtful things, she listened silently. Maybe somehow they'd help each other.

"I could try an' make excuses for why I done it, but no matter what I say, it was wrong. Hope one day I can ask Claire to forgive me. Back when I had a chance, I was too drunk to do anyone any good." He searched her eyes, then squeezed her hand. "I gave up drinkin' an' ain't never goin' back to it." A tear trickled down his face. "I won't never hurt you."

"I believe you." She nestled into him.

They stared out at the water. The waves lapped against the shore and time passed.

Safe in his arms, Melissa sighed.

Martha wouldn't be happy, but somehow, this felt right.

CHAPTER 38

Spring had come to Bridgeport.

Thank goodness.

Finally, Victoria could get out of the house and go for a stroll. The air had warmed enough so she could go out without a coat. That suited her. How else could she display the finest dresses in the city?

On the finest body, of course.

Ever since her birthday, John had been overly affectionate. He'd showered her with attention and a gorgeous, *expensive*, pearl necklace. In turn, she gave him whatever he asked for. Not difficult at all, since she enjoyed giving it.

Eventually, she'd go to the park, but today she decided to surprise John at work. She'd only been to his office twice since her arrival. It bored her. Too much paperwork and not nearly enough fun.

Appropriate for spring, she wore a floral-print dress. She set aside the necklace Andrew had given and donned John's pearls instead. John had told her they looked remarkable on her, even with the scarf she wouldn't shed. Not many folks knew of her scar, and she intended to keep it that way.

She opened the door of the brick office building and went in. Since John's office was at the back, she had to pass by James' first. She peeked inside, but found it empty, so she continued on.

Her husband stood facing the window. She was about to speak, when he turned and pound his fist on the desk.

"Damn!" he yelled, then startled when he noticed her. "Victoria? What are you doing here? Is something wrong?"

Luckily, he didn't appear to be angry *at her*, but something had obviously upset him. She doubted he'd randomly curse for no reason whatsoever.

"I'm fine," she said, stepping into the room. "I came to surprise you. Are *you* all right?"

"Yes." He smoothed the front of his suit jacket, then scanned his desk and lifted a sheet of paper. "It's this case I'm working on."

"Have you had, *lunch*?" She grinned saying the word. He'd schooled her in northern expressions. For some unknown reason, northerners had decided to create their own name for *dinner*. The silliest thing of all was that they often called supper, dinner. Why they had to make it so confusing was beyond her.

He raised a single brow and smiled. "No, I haven't. But I'm afraid I don't have time. I have a meeting in fifteen minutes." He drew out his watch chain and flipped open the thing. "Make that, *ten* minutes."

With a pout, she sighed. "Oh, well. I'll go on home and see what Jean-Pierre might cook for me."

John came out from behind his desk and placed his fingers to her lips. "Don't pout. It doesn't become you." He kissed her. "This is what your lips are for, my dear. I'll see you this evening."

She turned to leave and received a sound smack on her bottom. Even through her bustle, she could feel it. Enough to start her blood boiling. In a good way. Over her shoulder, she cast a look for him to remember.

In the short span of time she'd been with the man, he'd taught her a great deal. She had no doubt she knew more about pleasing a man than most women.

Andrew doesn't know what he's missin'.

Likely, Claire knew nothing at all.

Facing forward, she nearly toppled into James.

He stumbled backward. "Victoria? What a surprise!" The man beamed.

The way he's lookin' at me, I must truly look fine.

She struck a coy pose. "I'm glad to be here."

He acted like he was ready to burst at the seams—eyes wide and hardly able to stand still. "Did John tell you the good news?"

"News?" She glanced back at John, who immediately turned away. She tipped her head and studied James. "What news?"

He grabbed hold of her arms. "Emilie's going to have a baby! We just confirmed it. The doctor said she should deliver around Thanksgiving! We'll have even more to be thankful for. Isn't it wonderful?"

A baby? Victoria forced a smile. "I'm happy for you." She took hold of his hand and gave it a pat. "Please congratulate Emilie for me."

"I will." He nodded so hard it made her head hurt watching him. "I'm still having a hard time believing it myself. We've been hoping for some time it would happen." He peered over her shoulder into John's office. "I'm sure he's heard enough about it today. I've told everyone who's come in. I can't help myself!"

In a burst of even more energy, James hugged her. So tight she squealed.

"Just wait, Victoria," he said, thankfully releasing her. "One day you and John will share the same joy!"

He gave her a strange little bow, then scurried down the hallway to his office.

Before leaving, Victoria glanced a final time at John. He'd returned to the window, staring out the glass.

Definitely troubled 'bout sumthin'.

But what could be worse than her own troubles?

It's not fair. Why should Emilie have a baby when I'm not allowed?

Not wanting to dampen her appearance with tears, she pushed them down and refused to let them come. With her shoulders back and head held high, she returned home.

* * *

Damn it all.

Though tempted to thrust his fist through the window, John turned and struck the desk for a second time.

He knew it would happen eventually, but why now? Why so soon?

"Are you all right, John?"

He looked up at his business partner, who'd popped his fat head into his office.

John took a seat at his desk. "I'm fine."

"I heard you curse. Is it Victoria?"

"No. As I told you, I'm fine!" He lifted the same sheet of paper he'd shown Victoria. A mock excuse for what actually troubled him. "I have a difficult case. I'm frustrated."

"Anything I can help with?"

"No. This is a mess only I can fix. I simply have to work through it." He rubbed his temples with his forefingers. His head had started to ache.

"Well—let me know if you change your mind." *That won't happen.* "Oh, and by the way, I have to go out of town for a few days. I have a favor to ask." James moved from the doorway and stood in front of John's desk.

John sat fully upright. *Going out of town?* "Yes, of course. What can I do?"

"You may think me ridiculous, but . . . I'm worried about Emilie. I know she's young and healthy, but could you look in on her while I'm away?"

John's day had dramatically improved. "Of course. I understand why you're concerned. She's with child. You can never be too careful." He displayed his most gracious smile. "I'll take good care of her. There's no need for you to worry."

"Thank you. I've always been able to count on you. I leave tomorrow on the noon train. I'd appreciate if you'd stop in to see her on your way home."

"Consider it done." He shook James' hand.

* * *

As planned, James caught the noon train, and John decided to shorten his workday. The warm May sunshine felt good on his face, but even more pleasant was the thought of what awaited him.

He strutted down the brick sidewalk. Emilie likely wouldn't expect him this early, but James had to have told her he'd be coming by sometime today.

What will she be wearing?

He rapped on her door, but she scarcely opened it. Timid eyes peeked through the small crack.

"Open the door, Emilie," he said, as patiently as he could. "Let me in."

"Only if you promise you're not angry with me."

"Open the door." No longer patient, he demanded action.

Slowly, the door swung wide. She hid behind it.

John pushed it shut and stared at the girl. She wore nothing provocative. Only a simple day dress. Her hair hung loose around her shoulders. *Unkempt.* She stared downward and when he approached her, she backed away.

He folded his arms over his chest. "Is it mine?"

"It could be, but there's no way to know for certain." Her eyes remained affixed to the floor.

"Why don't you look at me, Emilie? This is what you wanted, remember?"

"*Oui.* But you said when my belly swelled you would no longer have me." She finally lifted her head. "I can't bear the thought of being without you."

Just what he wanted to hear. "Has it begun to swell?" He stepped close to her. This time, she didn't move.

She placed a single hand on her stomach. "Not yet. Why?"

"For now," he licked his lips, anticipating, "I still want you."

He threw her over his shoulder and she let out a small whimper. But he needed a way to vent his anger. He hauled her to the bedroom. After setting her down, he grabbed the top of her gown at the neckline and ripped it wide open. She gasped and shook, cowering into herself.

With a few more tugs, he ripped the horrid dress from her body, then pointed to the bed.

She lay down, trembling.

Not taking his eyes from her, he undressed.

He took her viciously. Forcefully. Determined to let her know how disappointed he was, he gave little thought to how she felt. He wouldn't hurt her, but he'd show her who was in control. He made it last, drawing pleasure from the fear in her eyes.

Once gratified, he fell back onto the pillows.

She rolled onto her side and draped a petite arm over his body. "You *are* angry, no?" With tear-filled eyes, she toyed with the hair on his chest. Likely trying to appease him.

"Disappointed is a better word. I thought we could carry on longer than this. Today might be our last time together." On their previous trysts, he'd caress her. But to further punish her, he didn't touch her.

"No, John, please don't say that. Promise we'll have at least one more time together." She rose up and began kissing his chest. "I need you."

"You don't need me. You have James, remember? He loves you." He spoke without emotion. "I've never seen a man more thrilled about the prospect of a child. He'll think differently when the brat bawls all night."

"John . . ." She put a hand against his cheek and turned his head to face her. "I understand. You are angry because you will miss me just as I will miss you." She placed a kiss on his lips. "I *do* love you. If only you loved me."

"You'd never have been happy with me. I don't want children. You know that."

"But what of Victoria? I can see she wants a baby. Women know these things." She lay her head down against him, and caressed his body.

"Yes, Victoria wants a child, but I won't allow it. If it were to happen, I'd have it removed from her body. I *won't* raise another child."

The movement of Emilie's hand stopped. "Removed? You would kill a child?"

"It wouldn't be a child. Not yet. It would be an . . . *inconvenience*. And yes, I'd rid her of it." Emilie inched away from him. *Don't make another mistake, woman.* "I'm her husband. She'll do as I tell her."

Emilie swung her legs over the side of the bed and stood. She then put on a silk robe. "I want you to leave."

"What?" He scowled at her.

"Leave." She pointed to the door. "*Now.*"

He jumped up from the bed. "I'm not ready to leave." No woman would tell him what to do.

Her body quivered. "You need to leave."

"I'm not going anywhere." He grabbed her by the arms and yanked her close. "I told James I'd look after you, and that's exactly what I'm going to do." He kissed her hard. "You said you love me."

"That was before—"

He stopped her with another kiss, then pushed the robe from her body. "I'm not done with you, Emilie. Not yet." He picked her up and flung her to the center of the bed.

She rapidly shook her head. "No, John. I don't want to."

"But *I* do!" Her rejection stirred his desire. He gave her no choice and took her again. This time, he purposefully did things she'd enjoy. He watched the expression on her face change until she grasped his back and drew him in, moaning with pleasure.

He delighted in changing a woman's mind.

Even if it had to be forced.

CHAPTER 39

Beth sat on the front porch, leisurely rocking. Her father-in-law rested beside her in a rocking chair of his own. The June sun beat down on the little farmhouse, and they enjoyed being outside on afternoons like this.

She'd adapted well to her new home. Especially after Valentine's Day. George was like a new man. Even Henry had remarked about a change in him. Said he showed more confidence in his work and rarely stammered.

Beth couldn't help but smile.

Love can make miracles happen.

"Want me to read to you, Daddy?" When his wife read to him, she always chose German books. Beth was trying to get him to appreciate some of the classics written in English.

She'd grown to love the man. Having lost both of her own folks, she felt truly blessed having the Barnhardts in her life.

"No," he said, barely moving his rocker. "I'm enjoying watching the grass grow." He grinned, making her laugh.

"All right. But if you change your mind, say so. I know you like the way I read."

"Yes, I do. You put more emotion into it than Freda does. It's that fine southern accent of yours. Quite different from Freda's German."

"Yep." Beth giggled. "Odd that George doesn't talk like y'all."

"No." The man grew quiet. Maybe it was because he was happy George talked at all. He'd sure gotten a lot better at it lately.

She squirmed in her chair, then gripped the armrest and pushed herself up to her feet. "Gotta use the outhouse." She scurried away with his chuckle following her.

He may have found humor in her reason for leaving, but she didn't feel right not telling him *why*.

Truthfully, she just plain didn't feel right. At first, she thought she'd come down with some horrible illness she'd likely die from. But then, sense gripped her.

I'm pregnant, that's all there is to it.

Feeling a little scared, as well as excited, she had no idea how to break the news to George. She hoped he'd be pleased.

She'd never forget how thrilled she'd been when Claire had told her she was with child.

Then everythin' changed.

She didn't want to think about that part of it. She wanted to remember the *happy* part. Claire had said that somehow she just knew.

Beth knew, too. She felt *different*. Since her cycle was late, it confirmed everything in her mind. She'd been stewing over how to tell George. She couldn't just come right out and say it. It had to be done in a special way.

Hoping something might come to mind, she returned to the porch and rocked with the unknowing, soon-to-be grandpa.

Night fell, and she and George went to bed. She'd still not come up with an idea.

He snuggled up to her. "Ya seem a might tense."

"Yep."

He nuzzled her neck. "I can help."

Of course he could. No matter how they felt, they both seemed to always benefit from a little gentle lovemaking. "I'd like that, George."

He wasted no time and pushed her gown up and out of the way, then climbed atop her.

They'd gotten good at being quiet, but even if they made a little noise, neither of them fretted over the slightest movement of the bed. She loved this time with him. It was theirs alone.

"George," she whispered.

"What?"

The room was completely dark. She couldn't see an expression on his face, even if she wanted to. "I just wanted to tell you, I reckon we've gotten real good at this." She made sure to keep her voice low.

His movement didn't stop. "Glad ya like it." Even without seeing him, she could tell he'd smiled.

"George?"

"What?" His breathing had quickened.

"What I meant to say is . . . we've gotten *real* good at this." She moved with him, enjoying the sensation, but determined to get her point across.

"Beth, I think ya might like it more if ya didn't talk so much. 'Sides, I'm tryin' to concentrate."

"You don't need to concentrate. You know what you're doin'." *Boy, did he ever.* It might not be the best time to do this, but she hadn't come up with another plan, so she pressed on. "Know how I've never told you *no*, unless it's that time?"

"Uh-huh." He moved much faster.

"Well . . ." She huffed, nearly losing her breath, trying to keep up with him. "Have you noticed I haven't said no . . . in a long . . . time?" *Oh, George . . .*

The rhythm slowed. "Come to think of it, you're right. I can't recall the last time you said *no*." He sped up again.

For a brief moment, she assumed he understood. But he obviously hadn't. He only seemed to be concerned with increasing his pace. She'd have to spell it out for him. "That's because that time hasn't come in a great while. I think we're gonna have a baby."

He froze.

Without saying a word, he rolled off her.

She turned onto her side. "You didn't hafta stop."

He pushed the covers back, sat up, then got out of bed and went to the window.

"You all right, George?" Beth scooched up and leaned against the backboard, then pulled the quilt up around her.

He glanced over his shoulder, then opened the curtains and pushed up the window. "It's might hot in here." He stuck his head outside, gasping for air.

He's upset.

Worry knotted her stomach. She wanted him to be happy.

This can't be good for the baby.

"George?"

He turned around and stared at her. With the curtains open, moonlight softly illuminated the room. Her naked husband looked like he might buckle at the knees.

He swallowed hard. "Do you know how beautiful you look right now?" He knelt on the bed next to her and cupped his hand over her cheek.

She leaned in to his touch. "You mean that?" Tears pooled in her eyes. She'd misread him. He wasn't angry at all.

"Yes, I do. You're gonna have my child." He broke out crying and she lost it. She bawled like the infant she'd soon hold in her arms.

He got under the covers and nestled against her. "You're gonna have a baby," he said through his tears, rubbing her belly.

She stroked his cheek. "I told you we got good at it. Can't believe it really worked."

His tears dampened her shoulder, but she'd never been happier. "George?"

"Yeah?"

"You know, I'm gonna get even bigger. Do you mind so much?"

"You'd *best* get bigger. You'll have a child in your belly." He kissed her lips. "Don't you ever fret 'bout your size. I think you're perfect."

"You do?"

"Yep. I do."

"Well . . . would you mind so much finishin' what you started?"

With a low chuckle, followed by an inviting growl, he moved onto her.

This time, Beth kept her mouth shut.

CHAPTER 40

John vigorously rubbed his hands together. They always tingled when he was about to come into money.

He'd invited a number of guests for a *friendly* game of poker. All men of course. Victoria had pouted in her usual fashion and complained that it would be no fun for her. After he gave her his best *don't challenge me* look, she donned a *please forgive me* smile and went off to their room for the night.

He had the girl well-trained. A pet he'd taught how to beg and roll over.

If only she didn't speak.

He chuckled and went to the kitchen to check on Jean-Pierre's progress.

The food wasn't nearly as important as the beverages. With enough alcohol, his guests wouldn't think clearly and make costly mistakes. Even without cheating, he could beat them at any hand.

Satisfied that his cook had things under control, John went to the parlor to finalize preparations. He planned to impress two guests in particular.

Raymond Wilson would be bringing both of his sons. John intended to find out how much sense the young men had. He wanted to see if their minds were moldable. If so, he could turn them into exceptional attorneys. After all, no one excelled at it better than he. Digging up dirt in order to bring a man to ruin was a skill he'd mastered. As long as it benefited his own wallet. He could create scandal when necessary. Ties to the press had always been a crucial ally.

He set out cigars at each table, as well as decks of cards and specially-made gambling chips crafted from ivory. They alone were symbols of his wealth and success.

As the men arrived, he guided them to the parlor. Most had already seen Victoria's painting, but the young Wilson *boys* were in for a treat. After what Raymond had told him about Randall, he assumed the elder of the two had seen a woman in all her glory. The younger likely hadn't. Then again, if he was anything like John, he'd have lost his virtue at sixteen and would already be well-skilled.

But, the average male is nothing like me.

When the Wilsons arrived, John studied the boys. Truthfully, it surprised him that they were separated by two years. They looked more like twins. Randall was slightly taller than Robert, but both had dark hair and eyes. From a distance, it would be impossible to tell them apart.

They eyed the interior as if looking for something. *What could it be?* They were no strangers to grandeur. Though he'd never been there, John had heard the Wilson home was twice the size of his residence and expensively furnished.

"Why don't you show your sons the poker room?" John suggested to Raymond. "If you don't mind, I must see to the food preparation." An unnecessary task, but he wanted to give the boys time to view the *art* without him looking over their shoulder.

"Of course," Raymond said and led them away.

John headed for the kitchen, but then spun on his heels and waited. After a good solid minute, he strode into the parlor.

Low-lying smoke hovered in the air. Muffled chatter and the clink of betting chips filled the room. He spied Raymond at one of the tables, engaged in conversation. And then, just as he'd thought, the younger Wilsons were standing at the bar, admiring the view.

As quietly as he could, John crept up behind them.

"I told you she was beautiful," Robert said.

"Yes, you did," his brother replied. "But I didn't expect *this*. She definitely rivals Susan."

More fun than I deserve. John covered his mouth to suppress a gloating chuckle.

"Brother," Robert said. "She puts Susan to shame. Just look at her eyes."

Eyes? Why on earth is he looking there?

"Her eyes?" Randall shook his head. "I find everything below her neck much more interesting."

Now, that's my boy.

"You would." Robert sounded genuinely disturbed. "Is that all you ever think about?"

Good thing I don't have to apprentice this young man right away. Maybe he'll mature and gain some common sense.

"And you don't?" Randall scoffed. "You're acting as though you've never bedded a woman. I know better."

Robert grunted.

"If she wasn't married . . ." Randall went on. "I'd have to sample her." He tipped a glass in her direction, then began to drink.

"But, she *is*. You don't want to cross John Martin."

John simultaneously slapped both of them hard on the back. Randall spewed his beverage.

Perfect timing.

Robert whipped around. "Mr. Martin!"

"Yes. Are you enjoying my wife?" John lifted a cigar from the bar and lit it.

"I'm so sorry, sir," Randall said, sputtering like a fool. "You startled me. I-I can get something to clean this up." With his coat sleeve, he dabbed at the vast amount of liquid he'd ejected on the bar.

John stood between them and draped an arm over their shoulders, his lit cigar close to Randall's head. "Don't worry yourself over that little spill." He took a drag, then blew out a plume of smoke. "I enjoy looking at her, too. She's even better in the flesh. I'm a lucky man."

"Yes, sir," Randall said. "You're *quite* lucky. She's extraordinary." His lips twitched into a nervous smile.

John reveled in having the upper hand. His apprentice would be groveling at his feet, begging to be taught. "You have no idea. Victoria has a way about herself. She *never* tires. She can go on for hours."

Both young men gaped, causing John to laugh aloud. "I know what's going on in those young minds of yours. You think I'm old, and wonder how I can keep up with her." He looked at both of them in turn, but neither responded. However, their mouths instantly snapped shut.

"Well," John said, standing a little taller. "I'll have you know, I'm more than capable. I keep her satisfied."

The younger Wilson sputtered out a cough. "You're fortunate, sir. Most men never have the opportunity to be with a woman of your wife's caliber. How did you meet her?"

Yes, the youthful Robert had more class than Randall and an obvious need to please. *A detriment to any lawyer.*

"She was to marry my son," John said, gazing at the image of his beautiful conquest. "She chose me instead. Sometimes women prefer a more experienced man. They don't want *boys.*" He accentuated his remark with another firm smack on their backs and walked away.

That'll give them something to think about.

* * *

Victoria sat on her favorite park bench, basking in the warmth of the pleasant summer sun. If she got too warm, she'd fan herself with an elegant fan John had given her for their anniversary. She could easily sit here for hours.

Besides, there was nothing better to do than watch folks pass by.

She'd worn a light cotton dress with an appropriate low-scooped neckline. Donning the pearls John had given her, she caught the eye of every man that passed. She chose to wear her hair high upon her head, purposefully displaying more skin. Of course, her scarf covered some of it, but she let it fall behind her back so as not to get in the way of the most important view.

With every eye she caught, she returned a devilish smile.

Being honest with herself, she was on the prowl. Looking for the perfect man to accomplish what John wouldn't. She'd get what she deserved.

The man had to be attractive, intelligent, and hopefully a good lover. And when she was done with him, she'd cast him aside without another thought. John would be none-the-wiser, and she'd have her baby.

His summer hours had begun to annoy her. He'd been staying longer at work, and they never seemed to manage a proper mealtime.

She sighed. Life as an attorney's wife wasn't what she'd hoped.

High noon and she wasn't a bit hungry. She fanned her face, waiting for someone to come by.

In the distance she spotted two young men approaching, so she sat fully upright, dropped the fan to her waist, and pulled her shoulders back. They deserved the best view possible.

Oh, my, they're handsome.

They got better looking the closer they came.

Her heart fluttered. She recognized one of them from last year's Christmas party. A face she'd never forget.

Robert Wilson.

Hunger instantly overwhelmed her. But not for food.

"Mrs. Martin?" Robert said with a smile that sent her heart soaring. "You *are* Victoria Martin, aren't you?"

"Yes, I am." She locked eyes with him, then extended her hand, which he feathered with a soft kiss. "I see you remembered my husband's lesson."

His eyes were almost as dark as Andrew's. She couldn't shift her gaze.

"Yes, I'm a fast learner." He nodded, then turned his head, gesturing to the man beside him. One almost identical to himself. "Mrs. Martin, I'd like you to meet my brother, Randall. He'll be your husband's apprentice next year."

She couldn't help but grin. The man's eyes were glued to her cleavage. "My pleasure," she said, extending her hand.

His eyes shifted to her hand as he took it in his own. He caressed it with his thumb, then moved it ever-so-slowly to his lips. "The pleasure's all mine." His mouth lingered on her hand, and before he released it, she could've sworn his tongue had been involved.

"Oh, my," she whispered, then composed herself. She had to keep her wits about her. Tilting her head, she intently studied them. "You two could be bookends. I know you're not the same age, but you *do* look alike."

Randall lifted his chin, standing taller. "Look closer. You'll find I'm more handsome than my *baby* brother."

She giggled. "From what I can see, he's no baby. Are you Mr. Wilson?" Something about Robert had her in knots. Once again, their eyes locked.

"Mr. Wilson?" Robert blinked, but didn't move his gaze. "Please. You make me sound so old. Call me Robert."

"Very well, *Robert*. You may call me . . ." She paused, delighting in the anticipation behind his eyes. She'd keep the upper hand. "*Mrs. Martin*." Casting her most wicked smile, she believed the young man might drop to his knees.

That could be fun.

Randall stepped forward and motioned to the bench. "May I?"

"Hmm . . ." She pursed her lips. "I suppose so. Robert, would you like to sit as well?"

His broad smile produced a desirable dimple. "Yes, I would."

They sat. One to each side of her. Pulling her shoulders back, she fluttered her fan. This day had taken a step in the right direction.

"Are you *hot*, Mrs. Martin?" Randall asked. He rested his arm on the back of the bench behind her shoulder.

When she turned her head to look at him, he licked his lips. *I know what you're thinkin'.* "I'm *always* hot," she replied, fluttering her fan for effect.

His eyebrows rose, nearly touching a tuft of thick dark hair that fell across his forehead. He scooted closer and leaned back against the seat.

Victoria turned away from him and focused on his brother. Randall was much too eager. He could get her into trouble. "So, Robert, why aren't you workin'? Did John give you the afternoon off?" He'd remarked to her that the young Wilson was a fine employee. She imagined he'd be just as fine at other things.

"No," Robert said. "It's my lunch break. Randall decided to join me. You see, he's a bit lonely. His *fiancée* is in Europe for the summer."

Victoria turned back to Randall. She caught a trace of a scowl aimed at Robert, before he turned it into a smile for her. "Yes," Randall said, nostrils flaring. "I'm engaged to a lovely girl. We're to be married at Christmas."

"Marriage is a fine thing," Victoria said, batting her lashes. "John takes good care of me." Knowing Randall had been attempting some form of seduction since the second he'd laid eyes on her, she decided not to give him another opportunity. How could she trust a man betrothed to another woman, who without a doubt would take *her* to his bed immediately? She rotated her body to face the better of the two. "How 'bout you, Robert? Has a woman captured *your* heart?"

"As a matter of fact . . . yes." He stared into her eyes, his meaning crystal clear.

"Isn't love grand?" she asked with a sigh. Switching her fan to her left hand, she lowered her right. It *accidentally* brushed Robert's leg.

He cleared his throat. "Yes, it is."

She nearly jumped when he moved his arm behind her back and glided his fingers across the thin fabric of her cotton dress.

Not wanting Randall to observe the actions of his younger brother, she faced him and positioned her body as a barrier to his line of sight. "So, Randall . . . tell me 'bout your fiancée." Tempted to close her eyes, she forced them to remain open. Robert's gentle caress continued and slowly intensified. *Don't stop.*

"Her name's Susan," Randall said. His smile broadened. *He thinks I want him . . . Silly boy.* "She comes from a prominent family here in Bridgeport. We've known each other since we were children."

"That's marvelous," Victoria said. How could she remain composed when she could hardly breathe? Robert had accompanied his strokes with tender squeezes. The heat in her core had become unbearable. She needed release. "My," she squeaked out. "It's truly warm." She waved her fan so hard, her wrist began to ache.

Robert slowed his hand, then traced along her side with a single finger. "Yes, it is. Warmer than usual, isn't it brother?"

"Yes. We should get out of the heat. Mrs. Martin, I'm afraid we must leave. We haven't had our lunch, and I'm sure Robert's as hungry as I am." Randall stood.

"Probably even hungrier," Robert said.

A slight rustling of her bustle, made her jump. Robert had made an extremely bold move. "I believe I was bit by a bug." She tittered, then covered her mouth. Randall's quizzical expression at her action had warranted a lie.

"A shame," Robert said, standing beside his brother. "Perhaps you should leave the park. Have *you* eaten?"

She moistened her lips. "I was about to go and see what Jean-Pierre might cook for me."

Robert extended his hand, and she took it, allowing him to lift her to her feet. "It's best never to stay in the heat for long."

"Thank you for your concern." Though she didn't want to, she let go of his hand and extended hers to Randall. "I'm happy to have met you."

Without verbally responding, he kissed her hand a final time. Much shorter and less *wet* than the previous kiss.

She strolled away. After several strides, she peered over her shoulder. "Perhaps I'll see you again sometime." Preferably Robert. *Alone.*

"You will," Robert said. The effect of his dimpled smile remained with her all the way home.

A level of desire she'd not had for John in quite a while began to awaken. The same stirrings she'd felt at Christmas.

John had become boring. Their lovemaking was routine. She always knew what he was going to do and when he'd do it. She'd endure him if the outcome would be a child, but that would never happen.

Robert's touch excited her. She wanted the young, handsome man, and his actions indicated he wanted her, too.

How, when, and where?

She had a lot to think about.

CHAPTER 41

Nothing stopped Victoria from taking her daily stroll to the park. Wanting to see a certain Wilson brother motivated her. He fit her plan perfectly.

Dark clouds overhead promised less than desirable weather, but she didn't care. It was still warm, and without rain falling she gladly headed out.

As she meandered along the pathway through the park, she envisioned Robert. His flawless face had filled her dreams more than once. John's age was showing, especially around his eyes. Wrinkles that confirmed the many years between them.

In another ten years, he'd be an old man, and she'd still be young and beautiful. She had no intention of leaving him, but why not be entertained by younger men? She craved their attention and more importantly wanted a child.

I'd never be lonely again.

Thunder rumbled. She'd have to shorten her walk. Already some distance into the park, she turned around to head home. Getting caught in the rain in her fine clothes wouldn't be wise.

A carriage approached. Uncommon here, but permitted nonetheless. It was an elaborate enclosed carriage, befitting someone of importance. Even the driver looked significant in his black suit and top hat. As he neared, he dipped his head and smiled. Strangely, he pulled the two horses to a stop beside her.

Who's inside?

The curtains were drawn making it impossible to see within. The door swung open. Startled, she stepped back.

An arm extended from the opening, beckoning her.

What? Confused, she stared, then tipped her head to the side and moved closer.

"Mrs. Martin," a man's voice said from the interior, "we haven't got all day." He motioned again for her to enter.

Recognizing the voice, her heart skipped a beat. Her throat dried, making her swallow hard. With anticipatory bravery, she took his extended hand and went inside.

She sat facing Robert Wilson. He patted the side of the carriage and closed the door. A slight jerk set them in motion and she steadied herself against the seat.

He didn't say a word, simply remained in the seat across from her, studying her. Unsure what *she* should say, she smoothed her dress and gazed around the interior.

Luxury unlike anything she'd seen in a moving vehicle —aside from the train. The seats were upholstered in heavy gold velvet. Matching gold curtains shielded them from the outside world. Aside from the driver, no one would know they were together.

Alone.

Light seeped through several small slits between the draperies. She could see him plainly. Every gorgeous detail.

I must remain in control.

She sat fully upright. "Mr. Wilson, do you always pick up ladies this way?"

He grinned, highlighting the dimple she loved. "We've reverted back to *Mr. Wilson*? Didn't I ask you to call me *Robert*?"

He'd avoided her question. "*Robert*." She gazed into his incredible brown eyes. "Why'd you stop?"

"I thought it might rain. Didn't want you to get wet." He leaned close and rested a hand on her knee.

Briefly, she shut her eyes, relishing his touch, then re-opened them and scrutinized his fingers. "You're touchin' my knee . . . *Robert*. You're playin' a dangerous game."

"I like games. Don't you?" He glided his hand further up her leg.

"Yes. *I'm* usually the one playin'." She knew what was about to happen.

Sitting back, he raised both hands into the air. "Well then. You can lead. Your move, *Mrs. Martin*." He folded his arms over his chest.

She let out a soft laugh. "By my rules, then. First, I'd like to talk. I rarely get to speak to someone my age. How old *are* you, Robert?"

"Nineteen. Old enough to know how to please a woman such as yourself."

"What makes you believe I'm seekin' pleasure?"

Once again, he leaned in, lessening the space between them. "When I caressed you the other day, you gave no indication I'd offended you. Honestly, I think you enjoyed it."

She pursed her lips, choosing not to respond. He'd read her well. She'd welcomed his advances. Letting out a huff of air, she started to speak, but didn't know what to say. So, she parted the curtain and peered outside.

"Mrs. Martin." His voice sounded richer than butter. Soft, smooth, and inviting. "From the first time I saw you, I couldn't erase you from my mind. I *had* to see you again. Then, when I saw your portrait, something in your eyes captivated me."

She let the curtain fall from her grasp and shifted to face him. His words warmed her in a new way. His sincerity charmed her. "You were lookin' at my eyes?"

"Oh, yes. They mesmerized me. And now, seeing you here, they entrance me even more." His gaze drove straight to her heart. "There's something special about you. And I believe you want something more than you already have . . . *Victoria*," he whispered.

The lump in her throat felt like a boulder wedged in place to keep her from speaking. "My . . ." she muttered, attempting to regain control. After all, this was her game, not his. "Takin' liberties? You're to refer to me as *Mrs. Martin.*"

"Mrs. Martin. Did the artist accurately capture you?" His brows lifted high. "*Every* detail?"

"I believe so. I was pleased with the paintin'. But I didn't want it hung in the parlor." Keeping her head held high, she looked away from him.

"If you didn't want the painting seen, why pose?"

"For John. *He* wanted it. But I didn't want other men to see it. I feared I wouldn't know how to act once they had. Do you understand?" She studied his reaction, hoping he comprehended her seriousness. "*I* want to decide who does and doesn't see me."

"I understand completely." His formerly raised brow dipped low. His face filled with concern. "Truthfully, I'm glad I saw it." He inched to the edge of his seat and bravely laid a hand on her leg again. "I'd like to see more. View what gave the artist his inspiration."

Her heart had increased its thumping speed from the second she heard his voice carry from the carriage, but she had to feign control. "You're touchin' me again. It's still my game, Robert. You've not been given permission."

Yet.

A sly smile formed on his luscious lips and he scooted back, once again folding his arms over his chest. "Foul on my part. I concede. It's your game. Your rules. Forgive me, Mrs. Martin."

"Don't let it happen again. *My* game. *My* rules." She'd affirmed their roles, taking full control. "As I said, I'll be the one to decide who does and doesn't see me."

Seductively licking her lips, she delighted in watching him sweat. One button at a time, she worked her way down the front of her dress. The neckline was high, but she never fastened it all the way up. So even before she began undoing the long line of pearls, he'd been able to see bare flesh.

With each new release, the rise and fall of his chest became more noticeable. The final button sat at her waistline. Once she popped it through its tiny hole, she opened the front of her dress wide to accentuate his view. Her corset had her breasts pushed up and full.

His hand quivered against his suit coat. She had to give him credit. The young man had great restraint.

I'll give him what he wants.

Her selfish desire would benefit both of them.

She took his hand and placed it over her breast. It hadn't stopped trembling, so she rested hers atop it and helped him glide it over her skin. Once his demeanor calmed, she allowed him his own exploration.

He moved it gently, feeling her. Unfortunately, the corset kept him from seeing everything.

Next time.

Breathless, she tipped her head back and closed her eyes. "Robert," she rasped. "John can never know."

"No one will know," he whispered.

The air began to heat. Robert's warm breath skimmed across her flesh as he moved closer.

Opening her eyes, she peered into his. "It's your move. Do whatever you'd like."

"Anything?" His eyes locked onto hers, hungry and fearless. Giving him permission had taken away every trace of trepidation.

"Yes."

Excitement coursed through her veins, wondering what liberties he'd take next.

He removed a hand from her breast, then worked it under her dress.

She trembled as he glided his fingers up her leg.

"No bloomers?" he asked, grinning.

"Not in this heat." She could barely get the words out. Her heart raced so hard and fast, she feared it might fail her.

But what a wonderful way to die.

"Your skin's so soft," he whispered. He'd reached the top of her stockings and touched bare flesh.

Keep going.

He hesitated, so she nodded her encouragement.

He moistened his lips, then continued up her thigh. His touch more tender than John's.

After blinking several times, he stared at her. His hand came to rest between her legs and she gasped. He gave her a look she'd seen on her own face when she gazed in the mirror. Sly, devious, and insatiably hungry.

She'd purposely worn a split undergarment. It made relieving herself easier, but the kind of relief she sought today could prove to be difficult in the carriage.

"You're beautiful, Victoria," he whispered, while his fingers explored.

"So are you."

He pulled away and she whimpered. But then he began working the buttons on his trousers.

Oh, my.

He openly displayed his arousal. Danger made her head reel, but she wouldn't stop him. She'd never felt so drawn to a man. His exposed flesh reminded her how much she hated John's *protection.*

It's his fault I'm doin' this.

Knowing herself to be a skilled lover, she wouldn't let this young man believe her to be timid. So she boldly stroked him.

"You're quite the man. You rival John. You're no baby."

"No, I'm not." His eyes closed as she skillfully worked her magic.

John had taught her what men liked. Robert's response proved he'd been a proficient teacher.

"Come here," he whispered. "Let me show you how much of a man I am."

She willingly obeyed.

Lifting her dress, she bundled up a great deal of fabric around her waist, then managed to straddle him on the seat. They'd both been more than ready and she easily took him into her. He clutched her bottom with both hands, then buried his face in her bosom. His mouth brushed along her skin, searching her breasts.

Moving his lips to her neck, he kissed lightly, then grinned and wrapped his tongue around her pearls.

She couldn't bear it any longer.

Ravenous, she took his face in her hands and kissed him. His full lips enticed her to deepen the kiss, lighting her on fire. "Oh, yes, Robert."

She pushed her hands into his thick hair and began to move. Flesh against flesh. Something almost forgotten, but what she craved.

"Victoria," he murmured, amidst numerous kisses across her upper body.

The movement of the carriage intensified the sensations of their lovemaking. Or maybe the sinful act itself caused her to want more. This could never be a single encounter.

I'm his as long as he'll have me.

Her skill and flexibility combined with his incredible drive accomplished what she'd hoped for. Neither held back, and they cried out with gratification. He screamed, then groaned, releasing his seed.

Exactly what she wanted.

It would likely take more than once, but she definitely found the process to her liking.

CHAPTER 42

Claire's pregnancy had her spent. She was exhausted all the time. More so than when she'd carried Michael.

Assuming her age to be a factor, she prayed she'd deliver without complications. Andrew had assured her he'd be there.

Least he won't be knittin' a sweater.

She giggled. Truthfully, it helped knowing she wouldn't have to endure Mary Margaret's bony fingers.

The sweltering August heat was unbearable. She'd been *retaining water*—as Andrew called it—and she'd started to swell in places other than her enormous belly. Not only were her ankles swollen, but her hands puffed up so much she couldn't wear her wedding ring.

Andrew insisted she remain in bed as much as possible until the baby came. But lying in the heat made her miserable.

Samuel kept watch over her. She appreciated him more than ever.

Soft rain pattered against the rooftop. Hoping it would cool things down, she closed her eyes and tried to sleep.

A sharp pain wrenched her wide awake.

She pushed herself upright and leaned against the head-board. While caressing her unborn child, another pain struck.

"Samuel!"

He raced into the room. "What's wrong, Miss Claire?"

"It's time. Go get Clay. Tell him I need Andrew."

"Now?"

"Yes!" She doubled over. The severe pain didn't feel right. Nothing like those she'd felt with Michael. "Hurry!"

"Yes, Miss Claire!" He bolted out the door.

"Take one a the horses!" she called out after him.

Michael wandered into the room and approached the bed. His little face scrunched with worry.

She stroked his head. "It's all right. Mama's gonna be just fine."

"Baby there," he said, pointing to her stomach.

"Yes, your baby sister wants to be born." She'd referred to her unborn child as a girl for so long that she believed it to be so. But another boy would suit her.

Just be healthy.

Michael lifted his arms. "Mama."

"No, baby, I can't hold you right now. Get your bunny and bring it back here. You can sit on Mama's bed." He toddled away, then returned with his toy in tow.

She smiled at her sweet son, but another contraction hit hard, making her wince. It increased the rate of her breathing.

What if Andrew doesn't get here in time?

Michael climbed up beside her, then placed his rabbit atop her tummy. "Bunny love baby."

"And I love *you*," she said, stroking his cheek. She bit her lower lip, holding back tears. She had to put on a brave face for Michael.

Her labor was advancing much too fast.

"Miss Claire?"

Jenny . . .

The front door shut and rapid footfalls beat against the floorboards. Jenny's timid face appeared in the bedroom doorway. "Mama sent me. Clay's gone for Doc." She glanced over her shoulder. "Sam, come get Michael. Tend him while I hep Miss Claire."

The girl rushed to Claire's side, examining her with a stern gaze. Samuel came in and took Michael, then rapidly left.

"I'll get more water," Jenny said. "You're gonna need it. You're sweatin' sumthin' awful."

"Thank you."

Jenny returned with a full glass of water as well as a small bowl. She set both down on the bed stand, then pushed the bedroom door shut. "Don't want Michael to be scared."

Smart girl.

After helping Claire readjust the pillows behind her back, Jenny dipped a cloth into the bowl.

Claire relaxed onto the feather pillows, then closed her eyes while Jenny dabbed at her forehead with the damp cloth.

"Does it hurt bad, Miss Claire?"

"Yes," she said, then groaned with pain. Not wanting to cry out, she pinched her lips tight.

"You can scream a might with a baby comin'," Jenny said. She rubbed Claire's arm. "Mama did."

The contraction ended and Claire blew out a long breath.

Jenny stared at Claire's enormous belly. "Don't reckon I'll ever have babies." She stood and smoothed her dress against her flat stomach. "Can't figger how it stretches."

"Oh!" Claire didn't hold back this time. "Andrew had best hurry! Otherwise, you'll hafta deliver this baby!"

"Uh-uh!" Jenny frantically shook her head. "I'll get Mama if'n I hafta."

"There's no time! The baby's comin' whether we like it or not." Claire jerked at the bottom of her gown. "Help me with my undergarment."

With shaking hands, Jenny obliged. She gaped at the puddle of water that seeped onto the bed. "No, Miss Claire. I can't." She backed away and froze with her back to the wall, breathing just as hard as Claire. "There's blood."

"Jenny . . ." Claire pinched her eyes shut, fighting the pain. "I need you." She pushed herself onto her elbows, attempting to sit upright. Drawing her legs up, she bent her knees. Without a doubt, the baby was coming.

I never dreamed I'd wish Mary Margaret was here.

The bedroom door burst open.

Andrew!

Tears trickled from the corners of Claire's eyes.

Thank God.

He stood beside her in two quick strides. "I'm here, sweetheart." He kissed her forehead, then nodded to Jenny. "Move around to the other side. I need some room." He sat on the edge of the bed; right below Claire's bent knees.

After giving him a quick hug, Jenny did as he asked. Relief flowed from her.

"The head's cresting," Andrew said. "I can't believe how quickly you've progressed. Clay indicated you'd just started having pains, but it's already time for you to push." He looked directly at her with the face of a doctor. Exactly what she needed. But something more lay behind his eyes. *He's worried.* "When the next contraction comes, push with all your strength."

Nothing about this birth felt right. From the very first pain, she'd grown weaker. "Andrew . . . I love you." She gasped for air.

He took her wrist, feeling her pulse. After a long minute, he set her arm to her side. "I love you, too. You can do this, Claire."

No, I can't.

By the look on his face, Andrew knew it, too.

"Jenny," he said. "Help Claire sit up. It'll help her push."

The girl's head bobbed up and down. She climbed onto the bed and positioned herself behind her. Claire lay back in her arms. She groaned as the contraction gripped her.

"Push!" Andrew yelled. His hands cupped over the baby's head.

Claire inhaled, then bore down with every ounce of her remaining strength, while Jenny kept her upright.

"Good!" Andrew grabbed a towel. "The head's through." He wiped the baby's face. "On the next contraction, you'll need to push harder to get the shoulders through."

"I can't," Claire panted. "I can't."

"Yes, you can. I won't let anything happen to you or this child, but you've got to give me another big push." His calm voice didn't mask his fear. And when she looked at his face, her heart sank.

He's so pale.

"It hurts," Claire whimpered.

How did he feel seeing their child wanting to be born, but stuck inside its mama?

I hafta do this for him.

* * *

Andrew's heart pounded hard.

She's slipping away.

Refusing to lose another woman he loved in childbirth, he had to be strong. All the signs had been there, but he hadn't wanted to believe them.

Claire's body tensed and she moaned.

"Jenny," Andrew said. "Lift her as best you can. Claire—*honey*—push." He kept his voice low, hoping to ease her.

She squinted her eyes tight bearing down, and he managed to get a grip on the baby's shoulders. Once through, he expelled their child. Gazing at his precious daughter, tears clouded his vision, but he managed to give her a swat on the behind, prompting her to cry.

The tiniest, most precious sound he'd ever heard.

"Doc!" Jenny cried. "What do I do?"

He shifted his gaze from his little girl to his wife. Her head had dropped back against Jenny's arm. Her eyes were shut and her breathing shallow.

Tears flowed down Jenny's cheeks. "I don't know what to do."

"Move out from behind her and lay her against the pillows. She's exhausted."

Jenny scooted away. The care she showed Claire was as fine as any nurse he'd worked with.

"You did well," he said. "I'd like you to boil some water so I can wash the baby. I'll take care of Claire now."

"She don't look good, Doc."

"She'll be fine." He gave her what he hoped was a reassuring smile, but his heart wasn't in it. Terrible memories of nearly losing her before flooded his mind.

Jenny left the room and closed the door.

Andrew quickly cut the umbilical cord, tied it off, then wrapped the baby in a blanket. He laid her on the bed beside Claire and tried to ignore her crying. She appeared healthy and strong, but her mother was anything but.

With a racing heart, he removed the afterbirth. Her blood flow looked normal. She hadn't hemorrhaged. But she still wasn't out of danger.

"Claire . . . Claire, please wake up." He'd said those words before. A stab of agony pierced his soul.

His infant daughter continued to cry. "Claire, we have a little girl. She's beautiful, just like you. Please wake up." With tears running down his face, he kissed her lips.

"Andrew . . ." Her eyes remained shut, but he didn't care. Hearing her say his name made him want to dance. "I'm so tired."

He stroked her cheek. "Rest. You've more than earned it."

"But, the baby needs me. Is it all right?"

"Yes. She's perfect."

"She?"

"You were right. We have a little girl."

The pain and defeat that had covered Claire's face transformed into a weak smile. "God's so gracious."

Joy surrounded him, radiating from Claire's beautiful smile. "Yes, He is." *Gracious.* He took Claire's hand, kissed it, then held it in his own. "Why don't we call her *Grace*?"

"Thought you wanted to name her after your mama?"

"Well . . ."

"We could call her Grace Elizabeth."

"I love it." He scooped up Grace Elizabeth Fletcher and kissed her tiny head. She had a headful of dark hair. "Did Michael have this much hair when he was born?"

"Yep." She reached for the baby. A rap on the door stopped her from taking her.

Andrew opened the door and Jenny came in with a pan of water. Her face lit up as she looked from Claire to Grace.

"We named her Grace," Andrew said, taking the pan.

Jenny beamed. "I'll leaves ya alone to wash. I'll tell Sam to stay here with Michael, but I's gonna go home an' let Mama know 'bout the baby."

She inched out the door, grinning all the while.

Andrew felt Claire's eyes on him as he washed their child. Then he laid her down on the bed and tenderly cleaned his wife. Once he'd finished, he helped her sit up-right and placed Grace into her arms.

Taking the place beside them, he supported Claire with one arm.

She stroked the baby's cheek with a single finger. "I'm glad you were here, Andrew. I know Jenny is, too."

"I promised I'd be here." He kept looking from his wife to his child. Love encircled them. "Of course, I had no idea you'd be in such a hurry, Mrs. Fletcher." He chose to tease, but knew neither of them would have survived the birth if he'd not been there.

"I wasn't," Claire whispered. "Grace was."

He stood from the bed. "You need to rest. Grace will be ready to nurse soon, but for now, sleep." He took their baby from her. "Doctor's orders."

She didn't argue. Lying back, she shut her eyes.

Andrew cradled his infant daughter, then bent down and gave his wife a kiss on the forehead.

He believed she'd be fine, but this would have to be their last child.

She'd never withstand another.

CHAPTER 43

Before leaving Robert in the carriage, Victoria told him she wanted him in her bed. He'd called her insane for wanting to take that risk. Seems they both knew John wouldn't take kindly to another man bedding her.

Even though Robert appeared nervous about the idea, they'd made a plan.

John would be out of town, so it was fairly fail-safe. Regardless, there was always a chance they'd be discovered.

Danger had become her new best friend.

Ever since the tryst with Robert, she'd acted overly affectionate with John. Not wanting him to suspect her infidelity, she did whatever he wanted.

Then the day she'd longed for finally arrived.

"Will you miss me, my dear?" John asked as he prepared to leave.

"Horribly." She displayed her best pout. "Please hurry home."

He jerked her body against his. "Think of me while I'm away."

"I will." After licking her lips, she gave him a kiss to remember her by. "When will you be back?"

"Day after tomorrow. My client has political connections. He'll be advising me on my campaign." With a proud smile, he smacked her rump and walked out the door.

Almost giddy, she floated across the floor.

Time to prepare for Robert.

She'd instructed him to enter through the back door, next to the bathing room. At the back of that room he'd find a stairway behind some shelving used for towels. Few people knew about the hidden stairway. It led directly to their bedroom.

The most important detail was to arrive after nine o'clock. Otherwise, he'd risk running into Jean-Pierre.

She hummed as she waltzed into the kitchen for a bite to eat. Though not necessarily hungry, she felt it wise to get some nourishment. It could be a very long night.

The day drug by and the butterflies in her stomach remained. She'd not felt this excited about making love since the first night she'd spent with John.

If only Robert could stay all night.

It would be fun waking up next to him. But that couldn't happen. *Too* dangerous. She'd have to make sure he was gone well before sunrise.

She'd experienced John's wrath before. He wasn't the kind of man to deceive. But he'd never harm her. He wouldn't risk that kind of scandal. Especially now. Who'd want a senator who abused his wife?

Even so, he could make her life miserable behind closed doors. But she didn't care. As long as she got the child she deserved. Once conceived, he'd have to learn to live with it. She'd find a way to make him believe it was his.

The piano keys plinked.

Victoria followed the sound into the ballroom. Willie was dusting.

"Willie," Victoria said. "Have I told you what a fine job you do for Mr. Martin and me?"

Holding the duster in midair, the woman's eyes drew wide. Probably because Victoria rarely spoke to her. "Thank you, Mrs. Martin."

"Because of your outstandin' work, I'm givin' you the rest of the day off. Go spend some time with your children."

"But . . ." She pointed to the piano. "I haven't finished."

"Don't worry 'bout that. And don't fret over your pay. You'll receive a full day's wage. Now, run along. Your children won't be young forever." Victoria shooed her out the door.

After pacing until her legs grew tired, Victoria ate a small bowl of soup for supper, then told Jean-Pierre she was retiring early.

She made certain the back door was unlocked, then went to the bathing room and prepared a bath. A good soak would not only relax her, but she wanted to be clean and fresh for her lover.

After drying off, she opened the passageway to the stairwell, then lit a lamp and ascended to her room. She never used these stairs, but somehow climbing them added to her anticipation. In just a few hours, Robert would be following in her footsteps.

She dabbed some vanilla between her breasts, set the lantern beside the bed, then misted the sheets with cologne.

After opening the window for a nice, pleasant breeze, she got into bed. Almost immediately she jumped up to lock the bedroom door. If John came home early, he'd have a hard time getting in. It'd give Robert time to exit down the back stairway.

"Perfect," she mumbled and slipped back into bed.

A simple satin sheet covered her naked body. Light from the lantern highlighted the view she'd prepared for him. He'd be able to see every curve of her form beneath the thin fabric.

She tried to sleep, but thoughts of Robert filled her mind. Would tonight be as good as it had been in the carriage? It was bound to be better. They'd been restricted on that plush velvet seat.

Time passed slowly. She drifted off, then woke again with a start. Her heart beat so hard she swore she heard it. Something overtook the sound. Footsteps on the hidden stairway.

Robert.

She ran her fingers through her hair, arranging it on the pillows. Then she moistened her lips for what she knew would be a night of heated kisses.

The door creaked open and he stepped through. *My lover.* The handsome young man who'd stolen a piece of her heart.

She nearly lost her breath.

He stepped closer. Without saying a word, he began removing his clothes. She'd seen very little of him bare—

aside from the most important part—but she appreciated *every* aspect of a man.

Robert Wilson didn't disappoint. His lean, muscular body had very little hair. And he was more than ready to make love. *So am I.*

Naked, he sat on the edge of the bed beside her. He brushed her cheek with his fingertips. "I'm here as you requested." He spoke barely above a whisper. But even if he'd been louder, they wouldn't be heard. Jean-Pierre's room was too far away.

"Yes, you are," she said, wanting to grab onto him and get down to business. But something about tonight was different. This man was tender. Completely different from John.

He bent down and kissed her. Light at first, but it intensified as his hand glided over the satin that covered her. "Very nice," he said. His hand stopped at her breast.

She lifted the sheet, giving him a peek beneath. "Even nicer," he said with a grin.

"You're quite fine yourself, Mr. Wilson. Now get between these sheets before I get angry." She cast a devilish smile, and he wasted no time doing her bidding.

Their hands freely roamed, exploring what they'd not been able to in the carriage. And between every touch, he placed kisses on her body. When he moved his lips across her neck, he paused, then pulled back. He touched the scar she despised.

"Don't mind that," she said, moving his hand. "I'll tell you 'bout it sometime."

He didn't question her further, and to her delight resumed his kisses and exploration. His mouth wandered over her entire body. Teasing and tasting. She simply lay there reveling in his affection. Eventually he returned to her breasts, then nuzzled at the center. "You smell incredible." After inhaling deeply, he ran his tongue around her nipple, then enthusiastically suckled.

The perfect breasts created for that very reason. For now, she'd let *him* enjoy them, but one day, she'd use them to feed their child.

He nestled himself atop her. "You're more woman than I deserve."

"We're both deservin'. So take me before I scream."

His dimpled smile made her squirm.

"I want you," he said, entering her. "And I want to make it last. Not like in the carriage."

"We have all night."

He kissed her, harder—almost desperate—and began to move.

She arched into his body, meeting every thrust. She'd take his seed and hold it inside.

Is it right to use him like this?

Right or wrong, she didn't care. She clasped onto him and savored every second, using her body to entice his release.

"Yes!" he cried out with a final thrust, then fell breathless upon her.

She'd not reached her own satisfaction, but that would come before night's end. For now, she caressed his smooth back, feeling his rapidly beating heart against her breasts.

With a loud sigh, he withdrew from her and rolled to the side. She cinched her legs tightly together.

He propped himself up on one arm, then glided his other hand over her body. "I've never met anyone like you. I'm afraid I'm falling in love with you."

No. That's not how it's supposed to be.

Her heart raced. "You can't. I'm a married woman. You knew that when we started." She shifted onto her side and looked in his eyes. This gorgeous man could be what she'd always searched for. *But it's too late.* She rested a hand on his cheek. "You don't love *me*. You love my body, nothin' more."

"You're wrong. That is . . . yes, I *do* love your body, but as I told you from the beginning, I see much more in you. You're special. I can't get enough of you." He climbed atop her once again, obviously wanting to prove his point. Unlike John, he didn't need time to regain his arousal. It had returned almost instantly.

She gladly accommodated him.

* * *

Well past midnight.

They'd made love for hours with little rest. Suddenly sleepy, Victoria laid her head on Robert's chest. His fingers raked tenderly through her hair.

"Tell me about your scar," he whispered.

She sighed. Why did he have to mention it? The night had been so perfect.

"If you'd rather not speak of it, I understand. But I care about you. I'd like to know."

Without looking at him, she decided to tell. If he truly cared, it wouldn't matter. "A Negro tried havin' his way with me. I fought him and made him angry." She swallowed hard, recalling the horrible ordeal. "He bit me."

Robert had been caressing her, but immediately stopped. "Did he have you?"

She lifted her head and met his gaze. "No. I stabbed him in the back with a hat pin and managed to get away. My daddy sent men after him. They hung him."

While she spoke, Robert had been holding his breath. When she finished, he blew it out slowly. "Good. That is—it's good he didn't have you. But I'm sorry he hurt you." His hand resumed its movement, then he kissed the top of her head. "Could you love me? If it weren't for John, could you be mine?"

After placing a kiss at the center of his chest, she peered deeply into his eyes. "Yes. But John would never let me go." She increased the intensity of her gaze. "Don't love me. You'll be hurt."

"It hurts me to leave you. I'll be returning to school in two weeks. I'll be home on weekends, but won't be able to see you as I want. I don't know when we can meet again." He drew her closer and kissed her lips. "I won't stop thinking about you."

"I don't want you to go, but we have no choice. I can go to the park on the weekends. You can come by in your carriage. It's not as pleasant as my bed, but if it's all we have, then that's what we'll do." She kissed him deeply. Even kissing him brought more pleasure than she felt with John. Oddly, along with his looks, Robert's kisses reminded her of Andrew. "I'll think of you, too."

Robert inched out of bed and began to dress. Because she didn't want to risk losing any of what he'd left inside her, she lay still. Would he discover her ploy?

No man would believe a woman would purposefully use him to father a child. Especially a married woman.

Fully dressed, he stood beside her, then bent down and kissed her a final time. "I love you, Victoria." She started to object, but he placed a single finger over her lips. "No. Don't say a word."

Her heart sank as he walked away. The doorway creaked, and soon his footsteps faded.

Gone.

She rubbed small circles around her flat abdomen. "Lord, I want a child. Please make it so."

Would God hear her prayer or turn His back on her for breaking her marriage vows?

It didn't matter. She'd continue with Robert until she succeeded.

ACKNOWLEDGMENTS

I can't begin to tell you how happy it makes me that you're enjoying my Southern Secrets Saga. Thank you for continuing to read this ongoing adventure! I appreciate all the warm comments I've received and the excitement you've related wondering what will happen next. I assure you that the journey is far from over.

Thank you to my editor, Cindy Brannam, for all the excellent suggestions and keeping me on track. As I'm sure you can imagine, it's not always easy keeping up with so many different characters and remembering who knows what and *when* they know it. This story has tumbled through my mind for many years, and I'm happy to get it all in print.

Thank you to Rae Monet, Karen Duvall, and Jesse Gordon for all their hard work on beautifully adding their talent to the final product. With their help, you'll continue to see gorgeous covers and well-formatted books.

I hope you're looking forward to the next installment. I know I am!

COMING SOON!

Incivilities
Southern Secrets Saga, Book 4

The *Southern Secrets Saga* continues . . .

Reconciliation may be achieved by some, but others will stray far in the opposite direction.

Revealed secrets lead to hate and revenge, until someone pays the ultimate price for their deceptions.

Drawing on raw, human rage, *Incivilities* abound.

If you're enjoying the *Southern Secrets Saga*,
you might also like these books by Jeanne Hardt!

The RIVER ROMANCE Series

Step back in time to 1850 and travel along the
Mississippi River in the *River Romance* series!

Marked
River Romance, Book 1

Cora Craighead wants more than anything to leave
Plum Point, Arkansas, aboard one of the fantastic steam-
boats that pass by her run-down home on the Mississippi
River. She's certain there's more to life out there...*somewhere*. Besides, anything has to be better than living with
her pa who spends his days and nights drinking and gambling.

Douglas Denton grew up on one of the wealthiest es-
tates in Memphis, Tennessee. Life filled with parties,
expensive clothing, and proper English never suited him.
He longs for simplicity and a woman with a pure heart—
not one who craves his money. Cora is that and more, but
she belongs to someone else.

Cora finally gets her wish, only to be taken down a road
of strife, uncertainty, and mysterious prophecies. When
she's finally discovered again by Douglas, she's a widow,
fearing for her life and that of her newborn child and blind
companion.

Full of emotions, family secrets, and the search for true
love, you'll find it's not just the cards that are marked.

Tainted
River Romance, Book 2

Despite her new position as manager of the *Bonny Lass,* Francine DuBois doubts her abilities. After all, the only skill she's ever been recognized for is entertaining men and giving them pleasure. But she'll never let her insecurities show in the presence of the new captain. He's too young to be a pilot and he'll never measure up to his predecessor. However, just below the surface, there's something about him she can't ignore.

Luke Waters may be young, but he's determined to prove he's more than capable. He'll show everyone he's the best pilot the Mississippi River has to offer. His only problem - the new crew manager. His religious upbringing taught him to frown on women of her profession, so how can he bring himself to overlook her way of life and give her the respect a workable relationship requires? Especially when he can't stop dreaming about her.

Which is worse? A tainted past, or a tainted opinion?

Forgotten
River Romance, Book 3

Rumor has it, the war is about to end. But that doesn't stop Billy Denton from running away to enlist. He's lived a privileged life on the Wellesley estate, where slavery is seen as a necessary means to operate their textile production. Believing no human should be enslaved by another, he's willing to fight—and even *die*—to change the future of the woman who holds his heart.

Living and working at the estate is all Angel knows. When Billy tells her he's joining the Union army, she begs him to stay, fearing she'll lose her best friend ... the only man she's ever loved. She'd rather remain a slave, than have him harmed in any way.

Angel attains freedom, but time passes and there's no sign of Billy. In her heart, she believes he'll come home to her. Their love may be forbidden, but can never be forgotten.

Holding on to hope ... Angel waits.

Also by Jeanne Hardt, another Southern Historical!

From the Ashes of Atlanta

After losing his Atlanta home and family to the war, Confederate soldier, Jeb Carter, somehow wakes up in a Boston hospital. Alone, desperate, and with a badly broken leg, he pretends to be mute to save himself from those he hates—Yankees.

Gwen Abbott, a student at Boston Women's Medical College, is elated when she's allowed to study under the guidance of a prominent doctor at Massachusetts General. While forced into a courtship with a man she can scarcely tolerate, her thoughts are consumed with their mysterious new patient. If only he could talk.

Two strangers from different worlds, joined by fate. Perhaps love can speak without words and win a war without a single shot being fired.

Also by Jeanne Hardt

A GOLDEN LIFE
(A slightly unusual contemporary tale...)

In the beautiful mountain setting of Gatlinburg, Tennessee, something magical is about to happen.

Traci Oliver may be a best-selling romance author, but for the first time in her writing career she can't type a word on the blank page. Book number fifty is supposed to be her best ever—her *golden* book—but inspiration joined her husband in the grave. How can she write about love with a shattered heart?

At the precise moment of the anniversary of his death, a knock on her door changes everything.

When characters from her books take on human form and tell her that they've come to help her, she doubts her sanity. Are they real, or has she lost her mind?

Her doctor says grieving is a process, but she never dreamed that part of the process would bring her heroes to life. She wonders if all people experience this kind of thing, or is it a weird phenomenon reserved solely for romance writers? Truthfully, the only hero she wants in her life is her husband, and she can never be with him again.

Or maybe she can ...

www.jeannehardt.com
www.facebook.com/JEANNEHARDTAUTHOR
www.amazon.com/author/jeannehardt

Made in the USA
Charleston, SC
09 February 2016